MR. LEMONCELLO, HIS BANANA SHOES BURP-SQUEAKING, STEPPED OUT OF A ROOM FILLED WITH DOZENS OF BLACK-AND-WHITE TELEVISION MONITORS—THE KIND SECURITY GUARDS WATCH AT THEIR WORKSTATIONS.

"Ladies and gentlemen, thank you for joining us on this grand and auspicious day.

"Today I am pleased to announce the most marvelously stupendous game ever created: Escape from Mr. Lemoncello's Library! The entire library will be the game board. Your children will be the game pieces. The winner will become famous all over the world."

PLAY ALL THE GAMES, SOLVE ALL THE PUZZLES— READ ALL THE LEMONCELLOS!

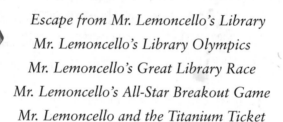

Escape from Mr. Lemoncello's Library
Mr. Lemoncello's Library Olympics
Mr. Lemoncello's Great Library Race
Mr. Lemoncello's All-Star Breakout Game
Mr. Lemoncello and the Titanium Ticket

ESCAPE FROM MR. LEMONCELLO'S LIBRARY

CHRIS GRABENSTEIN

Text copyright © 2013, 2016 by Chris Grabenstein
Cover art copyright © 2020 by James Lancett
Photograph credit: p. 269 of *Mr. Lemoncello's Library Olympics*
(MAD #105) ™ and © E. C. Publications, Inc.

All rights reserved. Published in the United States by Random House Children's Books, a division of Penguin Random House LLC, New York. The titles in this work were originally published separately in the United States by Random House Children's Books, a division of Penguin Random House LLC, New York, in 2013 and 2016.

Random House and the colophon are registered trademarks of Penguin Random House LLC.

Visit us on the Web!
rhcbooks.com

Educators and librarians, for a variety of teaching tools, visit us at RHTeachersLibrarians.com

The Library of Congress has cataloged the individual books under the following Control Numbers: 2012048122 (*Escape from Mr. Lemoncello's Library*) and 2015024473 (*Mr. Lemoncello's Library Olympics*).

ISBN 978-0-593-64654-0 (proprietary edition)

MANUFACTURED IN CHINA
10 9 8 7 6 5 4 3 2 1

For the late Jeanette P. Myers,
and all the other librarians who help us find
whatever we're looking for

This is how Kyle Keeley got grounded for a week.

First he took a shortcut through his mother's favorite rosebush.

Yes, the thorns hurt, but having crashed through the brambles and trampled a few petunias, he had a five-second jump on his oldest brother, Mike.

Both Kyle and his big brother knew exactly where to find what they needed to win the game: inside the house!

Kyle had already found the pinecone to complete his "outdoors" round. And he was pretty sure Mike had snagged his "yellow flower." Hey, it was June. Dandelions were everywhere.

"Give it up, Kyle!" shouted Mike as the brothers dashed up the driveway. "You don't stand a chance."

Mike zoomed past Kyle and headed for the front door, wiping out Kyle's temporary lead.

Of course he did.

Seventeen-year-old Mike Keeley was a total jock, a high school superstar. Football, basketball, baseball. If it had a ball, Mike Keeley was good at it.

Kyle, who was twelve, wasn't the star of anything.

Kyle's other brother, Curtis, who was fifteen, was still trapped over in the neighbor's yard, dealing with their dog. Curtis was the smartest Keeley. But for *his* "outdoors" round, he had pulled the always unfortunate Your Neighbor's Dog's Toy card. Any "dog" card was basically the same as a Lose a Turn.

As for why the three Keeley brothers were running around their neighborhood on a Sunday afternoon like crazed lunatics, grabbing all sorts of wacky stuff, well, it was their mother's fault.

She was the one who had suggested, "If you boys are bored, play a board game!"

So Kyle had gone down into the basement and dug up one of his all-time favorites: Mr. Lemoncello's Indoor-Outdoor Scavenger Hunt. It had been a huge hit for Mr. Lemoncello, the master game maker. Kyle and his brothers had played it so much when they were younger, Mrs. Keeley wrote to Mr. Lemoncello's company for a refresher pack of clue cards. The new cards listed all sorts of different bizarro stuff you needed to find, like "an adult's droopy underpants," "one dirty dish," and "a rotten banana peel."

(At the end of the game, the losers had to put everything back exactly where the items had been found. It was an official rule, printed inside the top of the box, and made winning the game that much more important!)

While Curtis was stranded next door, trying to talk the neighbor's Doberman, Twinky, out of his favorite tug toy, Kyle and Mike were both searching for the same two items, because for the final round, all the players were given the same Riddle Card.

That day's riddle, even though it was a card Kyle had never seen before, had been extra easy.

FIND TWO COINS FROM 1982 THAT ADD UP TO THIRTY CENTS AND ONE OF THEM CANNOT BE A NICKEL.

Duh. The answer was a quarter and a nickel because the riddle said only *one* of them couldn't be a nickel.

So to win, Kyle had to find a 1982 quarter *and* a 1982 nickel.

Also easy.

Their dad kept an apple cider jug filled with loose change down in his basement workshop.

That's why Kyle and Mike were racing to get there first.

Mike bolted through the front door.

Kyle grinned.

He loved playing games against his big brothers. As the youngest, it was just about the only chance he ever got to beat them fair and square. Board games leveled the playing field. You needed a good roll of the dice, a lucky draw of the cards, and some smarts, but if things went your way and you gave it your all, anyone could win.

Especially today, since Mike had blown his lead by choosing the standard route down to the basement. He'd go through the front door, tear to the back of the house, bound down the steps, and then run to their dad's workshop.

Kyle, on the other hand, would take a shortcut.

He hopped over a couple of boxy shrubs and kicked open the low-to-the-ground casement window. He heard something crackle when his tennis shoe hit the windowpane, but he couldn't worry about it. He had to beat his big brother.

He crawled through the narrow opening, dropped to the floor, and scrabbled over to the workbench, where he found the jug, dumped out the coins, and started sifting through the sea of pennies, nickels, dimes, and quarters.

Score!

Kyle quickly uncovered a 1982 nickel. He tucked it into his shirt pocket and sent pennies, nickels, and dimes skidding across the floor as he concentrated on quarters. 2010. 2003. 1986.

"Come on, come on," he muttered.

The workshop door swung open.

"What the . . . ?" Mike was surprised to see that Kyle had beaten him to the coin jar.

Mike fell to his knees and started searching for his own

coins just as Kyle shouted, "Got it!" and plucked a 1982 quarter out of the pile.

"What about the nickel?" demanded Mike.

Kyle pulled it out of his shirt pocket.

"You went through the window?" said a voice from outside.

It was Curtis. Kneeling in the flower beds.

"Yeah," said Kyle.

"I was going to do that. The shortest distance between two points is a straight line."

"I can't believe you won!" moaned Mike, who wasn't used to losing *anything*.

"Well," said Kyle, standing up and strutting a little, "believe it, brother. Because now you two *losers* have to put all the junk back."

"I am *not* taking this back to Twinky!" said Curtis. He held up a very slimy, knotted rope.

"Oh, yes you are," said Kyle. "Because you *lost*. Oh sure, you *thought* about using the window. . . ."

"Um, Kyle?" mumbled Curtis. "You might want to shut up. . . ."

"What? C'mon, Curtis. Don't be such a sore loser. Just because I was the one who took the shortcut and kicked open the window and—"

"You did this, Kyle?"

A new face appeared in the window.

Their dad's.

"Heh, heh, heh," chuckled Mike behind Kyle.

"You broke the glass?" Their father sounded ticked off. "Well, guess who's going to pay to have this window replaced."

That's why Kyle Keeley had fifty cents deducted from his allowance for the rest of the year.

And got grounded for a week.

Halfway across town, Dr. Yanina Zinchenko, the world-famous librarian, was walking briskly through the cavernous building that was only days away from its gala grand opening.

Alexandriaville's new public library had been under construction for five years. All work had been done with the utmost secrecy under the tightest possible security. One crew did the exterior renovations on what had once been the small Ohio city's most magnificent building, the Gold Leaf Bank. Other crews—carpenters, masons, electricians, and plumbers—worked on the interior.

No single construction crew stayed on the job longer than six weeks.

No crew knew what any of the other crews had done (or would be doing).

And when all those crews were finished, several

super-secret covert crews (highly paid workers who would deny ever having been near the library, Alexandriaville, *or* the state of Ohio) stealthily applied the final touches.

Dr. Zinchenko had supervised the construction project for her employer—a very eccentric (some would say loony) billionaire. Only she knew all the marvels and wonders the incredible new library would hold (and hide) within its walls.

Dr. Zinchenko was a tall woman with blazing-red hair. She wore an expensive, custom-tailored business suit, jazzy high-heeled shoes, a Bluetooth earpiece, and glasses with thick red frames.

Heels clicking on the marble floor, fingers tapping on the glass of her very advanced tablet computer, Dr. Zinchenko strode past the control center's red door, under an arch, and into the breathtakingly large circular reading room beneath the library's three-story-tall rotunda.

The bank building, which provided the shell for the new library, had been built in 1931. With towering Corinthian columns, an arched entryway, lots of fancy trim, and a mammoth shimmering gold dome, the building looked like it belonged next door to the triumphant memorials in Washington, D.C.—not on this small Ohio town's quaint streets.

Dr. Zinchenko paused to stare up at the library's most stunning visual effect: the Wonder Dome. Ten wedge-shaped, high-definition video screens—as brilliant as those in Times Square—lined the underbelly of the dome like so many orange slices. Each screen could operate independently or as part of a spectacular whole. The Wonder Dome could become the constellations of the night sky; a flight through the clouds that made viewers below sense that the whole building had somehow lifted off the ground; or, in Dewey decimal mode, ten sections depicting vibrant and constantly changing images associated with each category in the library cataloging system.

"I have the final numbers for the fourth sector of the Wonder Dome in Dewey mode," Dr. Zinchenko said into her Bluetooth earpiece. "364 point 1092." She carefully over-enunciated each word to make certain the video artist knew what specific numbers should occasionally drift across the fourth wedge amid the swirling social-sciences montage featuring a floating judge's gavel, a tumbling teacher's apple, and a gentle snowfall of holiday icons. "The numbers, however, should not appear until eleven a.m. Sunday. Is that clear?"

"Yes, Dr. Zinchenko," replied the tinny voice in her ear.

Next Dr. Zinchenko studied the holographic statues projected into black crepe-lined recesses cut into the massive stone piers that supported the arched windows from which the Wonder Dome rose.

"Why are Shakespeare and Dickens still here? They're not on the list for opening night."

"Sorry," replied the library's director of holographic imagery, who was also on the conference call. "I'll fix it."

"Thank you."

Exiting the rotunda, the librarian entered the Children's Room.

It was dim, with only a few work lights glowing, but Dr. Zinchenko had memorized the layout of the miniature tables and was able to march, without bumping her shins, to the Story Corner for a final check on her recently installed geese.

The flock of six audio-animatronic goslings—fluffy robots with ping-pongish eyeballs (created for the new library by imagineers who used to work at Disney World)—stood perched atop an angled bookcase in the corner. Mother Goose, in her bonnet and granny glasses, was frozen in the center.

"This is librarian One," said Dr. Zinchenko, loud enough for the microphones hidden in the ceiling to pick up her voice. "Initiate story-time sequence."

The geese sprang to mechanical life.

"Nursery rhyme."

The geese honked out "Baa-Baa Black Sheep" in six-part harmony.

"Treasure Island?"

The birds yo-ho-ho'ed their way through "Fifteen Men on a Dead Man's Chest."

Dr. Zinchenko clapped her hands. The rollicking geese stopped singing and swaying.

"One more," she said. Squinting, she saw a book sitting on a nearby table. *"Walter the Farting Dog."*

The six geese spun around and farted, their tail feathers flipping up in sync with the noisy blasts.

"Excellent. End story time."

The geese slumped back into their sleep mode. Dr. Zinchenko made one more tick on her computer tablet. Her final punch list was growing shorter and shorter, which was a very good thing. The library's grand opening was set for Friday night. Dr. Z and her army of associates had only a few days left to smooth out any kinks in the library's complex operating system.

Suddenly, Dr. Zinchenko heard a low, rumbling growl.

Turning around, she was eyeball to icy-blue eyeball with a very rare white tiger.

Dr. Zinchenko sighed and touched her Bluetooth earpiece.

"Ms. G? This is Dr. Z. What is our white Bengal tiger doing in the children's department? . . . I see. Apparently, there was a slight misunderstanding. We do not want him permanently positioned near *The Jungle Book*. Check the call number. 599 point 757. . . . Right. He should be in Zoology. . . . Yes, please. Right away. Thank you, Ms. G."

And like a vanishing mirage, the tiger disappeared.

3

Of course, even though he was grounded, Kyle Keeley still had to go to school.

"Mike, Curtis, Kyle, time to wake up!" his mother called from down in the kitchen.

Kyle plopped his feet on the floor, rubbed his eyes, and sleepily looked around his room.

The computer handed down from his brother Curtis was sitting on the desk that used to belong to his other brother, Mike. The rug on the floor, with its Cincinnati Reds logo, had also been Mike's when *he* was twelve years old. The books lined up in his bookcase had been lined up on Mike's and Curtis's shelves, except for the ones Kyle got each year for Christmas from his grandmother. He still hadn't read last year's addition.

Kyle wasn't big on books.

Unless they were the instruction manual or hint guide to a video game. He had a Sony PlayStation set up in the family room. It wasn't the high-def, Blu-ray PS3. It was the one Santa had brought Mike maybe four years earlier. (Mike kept the brand-new Blu-ray model locked up in his bedroom.)

But still, clunker that it was, the four-year-old gaming console in the family room worked.

Except this week.

Well, it *worked*, but Kyle's dad had taken away his TV and computer privileges, so unless he just wanted to hear the hard drive hum, there was really no point in firing up the PlayStation until the next Sunday, when his sentence ended.

"When you're grounded in this house," his father had said, "you're *grounded*."

If Kyle needed a computer for homework during this last week of school, he could use his mom's, the one in the kitchen.

His mom had no games on her computer.

Okay, she had Diner Dash, but that didn't really count.

Being grounded in the Keeley household meant you couldn't do anything except, as his dad put it, "think about what you did that caused you to be grounded."

Kyle knew what he had done: He'd broken a window.

But hey—I also beat my big brothers!

* * *

"Good morning, Kyle," his mom said when he hit the kitchen. She was sitting at her computer desk, sipping coffee and tapping keys. "Grab a Toaster Tart for breakfast."

Curtis and Mike were already in the kitchen, chowing down on the last of the good Toaster Tarts—the frosted cupcake swirls. They'd left Kyle the unfrosted brown sugar cinnamon. The ones that tasted like the box they came in.

"New library opens Friday, just in time for summer vacation," Kyle's mom mumbled, reading her computer screen. "Been twelve years since they tore down the old one. Listen to this, boys: Dr. Yanina Zinchenko, the new public library's head librarian, promises that 'patrons will be surprised' by what they find inside."

"Really?" said Kyle, who always liked a good surprise. "I wonder what they'll have in there."

"Um, books maybe?" said Mike. "It's a *library*, Kyle."

"Still," said Curtis, "I can't wait to get my new library card!"

"Because you're a nerd," said Mike.

"I prefer the term 'geek,' " said Curtis.

"Well, I gotta go," said Kyle, grabbing his backpack. "Don't want to miss the bus."

He hurried out the door. What Kyle really didn't want to miss were his friends. A lot of them had Sony PSPs and Nintendo 3DSs.

Loaded with lots and lots of games!

* * *

14

Kyle fist-bumped and knuckle-knocked his way up the bus aisle to his usual seat. Almost everybody wanted to say "Hey" to him, except, of course, Sierra Russell.

Like always, Sierra, who was also a seventh grader, was sitting in the back of the bus, her nose buried in a book—probably one of those about girls who lived in tiny homes on the prairie or something.

Ever since her parents divorced and her dad moved out of town, Sierra Russell had been incredibly quiet and spent all her free time reading.

"Nice shirt," said Akimi Hughes as Kyle slid into the seat beside her.

"Thanks. It used to be Mike's."

"Doesn't matter. It's still cool."

Akimi's mother was Asian, her dad Irish. She had very long jet-black hair, extremely blue eyes, and a ton of freckles.

"What're you playing?" Kyle asked, because Akimi was frantically working the controls on her PSP 3000.

"Squirrel Squad," said Akimi.

"One of Mr. Lemoncello's best," said Kyle, who had the same game on his PlayStation.

The one he couldn't play with for a week.

"You need a hand?"

"Nah."

"Watch out for the beehives. . . ."

"I know about the beehives, Kyle."

"I'm just saying . . ."

"Yes!"

"What?"

"I cleared level six! Finally."

"Awesome." Kyle did not mention that he was up to level twenty-seven. Akimi was his best friend. Friends don't gloat to friends.

"When I shot the squirrels at the falcons," said Akimi, "the pilots parachuted. If a squirrel bit the pilot in the butt, I got a fifty-point bonus."

Yes, in Mr. Lemoncello's catapulting critters game, there were all sorts of wacky jokes. The falcons weren't birds; they were F-16 Falcon Fighter Jets. And the squirrels? They were nuts. Totally bonkers. With swirly whirlpool eyes. They flew through the air jabbering gibberish. They bit butts.

This was one of the main reasons why Kyle thought everything that came out of Mr. Lemoncello's Imagination Factory—board games, puzzles, video games—was amazingly awesome. For Mr. Lemoncello, a game just wasn't a game if it wasn't a little goofy around the edges.

"So, did you pick up the bonus code?" asked Kyle.

"Huh?"

"In the freeze-frame there."

Akimi studied the screen.

"Turn it over."

Akimi did.

"See that number tucked into the corner? Type that in the next time the home screen asks you for your password."

16

"Why? What happens?"

"You'll see."

Akimi slugged him in the arm. "What?"

"Well, don't be surprised if you start flinging *flaming* squirrels on level seven."

"Get. Out!"

"Try it. You'll see."

"I will. This afternoon. So, did you write your extra-credit essay?"

"Huh? What essay?"

"Um, the one that's due today. About the new public library?"

"Refresh my memory."

Akimi sighed. "Because the old library was torn down twelve years ago, the twelve twelve-year-olds who write the best essays on 'Why I'm Excited About the New Public Library' will get to go to the library lock-in this Friday night."

"Huh?"

"The winners will spend the night in the new library before anybody else even gets to see the place!"

"Is this like that movie *Night at the Museum*? Will the books come alive and chase people around and junk?"

"No. But there will probably be free movies, and food, and prizes, and *games*."

All of a sudden, Kyle was interested.

4

"So, exactly what kind of games are we talking about?"

"I don't know," said Akimi. "Fun book stuff, I guess."

"And do you think this new library will have equally new computers?"

"Definitely."

"Wi-Fi?"

"Probably."

Kyle nodded slowly. "And this all takes place Friday night?"

"Yep."

"Akimi, I think you just discovered a way for me to shorten my most recent groundation."

"Your what?"

"My game-deprived parental punishment."

Kyle figured being locked in a library with computers

on Friday night would be better than being stuck at home without any gaming gear at all.

"Can I borrow a pen and a sheet of paper?"

"What? You're going to write your essay now? On the bus?"

"Better late than never."

"They're due in homeroom, Kyle. First thing."

"Fine. I'll keep it brief."

Akimi shook her head and handed Kyle a notebook and a pen. The bus bounced over a speed bump into the school driveway.

He would need to make his essay really, really short.

He was hoping the twelve winners would be randomly pulled out of a hat or something and, like the lottery people always said in their TV commercials, you just had to "be in it to win it."

Meanwhile, in another part of town, Charles Chiltington was sitting in his father's library, working with the college student who'd been hired to help him polish up his extra-credit essay.

He was dressed in his typical school uniform: khaki slacks, blue blazer, button-down shirt, and tastefully striped tie. He was the only student at Alexandriaville Middle School who dressed that way.

"What's a big word for 'library'?" Charles asked his tutor. "Teachers love big words."

" 'Book repository.' "

"Bigger, please."

"Um, 'athenaeum.' "

"Perfect! It's such a weird word, they'll have to look it up."

Charles made the change, saved the file, and sent the document off to the printer.

"Your dad sure reads a lot," said his ELA tutor, admiring the leather-bound books lining the walls of Mr. Chiltington's home library.

"Knowledge is power," said Charles. "It's one of our fundamental family philosophies."

Another was *We eat losers for breakfast.*

Kyle and Akimi climbed off the bus and headed into the school.

"You know," said Akimi, "my dad told me the library people had like a bazillion different architects doing drawings and blueprints that they couldn't share with each other."

"How come?"

"To keep everything super secret. My dad and his firm did the front door and that was it."

The second they stepped into Mrs. Cameron's classroom for homeroom period, Miguel Fernandez shouted, "Hey, Kyle! Check it out, bro." He held up a clear plastic binder maybe two inches thick. "I totally aced my essay, man!"

"The library dealio?"

"Yeah! I put in pictures and charts, plus a whole section about the Ancient Library of Alexandria, Egypt, since this is *Alexandria*ville, Ohio!"

"Cool," said Kyle.

Miguel Fernandez was super enthusiastic about everything. He was also president of the school's Library Aide Society. "Hey, Kyle—you know what they say about libraries?"

"Uh, not really."

"They have something for every chapter of your life!"

While Kyle groaned, the second bell rang.

"All right, everybody," said Mrs. Dana Cameron, Kyle's homeroom teacher. "Time to turn in your extra-credit essays." She started walking up and down the rows of desks. "The judges will be meeting in the faculty lounge this morning to make the preliminary cut. . . ."

Crap, thought Kyle. There were *judges.* This was not going to be a bingo-ball drawing like the lottery.

"Mr. Keeley?" The teacher hovered over his desk. "Did you write an essay?"

"Yeah. Sort of."

"I'm sorry. I don't understand. Either you wrote an essay or you didn't."

Kyle halfheartedly handed her his hastily scribbled sheet of paper.

And unfortunately, Mrs. Cameron read it. Out loud.

" 'Balloons. There might be balloons.' "

The classroom erupted with laughter.

Until Mrs. Cameron did that tilt-down-her-glasses-and-glare-over-them thing she did to terrify everybody into total silence.

"This is your essay, Kyle?"

"Yes, ma'am. We were supposed to write why we're excited about the grand opening and, well, balloons are always my favorite part."

"I see," said Mrs. Cameron. "You know, Kyle, your brother Curtis wrote excellent essays when he was in my class."

"Yes, Mrs. Cameron," mumbled Kyle.

Mrs. Cameron sighed contentedly. "Please give him my regards."

"Yes, ma'am."

Mrs. Cameron moved on to the next desk. Miguel eagerly handed her his thick booklet.

"Very well done, Miguel."

"Thank you, Mrs. Cameron!"

Kyle heard an odd noise out in the parking lot. A puttering, clunking, clanking sound.

"Oh, my," said Mrs. Cameron, "I wonder if that's *him*!"

She hurried to the window and pulled up the blinds. All the kids in the classroom followed her.

And then they saw it.

Out in the visitor parking lot. A car that looked like a giant red boot on wheels. It had a strip of notched black boot sole for its bumper. Thick shoelaces crisscrossed their way up from the windshield to the top of a ten-foot-tall boot collar.

"It looks just like the red boot from that game," said Miguel. "Family Frenzy."

Kyle nodded. Family Frenzy was Mr. Lemoncello's first and probably most famous game. The red boot was one of ten tokens you could pick to move around the board.

A tall, gangly man stepped out of the boot car.

"It's Mr. Lemoncello!" gasped Kyle, his heart racing. "What's *he* doing here?"

"It was just announced," said Mrs. Cameron. "This evening, Mr. Luigi Lemoncello himself will be the final judge."

"Of what?"

"Your library essays."

5

Eating lunch in the cafeteria, Kyle stared at his wilted fish
sticks, wishing he could pull a magic Take Another Turn
card out of thin air.

"I blew it," he mumbled.

"Yep," Akimi agreed. "You basically did."

"Can you imagine how awesome that new library's
gonna be if Mr. Lemoncello and his Imagination Factory
guys had anything to do with it?"

"Yes. I can. And I'm kind of hoping I get to see it,
too. After all, I wrote a real essay, not one sentence about
balloons."

"Thanks. Rub it in."

Akimi eased up a little. "Hey, Kyle—when you're playing a game like Sorry and you get bumped back three
spaces, do you usually quit?"

"No. If I get bumped, I play harder because I know I

need to find a way to get back those three spaces *and* pull ahead of the pack."

"Hey, guys!" Miguel Fernandez carried his tray over to join Kyle and Akimi.

He was being followed by a kid with spiky hair and glasses the size of welders' goggles.

"You two know Andrew Peckleman, right?"

"Hey," said Kyle and Akimi.

"Hello."

"Andrew is one of my top library aides," said Miguel.

"Cool," said Akimi.

"Mrs. Yunghans, the librarian, just confirmed that Mr. Lemoncello is the top-secret benefactor who donated all the money to build the new public library. Five hundred million dollars!"

"She heard it on NPR," added Peckleman, who more or less talked through his nose. "So we did some primary source research on Mr. Lemoncello and his connection to Alexandriaville."

"What'd you find out?" asked Kyle.

"First off," said Miguel, "he was born here."

"He had nine brothers and sisters," added Andrew.

"All of 'em crammed into a tiny apartment with only one bathroom over in Little Italy," said Miguel.

"And," said Peckleman, sounding like he wanted to one-up Miguel, "he *loved* the old public library down on Market Street. He used to go there when he was a kid and needed a quiet place to think and doodle his ideas."

"And get this," said Miguel eagerly. "Mrs. Tobin, the librarian back then, took an interest in little Luigi, even though he was just, you know, a kid like us. She kept the library open late some nights and let him borrow junk from her desk or her purse—thimbles and thumbtacks and glue bottles, even red Barbie doll boots—stuff he used for game pieces so he could map out his first ideas on a library table. Then . . ."

Andrew jumped in. "Then Mrs. Tobin took Mr. Lemoncello's sketch for Family Frenzy home to her husband, who ran a print shop. They signed some papers, created a company, and within a couple of years they were all millionaires."

But Miguel had the last word: "Now, of course, Mr. Lemoncello is a bazillionaire!"

"What are you four nerds so excited about?" said Haley Daley as she waltzed past with the gaggle of popular girls in her royal court. Haley was the princess of the seventh grade. Blond hair, blue eyes, blazingly bright smile. She looked like a walking toothpaste commercial.

"We're pumped about Mr. Lemoncello!" said Miguel.

"And the new library!" said Andrew.

"And," said Kyle melodramatically, "just seeing you, Haley."

"You are *so* immature. Come on, girls." Haley and her friends flounced away to the "cool kids" table.

"Check it out," said Akimi, gesturing toward the

cafeteria's food line, where Charles Chiltington was balancing two trays: his own and one for Mrs. Cameron.

"I'm so glad you have lunchroom duty today, Mrs. Cameron," Kyle heard Chiltington say. "If you don't mind, I have a few questions about how conventions within genres—such as poetry, drama, or essays—can affect meaning."

"Well, Charles, I'd be happy to discuss that with you."

"Thank you, Mrs. Cameron. And, may I say, that sweater certainly complements your eye color."

"What a suck-up," mumbled Akimi. "Chiltington's trying to use his weaselly charm to make sure Mrs. C sends his essay up the line to Mr. Lemoncello."

"Don't worry," said Kyle. "Mrs. Cameron isn't the final judge. Mr. Lemoncello is. And since he's a genius, he will definitely pick the essays you guys all wrote."

"Undoubtedly," said Peckleman.

"Thanks, Kyle," said Miguel.

"I just wish you could win with us," said Akimi.

"Well, maybe I can. Like you said, this is just a Move Back Three Spaces card. A Take a Walk on the Boardwalk when someone else owns it. It's a chute in Chutes and Ladders. A detour to the Molasses Swamp in Candy Land!"

"Yo, Kyle," said Miguel. "Exactly how many board games have you played?"

"Enough to know that you don't ever quit until

somebody else actually wins." He picked up his lunch and headed for the dirty-tray window.

Akimi called after him. "Where are you going?"

"I have the rest of lunch and all of study hall to work on a new essay."

"But Mrs. Cameron won't take it."

"Maybe. But I've got to roll the dice one more time. Maybe I'll get lucky."

"I hope so," said Akimi.

"Me too! See you guys on the bus!"

6

Working on his library essay like he'd never worked on any essay in his whole essay-writing life, Kyle crafted a killer thesis sentence that compared libraries to his favorite games.

"Using a library can make learning about anything (and everything) fun," he wrote. "When you're in a library, researching a topic, you're on a scavenger hunt, looking for clues and prizes in books instead of your attic or back-yard."

He put in points and sub-points.

He wrapped everything up with a tidy conclusion.

He even checked his spelling (twice).

But Akimi had been right.

"I'm sorry, Kyle," Mrs. Cameron said when he handed her his new paper at the end of the day. "This is very good and I am impressed by your extra effort. However, the deadline was this morning. Rules are rules. The same as they are in all the board games you mentioned in your essay."

She'd basically handed Kyle a Go Back Five Hundred Spaces card.

But Kyle refused to give up.

He remembered how his mother had written to Mr. Lemoncello's Imagination Factory when he and his brothers needed a fresh set of clue cards for the Indoor-Outdoor Scavenger Hunt.

Maybe he could send his essay directly to Mr. Lemoncello via email.

Maybe, if the game maker wasn't judging the essays until later that night, Kyle still had a shot. A long shot, but, hey, sometimes the long ones were the only shots you got.

The second he hit home he sat down at his mother's kitchen computer. He attached his essay file to a "high priority" email addressed to Mr. Lemoncello at the Imagination Factory.

"What are you doing, Kyle?" his mom asked when she came into the room and found him typing on her computer.

"Some extra-credit homework."

"Extra credit? School's out at the end of the week."

"So?"

"You're not playing my Diner Dash game, are you?"

"No, Mom. It's an essay. About Mr. Lemoncello's amazing new library downtown."

"Oh. Sounds interesting. I heard on the radio that there's going to be a gala grand opening reception this Friday night at the Parker House Hotel, right across the street from the old bank building. I mean, the *new* library."

Kyle typed in a P.S. to his email: "I hope at the party on Friday you have balloons."

He hit send.

"Who did you send your essay to?" his mother asked. "Your teacher?"

"No. Mr. Lemoncello himself. It took some digging, but I found his email address on his game company's website."

"Really? I'm impressed." His mom rubbed his hair. "You know, this morning, I said to your dad: 'Kyle can be just as smart as Curtis and just as focused as Mike—*when* he puts his mind to it.'"

Kyle smiled. "Thanks, Mom."

But his smile quickly disappeared when a *BONG!* alerted him to an incoming email.

From Mr. Lemoncello.

It was an auto-response form letter.

Dear Lemoncello Game Lover:

This is a no-reply mailbox. Your message did not go through. Do not try to resend it or you'll just hear another *BONG!* But thank you for playing our games.

7

Heading back to school on Tuesday, Kyle knew he had to put on a brave face.

He smiled as he walked with his class toward the auditorium for a special early-morning assembly. The one where Mr. Luigi L. Lemoncello himself would announce the winners of the Library Lock-In Essay Contest.

"I hope he picked yours," Kyle whispered to Akimi.

"Thanks. I do, too. But the lock-in won't be as much fun without you."

"Well, when it's over, and the library is officially open, you can take me on a tour."

"That's exactly what I'm going to do! *If* I win."

"If you don't, I'm sending a flaming squirrel after Mrs. Cameron."

For this assembly, the seventh graders, most of whom were twelve years old, were told to sit in the front rows, close to the stage. That made Kyle feel a little better. At least he'd get a chance to see Mr. Lemoncello up close and personal.

But his hero wasn't even onstage.

Just the principal; the school librarian, Mrs. Yunghans; and a redheaded woman in high-heeled shoes who Kyle didn't recognize. She sat up straight, like someone had slipped a yardstick down the back of her bright red business suit. Her glasses were bright red, too.

"That's Dr. Yanina Zinchenko!" gushed Miguel Fernandez, who was sitting on Kyle's right.

"Who's she?" asked Akimi, seated to Kyle's left.

"Just the most famous librarian in the whole wide world!"

"All right, boys and girls," said the principal at the podium. "Settle down. Quiet, please. It is my great honor to introduce the head librarian for the new Alexandriaville public library, Dr. Yanina Zinchenko."

Everybody clapped. The tall lady in the red outfit strode to the microphone.

"Good morning."

Her voice was breathy with just a hint of a Russian accent.

"Twelve years ago, this town lost its one and only public library when it was torn down to make room for an elevated parking garage. Back then, many said the Internet had rendered the 'old-fashioned' library obsolete, that a new parking garage would attract shoppers to the boutiques and dress shops near the old bank building. But the library's demolition also meant that those of you who are now twelve years old have lived your entire lives *without* a public library."

She looked down at the front rows.

"This is why, to kick off our summer reading program, twelve twelve-year-olds will be selected to be the very first to explore the wonders awaiting inside Mr. Lemoncello's extraordinary new library. You will, of course, need your parents' permission. We have slips for you to take home. You will also need a sleeping bag, a toothbrush, and, if you please, a change of clothes."

She smiled mysteriously.

"You might consider packing *two* pairs of underwear."

Oh-kay, thought Kyle. *That's bizarre.* Did the librarian really think seventh graders weren't toilet trained?

"There will be movies, food, fun, games, and prizes. Also, each of our twelve winners will receive a five-hundred-dollar gift card good toward the purchase of Lemoncello games and gizmos."

Oh, man. Five hundred bucks' worth of free games and gear? Kyle sank a little lower in his seat. The next time someone gave him an extra-credit essay assignment, he'd turn it in *early*!

"And now, here to announce our winners, the man behind the new library, the master gamester himself—Mr. Luigi Lemoncello!"

Dr. Zinchenko gestured to her left.

The whole auditorium swung their heads.

People were clapping and whistling and cheering.

But nobody came onstage.

The applause petered out.

And then, on the opposite side of the stage, Kyle heard a very peculiar sound.

It was a cross between a burp and the squeak from a squeeze toy.

8

Over on the side of the stage, a shoe that looked like a peeled-open banana appeared from behind a curtain.

When it landed, the shoe burp-squeaked.

As a second banana shoe burp-squeaked onto the floor, Kyle looked up and there he was—Mr. Lemoncello! He had loose and floppy limbs and was dressed in a three-piece black suit with a bright red tie. His black broad-brimmed hat was cocked at a crooked angle atop his curly white hair. Kyle was so close he could see a sly twinkle sparkling in Mr. Lemoncello's coal-black eyes.

Treading very carefully, Mr. Lemoncello walked toward the podium. The burp-squeaks in his shoes seemed to change pitch depending on how hard he landed on his heels. He added a couple of little jig steps, a quick hop and a stutter-step skip, and yes—his shoes were squeaking out a song.

"Pop Goes the Weasel."

On the *Pop!* Mr. Lemoncello popped behind the podium.

The crowd went wild.

Mr. Lemoncello politely bowed and said, very softly, "Tank you. Tank you. *Grazie. Grazie.*"

He bent forward so his mouth was maybe an inch away from the microphone.

"*Buon giorno,* boise and-uh girls-a." He spoke very timidly, very slowly. "Tees ees how my-uh momma and my-uh poppa teach-uh me to speak-eh de English."

He wiggled his ears. Straightened his back.

"But then," he said in a crisp, clear voice, "I went to the Alexandriaville Public Library, where a wonderful librarian named Mrs. Gail Tobin helped me learn how to speak like this: 'If two witches were watching two watches, which witch would watch which watch?' I can also speak while upside down and underwater, but not today because I just had this suit dry-cleaned and do *not* want to get it wet."

Mr. Lemoncello bounced across the stage like a happy grasshopper.

"Now then, children, if I may call you that—which I must because I have not yet memorized all of your names, even though I *am* working on it—what do you think is the most amazingly incredible thing you'll find inside your wondrous new library, besides, of course, all the knowledge you need to do anything and everything you ever want or need to do?"

No one said anything. They were too mesmerized by Mr. Lemoncello's rat-a-tat words.

"Would it be: A) robots silently whizzing their way through the library, restocking the shelves, B) the Electronic Learning Center, with three dozen plasma-screen TVs all connected to flight simulators and educational video games, or C) the Wonder Dome? Lined with ten giant video screens, it can make the whole building feel like a rocket ship blasting off into outer space!"

"The game room!" someone shouted.

"The robots!"

"The video dome!"

Mr. Lemoncello raced back to the podium and made a buzzing noise into the microphone.

"Sorry. The correct answer is—and not just because of Winn-Dixie—D) all of the above!"

The crowd went wild.

Mr. Lemoncello whirled around to face his head librarian.

"Dr. Zinchenko? Will you kindly help me pass out our first twelve library cards?"

It was time to announce the essay contest winners.

Dr. Zinchenko placed a stack of twelve shiny cards on the podium in front of Mr. Lemoncello.

"Please," he said, "as I call your name, come join me onstage. Miguel Fernandez."

"Yes!" Miguel jumped up out of his seat.

"Akimi Hughes."

"Whoo-hoo."

Kyle was thrilled to see his two friends be the first ones called to the stage.

"Andrew Peckleman, Bridgette Wadge, Sierra Russell, Yasmeen Smith-Snyder."

Yasmeen squealed when her name was called.

"Sean Keegan, Haley Daley, Rose Vermette, and Kayla Corson."

Ten kids, all the same age as Kyle, were up onstage with his idol, Mr. Lemoncello. He was not. Only two more chances.

As if reading his mind, Mr. Lemoncello said, "Only two more," and tapped a pair of library cards on the podium. "Charles Chiltington."

"Gosh, really?" He dashed up to the podium and started pumping Mr. Lemoncello's hand. "Thank you, sir. This is such an honor. Truly. I mean that."

"Thank you, Charles. May I have my hand back? I need it to flip over this final card."

"Of course, sir. But I cannot wait to spend the night in your library, or, as I like to call it, your athenaeum. Because, as I said in my essay, when you open a book, you open your mind!"

Finally, Charles the brownnoser let go of Mr. Lemoncello's hand and went over to line up with the other winners.

"And last but not least," said Mr. Lemoncello, "Kyle Keeley."

Kyle could not believe his ears. He thought he was dreaming.

But then Akimi started waving for him to come on up!

Dazed, Kyle made his way up the steps to join the others onstage. Mr. Lemoncello handed Kyle a library card. His name and the number twelve were printed on the front. Two book covers—*I Love You, Stinky Face* and *The Napping House*—were on the back.

"Let's all pose for a picture, please," said the principal.

When everybody moved into position for the photographer, Kyle found himself standing *right next to* Mr. Lemoncello.

He swallowed hard. "I'm a big fan, sir," he said, his voice kind of shaky.

"Why, thank you. And remind me—you are?"

"I'm Kyle, sir. Kyle Keeley."

"Ah, yes. The boy who proved what I've always known to be true: The game is never over till it's over. *BONG!*"

9

Kyle couldn't wait to tell his family the good news.

"I won the essay contest!" He showed them his shiny new library card.

"Congratulations!" said his mom.

"Way to go!" said his dad.

His brothers, Curtis and Mike, were more interested in Kyle's other card: his five-hundred-dollar Lemoncello gift card.

"It's good for twelve months," said Kyle.

"But you need to use it *now*," said Mike. "We need to go to the store tonight so you can buy me Mr. Lemoncello's Kooky-Wacky Hockey."

"I can't."

"Why not?"

"I have to show my library card at the store to cash it in."

"And?"

"Um, I'm grounded, remember?"

"You know, Kyle," said his dad, looking at his mother, who nodded, "since you worked extra hard and did such a bang-up job on your essay, I think we might consider suspending your punishment."

"Really?"

"Really."

Kyle's mom and dad smiled at him.

The way they smiled whenever Mike won a football game or Curtis won the science fair.

After supper, all five Keeleys piled into the family van and headed off to the local toy store.

"Lemoncello's hockey game is awesome," said Mike as they drove to the store. "Especially when the penguins play the polar bears."

"I'm hoping to find a classic board game," mused Curtis. "Mr. Lemoncello's Bewilderingly Baffling Bibliomania."

"Is that about the Bible?" asked their dad from behind the wheel.

"Not exactly," said Curtis, "although the Bible, especially a rare Gutenberg edition, may be one of the treasures you must find and collect, because the object of the game is to collect rare and valuable books by—"

"The penguins in Kooky-Wacky Hockey aren't from Pittsburgh like in the NHL," said Mike, cutting off Curtis.

"They're from Antarctica. And the polar bears? They're from Alaska."

Kyle had decided to divvy up his gift card five ways. To give everybody—including his mom and dad—one hundred dollars to play with.

As soon as they entered the toy store, the family split up, cruising the aisles with their own shopping carts. His mom was going to upgrade to Mr. Lemoncello's Restaurant Rush. His dad was looking for one of Mr. Lemoncello's complicated What If? historical games: What If the Romans Had Won the American Civil War?

Kyle hung with Curtis and Mike for a while. Being the one with the gift card made him feel like he was suddenly *their* big brother.

Mike quickly found his PlayStation hockey game and Curtis was in geek heaven when he finally found Bibliomania.

"They only have one left!" he gushed, tearing off the cellophane shrink-wrap and prying open the lid. He sat down right in the middle of the store and unfolded the game board on his lap. "You see, you start under the rotunda in this circular reading room. Then you go upstairs and enter each of these ten chambers, where you have to answer a question about a book. . . ."

"Um, I think I hear Mom calling me," said Kyle. "She must need the gift card. Enjoy!"

And Kyle took off.

"*The store will close in fifteen minutes,*" announced a voice from the ceiling speakers.

Kyle flew up and down the aisles and grabbed a couple of board games he didn't own yet, including Mr. Lemoncello's Absolutely Incredible Iron Horse—a game where you build your own transcontinental railroad, complete with locomotive game pieces that actually puff steam.

As Kyle was doing some quick math to see if he'd spent his one hundred dollars, Charles Chiltington rolled up the aisle with a cart crammed full with *five* hundred dollars' worth of loot. Games stacked on top of games were practically spilling over the sides. Mr. Lemoncello's Phenomenal Picture Word Puzzler, one of Kyle's favorites, was teetering on the top.

"Hello, Keeley," said Chiltington with a smirk. He looked down at the three games sitting in the bottom of Kyle's shopping cart. "Just getting started?"

"No. I shared my gift card with my family."

"Really? Well, that was a mistake, wasn't it?"

Kyle was about to answer when Chiltington said, "So long. See you on Friday." Kyle wasn't 100 percent sure but Charles might've also muttered, "Loser."

Since the store was about to close, Kyle headed toward the checkout lanes. When he passed the customer service department, he saw Haley Daley.

"No," Kyle heard Haley say in a hushed tone to the clerk working the Returns window. "I do not want to return these items for *store credit*. I would prefer cash."

Kyle finally found his family, showed the cashier his library card, and paid for everything with a single swipe of his gift card.

"You know, Kyle," said his dad as the family walked across the parking lot, "your mother and I are extremely proud of you. Writing a good essay isn't easy."

"Maybe you'll be an author someday," added his mom. "Then you could write books that'll be on the shelves of the new library."

"Thanks, little brother," said Curtis, practically hugging his Bibliomania box.

"Yeah," said Mike. "This was awesome. Way to win one for the team!"

"Best 'family game night' ever," joked their dad.

Kyle was enjoying his rare moment of glory, playing Santa Claus for his whole family. As the week dragged on, Friday night and the library lock-in started to remind Kyle of Christmas, too: It felt like they would never come.

Then, finally, they did.

10

"Now this is what I call a party," said Kyle's mother as she helped herself to a bacon-wrapped shrimp from a tray being carried by a waiter in a tuxedo.

Kyle and his parents were in the crowded ballroom of the Parker House Hotel for the Lemoncello Library's Gala Grand Opening Reception. The Parker House was located right across the street from the old Gold Leaf Bank building and the cluster of office buildings, craft shops, clothing stores, and restaurants called Old Town.

"I'm going to see if I can find Akimi," Kyle said to his mom and dad.

"Give her our congratulations!" said his mom.

"We're proud of *her,* too," added his dad.

Kyle made his way through the glittering sea of dressed-up adults.

Even though his parents had put on fancy clothes for

the reception, Kyle was wearing "something comfortable to go exploring in," as instructed by the Lock-In Guide he'd received on Wednesday. He'd packed a sleeping bag and a small suitcase with a change of clothes, toiletries, and yes, as requested, an extra pair of underpants.

Kyle saw Sierra Russell all alone in a corner near a clump of curtains. It didn't look like her mother had come to the party with her. Sierra, of course, had her nose buried in a book. Kyle shook his head. The girl was about to spend the night in a building filled with books and she was skipping all the free food and pop so she could read? That was just nutty.

Haley Daley, wearing a sparkly blouse, was posing for a wall of photographers who wanted to snap her picture. Her mother was at the party, too. While the cameras were focused on Haley's smile, Mrs. Daley wrapped up a couple of chicken kebabs in a napkin and slipped them inside her purse.

Now Kyle saw Charles Chiltington. Poor guy must not have read the memo about comfortable clothes. He was still wearing his khakis and blazer, just like his dad. Kyle figured the Chiltington family must own like three hundred pairs of pleated tan pants.

"Hey, Kyle!" Akimi waved at him from near a fake shrub curled to look like a Silly Straw.

"Hey," said Kyle.

"Did you remember to bring your library card?"

"Yep." Kyle pulled it out of his pocket.

"Huh," said Akimi. "I got different books on the back of mine. *One Fish Two Fish Red Fish Blue Fish* by Dr. Seuss and *Nine Stories* by J. D. Salinger."

"Guess they're like baseball cards," said Kyle. "They're all different."

"Hey, you guys!" Miguel Fernandez, more excited than usual (which was saying something), pushed through the mob to join them. "Did you try these puffy cheesy things?"

"Nah," said Kyle. "I'm sticking to food I recognize."

"The 'puffy cheesy things' are called fromage tartlets," said Andrew Peckleman, coming over to join the group.

"Huh," said Kyle. "Good to know."

A waiter passed by with a tray loaded down with small boxes of Mr. Lemoncello's Anagraham Cracker cookies.

"Oh, I love these," said Kyle, taking a box off the platter and opening it. "The cookies are in the shapes of letters. You have to see how many words you can spell."

"Cool," said Miguel, snagging a fistful of cookies out of Kyle's box. "Taste good, too!"

"Yep," said Kyle. "But the more you eat, the harder the game gets."

"Why?" asked Andrew Peckleman.

"Less letters," said Akimi, snatching two "B's" and a "Q" and wolfing them down. "Mmm. Barbecue-flavored."

Kyle spread out the remaining cookies in his palm: U N F E H A V. He grinned as he deciphered an easy anagram. "HAVE FUN. Sweet."

"Ladies and gentlemen? Boys and girls?" Dr. Zinchenko,

dressed in a bright red suit, strode to the center of the ballroom. "May I have your attention, please? Mr. Lemoncello will be arriving shortly to say a few brief words. After that, I will escort the twelve essay contest winners across the street to the library. Therefore, children, might I suggest that you eat up? Food and drink are not permitted anywhere in the library except in the Book Nook Café, conveniently located on the first floor."

Miguel grabbed a few more puffy cheesy things.

When she thought no one was looking, Mrs. Daley shoved a napkined bundle of bacon-wrapped shrimp into her purse.

Akimi nibbled a couple of chocolate-dipped pretzel sticks.

"Aren't you gonna grab some more grub?" she said to Kyle.

"No thanks. I only like food I can play with."

"One last thing," announced Dr. Zinchenko. "We, of course, want our winners to have fun tonight. However, I must insist that each of you respect my number one rule: Be gentle. With each other and, most especially, the library's books and exhibits. Can you do that for me?"

"Yes!" shouted all the winners except Charles Chiltington. He said, "Indubitably."

"Good thing the library has dictionaries," muttered Akimi. "Half the time, it's the only way to figure out what Chiltington's saying."

Suddenly, all the adults in the ballroom started clapping.

Mr. Lemoncello, looking like a beanpole wearing a tail-coat and a tiny birthday-party fireman's hat, strode into the room through a side door.

"Thank you, thank you," he said, stretching the elastic band to raise his kid-sized hat and tipping it toward the crowd. "You are too kind."

When he let go of the hat, it snapped back with a sharp *THWACK!*

"As Dr. Zinchenko informed you, I'd like to say a few brief words. Here they are: 'short,' 'memorandum,' and 'underpants.' And let us pause to remember the immortal words of Dr. Seuss: 'The more that you read, the more things you will know. The more that you learn, the more places you'll go.' Children? . . ."

Mr. Lemoncello flourished his arm toward the ball-room doors.

"It's time to go across the street. Your amazingly spectacular new public library awaits!"

Eager to see what was inside the new library, the twelve essay contest winners quickly gathered behind Dr. Zinchenko.

"This way, children," said the head librarian. "Follow me."

The crowd cheered as they marched out of the ballroom, all toting their sleeping bags and suitcases. There was more cheering (plus some hooting and hollering) when they reached the hotel lobby and went out the revolving doors into the street.

The new public library, with its glistening gold dome, took up half a downtown block, its back butting up against an old-fashioned office tower. The building was a boxy fortress, three stories tall, with stately columns that acted like bookends, because the windowless walls had been painted to resemble a row of giant books lined up on a shelf.

"It's like a majestic Greek temple," gushed Miguel.

"And the world's biggest bookcase," added Sierra Russell, who had finally put away her paperback.

Velvet ropes lined a path across Main Street that led to a red carpet leading up a flight of steps to the arched entryway and seriously steel (not to mention *round*) front door.

Kyle had to smile when he saw what was tethered to the railings on either side of the steps: balloons!

A big bruiser—maybe six four, 250 pounds—in sunglasses and a black sports coat stood in front of the library's circular door, which had several large valve wheels like you'd see on a submarine hatch. The burly guard wore his hair in long, ropy dreadlocks.

"What's with that door?" asked Haley Daley, who, of course, had pushed her way to the front. "It looks like it came from a bank vault or something."

"It is the door from the old Gold Leaf Bank's walk-in vault," said Dr. Zinchenko. "It weighs twenty tons."

Akimi turned around and whispered, "My dad designed the support structure for that thing. Check out the hinges."

Kyle nodded. He was impressed.

"Why a vault door?" asked Kayla Corson.

"Because," said Dr. Zinchenko, "one sleepy Saturday, when Mr. Lemoncello was your age, he was working in the old public library over on Market Street. He was so lost in his thoughts, he did not hear the sirens as police cars raced past the library to the bank, where a burglar alarm had just been activated. This door serves as a reminder to us all: Our thoughts are safe when they are inside a library. Not even a bank robbery can disturb them."

Miguel was nodding like crazy. He could relate.

"It also helps us keep our most valuable treasures secure."

"There aren't any windows," observed Andrew Peckleman. "Probably to stop bank robbers from busting in. But shouldn't you people have added windows when you turned it into a library?"

"A library doesn't need windows, Andrew. We have books, which are windows into worlds we never even dreamed possible."

"An open book is an open mind," added Charles Chiltington. "That's what I always say."

Dr. Zinchenko pulled out a bright red note card. "Before we enter, please listen very carefully. 'Your library cards are the keys to everything you will need,'" she read. "'The library staff is here to help you find whatever it is you are looking for.'"

She smiled slightly, tucked the card back into her pocket, turned to the security guard, and said, "Clarence? Will you do the honors?"

"With pleasure, Dr. Z."

Clarence turned one giant wheel, spun another, and cranked a third.

Noiselessly, the twenty-ton door swung open.

* * *

The first thing Kyle could see inside was a trickling fountain in a grand foyer of brilliant white marble. The fountain featured a life-size statue of Mr. Lemoncello standing on a lily pad in the middle of a shallow reflecting pool ten feet wide. His head was tilted back so water could spurt up from his mouth in an arc.

Kyle noticed a quote chiseled into the statue's pedestal: KNOWLEDGE NOT SHARED REMAINS UNKNOWN. —LUIGI L. LEMONCELLO

Beyond the fountain, through an arched walkway, was a huge room filled with desks.

When everybody had shuffled into the entrance hall, Dr. Zinchenko turned to the security guard.

"Clarence?"

Clarence hauled the heavy steel door shut. Kyle heard the whir of spinning wheels, the clink of grinding gears, and a reverberating clunk.

"Wow!" said Miguel. "Talk about a lock-in!"

"I'll be in the control center, Dr. Z," said the security guard.

"Very well, Clarence."

Clarence disappeared behind a red door.

"Now then, children," said the librarian, "if you will all follow me into the Rotunda Reading Room."

As the rest of the group started filing into the gigantic circular room, Kyle checked out a display case beside the red door. A sign over it read "Staff Picks: Our Most

Memorable Reads." A dozen books were lined up on four shelves.

One cover in the middle of the bottom row caught Kyle's eye. It showed a football player wearing a number nineteen jersey dropping back to hurl a pass. Kyle made a mental note of the title: *In the Pocket: Johnny Unitas and Me.* Tomorrow morning, when the lock-in was over, he might use his library card to check it out for his big brother, Mike.

"Wow!"

Everybody gasped as they stepped into the Rotunda Reading Room and looked up. The entire underside of the dome looked like space as seen from the Hubble telescope: A dusty spiral nebula billowed up, a galaxy of stars twinkled, and meteorites whizzed across the ceiling.

"Ooh!"

The space imagery on the ceiling dissolved into ten distinct panels, each one becoming a display of swirling graphics.

"Those are the ten categories of the Dewey decimal system," whispered Miguel, sounding awestruck. "See the panel with Cleopatra, the guy mountain climbing, and the Viking ship sailing across it? That's for 900 to 999. History and Geography."

"Cool," said Kyle.

Tucked beneath the ten screens in arched niches were incredible 3-D statues glowing a ghostly green.

"I believe those are holographic projections," said Andrew Peckleman, waving up at a statue that was waving down at him.

The room under the dome was huge. It was circular, with a round desk at the center that was surrounded by four rings of reading desks.

Kyle saw that half of the rotunda was filled with floor-to-ceiling bookshelves. The other half had balconies on the second and third floors that reminded him of the open atrium of a hotel he and his family had stayed at once.

While everybody was gawking at the architecture, Dr. Zinchenko said the words Kyle had been waiting to hear all day:

"Now then, who's ready for our first game?"

12

"Will everybody please line up behind that far desk in front of the Children's Room?" said Dr. Zinchenko, gesturing toward one of the wooden tables in the outermost ring of the room.

"How many of you are familiar with Mr. Lemoncello's classic board game Hurry to the Top of the Heap?"

Twelve hands shot up.

"Very good," said Dr. Zinchenko.

Overhead, the Wonder Dome dissolved into a gigantic, curved Heap box top.

"This will be a live, three-dimensional version of that game. Each of you will be asked a trivia question. If you are able to answer it correctly, you will roll the dice and advance the equivalent number of desks. When you return to the starting point, you will move into the next concentric circle of desks. When you complete that ring, you will move into the next, and so on. If one of you makes it all the way to my desk at the center, you will be declared the winner."

"But we don't have any dice," said Yasmeen Smith-Snyder.

"Yes you do. See that smoky glass panel in the center of the desk? It is actually a touch-screen computer, currently running Mr. Lemoncello's dice-rolling app. Simply swipe and flick your fingers across the glass to toss and tumble the animated dice."

Dr. Zinchenko placed a stack of red cards on her desk. She looked like the host of a TV game show. "Before we begin, are there any other questions?"

Charles Chiltington raised his hand.

"Yes, Mr. Chiltington?"

"What will the winner win? After all, the prize is the most important part of any game."

Kyle didn't totally agree, but he was too excited about playing the game to say anything.

"Tonight's first prize," said Dr. Zinchenko, "is this golden key granting the winner access to Mr. Lemoncello's private and very posh bedroom suite up on the library's third floor. Instead of spending the night on the floor in a sleeping bag, you will be relaxing in luxury with a feather bed, a seventy-two-inch television screen and a state-of-the-art gaming console."

Okay. Kyle was definitely interested in this particular prize.

Judging from the wide-open eyes and chorus of "oohs" and "wows" all around him, so was everybody else.

Dr. Zinchenko flipped over the first question card.

"What major-league pitcher was the last to win at least thirty games in one season?"

Six players got it wrong before Kyle got it right.

"Denny McLain."

"Correct."

He swiped the glass panel, rolled a ten, and advanced ten desks around the room.

"What United States Navy ship was once captured by the North Koreans?"

Miguel nailed that one: "The USS *Pueblo*." He flew twelve spaces around the room.

"What did *Apollo 8* accomplish that had never been done before?"

Akimi, Andrew Peckleman, and Kayla Corson struck out on that one.

But Charles Chiltington knew the answer: "It was the first spacecraft to orbit the moon."

"Correct."

Chiltington rolled a five, landing him in last place.

Kyle's next question was tougher:

"Who was famous for saying, 'Book 'em, Danno'?"

"Um, that guy on *Hawaii Five-0*?"

"Please be more specific."

"Uh, the one with the shiny hair. Jack Lord?"

"That is correct."

Kyle breathed a sigh of relief. Thank goodness he and his dad sometimes watched reruns of old TV shows from the 1960s.

But when he flicked the computerized dice, his luck hit a brick wall. He rolled snake eyes and moved up two measly desks.

Meanwhile, Miguel went down with a question about Barbra Streisand. (Kyle wasn't exactly sure who she was.)

And Charles Chiltington surged ahead with a correct answer about the Beatles' "Hey Jude" and a double-sixes roll.

As the game went on, Kyle and Chiltington, the only players still standing, kept answering correctly and moving around the room, until they were both seated at a desk in the innermost ring—only six spaces away from Dr. Zinchenko's desk and victory. Kyle was seriously glad he and his mom had played so many games of Trivial Pursuit—with the original, extremely *old* cards.

"Kyle, here is your next question: What song in the movie *Doctor Dolittle* won an Academy Award?"

Kyle squinted. He had that movie. An old VHS cassette tape that his mom had bought at a garage sale. Too bad they didn't have a VCR to watch it on. But even though he'd never seen the movie, he had read the front and back of the box a couple of times.

"Um, 'Talk to the Animals'?"

"Correct."

He started breathing again.

"Roll the dice, please, Mr. Keeley."

Kyle did.

Another pair of ones. He moved up two spaces. Now he was only four desks away from winning.

"Mr. Chiltington, here is your next question: Who was elected president in 1968?"

"I believe that was Richard Milhous Nixon."

"You are also correct."

Chiltington didn't wait for the librarian to tell him to roll the dice. He flicked his fingers across the glass pad.

"Yes! Double sixes. Again." He moved around the last ring of desks, tapping their tops, counting them off even though everybody knew his twelve was more than good enough to carry him to the finish line.

"Congratulations, Mr. Chiltington," Dr. Zinchenko said as she handed him the key to the private suite. "You are this evening's first winner."

"Thank you, Dr. Zinchenko. I am truly and sincerely honored."

"Congratulations, Charles," said Kyle. "Way to win."

"Get used to it, Keeley," he answered in a voice only the other kids could hear. "I'm a Chiltington. We never lose."

13

What happened next was extremely cool.

A holographic image of a second librarian appeared beside Dr. Zinchenko at the center desk. She looked a little like Princess Leia being beamed out of R2-D2 in *Star Wars*. Except she had an old-fashioned bubble-top hairdo, cat's-eye glasses, and a tweed jacket with patches on the elbows.

"Here to present our official library lock-in rules," said Dr. Zinchenko, "is Mrs. Gail Tobin, head librarian of the Alexandriaville Public Library back in the 1960s, when Mr. Lemoncello was your age."

Overhead, the Wonder Dome had shifted back to its ten Dewey decimal displays.

"How old is she?" asked Sean Keegan.

"She'd be a hundred and ten if she were still alive."

"But she's dead and working here?"

"Let's just say her spirit lives on in this hologram."

"Mrs. Tobin's the one who helped Mr. Lemoncello so much," Kyle whispered to Akimi. "When he was a kid."

"I know. Her hair looks like a beehive."

Kyle shrugged. "From what I've seen on TV, the 1960s were generally weird."

"Welcome, children, to the library of the future," said the flickering projection. "Dr. Zinchenko will now pass out Lemoncello Library floor plans—your map and guide to all that this extraordinary building has to offer. Your new library cards will grant you access to all rooms except the master control center—the red door you passed on your way in—and, of course, Mr. Lemoncello's private suite on the third floor."

Charles Chiltington dangled his golden key in front of his face. "I believe you need *this* to enter that."

Mrs. Tobin ignored him. She was a hologram. That made it easier.

"Security personnel are on duty twenty-four hours a day," she continued. "During your stay, all of your actions will be recorded by video cameras, as outlined in the consent agreements you and your parents signed earlier."

"Are we going to be on a reality TV show?" asked Haley, smiling up at a tiny camera with a blinking red light.

"It is a distinct possibility," said Dr. Zinchenko.

"I like television," said the ghostly image of Mrs. Tobin. "*Rowan and Martin's Laugh-In* is my favorite program. Returning to the rules. The use of personal electronic devices is strictly prohibited at all times during the lock-in."

The security guard, Clarence, and a guy who looked like his identical twin brother entered the rotunda, each of them carrying an aluminum attaché case.

"Kindly deposit all cell phones, iPods, and iPads in the receptacles provided by our security guards, Clarence and Clement. Your devices will be safely stored for the duration of your stay and will be returned to you at the conclusion of our activities. Also, you may use the desktop pad computers in this room to comb through our card catalog and conduct Internet research. However, these devices cannot send or receive email or text messages—whatever those might be. Remember, I retired in 1973. We still used carbon paper. And now Dr. Zinchenko will walk you through the floor plan."

Everybody unfolded their map pamphlets.

"As you can see," said Dr. Zinchenko, "fiction titles are located here in the reading room. The Children's Enrichment Room, with soundproof walls, is over there. Two fully equipped community meeting rooms as well as the Book Nook Café—behind those windows where the curtains are drawn—are also located on this floor. Upstairs on two, you will find ten numbered doors, each leading into a chamber filled with books, information, and, well, *displays* related to its corresponding Dewey decimal category."

Kyle raised his hand.

"Yes?"

"Where's the Electronic Learning Center?"

Dr. Zinchenko grinned. "Upstairs on the third floor, where you will also find the Board Room, the Art and Artifacts Room, the IMAX theater, the Lemoncello-abilia Room, the—"

"Can we go upstairs and play?" asked Bridgette Wadge. "I want to try out the space shuttle simulator."

"I want to learn how to drive a car!" said Sean Keegan. "A race car!"

"I want to conquer the world with Alexander the Great!" said Yasmeen Smith-Snyder.

Apparently, everybody was doing what Kyle had already done: checking out the "Available Educational Gameware" listed on the back of the floor plan.

"Early access to the Electronic Learning Center will be tonight's second prize," said Dr. Zinchenko. "To win it, you must use the library's resources to find dessert, which we have hidden somewhere in the building. Whoever does the research and locates the goodies first will also be the first one allowed into the Electronic Learning Center. So use your wits and use your library. Go find dessert!"

Everybody raced around the room and sat down at separate desks to start tapping on the glass computer pads.

Well, everybody except Sierra Russell. She spent like two seconds swiping her fingers across a screen, wrote something down with a stubby pencil on a slip of paper, then wandered off to inspect the three-story-tall curved bookcases lining the walls at the back half of the rotunda. Kyle watched as she stepped onto a slightly elevated platform with handles like you'd see on your grandmother's walker. It even had a basket attached to the front.

"Dr. Zinchenko?"

"Yes, Ms. Russell?"

"Is this safe? Because the book I want is all the way up at the top."

"Yes. Just make sure your feet are securely locked in."

Sierra wiggled her leg. Kyle heard a metallic snap.

"It's like a ski boot," said Sierra.

"That's right. Now use the keypad to tell the hover ladder the call number for the book you are interested in and hang on tight."

Sierra consulted the slip of paper and tapped some keys.

"The bottom of that platform you are standing on is a magnet," said Dr. Zinchenko. "There are ribbons of electromagnetic material in the lining of the bookcases. The strength of those magnets will be modulated by our maglev computer based on the call number you input."

Two seconds later, Sierra Russell was floating in the air, drifting up and to the left. It was absolutely awesome.

"The hover ladder must use advanced magnetic levitation technology," said Miguel, seated at the desk to Kyle's right. "Just like the maglev bullet trains in Japan."

"Cool," mumbled Kyle.

And for the first time in his life, Kyle Keeley wanted to check out a library book more than anything in the world.

"How about we work together?" said Akimi when she sat down at Kyle's table.

"Hmmm?"

Kyle couldn't take his eyes off Sierra Russell. She had drifted up about twenty-five feet and was leaning against the railings of her floating platform, completely lost in a new book.

"Hello? Earth to Kyle? Do you want somebody else to get first dibs on the Electronic Learning Center?"

"No."

"Then focus."

"Okay. So how do we use our wits and the library to find dessert?"

Akimi nodded toward Miguel, whose fingers were dancing across the screen of his desktop's tablet computer.

"I think he's doing a search in the card catalog," whispered Akimi.

"Why?"

"It's how you find stuff in a library, Kyle."

"I know that. But we're not looking for *books* about dessert. We need to find actual food."

Andrew Peckleman stood up from his desk and sprinted up a wrought-iron spiral staircase leading to the second floor. Two seconds later, Charles Chiltington was sprinting up the staircase behind him.

All the other players soon followed. Everybody was headed to the second floor and the Dewey decimal rooms. Miguel finally popped up from his desk and made a mad dash for the nearest staircase.

"It's got to be up in the six hundreds, you guys," he called out to Kyle and Akimi.

"Thanks," said Kyle. But he still didn't budge from his seat.

"I guess the six hundreds is the Dewey decimal category where you find books about desserts," said Akimi. "Maybe we should . . ."

"Wait a second," said Kyle.

"Um, Kyle, in case you haven't noticed, you, me, and glider girl Sierra are the only ones still on this floor, and Sierra isn't really *on* the floor because she's floating."

"Hang on, Akimi. I have an idea." Kyle pulled out his floor plan. "Dessert is probably hiding in plain sight. Just like the bonus codes in Squirrel Squad. Follow me."

"Where to?"

"The Book Nook Café. The one room in the library where, according to what Dr. Zinchenko told us back at the hotel, food and drinks are actually allowed."

They strolled into the cozy café.

"Whoo-hoo!" shouted Akimi.

The walls were decorated with shelves of cookbooks but several tables were loaded down with trays of cookies, cakes, ice cream, and fruit!

"That's why the curtains were closed behind the windows into the rotunda," said Akimi. "So we couldn't see all this food. Way to go, Kyle."

Kyle did his best imitation of Charles Chiltington: "I'm a Keeley, Akimi. We never lose. Except, of course, when we don't win."

After everyone had dessert, Kyle and Akimi were the first ones allowed to enter the Electronic Learning Center.

Kyle flew the space shuttle, making an excellent landing on Mars before crashing into one of Saturn's moons. Akimi rode a horse with Paul Revere. Then Kyle learned how to drive a stick-shift stock car on the Talladega racetrack while Akimi climbed into a tiny submarine to swim with sharks, dolphins, and sea turtles—all of which were projected on the glass walls of her undersea simulator.

All the educational video games had 3-D visuals, digital surround sound, and something new that Mr. Lemoncello was developing for his video games: smell-a-vision. When you sacked Rome with the Visigoths, you could smell the smoky scent of the burning city as well as the barbarians' b.o.

After an hour, Dr. Zinchenko ushered everybody else into the Electronic Learning Center. They'd been watching George Washington debate George W. Bush (both were audio-animatronic dummies) in the "town square" at the center of the 900s room.

At ten p.m. they all tromped into the IMAX theater, also on the third floor, to see a jukebox concert. 3-D images of the world's best musicians (living and dead) performed their hits "live." The best part was Mozart jamming with Metallica.

Finally, around three in the morning, Clarence and his twin brother, Clement, came to escort the kids to their sleeping quarters. The boys would roll out their sleeping bags in the Children's Room, just off the rotunda; the girls would be upstairs on the third floor in the Board Room. Charles Chiltington would be luxuriating all alone in Mr. Lemoncello's private suite.

Exhausted from the excitement of the day—and crashing after eating way too much sugar—Kyle slept like a baby.

He only woke up because he heard music.

Loud, blaring music.

The theme song from that boxing movie *Rocky*, his brother Mike's favorite.

"Whazzat?" he mumbled, crawling out of his sleeping bag.

Kyle glanced at his watch. It was eleven a.m. He figured the library lock-in was officially over and this was the group's wake-up call.

The music kept blaring.

"This is how they wake up astronauts," groaned Miguel.

"Turn it off!" moaned Andrew Peckleman.

Kyle slipped on his jeans and sneakers and staggered out into the giant reading room.

"Dr. Zinchenko?"

His voice echoed off the dome. No answer.

"Clarence? Clement?"

Nothing.

The *Rocky* music got louder.

Akimi leaned in from the third-floor balcony.

"What's going on down there?"

"I think they're trying to wake up astronauts," said Kyle. "On the moon."

He made his way to the front door and reached for the handle.

It wouldn't budge.

He jiggled it.

Nothing.

He jiggled harder.

Still nothing.

Kyle realized that the library lock-in might be over but they were still locked in the library.

15

"Everybody, please take your seats," Dr. Zinchenko said to the parents gathered in a conference room at the Parker House Hotel.

"When do our kids come home?" asked one of the mothers.

"Rose has soccer at two," said another.

The librarian nodded. "Mr. Lemoncello will—"

Just then, an accordion-panel door at the far end of the room flew open, revealing the eccentric billionaire dressed in a bright purple tracksuit and a plumed pirate hat. He was eating a slice of seven-layer birthday cake.

"Good morning or, as they're currently saying in Reykjavik, *gott síðdegi,* which means 'good afternoon,' because there is a four-hour time difference between Ohio and Iceland, a fact I first learned spinning a globe in my local library."

Mr. Lemoncello, his banana shoes burp-squeaking, stepped out of a room filled with dozens of black-and-white television monitors—the kind security guards watch at their workstations.

"Ladies and gentlemen, thank you for joining us on this grand and auspicious day. Today I am pleased to announce the most marvelously stupendous game ever created: Escape from Mr. Lemoncello's Library! The entire library will be the game board. Your children will be the game pieces. The winner will become famous all over the world."

"How?" asked one of the fathers.

"By starring in all of my commercials this holiday season. TV. Radio. Print. Billboards. Cardboard cutouts in toy stores. His or her face will be everywhere."

Mrs. Daley raised her hand. "Will they get paid?"

"Oh, yes. In fact, you'll probably want to call me The Giver."

"And what exactly does Haley have to do to win?"

"Escape! From the library. I thought the game's title more or less gave that bit away." Mr. Lemoncello tapped a button in his pirate hat and an animated version of the library's floor plan was instantly displayed on the conference room's plasma-screen TVs.

"Whoever is the first to use what they find *in* the library to find their way *out* of the library will be crowned the winner. Now then, the children cannot use the front door or the fire exits or set off any alarms. They cannot go out the way they went in. They can only use their wits, cunning, and intelligence to decipher clues and solve riddles that will eventually lead them to the location of the library's super-secret alternate exit. And, ladies and gentlemen, I assure you, such an alternate exit does indeed exist."

The parents around the table started buzzing with excitement.

"Participation, of course, will be purely optional and voluntary," said Mr. Lemoncello, clasping his hands behind his back and stalking around the room.

Several parents pulled out cell phones.

"And please—do *not* attempt to phone, email, text, fax, or send smoke signals to your children, encouraging them to enter the competition. We have blocked all communication into and out of the library. Only those who truly wish to stay and play shall stay and play. Anyone who chooses to leave the library will go home with lovely parting gifts and a souvenir pirate hat very similar to mine. They'll also be invited to my birthday party tomorrow afternoon." He held up his crumb-filled plate. "I've been sampling potential cake candidates for breakfast."

Mrs. Keegan crossed her arms over her chest. "Will this game be dangerous?"

"No," said Mr. Lemoncello. "Your children will be under constant video surveillance by security personnel in the library's control center. Dr. Zinchenko and I will also be monitoring their progress here in my private video-viewing suite. Should anything go wrong, we have paramedics, firefighters, and a team of former Navy SEALs—each with the heart of a samurai—standing by to swoop in and rescue your children. It'll be like *The Hunger Games* but with lots of food and no bows or arrows."

"Why not just have the kids play one of your other games?" a parent suggested. "Why all this fuss?"

"Because, my dear friends, these twelve children have lived their entire lives without a public library. As a result, they have no idea how extraordinarily useful, helpful, and funful—a word I recently invented—a library can be. This is their chance to discover that a library is more than a collection of dusty old books. It is a place to learn, explore, and grow!"

"Mr. Lemoncello, I think what you're doing is fantastic," said one of the mothers.

"Thank you," said Mr. Lemoncello, bowing and clicking his heels (which made them *bruck* like a chicken).

"If any of you would like to check up on your children," announced Dr. Zinchenko, "please join us in the adjoining room."

"Oh, they're a lot of fun to watch," said Mr. Lemoncello. "However, Mr. and Mrs. Keeley, I'm afraid your son Kyle does not enjoy the theme song from *Rocky* quite as much as I do!"

16

Rocky had done its job.

Kyle—and everybody else locked inside the library—was definitely awake.

Even Charles Chiltington had come down to the Rotunda Reading Room from Mr. Lemoncello's private suite. The only essay writer not with the group was Sierra Russell, who, Kyle figured, was off looking for another book to read.

"We're still locked in?" squealed Haley Daley.

"This is so lame," added Sean Keegan. "It's like eleven-thirty. I've got things to do. Places to be."

"Look, you guys," said Kyle, "they'll probably open the front door right after we eat or something."

"Well, where's that ridiculous librarian?" said Charles Chiltington, who was never very nice when there weren't any adults in the room.

"Yeah," said Rose Vermette. "I can't stay in here all day. I have a soccer game at two."

"And, dudes," said Sean Keegan, "*I* have a life."

"Do you children require assistance?" said a soft, motherly voice.

It was the semi-transparent holographic image of Mrs. Tobin, the librarian from the 1960s. She was hovering a few inches off the ground in front of the center desk.

"Yes," said Kayla Corson. "How do we get out of here?"

The librarian blinked, the way a secondhand calculator (the one your oldest brother dropped on the floor a billion times) does when it's figuring out a square root.

"I'm sorry," said the robotic librarian. "I have not been provided with the answer to that question."

"Will we be doing brunch here this morning?" Chiltington asked politely. "I'm not hungry, but some of my chums sure are. After all, it is eleven-thirty."

"The kitchen staff recently placed fresh food in the Book Nook Café."

"Thank you, Mrs. Tobin," said Chiltington. "Would you like anything? A bowl of oatmeal, perhaps."

"No. Thank you, CHARLES. I am a hologram. I do not eat food."

"I guess that's how you stay so super skinny."

Kyle shook his head. The smarmy guy was oilier than a soggy sack of fries. He was even sucking up to a hologram.

Chiltington and the others traipsed off to have

breakfast, but Kyle and Akimi stayed with the holographic librarian.

"Um, I have a question," said Kyle.

"I'm listening."

"Is the library lock-in over? Are we supposed to go home now?"

"Mr. Lemoncello will be addressing that issue shortly."

"Okay. Thanks, Mrs. Tobin."

"You are welcome, KYLE."

After the librarian faded to a flicker, Akimi said, "By the way, Kyle, before we leave, you need to check out that room I slept in last night."

"The Board Room?"

"Yeah. They call it that because, guess what? It's filled with board games!"

"All Lemoncellos?"

"Nuh-uh. Stuff from other companies. Some of it goes way back to the 1890s. I think it's Mr. Lemoncello's personal collection. It's like a museum up there."

Kyle's eyes went wide. "You hungry?" he asked.

"Not really. We ate so much last night."

"You think we have time to check out this game museum?"

"Follow me."

The two friends bounded up a spiral staircase to the second floor, where they found another set of steps to take them up to the third.

When he entered the Board Room, Kyle was blown away. "Wow!"

The walls were lined with bookcases filled with antique games, tin toys, and card games.

"This is incredible."

"I guess," said Akimi. "If, you know, you like games."

Kyle smiled. "Which, you know, I do."

They spent several quiet minutes wandering around the room, taking in all the wacky games that people used to play. There was one display case featuring eight games with amazingly illustrated box tops. A tiny spotlight illuminated each one.

"Wonder what's so special about these games," said Kyle.

"Maybe those were Mr. Lemoncello's favorites when he was a kid."

"Maybe." But the slogan etched into the glass case confused Kyle: "Luigi Lemoncello: the first and last word in games."

"But these aren't Lemoncello games," he mumbled.

The first spotlighted game in the case was Howdy Doody's TV Game. After that came Hüsker Dü?, You Don't Say!, Like Minds, Fun City, Big 6 Sports Games, Get the Message, and Ruff and Reddy.

"It's a puzzle," Kyle said with a grin.

"I thought they were games."

"They are. But if you string together the first or last

word of each game title . . ." He tapped the glass in front of the first box on the bottom shelf. "You *get the message.*"

"Really?" said Akimi, sounding extremely skeptical. "You're sure it's not just a bunch of junk somebody picked up for like fifty cents at a yard sale?"

"Positive." Kyle pointed to each box top as he cracked the code. "Howdy. Dü you like fun games? Get Reddy."

Miguel Fernandez barged into the Board Room.

"Here you are! We need you guys in the Electronic Learning Center. Now."

"Why?"

"Charles Chiltington wolfed down his breakfast, then raced up here to finish the game he started last night so he can enter his name as the first high scorer."

"So?"

"The game he's playing is all about medieval castles and dungeons!"

This time Akimi said it: "So?"

"He's escaping through the sewers. The game has smell-a-vision. You ever smell a medieval sewer? Trust me, it is foul *and* disgusting."

The three of them dashed up the hall and entered the stinky room where Charles was sitting in a vibrating pedestal chair, thumbing his controller. As his avatar sloshed through a sewer pipe, the subwoofers built into his seat made every *SQUISH!* and *SPLAT!* rumble across the floor.

"Whoa!" said Kyle. "Knock it off, Charles. You're pumping out total tear gas."

"Because I'm in the sewers underneath the horse stables. It's the secret way out of the castle. I'm going to win another game. That's two for me, Keeley. How many for you?"

"Yo," said Miguel. "This room is two stories above the café. The ductwork is connected."

"What's your point?"

"You're making everybody's food downstairs smell like horse manure!"

"Who cares? I'm winning."

Charles's chair went *FLUMP!* again.

But this time, Kyle smelled . . . pine trees?

Like one of those evergreen air fresheners people hang inside their cars.

"Aw, this stupid thing is broken." Charles jumped out of the chair and reared back to kick it.

"Um, I wouldn't do that if I were you," said Kyle.

"Why not?"

"Because there's a security camera over there and it's aimed right at you."

"What? Where?"

"See the blinking red light?"

Suddenly, an image of Kyle pointing up at the camera lens appeared on every video screen in the Electronic Learning Center.

Until he was replaced by Mr. Lemoncello.

"Excellent escape plan, Charles," said Mr. Lemoncello on the video screens.

"Thank you, sir," said Chiltington, smoothing out his khaki pants. "And just so you know, I saw an ant crawling up the side of this seat. That's why I almost kicked it."

"How very thoughtful of you, Charles."

"Mr. Lemoncello?" said Akimi.

"Yes?"

"How come the sewer started smelling like a pine tree?"

"Because I enjoy the odor of pine trees much more than the stench of horse poop. How about you?"

"Definitely."

"Now then, will everybody else please join us upstairs in the Electronic Learning Center? I have a very important announcement to make."

Kyle heard feet clomping up the stairs and soon Andrew, Bridgette, Yasmeen, Sean, Haley, Rose, and Kayla hurried into the room.

"Are we all here?" said Mr. Lemoncello.

"Everybody except Sierra Russell," said Kyle.

"Ah, yes. I saw her downstairs reading *When You Reach Me* by Rebecca Stead. We'll reach her later. It's nearly noon and I'm eager to move on to the next round of our competition."

"What competition?" asked Yasmeen Smith-Snyder.

"The one we are about to begin."

"Sir?" said Sean Keegan. "I have stuff to do today."

"That's fine, Sean. You are, of course, free to leave. If any of the rest of you do not wish to stay and play, kindly deposit your library cards in the discard pile."

A tile in the floor popped open and an empty goldfish bowl atop an ornate column rose up about three feet.

"Just drop it in the bowl there, Sean. Attaboy. Follow the flashing red arrows in the floor to the nearest exit, where you will receive a lovely parting gift along with my everlasting admiration for your essay-writing abilities."

Bright red arrows danced across the floor. Sean followed them.

"What happens if we decide to stay?" asked Akimi.

"You will be given the chance to play a brand-new, exciting game!"

"Is there a prize for the winner?" demanded Haley Daley.

"Oh, yes."

Now Miguel shot up his hand. "Mr. Lemoncello? What do we have to do to win?"

"Simple: Find your way *out* of the library using only what's *in* the library."

"Awesome!"

"Lame," mumbled Kayla Corson. "I'm outta here."

She plunked her library card into the fishbowl and followed the blinking arrows out the door.

"Does anyone else want or need to leave?"

"Sorry, sir. I have soccer at two," said Rose Vermette. "See you guys later." She dropped her card into the discard bowl.

The instant she did, bells rang, confetti fell from the ceiling, and every electronic console in the game room started *ding-ding-ding*ing.

"Congratulations, Rose!" cried Mr. Lemoncello, who had put on a pointy party hat. "For sticking to your prior commitments, you will receive our special Prior Commitment Sticker prize: a complete set of Lemoncello Sticker Picture Games and a laptop computer to play them on! Enjoy."

Charles Chiltington stepped a little closer to the security camera as Rose Vermette skipped out of the room.

"Sir, might we assume that the prize for winning your brand-new game will be even better than a laptop computer?"

"Yes," said Mr. Lemoncello, taking off his party hat. "You may so assume."

"I'm in," said Chiltington.

"Me too," said Kyle.

"Me too," added Akimi, Miguel, Andrew, Bridgette, Yasmeen, and Haley.

Sierra Russell wandered into the room. Her nose was buried so deep in her book she didn't even notice Mr. Lemoncello's gigantic face on all the video screens.

"Is something going on?" she said, mostly to her book pages.

"You bet!" boomed Mr. Lemoncello.

Sierra's head snapped up.

"Oh. Hello, sir."

"Greetings, Sierra. Sorry to interrupt your reading. Just have a quick question: Will you be staying or leaving?"

"Well, sir, I'd like to stay. If that's okay?"

"Okay? It is *wondermous,* another word I just made up. Now then, to read you the rules of the game—because every game needs rules—here is your friend and mine, Dr. Yanina Zinchenko!"

The video screens switched to a close-up of the librarian with the red hair and glasses.

"Your exit from the library must be completed between noon today and noon tomorrow," said Dr. Zinchenko.

Mr. Lemoncello's head popped into a corner of her screen.

"Tomorrow's my birthday, by the way. Mark your calendars."

And he ducked back out of the frame.

"Our security guards will continue holding your cell phones," said Dr. Zinchenko. "You may not use the library computers to contact anyone outside the building. You may, however, use them to conduct research.

"You may also request three different types of outside assistance: one 'Ask an Expert,' one 'Librarian Consultation,' and one 'Extreme Challenge.' Please be advised: The Extreme Challenges are, as the name implies, extremely difficult. If you pass the challenge, your reward will be great. However, if you fail, you will be eliminated from the competition."

Kyle figured he'd avoid asking for one of those—unless he extremely needed to.

"To use any of these 'lifelines,'" Dr. Zinchenko continued, "simply summon Mrs. Tobin."

Chiltington raised his hand.

"Yes, Charles?"

"Would you mind telling us what the prize will be for the winner?"

The video screen switched to an image of Mr. Lemoncello, who had done some sort of quick change. Now he was wearing sunglasses and had a silk ascot tucked into his shirt collar. He looked like a flashy Hollywood movie star. From 1939.

"Fame and glory! The winner will become my new spokesperson and will star in all of my holiday promotions."

"We'll be famous?" gushed Yasmeen, fluffing up her hair and smiling at the security camera.

Haley stepped in front of Yasmeen. "I've done some modeling work. For Sherman's Shoes in Old Town."

Yasmeen stepped in front of Haley. "I was an extra in a hot dog commercial once. . . ."

"Well, I'm a cheerleader; Yasmeen isn't. . . ."

While the two girls continued primping and posing for the camera, Dr. Zinchenko came back on-screen to quickly rattle off some final words.

"Your library cards are the keys to everything you will need. The library staff is here to help you find whatever it is you are looking for. The way out is not the way you came in. You may *not* use any of the fire exits. If you do, an alarm will sound and you will be immediately eliminated from the game. For safety purposes, you will be under constant video surveillance and you will be recorded. In the unlikely event of an emergency, you will be evacuated from the building. Creating an incident that requires evacuation will not count as having discovered a way to exit the library. Any questions?"

"Just one," said Andrew Peckleman, adjusting his goggle-sized glasses with his fingertip. "When exactly will the game begin?"

Mr. Lemoncello's face reappeared on the screens.

"Good question, Andrew! Oh, my. It's noon! How about . . . let's say . . . oh, I don't know . . . *now*!"

18

The contestants raced down the stairs to the Rotunda Reading Room.

Kyle saw Haley Daley dash down another set of steps into the basement, to what the floor plan called the Stacks.

Miguel and Andrew, the two library experts, grabbed separate tables and started working the touch-screen computers. Bridgette Wadge did the same thing.

Charles Chiltington strolled out the arched doorway and into the foyer with the fountain.

Yasmeen Smith-Snyder was running around the circular room with her floor plan in front of her face, like someone frantically checking their text messages while racing down a crowded sidewalk.

Sierra Russell found a comfy chair and sat down.

To finish her book.

The girl definitely wasn't into the whole spirit of The Game.

"So, Kyle," said Akimi, "you want to form an alliance?"

"What do you mean?"

"It's what people do on reality shows like *Survivor*. We help each other until, you know, everybody else is eliminated and we have to stab each other in the back."

"Um, I don't remember hearing anything about 'eliminations.'"

"Oh. Right."

"But, hey, there was nothing in the rules that said we couldn't share the top prize. I just want to *win*!"

"Cool. So, we're a team?"

"Sure."

"Great," said Akimi. "I nominate you to be our captain. All in favor raise their hands."

Kyle and Akimi both raised their hands.

"It's unanimous," said Akimi. "Okay. Let's go ask that antique librarian a question."

"What?"

"We both get to ask one question, right?"

"Right."

"Okay, here's mine: 'Hey, lady—how do we get out of here?'"

"And you think she'll tell you?"

"No. Not really. So, what's your plan?"

"Well, I was thinking—"

Suddenly, Yasmeen shouted, "I win!"

The rest of them stopped whatever they were doing.

"It's just like last night when Kyle found dessert in the most obvious place. To get out of the library, all we have to do is use one of the fire exits. Duh."

She headed toward a hallway between the Book Nook Café and Community Meeting Room A.

Kyle stood up. "Um, Yasmeen? I think maybe you missed some of what . . ."

Charles Chiltington dashed into the room and shouted, "You're not going to win, Yasmeen. Not unless you beat me to that fire exit!"

He bolted toward the corridor.

Yasmeen bolted toward it, too.

"You guys?" said Kyle.

Kyle could see a red Exit light glowing at the far end of the hallway Charles and Yasmeen were sprinting down. Charles stumbled and fell. Yasmeen kept running. Harder. Faster. She slammed into the exit bar on the metal door.

Alarms sounded. Flashing red lights swirled. Somewhere, a tiger roared. Mr. Lemoncello's voice rang out of the overhead speakers. "Sorry, Yasmeen. That's where your sidewalk ends. You broke the rules. You are out of the game. Your library card will be placed in the discard bowl and you will be going home."

As the fire exit door slowly swung shut and Yasmeen disappeared into the bright sunshine outside the library,

Kyle checked out Charles Chiltington, who would've been sent home if he hadn't stumbled and had reached the exit first.

The guy was smirking.

That was when it hit Kyle: Chiltington had faked Yasmeen out. He knew she couldn't win by going out a fire exit. But he ran down the hall to fool her into thinking she was doing the right thing.

Oh, yeah. Chiltington was definitely in it to win it.

No matter who he had to trample.

Whistling casually, Charles strolled back to the lobby.

"What's Chiltington doing out in the entrance hall?" said Akimi. "They told us the way out isn't the way in."

Before Kyle could answer, Andrew Peckleman started shouting at Miguel, who had wandered over to Peckleman's table.

"Get away! You're trying to steal my idea!"

"No, man," said Miguel. "I just happened to see your screen and I don't think that particular periodical—"

"You know what, Miguel? I don't really care what you think! This isn't school. This is the *public* library and you're not the boss in here, so just leave me alone!"

Miguel tossed up his hands. "No problem, bro. I was just trying to help."

"Ha! You mean help me lose." Andrew stormed up the closest spiral staircase to the second floor and the Dewey decimal rooms. Miguel, looking sort of sad, headed up a separate spiral staircase. Bridgette Wadge trailed after them.

"Want to follow those guys like Bridgette did?" whispered Akimi. "I'll take Peckleman, you take Miguel."

"No thanks," said Kyle, looking up at the domed ceiling. "I'm much more interested in the windows up there."

Three stories above the rotunda floor, just below the Wonder Dome, there was a series of ten arched windows set between the recessed statue nooks. The windows acted like skylights at the base of the dome, allowing sunshine to flood into the room below.

"Do you think those windows open?" asked Akimi.

"Maybe. Maybe not. But I've never let a closed or locked window stand between me and winning a game. Just ask my dad."

"What?"

"Never mind. Come on." Kyle trotted over to the cushy chair where Sierra Russell was peacefully reading her book.

"Um, excuse me, hate to interrupt . . ."

Sierra raised her head. She had a very dreamy look in her eyes.

"I need a book."

"Really?" said Sierra. "What kind?"

"Like the one you found. Up there." He gestured to the curving bookcases climbing up the back half of the rotunda.

"Fiction," said Sierra.

"Right," said Kyle. "Love me some fiction."

"Well, what sort of story do you like?"

"Something way up high," said Kyle. "The higher the better."

"Really?"

"Yep."

"Well, that's an interesting way to put together a reading list, basing it on bookcase elevation. . . ."

"I'd like something on the top shelf. Maybe right under the hologram statue of that guy hanging out with the Cat in the Hat."

"That's Dr. Seuss," said Sierra. "He wrote *The Cat in the Hat.*"

"Sweet," said Kyle. "But I just like how close he is to that window."

19

"Oh, Mrs. Tobin?" Akimi called out. "I need to use my Librarian Consultation."

"You sure about this?" said Kyle.

"That's the beauty of being a team. After we burn through mine, we'll still have yours."

The hologram librarian appeared and advised Akimi that *Huckleberry Finn* by Mark Twain was the book located right underneath the holographic image of Dr. Seuss and the Cat in the Hat.

After Mrs. Tobin vanished, Kyle and Akimi used their desktop computer to find the call number for *Huckleberry Finn.* Kyle grabbed a pen and scribbled it down on his palm.

"Are you going to do what I think you're going to do?" said Akimi.

"Yep. I'm going to float up there, hoist myself into that nook where the hologram is, reach over to the window, push it open, and stick out my hand. Technically, I will have found my way *out* of the library. Nothing in the rules said anything about how *far* outside we had to go to win."

"You could fall."

"I don't think so. I'm wiry, like a monkey."

"Seriously, Kyle. It isn't worth it."

"Um, yes it is. Did I mention I want to *win?*"

"You should improvise a safety harness," suggested Sierra Russell.

"Huh?"

"Well, in this adventure book I read once, the hero was in a very similar predicament. So he removed the curled handset wires from several telephones, bundled them together, and made a safety rope."

Ten minutes later, Kyle, Akimi, and Sierra had stripped the sproingy wires off a couple of telephone handsets. Kyle looped the cables around his waist and tied the other end to the handrail of the hover ladder. When fully extended, the safety rope would stretch out to a little more than twenty feet.

It should work.

"Be careful up there," said Akimi.

"Yes," said Sierra, who wasn't reading her book anymore. Apparently, watching a real live person risk his real live life by doing something really, really scary was one thing more exciting than reading.

Kyle locked his feet into the hover ladder's ski boot brackets. "Here we go."

Serious adrenaline raced through his body as he tapped the call number for *Huckleberry Finn* into the hover ladder's book locator keypad.

"When you open the window," said Akimi, "just shout, 'I found the way out!' and we win."

"Right," said Kyle. "All three of us."

"Huh?"

"Hey, Sierra came up with the safety rope idea. She's on our team now, too."

"Fine. Whatever. Just don't break your neck."

"Not part of the plan."

Kyle pressed the enter button on the control panel. The platform floated up off the ground and drifted slightly to the right.

"Be careful!" said Akimi. "Watch it!"

"I'm not doing anything," said Kyle. "This thingama-jiggy is doing all the work. I'm just along for the ride."

Kyle gripped the handles as the platform rose higher and higher. He sailed past books by Tolstoy and Thackeray. Tilting back his head, he looked up at the semi-transparent statues projected into the curved niches next to the arched windows.

They were a weird mix. A thoughtful African American man in a three-piece suit and a bow tie. A guy with long curly hair, old-fashioned clothes, and a looking glass. A long-haired dude in a scruffy shirt hiding behind cutouts of the letters "P" and "B." A bald guy with a beard.

Since the statues were really holographic projections, they had chisel-type labels floating in front of their pedestals identifying who the famous people were. The ones closest to Kyle were George Orwell, Lewis Carroll, Dr. Seuss, and Maya Angelou.

As he continued to climb, Kyle could hear the soft whir of the electromagnets invisibly lifting him toward the ceiling.

And then he heard something much louder.

"What a ridiculous idea!"

Charles Chiltington. He was standing on the second-floor balcony at the far side of the rotunda.

"You know, Keeley, I thought about doing the same thing. But then I noticed something you obviously overlooked: There's a wire mesh security screen on the other side of those windows."

The levitating platform stuttered to a stop.

"Enjoy staring at the ceiling, Keeley. I'm off to win yet another game!"

Kyle ignored Chiltington and grabbed hold of the ledge beneath Dr. Seuss's berth. He tried to haul himself up but his feet wouldn't budge.

They were locked in place by those ski boot clamps.

And this close to the skylights, Kyle could see that Chiltington was right—there was a security screen on the other side of the windows.

Kyle checked his wristwatch. It was one p.m. He and

his teammates had wasted an hour on the lame window idea. He sighed heavily and stared up at the quivering Seuss projection in the bowed niche above his head.

The Cat in the Hat's mouth started to move.

" 'Think left and think right and think low and think high.' "

Kyle recognized the voice.

It was Mr. Lemoncello.

" 'Oh, the thinks you can think up if only you try!' "

In other words, Kyle was back to square one. He needed to think up a whole new escape plan.

The ladder began a slow and steady descent to the floor—even though Kyle hadn't pushed a button.

"Don't listen to smarmypants Charles," Akimi coached as Kyle coasted toward the floor. "It was worth a shot."

"I agree," said Sierra.

A bloodcurdling scream came ringing up the staircase from the basement.

"That's Haley!" said Akimi. "I saw her go downstairs."

"That's where the Stacks are," added Sierra.

"Come on," said Kyle. "She could be in serious trouble."

"You should never help your competition, Keeley," scoffed Charles as he casually strolled down a spiral staircase. "Unless, of course, you *always* play to lose!"

Losers.

That's what Charles Chiltington thought about sentimental saps like Kyle Keeley. A damsel in distress starts
screaming and he forgets all about winning the game to go
rescue her?

What a pathetic loser.

Unless, of course, Haley Daley was screaming because
she had already found the alternate exit.

That made Charles laugh.

Impossible.

Although quite pretty, Haley Daley, the princess of the
seventh grade, was a total airhead. There was no way a
dumb girl like her could've outsmarted Charles Chiltington.

It was time to play his hunch.

Twice already, the head librarian, Dr. Zinchenko, had
said, "The library staff is here to help you find whatever it

is you are looking for." She said it once when they were just about to enter the library, again when she was reading the laundry list of rules.

Well, what Charles was looking for was a way out of the building that wasn't the front door and wouldn't set off any alarms.

That was why he kept coming back to the lobby with the gurgling fountain. Why he kept studying the display case labeled "Staff Picks: Our Most Memorable Reads."

"The staff is here to help," he muttered. "These are staff picks. Ipso facto, this has to be some sort of enormous clue."

Inside the sealed bookcase, Charles saw twelve book covers.

One for each of the twelve twelve-year-old players? he wondered.

The display items weren't actual books. They were cover art mounted on book-sized foam core. Three covers were lined up on each of the case's four shelves. Since they weren't actual books with spines, none of the covers included their call numbers.

Charles focused on the three books lined up on the bottom row.

Hoosier Hospitality was on the left. *In the Pocket: Johnny Unitas and Me* was in the middle. *The Dinner Party* was on the right.

Charles decided to concentrate on the Johnny Unitas

title. He moved into the rotunda and did a quick card catalog search on one of the desktop computers. When he typed *"In the Pocket,"* a matching cover image popped up.

But still no call number.

In the spot where the identifier should have been, there were instead a censor's thick black box and the words "I.D. Temporarily Removed from System."

Scrolling further down the screen, Charles came across a rather unusual annotation: "You didn't really think we'd make it that easy, did you?"

Charles grinned.

The computer was telling him he was on the right track.

He glanced up from the desk. The Children's Room was directly in front of him. The book about Johnny Unitas, with its cartoony cover depicting a football player wearing a number nineteen jersey and dropping back to launch a pass, was most likely a children's book.

Of course, it was also a sports biography.

So would it be shelved with sports books, biographies, or children's books?

Charles went back to the computerized card catalog. He read the book's description: "Billy wants to be a great quarterback like his hero, Johnny Unitas, but his coach is worried he'll get hurt."

It sounded like fiction. A made-up story. It had to be in the Children's Room.

As Charles crossed the slick marble floor, something else struck him.

This was like Hüsker Dü?, a memory game he had played when he was in kindergarten. He was on a hunt to find a hidden match for the football book cover he had just memorized. This was, in short, another memory game— that was why the Staff Picks display had been subtitled "Our Most *Memorable* Reads."

"Clever, Lemoncello," he mumbled. "Very clever indeed."

Charles entered the children's department. It didn't take him very long to find the book, because *In the Pocket* was propped up on a miniature stand on top of a shelf.

"Found it!" Charles proclaimed. Then, savoring the moment, he picked up the book and read the title out loud: *"In the Pocket: Johnny Unitas and Me."*

All of a sudden, a row of animatronic geese tucked into a corner of the room started honking and singing.

"They call him Mr. Touchdown, yes, they call him Mr. T."

The squawking birds startled Charles so much he dropped the book.

When he did, a four-by-four card fluttered out from behind its cover.

Charles bent down to pick it up.

Printed on the card was a black-and-white silhouette. A quarterback, wearing a number nineteen jersey (just like Johnny Unitas), was arching back his arm to throw a pass.

Charles grinned.

He was definitely on the right track.

He tucked the silhouette card into his pocket and hurried back to the lobby to memorize more book covers.

21

"Ouch! I'm stuck! Help!"

Haley Daley's cries sailed up the staircase as Kyle led the charge down the steps into the Stacks.

"So, what exactly are the Stacks?" asked Akimi, three steps behind Kyle.

"It's where the library stores its collection of research material," said Sierra, who was two stairs behind Akimi.

The three of them reached the basement. It was filled with tidy rows of floor-to-ceiling shelving units.

"Help!"

Haley sounded like she was on the far side of the room, behind the walls of metal storage racks crowded with boxes, books, and bins.

"What is all this stuff?" said Kyle, looking for a passageway, trying to figure out how to get to wherever Haley was.

"Mostly rare books and documents you can't check out," said Sierra. "But if you fill out a call slip, you can use this material up in the reading room."

With a whir and whoosh of its electric motor, a shiny robot the color of the storm troopers in *Star Wars* scooted across an intersection between bookshelves. It moved on tank treads and had what looked like a shopping cart attached to its front.

"Let's follow that robot!" said Kyle. "It might know the fastest way to reach Haley."

The trio dashed up a narrow pathway to where they saw the robot extending its quadruple-jointed mechanical arm to pluck a flat metal box out of a slide-in compartment. The box had been stored in a section of shelving with a flashing LCD that read "Magazines & Periodicals. 1930s."

"Somebody upstairs wants an old magazine?" said Akimi.

"They're probably researching the Gold Leaf Bank building," said Sierra. "I think it was built in the 1930s."

"Help!" screamed Haley. "I'm stuck."

"Hang on!" shouted Kyle. "We're coming."

"Well, hurry up already!"

"This way," said Kyle.

They scampered up another aisle, turned right, and saw Haley, her hand jammed through a horizontal slot near the top of the basement wall. To reach it, she'd had to stand on an elevated treadmill maybe thirty feet long. Since the thing was rolling, Haley was jogging in place so she wouldn't fall on her face. The high-tech conveyor belt was actually a series of rollers. Ten robot carts—staggered so no two were directly across from each other—were lined up on either side.

"I think it's an automatic book sorter," said Sierra. "That laser beam near Haley's ankles probably scans a book's tag and tells the conveyor belt which of the ten sorting trays to shove it into."

"You guys?" screamed Haley. "Hurry up and rescue me!"

Kyle stepped back. Tried to assess the situation.

"What is that slot you're hanging on to?"

"The bottom of the stupid book drop," said Haley, trotting on the treadmill. "I saw it on the floor plan. People can walk up to it on the sidewalk and return their books. I figured it had to lead down here."

"Smart move," said Kyle. "You could crawl through the slot and escape."

"*If* you were the size of a book," Akimi said sarcastically.

"I never got that far," said Haley. "The minute I stepped onto this belt thing, it started moving."

Kyle nodded. "Probably a weight-activated switch."

"A book falls in," said Akimi. "The sorter starts up."

"Clever," said Kyle. "Plus, it gives our game its first booby trap."

"Well, the game is no fun if you're the booby stuck in the trap!" said Haley.

Kyle turned to Sierra. "We need to stop the belt so Haley can yank her hand out of that slot without falling on her butt or cracking open her skull. Have you ever read a book where the hero outwits an escalator or a rolling checkout belt in the grocery store or something?"

"No," said Sierra. "Not really."

"How about one where the hero just flips an emergency shutoff switch?" asked Akimi. "Because that's what I'd do if, you know, I found one."

Akimi was standing next to a wall-mounted switch box. She flicked it down. The conveyor belt slowed to a stop.

"Ta-da! Another chapter for my amazingly awesome autobiography—if I ever write one."

Haley yanked her hand out of the book return slot. It sort of popped when it finally sprang free. She collapsed to her knees on the frozen treadmill.

"My hand feels flatter than a pancake," she moaned.

"Are you hurt?" asked Kyle. "Maybe we should tell the security guys that . . ."

"What? That I have a boo-boo and need to go home? Forget it, Kyle Keeley. You're not going to beat me that easily."

"I'm not trying to—"

Haley showed him the palm of her hand. "Save it, Keeley." She crawled off the conveyor belt. "One way or another, I'm going to win this game. I just hope starring in Mr. Lemoncello's commercials earns me some decent money."

She hobbled around the bookshelves toward the staircase up to the reading room.

When she was gone, Akimi raised her hand. "Question?"

"Yeah?" said Kyle.

"How come the guys inside the control room didn't flip a switch to shut down the book sorter when they saw Haley doing her cardio cha-cha-cha on it?"

Kyle shrugged. "Maybe they weren't watching."

"Actually," said Sierra, pointing to a square tile on the floor near the book sorter, "I think they were."

Kyle looked down. The tile was glowing like one of the tablet computer screens upstairs in the rotunda. Kyle read the words zipping across the illuminated square.

" 'Congratulations,' " he read out loud. " 'For helping Haley and being a sport, you've earned much more than a good report.' "

The tile popped open.

Inside a small compartment was a rolled-up tube of paper with a yellow card clipped to its end.

"Huh," said Akimi. "I guess somebody *was* watching."

Kyle pulled the yellow card off the paper tube. It smelled like lemons.

"What's it say?" asked Sierra.

Kyle flipped the card over so Sierra and Akimi could see what was printed on it:

SUPER-DOOPER BONUS CLUE.

22

"Oh, man, that was so dumb!"

Haley could not believe how idiotic she had been.

"Trying to crawl out of a book return slot? Chya. Like that was going to work."

She was giving herself a good talking-to as she trudged up the steps to the first floor.

When she entered the rotunda, she saw Charles Chiltington slipping out into the lobby again.

Chiltington was a snake. Worse. A garden slug. Maybe a leech. Something oily and slimy that left a greasy trail and liked to mooch off other people's ideas. That was why Chiltington had tailed the twin library nerds, Peckleman and Fernandez, upstairs during last night's dessert hunt. Haley was smart enough to know that Chiltington was hoping to steal the book geeks' ideas.

Actually, Haley was a lot smarter than anybody (except

her teachers and whoever scored her IQ tests) knew. With certain people, mainly grown-ups and silly boys, pretending to be a ditzy princess made getting what she wanted a whole lot easier.

And what she wanted right now was money. Lots of money. Her dad had been out of work for nearly a year. They'd run through all their rainy-day savings. They'd had to borrow from relatives and in-laws.

If Haley could win this competition and become Mr. Lemoncello's spokesmodel, her family's money woes would be over and they wouldn't have to sell their home. And once other people saw her on TV for Lemoncello games, they'd want her for their commercials, too. And movies. Maybe her own sitcom. Something on the Disney Channel.

But for all that to happen, Haley needed a winning idea—and fast. Something better than "crawl through a slot that's barely wide enough for your wrist." Maybe she should flush herself down the toilet and escape through the sewers like Charles did in that video game.

She headed over to the Book Nook Café so she could sit down and think.

She stepped into the room and checked out the snack table. There were trays of cookies, strawberries, bananas, and brownies. Sitting down to nibble on a macaroon, she studied the row of cookbooks displayed on the bookshelves lining the wall.

One in particular caught her eye: *Cupcakes, Cookies & Pie, Oh, My!*

Because the cover looked extremely familiar: two googly-eyed sheep made out of chocolate-frosted cakes with gobs of mini marshmallows for fleece. Haley had seen the cover before.

In the lobby!

It was in that glass case of memorable reads selected by the library staff.

She went over to the shelf and picked up the book. When she opened the cover, she discovered two cards.

One was a four-by-four piece of white cardboard with the black silhouette of a sheep on it.

The second card was yellow and about the same size as a Community Chest card in Monopoly. Haley sniffed the card. It smelled like lemons.

She grinned. "For *Lemon*cello!"

On one side of the yellow card was printed:

SUPER-DOOPER BONUS CLUE

On the other was the clue:

YOUR MARVELOUS MEMORY HAS EARNED YOU EVEN MORE MEMORIES. PROCEED TO THE LEMONCELLO-ABILIA ROOM.

LOOK FOR ITEM #12.

Haley slid both cards into the back pocket of her jeans,

pulled out her library floor plan, and found the Lemoncello-abilia Room. It was up on the third floor.

Making certain nobody (i.e., Charles Chiltington) was following her, Haley quietly dashed up a spiral staircase to the second floor. Checking for Chiltington one more time, she tiptoed up to the third floor, where she found the room labeled "Lemoncello-abilia: Mini-Museum of Personally Interesting and Somewhat Quirky Junk."

Haley opened the door and stepped inside.

The front room was like a storage warehouse. Cardboard boxes were stacked on top of wooden crates sitting on plastic bins stuffed with papers. All the boxes, bins, and crates were numbered. She saw one labeled "#576."

"Guess Mr. Lemoncello never throws anything away," Haley remarked as she scanned the heaps, looking for the #12 mentioned on her bonus card.

Weaving her way through the stacks and columns, Haley finally found her Super-Dooper Bonus. Item #12 was an old boot box from an Alexandriaville shoe store Haley had never heard of. Someone had taped a label on the lid: "Paraphernalia, Accoutrements, and Doodads from Mr. Lemoncello's 12th Year."

Haley lifted the lid. The box was filled with all sorts of confusing knickknacks: hand-whittled prototypes for game pieces; a star-spangled, red-white-and-blue "H-H-H Humphrey" button; a battered clasp envelope sealed up with tons of tape.

Someone had scribbled "First and Worst Idea Ever" on the front of the envelope with a Magic Marker.

There were also a felt pennant from Disneyland and a rubber-banded stack of cartoony cards for something called Wacky Packages. (The card on top was Weakies, Breakfast of Chumps.)

Haley knew this memory box had to be an important clue.

Why? She had absolutely no idea.

23

Kyle flipped over his lemon-scented Super-Dooper Bonus card and read what was written on the other side.

YOU WILL FIND THE ULTIMATE VERSION OF THIS BOARD GAME ON THE SECOND-FLOOR BALCONY CIRCLING THE ROTUNDA.

"Huh?" said Akimi. "What's that mean?"

"I don't know. Let's roll out the paper and see."

Akimi and Sierra helped Kyle anchor the edges of the scroll on the tiled floor.

"Okay," said Kyle. "It looks like the early sketch for a board game. See the circle in the center of the other circle? That's probably where you place the spinner. You move your pieces around the ten rooms. . . ."

He stopped.

"Wait a second."

"What?" said Akimi.

"Do you recognize the game?" asked Sierra.

"Yep," said Kyle. "I played it this week with my brother Curtis. It's Mr. Lemoncello's Bewilderingly Baffling Bibliomania. It takes place in a make-believe *library*."

"What about finding the 'ultimate version' up on the second-floor balcony?" asked Sierra.

Kyle grinned. "You'll see."

Coming up from the basement, Kyle saw Andrew Peckleman in the middle of the Rotunda Reading Room, opening a long metal box sitting on top of the center desk.

The holographic image of Mrs. Tobin was there, smiling patiently, as Peckleman pulled some kind of magazine out of the box. Miguel was also near the librarian's desk, apparently waiting his turn for a consultation.

"That's the box we saw the robot pluck off the shelf," whispered Akimi.

Kyle nodded. He motioned for the others to follow him and slipped around the circumference of the rotunda. Akimi and Sierra slunk after him.

In the shadows on the far side of the room, they saw Haley Daley heading for the staircase they'd just come up: steps that would take her back to the basement.

Kyle wondered if she'd found something else to crawl through. If so, he hoped it was bigger than a mailbox.

"Is this the *real* magazine?" he heard Peckleman shout at the hologram.

"Yes, ANDREW. This concludes your Librarian Consultation. Next? How may I help you, MIGUEL?"

"Not so fast," snapped Andrew. "I'm not done."

"Um, your consultation just concluded," said Miguel.

"Says who?"

"The librarian."

"MIGUEL?" said the hologram of Mrs. Tobin. "What is *your* question?"

"Sorry, bro. I told you."

"She's just like Mrs. Yunghans at school," snapped Peckleman. "All the librarians like you better than me!"

"Yo. Ease up."

"You'll see, Mrs. Tobin! You'll all see. I'm gonna beat Miguel Fernandez, big-time! And when I win, I'm gonna tell Mr. Lemoncello to fire you!"

"She's a hologram," said Miguel with a laugh. "You can't fire somebody who doesn't actually exist."

"Then I'll tell Lemoncello to pull her plug." Peckleman grabbed his magazine and stormed out of the rotunda into the lobby.

"I guess Andrew's planning on doing something with the front door," Kyle whispered to Akimi.

"Well, that's totally dumb. They already told us the way out isn't the way we came in."

"Maybe Andrew doesn't think Dr. Zinchenko was telling us the truth," suggested Sierra.

"Come on," said Kyle, leading his team toward the closest staircase up to the second floor. Glancing over his shoulder, he watched Miguel place a slip of paper on the table in front of the semi-translucent librarian.

"This item has been temporarily removed from the Stacks, MIGUEL," said Mrs. Tobin. "You will find it in a display case next to the original Winkle and Grimble scale model. Let me give you that location."

There was a grinding sound, like when movie tickets shoot up through the slot at the box office. Miguel snatched the small square of paper that popped up from the librarian's desk and spun around.

He froze the instant he saw Kyle, Akimi, and Sierra sneaking around the room behind him.

"Hey," said Miguel, hiding the tiny square of paper behind his back. "Yo."

"Yo," said Kyle. "Whazzup?"

"Nothin'. Just, you know, workin' the puzzle."

"Yeah. Us too."

"Okay. Later."

"Later."

Both boys thumped their fists on their chests like baseball players do. Miguel turned and ran for a staircase winding up to the second floor.

"Come on, you guys," said Kyle as he took off running for a different set of steps.

When Kyle, Akimi, and Sierra made it up to the balcony, they watched Miguel run up to the third floor. As soon as he disappeared into a room up there, Kyle unrolled the game sketch.

118

"Look at the drawing, then look down at the floor," said Kyle.

"They're the same!" said Sierra.

"Exactly. A circular room with a round desk at the center of that circle."

"Awesome," said Akimi. "And there are ten doors ringed around the balcony up here on the second floor, just like on the game board."

Kyle tapped the rendering of the spinner in the right-hand corner of the game plans. "See how the spinner is divided into ten different-colored sections numbered zero to nine?"

"It looks like the Wonder Dome," said Akimi, "when it's not doing its kaleidoscope thing or running a video that makes you think the building is hang gliding across Alaska, which totally made me airsick."

"Well, in the game, you have to go into all ten Dewey decimal book rooms and answer a trivia question about a book. If you answer correctly, you slip a book into your bookshelf and move on to another part of the library. When you have ten books, one from each room, it's basically a race to see who can exit the library first."

"Okay," said Akimi, sounding pumped. "This is good. This is major."

"Except one thing's missing," said Kyle.

"What?" asked Sierra.

"Mr. Lemoncello always works a clever back-door shortcut into his games. For instance, in Family Frenzy . . ."

"You can use the coal chute to slide into the millionaire's mansion at the end," said Akimi.

"Exactly. And in that castle game, Charles snuck out through the sewers. Anyway, when my brother Curtis beat me at Bibliomania . . ."

"You lost?" Akimi acted surprised.

"It happens. Occasionally. But only because Curtis used this shortcut." Kyle tapped a black square on the game diagram. "It took him straight out to the street. He beat me by one spin of the spinner."

"I don't see any black squares in the floor of our rotunda," said Akimi.

"Maybe," said Sierra, "for this new game, Mr. Lemoncello put the secret square someplace besides the main room."

Kyle nodded. "And maybe to win this *new* game we need to play the *old* one."

"You're a genius!" said Akimi.

"No. My brother Curtis is the genius. I just like to play games. So, do libraries even have board games?"

"Sure," said Sierra. "I think. I mean, the library in my dad's town has them."

"Which department?" asked Akimi, pulling out her floor plan.

"Young adult."

Akimi tapped her map. "Third floor. Stairs over there."

"Let's go!" said Kyle.

But before they could take off, they heard Mr. Lemoncello's voice echoing in the rotunda.

"Are you ready for your Extreme Challenge, Bridgette?"

Kyle and his teammates peered over the ledge of the balcony. Bridgette Wadge was alone in front of the librarian's desk, staring up at the ceiling.

"Yes, sir," she said.

"Are you sure?" Mr. Lemoncello's voice boomed out of hidden speakers. "You still have twenty-two hours to find the exit."

"I want to go for it now, sir. Get a jump on everybody else."

"Very well. Dr. Zinchenko? Reset the statues."

The ten holographic statues in their recessed nooks flickered off, leaving black and empty spaces.

"This Extreme Challenge is based on the classic Game of Authors card game," said Mr. Lemoncello. "Here are the authors in your deck."

Magically, new holographic statues appeared as Mr. Lemoncello rattled off the authors' names. "Charles Dickens, Raymond Chandler, Edgar Allan Poe, Agatha Christie, Patricia Highsmith, Mario Puzo, Frederick Forsyth, John Le Carré, Dashiell Hammett, and Fyodor Dostoyevsky."

"He wrote *Crime and Punishment,*" said Bridgette excitedly.

"Indeed he did."

"In fact," said Bridgette, "all those authors wrote crime novels."

"Correct again. However, that's the easy part. Dr. Z?

How do we make this authors game ridiculously difficult enough to qualify as an Extreme Challenge?"

"Simple," the librarian's voice echoed under the dome. "You will have two minutes, Bridgette, to name four books written by each of our authors."

Kyle gulped. "That's impossible," he whispered.

"Not really," said Sierra. She was about to start rattling off titles when Mr. Lemoncello said, "Go!" The sound of a ticking clock reverberated around the room.

"Um, okay," said Bridgette down on the main floor. "Agatha Christie. *Murder on the Orient Express, Ten Little Indians, Death on the Nile, The Mousetrap.*"

Somewhere, a bell dinged, and the British lady in the sensible shoes disappeared.

"Poe. *The Murders in the Rue Morgue, The Masque of the Red Death, The Purloined Letter, The Cask of Amontillado.*"

Another ding. Another statue vanished.

Bridgette kept going.

"Man," whispered Kyle, "what grade is she in? College?"

"Seventh," said Akimi, "just like us."

Bridgette Wadge kept tearing through the authors. The bell kept dinging.

But the clock kept ticking, too.

"Ten seconds," said Mr. Lemoncello.

Bridgette had saved the worst for last.

"Fyodor Dostoyevsky. *Crime and Punishment.* Um,

Crime and Punishment . . . The one about the brothers . . . *The Brothers* . . .”

And then she stalled.

She'd run out of gas.

A buzzer sounded.

“I'm sorry, Bridgette,” said Dr. Zinchenko. “But, as we advised you, the Extreme Challenges are extremely difficult. You will be going home with lovely parting gifts. Kindly hand your library card to Clarence and thank you for playing Escape from Mr. Lemoncello's Library.”

“That settles it,” muttered Kyle. “I am *never, ever* asking for one of those Extreme Challenge dealios.”

“Me neither,” said Akimi.

“I might,” said Sierra. “Maybe.”

And then she showed Kyle and Akimi the rumpled sheet of paper where she had written down *five* book titles for all ten authors.

25

Akimi grabbed the door handle to the Young Adult Room. "It's locked."

"Here," said Sierra. "Use my library card."

"Huh," said Akimi. "Your books on the back are different, too."

"I think they all are. I got *The Egypt Game* and *The Westing Game*."

"Two books about games?" said Kyle. "Sweet."

Akimi slipped Sierra's card into a reader slot above the doorknob. The door clicked. Kyle pushed it open.

The walls of the Young Adult Room were painted purple and yellow. There were swirly zebra-print rugs on the floor and a lumpy cluster of beanbag chairs. A couple of sofas were designed to look like Scrabble trays, with letter-square pillows.

Akimi nudged Kyle in the ribs. "Check it out."

In the far corner stood a carnival ticket booth with a mechanical dummy seated inside. A "Fun & Games" banner hung off the booth's striped roof. The dummy inside the glass booth?

He looked like Mr. Lemoncello.

He wasn't wearing a turban, but the Mr. Lemoncello mannequin reminded Kyle of the Zoltar Speaks fortune-teller booths he'd seen in video game arcades.

"That's not really him, is it?" said Akimi, who was right behind Kyle.

"No. It's a mechanical doll."

The frozen automaton was dressed in a black top hat and a bright red ringmaster jacket. Since the booth had the "Fun & Games" banner, Kyle figured you might have to talk to the dummy to get a game.

"Um, hello," he said. "We'd like to play a board game."

Bells rang, whistles whistled, and chaser lights blinked. The mechanical Mr. Lemoncello jostled to life.

"If you want a game, just say its name." The life-size puppet's blocky jaw flapped open and shut—almost in sync with the words.

"Do you have Mr. Lemoncello's Bewilderingly Baffling Bibliomania?"

"Did Joey Pigza lose control? Was Ella enchanted?"

"Huh?"

"Just say yes," suggested Sierra.

"Yes," said Kyle.

"Well, great Gilly Hopkins," said the Lemoncello dummy, "here you go!"

Kyle heard some mechanical noises and some whirring. Then, with a clunk, a wide slot popped open in the front of the booth and a game box slid out.

"Enjoy!" said the dummy. "And remember, it's not whether you win or lose, it's how you play the game. So be sure to read the instructions—so you'll know how to *play the game*."

Kyle took the box to a table.

"Okay," he said, raising the lid, "let's set it up and—"

There was a beep and the door opened. . . .

"Where is he?"

Andrew Peckleman barged into the room waving his antique magazine—something called *Popular Science Monthly*.

"Who're you looking for?" said Kyle.

"Mr. Lemoncello. I heard him. Is he in here?"

Kyle pointed toward the frozen Lemoncello doll sitting in the carnie booth. "It's a dummy."

Peckleman whipped his head around from side to side. "Is there a camera in here?"

"Right over the door."

Peckleman spun around to face it. Kyle, Akimi, and Sierra formed a human shield to hide their Bibliomania box.

"I want to use a second lifeline!" Peckleman shouted at the camera. "I want to talk to an expert!"

126

"Very well," said a calm voice Kyle immediately recognized as belonging to Dr. Zinchenko. "With whom do you wish to speak?"

"The guy who wrote this stupid magazine article about cracking open bank vaults in the 1930s!"

"I'm afraid we cannot arrange that for you, Andrew."

"Why not? The guy's a moron. He didn't tell me anything about how to open the front door, which is what my Google search said this magazine would do!"

"We told you the way out isn't the way in."

"That was just a red herring! A trick, to throw us off course."

"No, Andrew. It was not. What is the title of the article?"

" 'Newest Bank Vaults Defy the Cracksman.' "

"Ah. Well, that should have been a hint. Apparently, the reporter concluded that thieves could *not* break open the vault doors. When doing Internet research, it is important to—"

"Let me talk to the stupid idiot!"

"I am sorry. That magazine was published in 1936. The reporter is dead."

"Well, then, I want to talk to Mr. Lemoncello!"

"Excuse me?"

"I want to talk to Mr. Lemoncello!"

"This is highly irregular. . . ."

"And so's this game. You people have it rigged so

Miguel Fernandez will win. I know you do! That's why Mr. Lemoncello is afraid to talk to me."

Kyle heard the carnival booth dummy clatter back to life.

"Hello, Andrew. How may I help you?"

This Lemoncello didn't sound prerecorded. Apparently, the real deal was using the dummy to do his talking.

"Your library stinks!" shouted Peckleman.

"Oh, dear. Have you boys been playing that castle sewer game again?"

"No! But this stupid article should've given me the stupid answer but the stupid writer didn't write what he should've written."

"I see. And can you rephrase that in the form of a question?"

"How many can I ask you?"

"Just one. And then we're done."

"Okay. You're the expert on this stupid new library game. So where's your favorite contestant? Where's Miguel?"

"Is that your final question?"

"Yes!"

"Assuming our video monitors are correct, Mr. Fernandez is on the other side of the third floor, doing research in the Art and Artifacts Room."

"Thanks!"

Andrew bolted out the door.

The Lemoncello puppet bucked and drooped into its "off" mode.

Kyle sprang up from the table. "Come on," he said to Akimi and Sierra.

Akimi sighed. "*Now* where are we going?"

"To make sure Peckleman doesn't do something stupid that gets Miguel kicked out of the game."

"And why would we do that?"

"Because Miguel's our friend."

Akimi glanced at her floor plan. "The Art and Artifacts Room is on the other side of the circle."

"Sierra—stay here and guard the game box. Come on, Akimi."

Kyle and Akimi looped around the third-floor balcony to the other side. Kyle glanced at his watch. It was almost three p.m. They really needed to start focusing on The Game and not all this other monkey junk.

As they neared the Art & Artifacts Room, there was a shout, and the door flew open. Andrew Peckleman came running out.

Behind him were a woman with the head and tail of a lioness, and a Pharaoh in a cobra headpiece.

The Pharaoh stopped. "May onions grow in your earwax!" And a series of holographic hieroglyphics danced across the air.

Andrew Peckleman raced to a staircase, grabbed both handrails, and hurried down to the second floor. The Egyptians vanished.

129

Kyle and Akimi entered the Art & Artifacts Room and found Miguel seated at a desk with what looked like blueprints.

"You okay?" asked Kyle.

"Yeah, man. I'm fine. Thanks."

"Those guys chasing Andrew. Where'd they come from?"

"Holograms from the giant Lego Sphinx and Pyramid exhibit."

"So why'd they turn on Andrew?" asked Akimi.

"I don't know. One minute he's yelling at me. The next, the Pharaoh and Sekhmet are yelling at him."

"Sek-who?" said Kyle.

"Sekhmet," said Akimi. "The Egyptian lion goddess and warrior. Haven't you read *The Red Pyramid* by Rick Riordan?"

"It's on my list," said Kyle. Or it would be. He definitely needed to start a reading list soon so he could catch up with everybody else.

"I bet the security guards in the control room fired up the Egyptian holograms when they saw Andrew going berserk in here," said Akimi.

"Good," said Miguel. "A library is supposed to be a place for peaceful contemplation."

That was when Sierra Russell rushed into the room.

"You guys! Right after you left! The Mr. Lemoncello dummy spit out a bonus card!"

"Very clever," said Charles, pulling another silhouette card out of a book.

This cover had been easy to find. It was the third book on the top shelf of the Staff Picks display. The image on the front was a bright yellow yield sign. The title? *Universal Road Signs* by "renowned trafficologist" Abigail Rose Painter. Charles had found the matching book in the 300s room on the second floor. The 300s were all about social sciences, including things like commerce, communications, and—ta-da!—transportation.

The image also fit nicely with the pictogram he had found in the 700s room in a book called *The Umpire Strikes Back*. That baseball book was the first cover on the *second* shelf in the display case and had given Charles a card with the classic pose of an umpire calling an out.

Reading the images from left to right, then down—just like you'd read a book—Charles knew he was on the right track. The traffic sign book gave him "walk" and the umpire book gave him "out."

Put the two picture words together and he had "walk out."

Clearly, if he could find all twelve silhouettes, the Staff Picks display would tell him how to "walk out" of the library (although he had absolutely no idea what the first image he had found, the quarterback tossing a pass, had to do with escaping the library—not yet, anyway).

"Three down, nine to go," said Charles, winking up at the closest security camera. "And, Mr. Lemoncello, if you're watching, may I just say that you are an extremely brilliant man?"

Charles had never sucked up to a video camera before. He figured it was worth a shot. Maybe Mr. Lemoncello would send him a bonus clue or something.

Instead, when Charles stepped out of the 300s room, somebody sent him Andrew Peckleman. The goggle-eyed library geek was sputtering mad as he rushed down the steps and stomped around the second-floor balcony.

"Stupid library. Stupid Lemoncello. Stupid sphinx and Sekhmet."

"Why so glum, Andrew?" Charles called out.

"Because this game stinks. Mr. Lemoncello just sent a bunch of holograms hurling hieroglyphics after me. He could put somebody's eye out with those things."

"Really? With a hologram?"

"Hey, they're made with lasers, aren't they?"

"Indeed. Say, speaking of hieroglyphics, where might I find a book about picture languages?"

"Ha! Why should I help you?"

"Because Kyle Keeley is working with Akimi Hughes *and* Sierra Russell. I imagine it is only a matter of time before your friend Miguel Fernandez joins their team, too."

"Miguel isn't my friend! Besides, I'm better at navigating my way through a library than he'll ever be."

"I know. That's why I want you on my team."

"Really?"

Charles smiled. Kids like Andrew Peckleman were so easy to manipulate.

"Oh, yes. Work with me and I guarantee you the

world will know that *you* should be the head library aide at Alexandriaville Middle School."

"The four hundreds!" blurted Peckleman.

"Pardon?"

"That's where you'll find books on hieroglyphics and all kinds of languages. If you want secret codes, those are in the six hundreds room. The six-fifties, to be exact."

Charles shot out his hand. "Welcome to Team Charles, Andrew."

The new teammates stepped into the 400s room. For some reason, it was pitch dark and smelled like pine trees.

"Bienvenida! Bienvenue! Witamy! Kuwakaribisha! Welcome!" boomed a voice from the ceiling speakers. "This is the four hundreds room, home of foreign languages. Here, CHARLES and ANDREW, you can learn all about your American heritage."

A bank of spotlights thumped on.

Charles and Andrew were face-to-blank-face with a row of four featureless mannequins. An overhead projector beamed a movie onto dummy number two, turning it into a perky woman who looked like a flight attendant.

"Hello, and welcome to *your* American heritage. I'm Debbie. Let's begin your voyage!"

"That's okay," said Charles. "We're rather busy."

"Let's begin your voyage," the mannequin repeated.

Charles sighed. Obviously, there was no way to turn

this silly display off. He might as well speed things along by telling the dummy what it wanted to hear.

"Fine. But can we go with the abridged version? We're in a bit of a rush."

"Yeah," added Andrew, "we have to escape before noon tomorrow."

The woman, whose body remained frozen while a movie made her face and costume spring to life, reminded Charles of the graveyard statues from the Haunted Mansion ride at Disney World.

"While we research your family trees," she said, "please enjoy this short and informative film."

"Is this part of the game?" Andrew whispered to Charles.

"Possibly. Pay attention for any bonus clues."

"Okay. What do they look like?"

"Who can ever say?"

A screen behind the life-size dummies leapt to life with all sorts of scratchy images of people huddled together on the deck of a boat near the Statue of Liberty.

"For decades," narrated the ceiling voice, "public libraries have proudly served America's newest citizens— the immigrants who flock to these shores yearning for the freedom to build their own American dreams."

Charles really wasn't interested in this kind of stuff. His ancestors were all *Americans;* the only language they spoke was English.

"Yes, the library is where many new arrivals journey

first. To learn their new homeland's language. To keep in touch with the world they left behind. To search for the gainful employment that will make them productive residents of their newly adopted home!"

The movie dissolved into blackness.

"Thank you for your kind attention," chirped the cheerful Debbie. "We have completed your American family tree. Let's meet your first American ancestors!"

Two mannequins sprang to illuminated life, both of them dressed in traditional Thanksgiving pilgrim costumes.

"I know who they are already," said Charles. "That's John Chiltington and his wife, Elinor. They came to Plymouth Colony on the *Mayflower.* Can we move on to Andrew's family? Please?"

"Of course," said Debbie.

The mannequins quickly went through Andrew Peckleman's ancestry. Apparently, the family name had originally been Pickleman, because they made pickles. After a prolonged parade of pickle people, the dummies took on the guise of Andrew's most famous ancestor, a guy in horn-rimmed glasses and a tweed sports coat named Peter Paul Peckleman.

"I appeared on the TV game show *Concentration* in 1968," he announced, "and won a roomful of furniture and wood paneling for my rumpus room."

Charles smiled. He knew the TV game show *Concentration* was very similar to Mr. Lemoncello's Phenomenal

Picture Word Puzzler, one of the games he had picked up at the toy store. Peter Paul Peckleman's claim to fame was further confirmation that piecing together the picture puzzle would show Charles how to escape from the library.

He'd been right.

The dummies had just given him a bonus clue.

27

Excited by the sudden appearance of a second bonus card, Sierra read it out loud:

" 'Two plus two can equal more than four. Put two and two together and you'll be closer than before.' "

Akimi raised her hand.

"Yes?" said Sierra.

"You do realize that Miguel here isn't on our team?"

"Oh. Right. Sorry."

Miguel turned to Kyle. "You guys are a team?"

"Yep. You want to join?"

"Maybe. Not sure. Check back with me later, man."

"No problem," said Kyle.

He fist-thumped his chest. Miguel fist-thumped his. They were flashing each other peace signs when Sierra said, "I think this means we should all play together as a team. Remember what it says on the fountain down in the lobby: 'Knowledge not shared remains unknown.'"

"Maybe," said Miguel. "Like I said—let me get back to you guys. I'm workin' on a few angles of my own. Flying solo."

"Sure. No problem." Kyle was about to do the whole fist-chest-bump-peace-sign thing again when he had a brainstorm. "Miguel? Quick question. What's on your library card?"

Miguel shrugged. "My name and the number one."

"Anything else? Like on the back?"

"Nothing really. Couple of books."

"Two?"

"Yeah."

"What're their titles?"

Miguel bit his lip. "Don't want to say."

"Because you think they might be clues?"

"Not saying what I might or might not be thinking, bro."

Kyle nodded.

"There are two different books on the back of everybody's library cards," said Akimi, thinking out loud. "'Put two and two together and you'll be closer than before.' The book titles *are* some sort of clue. My books are *One*—"

"Um, Akimi?" Kyle shook his head. Nodded toward Miguel.

"Right. Sorry. My bad."

"Oh-kay, Miguel," said Kyle. "If and when you decide to team up with us, you can show us the two books on the back of your card; we'll all show you ours. We'll also split the prize four ways. Deal?"

"Deal."

"Come on, guys." Kyle gestured toward the exit.

"Where are we going?" asked Sierra.

Kyle dropped his voice. "The Electronic Learning Center."

"You want to play video games?" said Akimi. "Now? Seriously, Kyle, we may need to rethink your status as team captain."

"I don't want to play video games. I want to check out the discard pile."

"Huh?"

"The cards the players who went home early dumped into that goldfish bowl!"

"I'm comin' with you guys," said Miguel. "I've been thinking about those extra cards, too."

"Fine," said Kyle. "Whatever."

When they entered the game room, they saw Clarence, his arms folded across his chest genie-style. He was standing guard in front of the discard pile.

"May I help you?" he asked.

"Um, yeah," said Kyle. "We want to check out the cards in the bowl."

"Sorry," said Clarence. "You can't have them."

"But," said Mr. Lemoncello, his face suddenly appearing on every video screen in the room, "you can win them!"

Dressed in a polka-dotted bow tie and snazzy jacket like a game show host, Mr. Lemoncello had one arm resting on a slender Plexiglas podium. Behind him, Dr. Zinchenko—all decked out in a sparkly red minidress—looked like the models that point at prizes on TV.

"Are the four of you ready to play Let's Do a Deal?" When Mr. Lemoncello said that, he pushed a big red button in his podium. A prerecorded studio audience whistled, cheered, and applauded.

"Um, what's Let's Do a Deal?" asked Kyle.

"My first game to ever be turned into a TV show. Brought to you by lemon Pledge!"

Dr. Zinchenko started singing: *"Lemon Pledge, very pretty. Put the shine down, lemon good . . ."*

"Thank you, Dr. Z!" said Mr. Lemoncello, bopping the button to make the audience cheer again. "Now then, kids, here's the deal: Solve one simple picture puzzle and you four win the five library cards in the bowl."

"And if we lose?"

"Simple. Each of you loses his or her library card and adds it to the discard bowl for our next lucky contestants to try and win."

He banged the red button again. The audience cheered exactly the same way they cheered before.

Kyle turned to the others. "What do you say, guys?"

"Let's go for it," said Akimi.

Sierra nodded.

"Miguel?"

"I'm in, bro."

"You're joining our team?"

"Absolutely." They knocked knuckles to seal the deal.

Mr. Lemoncello must've whacked his button again, because the canned studio audience started cheering.

Kyle wondered what the sound effects would be if he and his friends lost their library cards playing Let's Do a Deal.

Probably groans.

And weeping. Lots and lots of weeping.

28

"Now then," said Mr. Lemoncello, "are you ready to play Risking Everything for Five Little Library Cards?"

Kyle swallowed hard. Then he nodded.

"All right, you Maniac Magees, here is your picture puzzle. The category is Famous Quotes. You have sixty seconds to solve this rebus."

"Wait a second," said Akimi. "What's a rebus?"

"You figure out the words in a phrase by looking at pictures and symbols," said Kyle.

"For instance," added Miguel, "the letters 'R' and 'E' plus a picture of a school bus would equal 'rebus.'"

"Oh. Okay," said Akimi. "If you guys say so."

"Are you ready to play?" asked Mr. Lemoncello.

Kyle looked at his teammates, who nodded.

"Yes, sir."

"Then on your mark . . . get set . . . go, dog, go!"

Mr. Lemoncello's image disappeared. Ticktock clock music started playing. The video screens all projected the same picture:

"We're officially dead," said Akimi.

"Fifty-five seconds," said Mr. Lemoncello.

"Okay, we break it up four ways," said Kyle. "The first and third rows are similar, I'll do them."

"I'll do the last one," said Akimi.

"I'll take the second row," said Miguel.

"I'm four," said Sierra.

"Fifty seconds," said Mr. Lemoncello.

Everyone went to work.

"Mine is some guy hitting himself in the thumb but with a 'gr' and an 'o'?" muttered Akimi. "Then the male symbol where the 'le' equals 'rx'? 'Marx'? Does that make sense? Hello? Kyle? Is my second half 'Marx'?"

Kyle didn't answer. He was too busy deciphering his own clue lines. " 'Outlet,' change the 'let' to 'side,' " he mumbled. " 'Golf' minus the 'g' and the 'l.' The letter 'A.' "

"Forty seconds."

" 'Dog.' " He dropped to the third line. He just needed the first word. " 'Bowling *pins*' without the 'p' but add an 'ide.' "

"Thirty seconds."

Kyle glanced at Miguel. He was moving his lips, mouthing out his part of the quote. Sierra, too.

"You guys ready?" Kyle whispered.

"Hang on," said Miguel.

"Twenty seconds."

"Okay. Go."

Kyle read the first line: " 'Outside of a dog . . .' "

Miguel picked up the thread: " '. . . a book is man's best friend.' "

Kyle continued. " 'Inside of a dog . . .' "

Sierra took over. " '. . . it's too dark to read.' "

Akimi brought them home: " 'Groucho Marx!' "

"Is that your final answer?" asked Mr. Lemoncello.

"Yes," said Kyle, and then he repeated the entire quote: " 'Outside of a dog, a book is man's best friend. Inside of a dog, it's too dark to read.'—Groucho Marx."

Bells rang. Chaser lights flashed. The audience went wild. Akimi and Sierra actually squealed and hugged each other.

"You are correct!" shouted Mr. Lemoncello. "There's no dead end in Norvelt, not today! Take those five library cards, Team Kyle! You won them fair and square!"

Charles and Andrew heard a commotion on the third floor. Bells ringing. An audience whooping it up. Girls squealing.

"Come on," said Charles.

They raced up the stairs and peeked into the Electronic Learning Center. Kyle Keeley and his teammates were all hugging each other and slapping high fives. On every video screen in the game room, Charles could see a pictogram puzzle.

"What's going on in there?" whispered Andrew.

"They might be gaining on us," Charles whispered back. "We need to pick up our pace. Quick—where would I find a book called *Hoosier Hospitality* written by Eve Healy Aresty?"

"The nine hundreds room."

"Let's go."

Charles and Andrew scurried back to the second floor and the 900s room.

Where they found Haley Daley holding *Hoosier Hospitality* by Eve Healy Aresty.

"Oh, hello, you guys," she said, slamming the book shut.

Charles moved toward her. Slowly.

"Find anything interesting in that book, Haley?"

"Not really." She giggled. "Just a bunch of dumb junk about Indiana."

Charles knew she was hiding something.

"I wonder, Haley, if you and I might share a quiet word?" He turned to Andrew. "In private."

"Does that mean I'm supposed to leave?"

"Yes, Andrew. It's for the good of the team. Trust me."

"Okay. But I'll be right outside that door if you decide to double-cross me or something."

"Thank you, Andrew. This will only take a quick minute."

Peckleman left the room.

Smiling, Charles moved even closer to Haley. So close he could smell her bubble gum. Or shampoo. Maybe both.

"Let's step over here," he said, taking Haley by the elbow. "I found another fascinating book that I think you'll just love." He guided her to a spot behind a bookcase where their conversation couldn't be observed by the security camera blinking up in the ceiling.

Haley went with Charles.

If he had been looking for the same book she'd just found, that meant he was playing the library escape game along a similar path. Charles Chiltington might have clues Haley could use. Clues she needed.

"Rumor has it," Charles whispered, "that your parents wrote your library essay for you."

Inside, Haley was grinning. Obviously, Charles would try to bully her into joining his team. Fine. She'd pretend to be frightened.

"What?" she whispered back, pretending to be terrified. "That's a lie. My dad just helped me with some of the spelling."

"Aha! So you admit it. All the spelling in your essay wasn't your own?"

Okay. This was going to take more acting skill than usual. Having someone check your spelling wasn't against anybody's rules for anything.

She widened her eyes. Made her lips quiver. "What do you want, Charles?"

"For you to join my team."

"Why should I do that?"

"Two reasons. One, if you're on my side, your flagrant plagiarism remains our dirty little secret. Two, I know what to do with that silhouette card you just found in the *Hoosier Hospitality* book."

"You do?"

"Oh, yes. If we share our clues, the pictures will create a phrase telling us how to find the alternate exit."

Haley smiled. For real. This was working out perfectly. She'd get all their clues, and even if they all won together, Mr. Lemoncello would definitely make her the real star of his TV commercials. She had "zazz." Charles and Andrew did not.

"Okay," she said. "Deal. I'm on your team."

Then she handed Charles the clue she had found in the *Hoosier* book:

"Of course!" said Charles. "After all, Indiana is the Hoosier State."

29

"Oh, man," said Kyle, leading his team around the balcony, back to the Young Adult Room. "Nine library cards. This is fantastic!"

They gathered around a table.

"Okay, guys. Time for everybody to put their cards on the table. Literally."

The teammates set down their cards. Kyle spread out the five from the discard bowl. Akimi pulled out a pad and wrote all the information on one master list:

BOOKS/AUTHORS ON THE BACKS OF
LIBRARY CARDS

#1 Miguel Fernandez
Incident at Hawk's Hill by Allan W. Eckert/
No, David! by David Shannon

#2 Akimi Hughes
One Fish Two Fish Red Fish Blue Fish
by Dr. Seuss/Nine Stories by J. D. Salinger

#3 UNKNOWN

#4 Bridgette Wadge
Tales of a Fourth Grade Nothing
by Judy Blume/Harry Potter and the
Sorcerer's Stone by J. K. Rowling

#5 Sierra Russell
The Egypt Game by Zilpha Keatley Snyder/
The Westing Game by Ellen Raskin

#6 Yasmeen Smith-Snyder
Around the World in Eighty Days
by Jules Verne/The Yak Who Yelled Yuck
by Carol Pugliano-Martin

#7 Sean Keegan
Olivia by Ian Falconer/Unreal! by Paul Jennings

#8 UNKNOWN

#9 Rose Vermette
All-of-a-Kind Family by Sydney Taylor/
Scat by Carl Hiaasen

#10 Kayla Corson
Anna to the Infinite Power
by Mildred Ames/Where the Sidewalk
Ends by Shel Silverstein

#11 UNKNOWN

#12 Kyle Keeley
I Love You, Stinky Face by Lisa McCourt/
The Napping House by Audrey Wood

"Wow," said Sierra. "That's a lot of good books. But what do all those authors and titles mean?"

"It means we need Charles's, Andrew's, and Haley's cards," said Kyle.

"Really?" said Akimi. "Because if you ask me, we already have way too much information."

"Well," said Kyle, "maybe later we'll find a clue that'll tell us how to read *this* clue."

"And how are we going to do that?" asked Miguel.

"Have you ever played this?" Kyle pointed to the Bibliomania box.

"Nope. Always wanted to."

"We were just about to get up a game."

"Does this have anything to do with finding our way out of the library?"

"We sure hope so," said Akimi.

"Awesome."

"By the way," Kyle said to Miguel, "what'd you find in the Art and Artifacts Room?"

"Yeah," said Akimi. "All those papers you kept trying to hide from us."

Miguel grinned. "The original blueprints for the Gold Leaf Bank building."

"Clever," said Kyle. "That way you could look for old exits that might still exist behind new walls."

"Exactly."

"Find any extra exits?" asked Akimi.

"Nope. No hidden windows, either."

"Yeah, what's up with that? How come they built this place with so few windows?"

"To discourage bank robbers, I guess," said Kyle.

"Yep," said Miguel. "The only way in was through the front door. The fire exits could only be opened from the inside, like at a movie theater. The vault itself was all the way down in the basement."

"Mr. Lemoncello kept all that security," said Kyle, "and added his own."

"So it would seem."

"Well, hopefully Bibliomania will lead us to some kind of alternate exit."

"And fast," said Akimi. "Don't forget, we're not the only ones playing this game. One of those other guys is probably halfway out the door already."

"Okay," said Kyle, "game play is pretty simple. You spin the spinner and advance your piece the number of spaces the needle points to. You move around the library and go into each of the ten Dewey decimal rooms, where you can pick up a book by answering a clue card. If you guess wrong, you get a new clue card in the same room on your next turn. The first person to fill the ten slots in their 'bookshelf' and spin their way out of the library wins."

"It's sort of like Trivial Pursuit," said Sierra. "And the questions aren't all that hard because they're mostly multiple-choice."

"Let's hear one!" said Miguel eagerly.

The cards were separated into ten multicolored mini-stacks, one for each room. Kyle grabbed a green card.

"Okay, this is for the eight hundreds room. Literature. 'Deathly ill and pursued by the Ringwraiths, Frodo Baggins was carried safely across the River Bruinen on the gleaming white elf-horse of Glorfindel named: A) Asphodel, B) Asfaloth, C) Almarian, D) Anglachel.'"

Akimi shook her head like she was having a brain freeze. "Wha-huh?"

"I think the answer might be 'A,'" said Miguel.

"They're all 'A's,'" said Kyle. "Asphodel, Asfaloth, Al—"

"It's 'B) Asfaloth,'" said Sierra. "It's from J. R. R. Tolkien's *Lord of the Rings*."

Kyle flipped the card over and read the answer. "'You are correct. You get a copy of *Lord of the Rings* to put in your bookshelf.'"

"So, Kyle," said Akimi, "how exactly is knowing the name of an elf-horse going to help us get out of the library?"

"Maybe it's like a secret code," suggested Miguel. "And the ten book titles will form a sentence telling us how to get out."

"Possibly," said Kyle. "But I see one problem."

"What's that?"

"It's too random. Mr. Lemoncello would have no idea which ten cards we might pick."

"Well," said Sierra, "maybe there are only *ten* questions. One for each room."

Akimi grabbed the card stacks, fanned them out. "Nope. They're all different."

"Hang on," said Kyle.

He was remembering something about another game: Mr. Lemoncello's Indoor-Outdoor Scavenger Hunt.

How his mother had been able to write to the company and request a fresh set of cards.

He turned to the video camera mounted in a corner. "I'd like my Librarian Consultation, please."

"What's up, Kyle?" asked Miguel.

"I'm playing a hunch."

The holographic Mrs. Tobin appeared behind the young adult librarian's desk.

"How may I help you, KYLE?"

"My friends and I want to play Bibliomania but we were wondering: Is there a new set of cards?"

"Yes, KYLE. There is."

And a fresh deck of cards popped up through a slot in the desk.

"We'll just play one bookshelf," said Kyle.

"Because we're a team now, right, bro?" said Miguel.

"Right. Plus, we don't have all day."

"Well," said Akimi, "technically we do. In fact, we have the rest of today and tomorrow till noon."

"We've got like nineteen hours left," said Miguel.

"But Charles and the others," said Sierra. "They could beat us."

"Right," said Kyle. "After all, he *is* a Chiltington. And according to Sir Charles, they never lose. Miguel, you're the newest member of the team. You spin first."

Miguel rubbed his hands together. Limbered up his fingers. Practiced flicking his index finger off his thumb. Made sure he had a good snap and follow-through.

"Would you hurry up and spin before my brain explodes?" pleaded Akimi.

"No problem." Miguel flicked the plastic pointer. It whirled around the cardboard square decorated with a sunburst of ten colorful triangles.

"Boo-yah! The triple zeros. General Knowledge."

"Um, that's not so great," said Kyle.

"How come?"

"You get to move zero spaces."

"Oh. Bummer."

Akimi shot up her hand.

"Yes?" said Kyle.

"Do we really have to spin and count spaces and all that junk? We have a deadline. Clocks everywhere are ticking against us."

"Maybe we can just pull a pink card," suggested Sierra.

"It's really not how you play the game," said Kyle.

"Um, we're not really playing this game, Kyle," said Akimi. "We're playing the other one. The Big Game. The one with the ginormous prize."

"I have to agree with Akimi," said Miguel.

"Fine," said Kyle. "It's against the rules, but pull a pink card."

"You sure, bro?"

"Just pull a pink!"

Miguel quickly sorted the new deck into ten stacks of different colors. He pulled the pink on the top of its pile.

"Hmmm. These are different from the regular cards."

He turned it over and showed it to the group.

$0 + 27 + 0.4 = ????$

157

"Easy-peasy," said Akimi. "The answer is twenty-seven-point-four, because the zero doesn't change the sum."

"Not in math," said Miguel. "But this isn't math. This is the Dewey decimal system and there's always three numbers to the left of the decimal point."

"We need to find a book with the call number 027.4," added Sierra.

"Fine," said Akimi. "But I guarantee you it isn't a math book!"

The team made their way around the balcony circling the Dewey decimal doors.

"Here we go," said Miguel. He slid his library card into a reader on a door labeled "000s."

"Okay," said Miguel, "in here we're gonna find General Knowledge. Almanacs, encyclopedias, bibliographies, books about library science . . ."

"It's a science?" said Akimi. "Where do they keep the chemicals?"

"In the library paste," joked Sierra, who was loosening up. She hadn't read one page of a book in hours.

"Found it," said Miguel, reaching up to pull a book off a shelf. "027.4. Man, it's old. Look how yellow the pages are."

"So what's the antique's title?" asked Akimi.

"*Get to Know Your Local Library* by Amy Alessio and Erin Downey."

Miguel held the book so everybody could see the cover. It was illustrated with a cartoony-looking detective in a checkered hat who was holding up a magnifying glass to examine books on a shelf.

"Looks like a library guide for kids," said Miguel, opening the cover to read one of the inside pages. "First publication was way back in 1952." He flipped through a few pages. "It explains the Dewey decimal system. Contains a glossary of library terms. A brief history of libraries . . ."

He reached the back of the book.

"Awesome."

"What?" asked Kyle as he and the others moved closer to see what Miguel had found.

"It's an old-fashioned book slip. From the Alexandria-ville Public Library."

"The one they tore down?"

"Yep. And this card, tucked into a sleeve glued to the back cover, comes from the olden days when they used to stamp the date the book was due on a grid and you had to fill in your name under 'issued to.'"

"And?"

"Look who checked this book out on 26 May '64!"

Kyle and the others looked.

"Luigi Lemoncello!"

* * *

Down on the first floor, Charles used his library card to open the door to Community Meeting Room A.

"Who is to have access to this room?" cooed a soothing voice from the ceiling.

"Me and my teammates," said Charles. "Andrew Peckleman and Haley Daley."

"Thank you. Please have ANDREW PECKLEMAN and HALEY DALEY swipe their cards through the reader now."

Both of them did.

"Thank you. Entrance to Community Meeting Room A will be limited to those approved by the host, CHARLES CHILTINGTON. Have a good meeting."

Charles and his team entered the sleek, ultramodern, white-on-white conference room. There were twelve comfy chairs set up around a glass-topped table and a cabinet filled with top-of-the-line audiovisual equipment.

"You can write on the walls," said Andrew. "They're like the Smart Boards at school."

"Excellent," said Charles, clasping his hands behind his back and pacing around the room. "Now, when we find all twelve pictograms and lay them out according to their position in the Staff Picks display case, they will create a rebus for a phrase that, I am quite certain, will tell us exactly how to exit this library without triggering any alarms. Therefore, it is time for all of us to lay our cards on the table."

Haley nodded. And pulled two more silhouettes out of the back pocket of her jeans.

"I found one of these in a cookbook," she said. "The other was in juvenile fiction. *Nancy Drew: The Mystery at Lilac Inn.*"

"There are blank note cards in this drawer," announced Andrew. "We should use them as placeholders for the books we still need to find."

They laid out a three-by-four grid of cards on the tabletop:

"What does it mean?" said Andrew.

"Simple," said Charles. "It means we need to find those other six books!"

31

"So, does anybody have a clue as to why we were supposed to find this book?" asked Kyle.

He and his teammates were back in the Young Adult Room staring at the cover of *Get to Know Your Local Library*.

"Too early to tell," said Miguel. "Let's keep playing. This book will probably make more sense once we go into the other rooms and pick up more clues."

"Whose turn is it?" asked Akimi.

"Yours," said Kyle. "Flick the spinner."

Akimi finger-kicked the plastic pointer.

"Purple!" she yelled when the arrow slid to a stop. "The eight hundreds."

"That means you move eight spaces," mumbled Kyle.

"Except today." Akimi reached for the card on top of

the purple stack. When she saw what was written on it, she frowned.

"What's the clue?" asked Kyle.

"Something about Literature, Rhetoric, or Criticism?" asked Miguel.

"Nope," said Akimi. "It's a wild card. With a riddle."

"Read it!" said Sierra.

"'I rhyme with dart and crackerjacks. Visit me and find a rhyme for Andy.'"

"Peckleman?" said Kyle. "How'd he get his name on a game card?"

"Bro," said Miguel, "nobody calls Andrew Peckleman 'Andy.' Of course, it could mean Andrew Jackson. The seventh president of the United States."

"Or Andy Panda," said Akimi.

"Or Andrew Carnegie," said Sierra. "He was a generous supporter of libraries."

"Okay," said Kyle. "Let's concentrate on the first part of the riddle. What rhymes with 'dart and crackerjacks'?"

"Smart and heart attacks?" suggested Miguel.

"Art and bric-a-bracs?" said Sierra.

"Art and *Artifacts*!" said Akimi, nailing it.

They hurried over to the Art & Artifacts Room.

"Everybody—check out the display cases," said Kyle. "See if anything rhymes with the word 'Andy.'"

"Well, this model of the old bank building is certainly 'grandy,'" said Miguel. "And the Pharaoh's pyramid and sphinx would be *sandy* if they weren't made out of Legos."

"True," said Kyle, sounding unconvinced about both.

"Check it out, you guys," cried Akimi, who was studying a row of Styrofoam heads sporting hats. "This plaid fedora from 1968 was worn by a guy named Leopold Loblolly."

"So?" said Kyle.

"According to this plaque, Loblolly was 'one of the notorious *Dandy* Bandits.' 'Dandy' rhymes with 'Andy.'"

"That it does," said Miguel. "However, 'Loblolly' does not."

"Neither does 'Leopold,'" added Kyle.

"'Candy' rhymes with 'Andy'!" said Sierra. She was staring at the objects in a display case under a banner reading "Welcome to the Wonderful World of Willy Wonka."

"Awesome!" said Miguel, hurrying over to admire the collection of Everlasting Gobstoppers, Glumptious Globgobblers, Laffy Taffy, and Pixy Stix displayed under glass in a sea of purple velvet.

"Mr. Lemoncello is a lot like Willy Wonka," said Kyle.

"You mean crazy?" said Akimi.

"I prefer the term 'eccentric.'"

"And Dr. Zinchenko is his Oompa-Loompa," said Sierra.

Everybody started giggling.

"Nah," Akimi joked, "she's too tall."

"And not nearly orange enough," added Miguel.

"The Willy Wonka book was written by Roald Dahl," said Sierra, who, Kyle figured, could name twelve other books the guy wrote, too. "In it, Mr. Wonka takes Charlie and Grandpa Joe home in a flying glass elevator that crashes through the roof of his chocolate factory."

Everybody thought about that for a second.

"So now we have to find a glass elevator?" said Akimi. "Because there isn't one on the floor plan."

"But Mr. Lemoncello is just wild enough to build one," said Kyle. "And if he did, he probably wouldn't put it on the floor plan."

"No way," said Miguel. "Everybody would want to ride on it."

"I know I would," said Sierra.

"So we're seriously searching for a secret glass elevator?" said Akimi.

"Maybe," said Kyle. "Maybe not. This is just another piece of a gigantic jigsaw puzzle. We won't see the whole picture until we collect all the pieces."

"Or someone shows us the box lid," cracked Akimi.

"Look, it's only six p.m.," said Kyle. "And we're collecting a ton of good information."

"You mean a ton of *random* information," said Akimi.

"Well," said Miguel, "once we have more clues, we can use Sherlock Holmes's famous 'deductive reasoning' method to make logical connections between all the random junk."

165

"Works for me," said Kyle. "But if we're going to play Sherlock Holmes, we need to go spin that spinner and dig up more clues."

"The game's afoot," said Sierra.

"Huh?" Kyle and Akimi said it together.

"Sorry. It's just something Sherlock says to Watson whenever he gets excited."

Sherlock Holmes. Kyle had just found another bunch of books to add to his reading list.

32

"Okay, Sierra," said Kyle, "your turn."

Sierra flicked the spinner. The pointy tip ended up in the yellow 200s zone, so she went ahead and pulled a yellow card.

"It's definitely for the two hundreds section," she said, showing her clue to Miguel before revealing it to Kyle and Akimi.

"Weird," said Miguel.

"What?" said Akimi before Kyle could.

"Well, the two hundreds are where they keep books on world religions."

"But there are *two* numbers on this card," said Sierra.

"Maybe this time we need to find *two* books?" suggested Kyle.

"I don't know," said Sierra, studying her card. " '220.5203' is obviously a call number."

"Obviously," said Akimi.

"But this other number isn't in the proper format. 'Two-twenty-fifteen.'"

"February twentieth, 2015!" said Akimi. "Quick—what happened on that date?"

"Um, nobody knows," said Kyle. "Because *it hasn't happened yet*."

"Oh. Right. Okay—how about February twentieth, *1915*?"

"That was the opening day of the Panama-Pacific International Exposition in San Francisco," said Sierra.

Jaws dropped.

"Sorry. I'm a big world's fair fan."

Everybody else just nodded.

Finally, Miguel spoke up. "Look, let's just go down to the two hundreds room and find 220.5203. We can figure out the second chunk later."

The team once again trooped down to the second floor and worked their way around the circular balcony.

"You guys?" said Sierra, looking across the atrium at the statues. "Remember how they switched all the hologram authors when Bridgette Wadge did her Extreme Challenge?"

"Yep," said Kyle. "She was doing good till she got to the Russian dude."

"What Russian dude?" asked Miguel, who hadn't witnessed Bridgette's elimination.

"Guy who wrote five or six books Sierra could tell you about."

"But look," said Sierra. "Now all the author statues are the same ones they were last night."

"So," said Kyle thoughtfully, "if they can switch 'em around . . ."

"These must be clues for our game!" blurted Akimi. She pulled out a pen and her notepad. "I'll write down their names."

"Start with the guy under the triple zeros wedge of the Wonder Dome," suggested Kyle.

"Right."

Akimi read the labeled pedestals and jotted down all the authors' names:

Thomas Wolfe, Booker T. Washington, Stephen Sondheim, George Orwell, Lewis Carroll, Dr. Seuss, Maya Angelou, Shel Silverstein, Pseudonymous Bosch, Todd Strasser.

"So," said Akimi when she'd finished writing, "do you think this game could get any more complicated?"

"Maybe," said Kyle. "It's possible that Mr. Lemoncello left a couple different paths to the same solution."

"Well, personally, I can only take one path at a time," said Akimi. "So let's go find two-twenty-point-whatever."

*　*　*

"Should be in the next row of bookcases," said Miguel. "Here we go. 220.5203. The King James Bible."

"*Ach der lieber!* An excellent choice," said a man with a thick German accent.

The four teammates spun around.

And were face to face with a semi-transparent guy in medieval garb with a fur-trimmed cap and a beard that looked like two raccoon tails sewn together under his nose and chin.

"I am Johannes Gensfleisch zur Laden zum Gutenberg," said the holographic image, who had ink stains all over his fingertips.

"You created the Gutenberg Bibles on your printing press!" gushed Sierra.

"Ja, ja, ja. Big bestseller. You need help with der Bible, I am at your service." He bowed.

"Oh-kay," said Akimi, turning to Miguel. "Take it away, Miguel."

"Herr Gutenberg, sir, we're looking for two-twenty-fifteen."

"*Das ist einfach.*"

"Huh?"

"That is easy. TWO, TWENTY, FIFTEEN is EXODUS, chapter TWENTY, verse FIFTEEN."

"Of course!" said Miguel. "Exodus is the second book of the Bible. Twenty and fifteen are the chapter and verse." He flipped through some pages. "Here we go. Exodus, chapter twenty, verse fifteen. It's one of the Ten Commandments: 'Thou shalt not steal.'"

33

"Let's put the two new cards on the table," said Charles.

He and his so-called teammates, Andrew and Haley (Charles planned on dumping them both right before he made his glorious solo exit from the library), had scoured the library together for hours looking for more book cover matches.

Peckleman wasn't nearly as good with the Dewey decimal system as he had claimed to be. And Charles needed someone to do that sort of thing for him. His father always hired tutors or research assistants for him whenever Charles had to do a major paper or report.

Finally, around six in, coincidentally, the 600s room, they scored twice, finding *Tea for You and Me* (641.3372) and *Why Wait to Lose Weight?* (613.2522).

Now their picture puzzle had only four blanks remaining:

"Okay," said Andrew, "I think it's pretty clear. 'Woolly BLANK walk up the skinny BLANK BLANK house Indian and nineteen BLANK.'"

Charles nodded and said, "Interesting," even though he knew Peckleman was way off.

"Uh, hello?" said Haley. "That doesn't make any sense."

"Sure it does," said Andrew.

"Uh, no it doesn't."

In his head, Charles had decoded the clues so far as

"Ewe (a female sheep) BLANK walk out the (t+h+e) way (weigh) BLANK BLANK Inn in passed (past) BLANK."

But out loud, he said, "I think we just need to tweak Andrew's translation a little."

"Fine. Go ahead. I don't care." Andrew slumped down in his seat to sulk.

"How about 'She BLANK walks out the skinny BLANK BLANK house five hundred and past BLANK.'"

"Where'd you get 'she'?" asked Haley.

"From 'sheep.' The card you gave us."

"Actually, I think the sheep is supposed to represent 'you.' Because a ewe is a female sheep."

"Fascinating," said Charles. "I didn't figure that out."

What he did figure out was that Haley Daley was much smarter than he had assumed. She could be a serious threat. And no way was Charles sharing his prize with anybody, especially her.

"And how did you get 'five hundred' from Indiana?" she asked.

"Simple. Indianapolis, the capital of Indiana, is home to a race known as the Indy 500."

"Okay. So how about 'You BLANK walk out the skinny BLANK BLANK in—because the Nancy Drew book was about an inn—five hundred pass, or *past*, BLANK."

Now Peckleman piped up. "That makes more sense than what you said, Charles."

"Indeed," said Charles, sounding magnanimous.

"Perhaps the clues are telling us to locate a secret skinny passageway five hundred paces past some landmark here in the library."

Andrew was excited. "This is like the pirate map from *Treasure Island*!"

"Or," said Haley, "maybe these clues are telling us we need to go out and find the four books we haven't found yet. We should split up. I'll go back to the four hundreds room."

"We've already been there," said Andrew.

"Well, you guys might've missed something."

"Good idea," said Charles. He figured if Haley Daley wasted time retracing steps he and Andrew had already taken, she would find nothing new and become less of a threat. "Let's meet back here at, say, seven."

"Fine."

Haley left the meeting room.

Charles went to the door and closed it.

"You know what we really need?" he said to Andrew.

"Chocolate milk and maybe some cookies?"

Charles shook his head. "No, Andrew. We need whatever clues Kyle Keeley and his team have found. Especially if they have our missing cards."

Veering left the instant she reached the second floor, Haley made her way toward the 400s room.

She figured that Charles and Andrew had probably missed something important in the foreign languages room because they'd spent too much time talking to "these awesome mannequins" that told them all about their "American heritage."

As she rounded the bend, Haley saw Kyle Keeley and his crew tumble out of the 200s room.

It looked like Miguel was carrying a Bible.

But a Bible wasn't one of the books on display in the Staff Picks case.

We're following separate paths to the same goal, Haley thought. *And somewhere, those two paths are going to collide.*

Haley slid her card key down the reader slot in the 400s door. The lock clicked and she pushed the door open.

The room was dimly lit.

"*Bienvenida! Bienvenue! Witamy! Kuwakaribisha!* Welcome!" boomed a voice from the ceiling speakers.

"Sorry," said Haley, blindly feeling her way forward and bumping into something hard and lumpy.

"This is the four hundreds room, home of foreign languages. Here, HALEY, you can learn all about your American heritage."

A bank of spotlights thumped on.

Haley was basically hugging a department store mannequin.

An overhead projector beamed a movie onto the dummy to her left, turning it into a perky woman who looked like Haley would probably look a couple of years after she graduated from college.

"Hello, HALEY. Welcome to *your* American heritage. Let's begin your voyage!"

"That's okay, I don't have time right now. I'm Haley Daley. My ancestors were Irish, okay? So can we skip the history lesson and . . ."

Suddenly, the two mannequins at the far end of the row turned into sepia-toned versions of her great-great-great-grandmother and great-great-great-grandfather. Haley knew it was them because her dad had a bunch of old photos hanging in their family room. The two dummies looked exactly like Patrick and Oona Daley did in their wedding portrait.

"No man ever wore a scarf as warm as his daughter's arm around his neck," said Patrick in his thick Irish brogue. "Yer da is proud of you, Haley."

"Thanks. But I really need to win this competition."

"Watch out for sneaky rascals," said Oona. "Them that would steal the sugar out of your punch."

Haley had to smile. It sounded like her ancestor had met Charles Chiltington.

"And always remember, Haley," said her great-great-great-grandfather, "every woman's mind is her kingdom. Rule it wisely, lassie."

"I'm trying!"

"This library can help," said her great-great-great-grandmother with a wink.

And when she did, a secret panel in the wall slid open.

"What's going on?" said Haley.

"You're our third visitor!" boomed the jolly announcer in the ceiling.

"So?"

"According to *The American Heritage Dictionary of Idioms*—available in our reference department, by the way—'the third time is a charm'! Therefore, as our third visitor, you have won this charming bonus."

Two bonuses in one day?

She was right! Mr. Lemoncello definitely wanted Haley Daley to win this game, because clearly he knew she'd be the perfect, best-looking spokesmodel for his holiday commercials.

"Don't worry, sir!" Haley said to the nearest TV camera. "I won't let you down."

She hurried through the open wall panel and into the 300s room on the other side.

Ta-da!

The first thing she saw was one of the books they'd been searching for all day long: *True Crime Ohio: The Buckeye State's Most Notorious Brigands, Burglars, and Bandits* by Clare Taylor-Winters.

She quickly opened the cover and found the hidden four-by-four card. It took her two seconds to decipher the clue:

"Bandits."

Haley remembered another bit of Irish wisdom, something her dad said all the time: "Never bolt your door with a boiled carrot!"

She decided to keep this new clue secret and secure. She wouldn't share it with Charles or Andrew.

Haley took off her left sneaker, folded the card in half, and slid the clue into her shoe for safekeeping. When her sneak was laced up tight again, she took the *True Crime Ohio* book off its display stand and tucked it into the bookshelf, making sure it was in the proper position: right between 364.1091 and 364.1093. That way, she'd know where to find it if, for whatever reason, she needed the book again.

Haley looked up at the nearest camera and flashed it her brightest toothpaste-commercial smile.

"Goooo, Le-moncell-ooooo! That's a cheer I just made up. We can use it in one of the commercials—after I win!"

35

"Entrance to Community Meeting Room B will only be granted to KYLE KEELEY, SIERRA RUSSELL, AKIMI HUGHES, and MIGUEL FERNANDEZ," said the soothing female voice in the ceiling after the four teammates had swiped their cards through the meeting room door's reader slot.

"This makes sense," said Akimi. "We needed a place to organize all this material, put it on the walls, and draw a chart like the FBI always does on TV when they're tailing the mob."

"Stole the meeting room idea from me, eh, Keeley?"

Charles Chiltington was standing in the doorway to Meeting Room A on the far side of the rotunda.

"No," said Kyle. "We just needed someplace to throw our victory party after we win."

"Not going to happen," Charles said smugly. "Must

I remind you? I'm a Chiltington. We never lose." And he disappeared back into Meeting Room A.

After Charles was gone, Kyle led his team into Meeting Room B.

Miguel posted the bank blueprints he had found up on the walls while Sierra set up the Bibliomania game board on the conference table.

"I'm glad this room won't let anybody else in," said Kyle.

"And by 'anybody' you mean Charles Chiltington, right?" said Akimi.

"Totally."

Akimi grabbed a marker and wrote a neat outline on the dry-erase walls:

CLUES SO FAR

DEFINITE CLUES

1) From the 000s room:
Get to Know Your Local Library book

2) From the Art & Artifacts Room:
Willy Wonka candy (rhymes with "Andy").
Find glass elevator?

3) From the 200s room:
Bible verse—"Thou shalt not steal."

PROBABLY CLUES

BOOKS/AUTHORS ON THE BACKS OF
LIBRARY CARDS

#1 Miguel Fernandez
Incident at Hawk's Hill by Allan W. Eckert/
No, David! by David Shannon

#2 Akimi Hughes
One Fish Two Fish Red Fish Blue Fish
by Dr. Seuss/Nine Stories by J. D. Salinger

#3 UNKNOWN

#4 Bridgette Wadge
Tales of a Fourth Grade Nothing
by Judy Blume/Harry Potter and the
Sorcerer's Stone by J. K. Rowling

#5 Sierra Russell
The Egypt Game by Zilpha Keatley Snyder/
The Westing Game by Ellen Raskin

#6 Yasmeen Smith-Snyder
Around the World in Eighty Days
by Jules Verne/The Yak Who Yelled Yuck
by Carol Pugliano-Martin

#7 Sean Keegan
Olivia by Ian Falconer/Unreal! by Paul Jennings

#8 UNKNOWN

#9 Rose Vermette
All-of-a-Kind Family by Sydney Taylor/
Scat by Carl Hiaasen

#10 Kayla Corson
Anna to the Infinite Power
by Mildred Ames/Where the Sidewalk
Ends by Shel Silverstein

#11 UNKNOWN

#12 Kyle Keeley
I Love You, Stinky Face by Lisa McCourt/
The Napping House by Audrey Wood

MAYBE CLUES???

Statues ringed around the dome:

Thomas Wolfe, Booker T. Washington, Stephen
Sondheim, George Orwell, Lewis Carroll,
Dr. Seuss, Maya Angelou, Shel Silverstein,
Pseudonymous Bosch, Todd Strasser

"Wow," said Akimi, stepping back to study the walls. "What an incredible mess."

"Yeah," said Kyle. "Okay, guys—there are eight more book rooms to explore and who knows how many more wild cards. Whose turn is it?"

"Yours," said Sierra.

Kyle flicked the spinner. "Green. The five hundreds. Science."

He pulled the first green card from the deck.

" 'Four and twenty were once in a pie. 598.367 might tell you why.' "

"Blackbirds?" said Miguel.

"I guess."

"Well," sighed Akimi, "let's go check out *another* book. There's still like an inch or two left on our whiteboard."

The 500s room was like a miniature museum of natural history.

In addition to towering walls of books, there was a whole planetarium of stars and constellations projected on the ceiling. Models of planets whirled in their orbits. Sparkle-tailed comets shot around the corners of bookshelves.

Kyle and his teammates made their way back to the 590s—Zoology.

Shelving units were arranged in a square around an open area, maybe twenty feet by twenty feet wide. When the team entered the empty space, the lights dimmed and a guy with long wavy hair who looked like an artistic Daniel Boone faded into view. He was wearing some kind of bear-fur coat and toting a musket.

"*Bonjour,*" said the hologram.

"It's John James Audubon," said Sierra. "The famous ornithologist."

"He gives people braces?" said Kyle.

"No," Sierra said with a laugh. "He studied and painted birds."

A blackbird with a yellow beak flew into the open area and roosted on a tree branch. The bird and the tree were both holograms, too.

"This beautiful blackbird from Alexandriaville, Ohio," said the semi-transparent Audubon image, "can mimic in song the sounds it has heard."

And the bird started wailing.

"Wow," said Akimi. "That sounds exactly like a police siren!"

"Yo," said Miguel. "Freaky."

"To learn more," said Audubon, "be sure to read *Bird Songs, Warbles, and Whistles* written by Dr. Diana Victoria Garcia, with classic illustrations by *moi.*"

With that, Audubon sat down on a campstool. An easel appeared, the blackbird struck a pose, and the outdoorsy artist started painting the bird's portrait, while humming "Blackbird" by the Beatles.

"Okay," said Kyle. "This is the strangest clue yet."

"Well, here's the book at least," said Sierra, who had found 598.367 on the shelf.

"So what do a blackbird's wails and warbles have to do with finding our way out of the library?" said Akimi.

Just then, they heard a very different sound.

Behind one of the bookcases, something growled, then roared.

"Did you guys hear that?" said Sierra.

"Yeah," said Akimi. "I don't think it's a robin red-breast."

A very rare white Bengal tiger, with icy-blue eyeballs, crept out from behind a wall of bookshelves and stalked into the open area where Audubon sat painting his bird portrait.

"Uh, is that another hologram?" asked Miguel.

ROAR!

No one stuck around to find out.

36

Down on the first floor, Charles and Andrew were working their way around the semicircle of three-story-tall floor-to-dome bookcases filled with fiction.

It was nearly eight p.m.

"We need to find that blasted book," said Charles, craning his neck to study the shelves.

"I'm getting kind of hungry," mumbled Andrew.

"You had a snack this afternoon," snapped Charles.

"Well, now it's time for dinner."

"No. We need to find *Anne of Green Gables* first."

The classic by Lucy Maud Montgomery was the middle book on the top shelf in the Staff Picks display case. So far, Charles, Haley, and Andrew had not been able to find it anywhere in the library.

"Unfortunately," said Andrew, "they've temporarily erased the book's call number from the database."

"So we wouldn't know what to punch into the hover ladder's control panel," grumbled Charles.

"Actually," said Andrew, "they might've shelved it in the Children's Room. Or maybe the eight hundreds, with Literature. Could be in the four hundreds, too, because it was originally written in Canadian, which is, technically, a foreign language."

"So you have said, Andrew. Repeatedly. But we've already searched those other locations. Several times. It has to be here with the other fiction titles. You just need to fly up and find it."

"Well," said Andrew, "I'm kind of afraid of heights."

"Fine. Whatever. I'll go up and grab it. But you have to give me some kind of call number to enter into the hover ladder."

"Lucy Maud Montgomery wrote other Anne books. There's *Anne of Avonlea*. . . ."

Charles dashed over to the nearest library table and swiped his fingers across the glass face of its built-in computer pad.

"Here we go. *Anne of Avonlea* by Lucy Maud Montgomery. F-MON."

"Yes," said Andrew. "Fiction books are usually put on the shelf in alphabetical order by the author's last name. Nonfiction titles are classified according to the Dewey decimal system."

"How long have you known this?"

Andrew's nose twitched. "Since second grade."

"So all we ever needed was 'F-MON'? We could've found this book hours ago?"

Andrew gulped.

"You are such a disappointment." Shaking his head, Charles huffed over to one of the hover ladders. He quickly jabbed "F," "M," "O," and "N" into the keypad. The boot clamps locked into place around his ankles. "You owe me for wasting all this time, Andrew. You owe me big-time. If you let me down once more, I swear I will tell everybody you're a big blubbering baby. I'll Twitter it *and* post it on Facebook."

"Don't worry. I'll make you glad you picked me for your team, Charles! I promise."

The hover ladder lifted off the floor and gently glided up to the M section of the fiction wall. Shuttling sideways, it carried Charles over to a shelf displaying all the Anne books.

He grabbed a copy of *Anne of Green Gables.*

As soon as he did, the ladder started its slow descent to the floor.

"What'd you find?" asked Andrew when Charles landed.

"The clue we needed."

He showed Andrew the card that had been tucked inside the front cover.

"Okay," said Andrew. "It's 'C plus hat'! So the word is 'chat,' which, by the way, could also be *'chat,'* the French word for cat!"

"Well done, Andrew," said Charles, even though he knew the clue was really "C plus Anne," equaling "can," thereby making the puzzle "You *can* walk out the way BLANK BLANK inn in past BLANK."

The way what did what? he wondered. *And what does "inn in" mean?*

Charles desperately needed to find the three missing pictograms.

Suddenly, Mr. Lemoncello's voice boomed out of speakers ringing the rotunda.

"Hey, Charles! Hey, Andrew! Let's Do a Deal!"

Game show music blared. A canned crowd cheered.

Charles turned around and saw shafts of colored light illuminating three envelopes perched on top of the librarian's round desk. Clarence the security guard marched into the reading room and, folding his arms over his chest, took up a position near the three envelopes.

"We have a green envelope, a blue envelope, and a red envelope," said Mr. Lemoncello. "In two of those three envelopes are copies of two of the three pictogram clues you still need. In one, there is a Clunker Card. If you pick an envelope with a clue, you get to keep it—and you get to keep going. But once you pick the Clunker Card, you're done . . . and you must suffer the consequences."

Andrew raised his hand.

"Yes, Andrew?"

"What are the consequences?"

"Something bad," said Mr. Lemoncello. "In fact, something wicked this way will probably come. Do you want to do a deal?"

"Yes!" said Charles.

The canned audience cheered.

"All right, then! Charles, you roll first."

"Pardon?"

"Swipe your fingers across the nearest desktop computer panel. The dice tumbler app is up and running!"

Again, the prerecorded audience cheered. They sounded like they loved watching dice tumble more than anything in the world.

Charles slid his fingers across a glass pane. The animated dice rolled.

"Oooh!" cried Mr. Lemoncello. "Double sixes. That gives you a twelve."

"Is that good, sir?"

"Maybe. Maybe not. Okay, Andrew—your turn!"

Peckleman tapped the glass. The dice flipped over.

"Another set of doubles!" said Mr. Lemoncello.

"Yeah," muttered Charles. "Two ones. Snake eyes."

"Is that bad?" asked Andrew.

"Maybe," said Mr. Lemoncello. "Maybe not. Okay, guys—which envelope would you like to open?"

Charles thought about it while ticktock music played. They were given this chance to play Let's Do a Deal after they located the *Anne of Green Gables* clue. Coincidence? He didn't think so.

"We'll take the green envelope, sir."

Clarence presented the green envelope to Charles.

"Open it!" said Andrew. "Open it."

Charles undid the clasp. Pulled out a card.

A loud *ZONK!* rocked the room.

The card was black. With blocky white type.

"Uh-oh," mumbled Andrew. "What's it say on that card?"

" 'Sorry, kids, you're out of luck,' " read Charles. " 'So out of doors you're all now stuck.' "

Clarence picked up the blue and red envelopes and marched back toward the entrance hall.

"What's that mean?" said Andrew.

"Well," said Mr. Lemoncello, "Charles rolled a twelve and you rolled a two. What's twelve plus two?"

"Fourteen," said Charles eagerly, the way he always did in math when he wanted to remind the teacher that he was the smartest kid in the class.

"Oooh," said Mr. Lemoncello. "This is not good. In fact, I'd say it's stinkerrific."

"Stinkerrific?" said Andrew. "Is that even a word?"

"It is now," said Mr. Lemoncello. "J.J.? Tell them what they've lost."

An authoritative female voice boomed out of the ceiling speakers:

"Warning: Due to a Clunker Card, all ten Dewey decimal doors will lock in ten minutes, at exactly eight o'clock. If you are in one of those rooms, kindly leave immediately. The ten doors on the second floor will remain locked for fourteen hours."

Andrew panicked. "What? Fourteen hours?"

"I told you twelve plus two was bad," quipped Mr. Lemoncello. "Of course, it could've been good. If you had picked one of the other envelopes, you would've received a clue and a free fourteen-month subscription to *Library Journal*."

Charles did some quick math. "Sir? Does this mean we'll be locked out of the ten Dewey decimal rooms until ten o'clock tomorrow morning?"

"Bingo!" said Mr. Lemoncello. "It sure does!"

"This stinks," whined Andrew. "We need those stupid rooms to solve your stupid puzzle! Clunker Cards stink. This game stinks. Fourteen-hour penalties stink."

Charles did his best to block out Andrew's rant.

He needed to think.

And then it hit him: *Kyle Keeley's team had to be working on some other solution to the bigger puzzle of how to escape from the library.* Otherwise, Charles and his team would not have been able to find the nine clues they'd already picked up. Surely, if Keeley's team had been playing the same memory match game, they would've found at least one of the pictograms before Charles, Andrew, or Haley did.

They must be working a completely different angle.

Charles was certain that if he could use this downtime

to learn what Keeley and his team had in their meeting room, and combined it with his picture puzzle, he would emerge from the library victorious.

"Do not despair, Andrew," Charles said confidently. "We are still going to win."

"How?"

Charles leaned in and cupped a hand around his mouth so no security cameras could read his lips.

"Remember," he whispered, "you need to pay me back for wasting a ton of time in finding *Anne of Green Gables*."

"What? You're the one who picked the stupid green envelope with the stupid Clunker Card!"

Charles narrowed his eyes and chilled his hushed voice. "So?"

"Um, nothing," said Andrew nervously. "Just thought I'd, you know, point it out."

Charles turned his eyes into blue ice.

"So," whispered Andrew, swallowing hard, "what exactly do you want me to do?"

"Find a way to sneak into Community Meeting Room *B*."

Andrew wheezed in panic. "That's impossible."

"Don't worry. I have an idea."

"What is it?"

"Two words: Sierra Russell."

37

"Ever wonder if this could reek any worse?" said Akimi. "Because it couldn't."

"Yo, none of us pulled a Clunker Card," groused Miguel. "That means somebody on Charles's team did it."

"Akimi and Miguel are right, Kyle," said Sierra. "This really isn't fair."

"I know," was all Kyle could say. "But it's like in Mr. Lemoncello's Family Frenzy, where one player pulls the Orthodontist card and *everybody* has to move back seven spaces to buy their kids braces."

Kyle and his teammates were back in Community Meeting Room B. They'd been staring at the clue board, wondering what a wailing blackbird had to do with Willy Wonka and the Ten Commandments—not to mention that long list of books and all the statues—when the voice in the ceiling made its announcement about the Dewey decimal doors being locked for fourteen hours.

"Well, Mr. Lemoncello better have a *good* reason," said Akimi.

"Oh, I do," said Mr. Lemoncello.

His face appeared on one of the meeting room walls, which was really a giant plasma-screen video monitor.

"Team Kyle is not being penalized for Team Charles's blunder," he said. "Far from it. In fact, you are being rewarded."

Akimi arched her eyebrows in disbelief. "Really? How?"

"The other team's penalty gives you a wrinkle in time."

"A wrinkle in time?" said Kyle. "Is that a clue?"

"No. It's a book. And sometimes, Kyle, a book is just a book. But thanks to the Clunker Card, you have the gift of wrinkled time to seek clues *outside* the ten Dewey decimal rooms. Speaking of *Time*, a magazine available in our periodicals section, it's dinnertime!"

"So the game is basically suspended until ten o'clock tomorrow?" said Kyle.

"Well, Kyle, that's up to you. You can use this time as a bonus, to think, read, and explore. Or you can run upstairs and play video games all night long. The choice is yours."

"We want to win *this* game," said Kyle. His teammates nodded in agreement.

"Wondermous!" said Mr. Lemoncello. "Keep working the puzzle but try to avoid Mrs. Basil E. Frankweiler's files.

They're all mixed up. And before you turn in this evening, you might want to spend some time curled up with a good book."

"Um, they just said the book rooms are locked," said Akimi.

"The nice lady in the ceiling was only talking about the ten Dewey decimal rooms. There is plenty of first-class fiction in the Rotunda Reading Room. Dr. Zinchenko has even selected seven books specifically for our seven remaining contestants. After dinner, you'll find those books on her desk."

When he said that, Mr. Lemoncello started winking.

"I think you'll find the books to be very *enlightening*. Inspirational, even."

And then he winked some more.

"And now, I must return to my side of the mountain. See you in the morning, children! I have great expectations for you all!"

Mr. Lemoncello's image disappeared from the wall.

"Okay," said Akimi, "from the way Mr. Lemoncello was just winking, either somebody kicked a bucket of sand in his face or our recommended reading list is another clue."

On the other side of the rotunda, Charles huddled with Andrew in Meeting Room A.

"I don't trust Haley," he said.

"Why not?"

Charles placed his hand on Andrew's shoulder. "Well, my friend, I'm not sure if I should tell you this, but Haley told me she didn't think you were 'handsome enough' to appear in Mr. Lemoncello's holiday commercials with us when we win."

"Because of my glasses?"

Charles bit his lip. Nodded. "Of course, I totally disagree."

"I see," said Andrew, his ears burning bright red. "Then she doesn't get to see what we found in that *Anne of Green Gables* book."

"Very well, Andrew. If that's how you want to play it."

"You bet I do."

"Fine. Let's go see what's for dinner. I'm starving."

When Charles and Andrew entered the café, the Keeley team was already inside, filling their trays.

"Hey, way to go, Charles!" joked Miguel Fernandez. "You guys pulled a Clunker Card?"

"Indeed we did. However, not even that bit of bad luck can derail our juggernaut!"

"Huh?" said Akimi.

"He means we're still gonna win!" said Andrew.

Charles and Andrew crossed to the far side of the room to join Haley, who was sitting in a corner.

"You guys find any clues this afternoon?" she asked.

"Sadly, no," said Charles.

"All we found was that door-locking penalty," said Andrew, who could lie almost as well as Charles.

"How about you, Haley?" Charles asked. "Find anything interesting?"

"Nope. Nada." Then she yawned and finished her dinner. "I think I'll head upstairs and sack out."

"Really? It's only eight-forty-eight."

"I know. But I'm totally pooped." She yawned again. "Plus, I want to be up bright and early, before the Dewey decimal doors reopen. We have more clues to find. See you guys tomorrow. Unless we have more team business to discuss?"

"No. Nothing."

She walked out of the café.

38

"Very interesting," said Akimi, looking through the café's glass walls and into the Rotunda Reading Room.

"What?" said Miguel.

"I think Clarence just dropped off our books."

Kyle pushed back from the table. He could see the shadowy figure of the bulky security guard slinking away from the round desk at the center of the rotunda. He left behind a stack of books.

"Come on," he said. "Let's go see what sort of 'inspirational' reading Dr. Zinchenko has selected for us."

"What about those guys?" said Miguel, gesturing toward the table where Charles and Andrew were finishing their desserts.

Kyle was torn.

On one hand, he didn't want to give away the bonus his team had received thanks to the other team's penalty.

On the other hand, he didn't want people saying he and his friends won because Mr. Lemoncello had tossed them an extra clue.

He came up with a compromise.

"Hey, Charles? Andrew? We're all going to go grab some books to read to kill time till tomorrow morning. You two might want to do the same thing."

"No thanks." Charles stood up. "We pretty much have this thing figured out. In fact, I think Mr. Lemoncello steered us toward the Clunker Card so we wouldn't win too easily. I mean, how would it look if we escaped from his library in less than twenty-four hours?"

"Bad," said Andrew. "Real bad."

"Indeed," said Charles. "In fact, I suspect nobody would buy Lemoncello games anymore if we showed them how consistently easy they are to win. Anyway, we're going upstairs so I can give Andrew a tour of my private suite. Would any of you care to join us?"

"No thanks," said Akimi.

"Suit yourself. Oh, by the way, Mr. Lemoncello has a real video game console upstairs."

Kyle felt his mouth going dry.

"It's top-of-the-line equipment. And it plays real games. Not just educational stuff. Care to join us, Keeley?"

"Um . . ."

"We're going to play Squirrel Squad Six. The new edition. According to the game box, it won't be released to the general public until early December."

Kyle felt sweat beading on his forehead. His palms were moist. His fingers were twitching, itching to thumb-toggle a joystick.

But finally, after the inside of his mouth had turned to sandpaper, he said, "No thanks, Charles. We're just gonna, you know, read."

After Charles and Andrew headed up to the third floor to play what was probably the most awesome version ever of Mr. Lemoncello's most awesome video game ever (if Charles Chiltington was actually telling the truth), Kyle and his teammates hurried out to see what books were waiting for them on the librarian's table.

They found seven different versions of the same book: *The Complete Sherlock Holmes*. One was a leather-bound limited edition; another was a tattered paperback; three were hardcovers with different illustrations on their fronts; one was a bigger kind of paperback with lots of scholarly essays; and the seventh was an e-reader with only the one title loaded onto it.

"I think Mr. Lemoncello wants us to start a book club," said Sierra.

"What do you mean?" asked Kyle.

"You know—we all read the same book and then get together later to discuss it and share our opinions."

"It's fun," said Miguel. "We have a book group at school."

"Are you in it?" asked Sierra.

"Yeah. Maybe you'd like to join us sometime?"

"I would. Thank you, Miguel."

Akimi cleared her throat. "Now what?" she said to Kyle.

Kyle shrugged. "Like I told Charles. We read."

Everybody grabbed a copy of the Sherlock Holmes book.

Nobody went for the e-reader.

Upstairs on the third floor, Haley tiptoed around the Lemoncello-abilia Room.

When she had visited the mini-museum earlier, she hadn't really looked around. Now she hoped to find another book from the "memorable reads" display, a Little Golden Book called *Baby's Mother Goose: Pat-a-Cake*, which could've been something Mr. Lemoncello read (or had read to him) when he was a very young boy.

Haley made her way past the orderly stacks of boxes through a doorway and into what looked like a re-creation of Mr. Lemoncello's childhood bedroom—a cramped space crammed with two bunk beds that he had shared with his three brothers. Next to one of the lower bunks was a bookcase made out of plastic milk crates.

There it was, filed away with maybe three dozen other skinny, hardboard-covered picture books.

Haley pried open the cover.

Out plopped a four-by-four art card:

She quickly folded it in half and stuffed it inside her sneaker with her "BANDITS" clue.

Because now she was pretty certain that "bandits" had, at one time or another, "crawled in" to this building back when it was a bank.

The silhouette of Indiana didn't represent the Indianapolis 500 like Charles had insisted.

It stood for "IN," the official post office abbreviation for the Hoosier State.

First thing in the morning, when the doors reopened, she needed to search through the Dewey decimal rooms to find a clue that would tell her exactly how and where the bandits had crawled in.

A tunnel? An air vent? A secret passageway on the first, second, or third floor between the old bank and the office building behind it?

There was only one thing Haley was certain of: They hadn't crawled in through a book return slot.

39

Everyone in the reading room was quietly lost in the adventures of Sherlock Holmes.

Kyle had just finished a pretty cool story called "A Scandal in Bohemia," about a king who was going to get married to a royal heiress with maybe six names. But the king was being blackmailed by an old girlfriend, an opera singer from New Jersey named Irene Adler.

Something Sherlock Holmes said to Dr. Watson early in the story really stuck with Kyle: "You see, but you do not observe."

Kyle figured that was why Mr. Lemoncello wanted them all to take a break from chasing clues and read these classic mysteries. Not to find new clues but to become better puzzle solvers. Had they been seeing things without really observing them? Probably.

Reading the story was also kind of fun. Kyle could

totally see Holmes's apartment at 221b Baker Street and the snooty king and the horse-drawn carriages on the foggy London streets and the disguises Holmes wore and the smoke bomb Dr. Watson tossed through a window and everybody on the street screaming, "Fire!"

It was like he was watching a 3-D IMAX movie in his head. Kyle couldn't wait to start the second story in the book, "The Adventure of the Red-Headed League."

"How's it going?" whispered Akimi.

"This book is pretty cool. This Sir Arthur Conan Doyle guy knows how to keep his readers hooked."

"His characters leap off the pages," said Sierra.

"Yeah," said Miguel. "I dig the 'consulting detective.'"

"Huh?" said Kyle.

"That's what Holmes calls himself sometimes."

"Oh. I've only read one story so far and . . ."

Suddenly, something seemed odd to Kyle.

"Hey—how come Conan Doyle isn't one of those statues up there?"

"What do you mean?" said Akimi.

"He's a famous author, right? How come they're projecting a statue of a modern writer like Pseudonymous Bosch but not the author who created a classic like Sherlock Holmes?"

"Good question, bro," said Miguel.

"I need to *consult* with my brother Curtis."

"How come?"

"Curtis has read more books than anyone I know,

except maybe Sierra. He scored an 808 on his SAT Subject Test in Literature."

"Uh, Kyle?" said Akimi. "I think the top score for any SAT test is 800."

"Yep. Then Curtis took it. They had to raise it."

"So maybe he can help us figure out what's up with all the statues," said Miguel.

"Exactly. Why these ten? Why not ten other writers?"

"Why not the same ten Bridgette Wadge had for her Extreme Challenge?" added Sierra.

Kyle looked around the room.

"Mrs. Tobin? Hello? Mrs. Tobin?"

The hazy holographic image of the 1960s librarian flickered into view.

"How may I help you, KYLE?"

"I'd like to talk to an expert."

"And whom do you wish to speak to?"

"Mr. Curtis Keeley."

"Your brother?"

"And an SAT-certified expert on the subject of literature and authors and other literary-type junk."

Suddenly, the hologram vanished and Dr. Zinchenko's voice came over the ceiling speakers.

"This is a rather irregular request, Mr. Keeley."

"Hey," said Akimi, "this whole game is rather irregular, don't ya think?"

"We just need some more data," said Kyle. "Because,

like Sherlock says to Dr. Watson, 'it is a capital mistake to theorize before one has data.' "

"I take it you're enjoying your book?" said the librarian.

Kyle gave the closest security camera a big thumbs-up. "Boo-yeah. Can't wait to see what's up with that league of redheaded gentlemen."

"Ah, yes," said Dr. Zinchenko. "A fascinating story. I recently reread it myself. Very well, Kyle. We will contact your brother to determine if he does indeed qualify as a literary expert. It may take a while."

"No rush," said Kyle. "I've got a good book."

Kyle was busy helping Holmes figure out that the Red-Headed League was just a clever ploy pulled by some robbers to get a red-haired pawnbroker to leave his shop long enough for them to dig a tunnel from his basement to the bank next door when the librarian's voice jolted him out of London and brought him home to Ohio.

"My apologies for the interruption."

Akimi, Miguel, and Sierra closed their books, too. It was eleven-fifteen. Everyone had sleepy, dreamy looks in their eyes because they'd been kind of drifting off in their comfy reading chairs.

"What's up?" said Kyle.

"We have arranged for your expert consultation with Mr. Curtis Keeley."

"Awesome! How do we do it?"

"You and your expert may have a five-minute video chat on my computer terminal, which is located behind the main desk."

Kyle hurried over to the round desk in the center of the room. His three teammates hurried right behind him.

"Your consultation begins . . . now."

And there was Curtis. Sitting at his computer in his bedroom.

"Hey, Curtis!"

"Hi, Kyle. How's it going in there?"

"Great."

Kyle's oldest brother, Mike, popped into the doorway behind Curtis.

"Ky-le, Ky-le," Mike chanted. "Whoo-hoo!"

Kyle had never had his own cheerleader before.

"We need you to give us one hundred and ten percent in there, li'l brother!" Mike squinted at the screen over Curtis's shoulder. "Who are those other guys?"

"My teammates, Miguel, Sierra, and you know Akimi."

"You guys are a team? Smart move. Even I can't win football games without help from ten other guys."

"Um, Mike?" said Kyle. "Curtis and I only have five minutes to chat."

"Cool. I'm outta here. Win, baby, win!"

Mike backpedaled out of the bedroom, making double fist pumps the whole way.

"You have four minutes remaining," advised Dr. Zinchenko.

"Okay, Curtis, here's my question. What do these authors have in common?"

Kyle rattled off the list of the statues in order.

And Curtis stared blankly into his computer cam.

For a real long time.

Then he shook his head. "I'm sorry, Kyle. I have no earthly idea."

"Really?" Kyle was astonished. "You've got nothing?"

"Well," said Curtis, "the only connection I can see is Thomas Wolfe wrote *Look Homeward, Angel* and Lewis Carroll wrote *Through the Looking-Glass*. Both titles have the word 'look' in them. But the two books are otherwise completely different. The two authors as well."

Kyle and his whole team stood in stunned silence.

Until Sierra started jumping up and down.

"Of course!" she shouted.

"Your time is up," announced Dr. Zinchenko.

"Um, okay," Kyle said to the computer screen. "Thanks, Curtis. That was, uh, really helpful."

"It was!" said Sierra, daintily clapping her hands together like a very polite seal. The computer screen faded to black.

"What's up?" asked Miguel.

"I think I know how to crack the statue code."

"There's a code?" said Akimi. "Who knew?"

"It'll take time," said Sierra. "And I need a computer."

"Oh-kay," said Kyle, who was sort of shocked to see Sierra so completely jazzed. "We'll be in our meeting room, putting together a list of new Dewey decimal numbers from the Bibliomania cards so we're ready to hit the ground running when the doors reopen at ten tomorrow morning."

While Sierra settled in at a desktop computer pad, the rest of the team returned to the Bibliomania board game.

"We should just start flipping over cards and putting together a list of call numbers," Kyle suggested.

"Sounds like a plan," said Akimi.

She plucked a purple card out of the pile.

Lose a Turn was all that was printed on the other side.

"Try a different color," urged Miguel.

Akimi flipped up a blue card.

Take an Extra Turn was printed on it. So Akimi flipped over all the other blue cards while Miguel flipped over all the purples.

The purple cards all said **Lose a Turn**. The blue ones all said **Take an Extra Turn**.

Kyle had been checking out the red and maroon piles.

"The reds all say 'Pick a Yellow Card,'" he reported. "The maroons say 'Grab a Green.'"

"The grays do the same thing," said Miguel. "Only they say 'Pick a Pink.' The tan cards say 'Go Grab an Orange.'"

"So that leaves the colors we've already played." Kyle flipped over a yellow card. "'In the square root of 48,629.20271209 . . .'"

"What the . . . ?" said Akimi.

"Hang on," said Miguel. "There's a calculator app in this desktop computer."

Kyle read the rest of the card: ". . . 'find half of 4-40-30.'"

"Well, that's 2-20-15, again," said Akimi.

"And the square root of forty-eight thousand whatever is 220.5203," said Miguel. "The King James Bible we already found."

Akimi flipped through the rest of the yellow cards. "Same with these. They all send us into the Religion section to find that Bible verse."

"Ditto with the greens," reported Miguel. "All clues leading to *Bird Songs, Warbles, and Whistles.*"

"And the pinks all lead back to 027.4," said Kyle. "I guess they really wanted to make sure we found *Get to Know Your Local Library.*"

"Which leaves the wild cards," said Akimi. She examined the orange deck. "Find a rhyme for 'cart and paperbacks,' 'smart and zodiacs,' 'tart and potato sacks.'"

"The Art and Artifacts Room," said Miguel with a sigh.

"Where," Akimi continued, "we need to find a rhyme for 'Randy,' 'Sandy,' or 'Brandi.'"

"The Willy Wonka candy," said Miguel.

"So," said Kyle, "I'm guessing the Bibliomania game was only supposed to help us find the four clues we've already found."

"But we need to know more numbers," said Miguel. "Because a library should be a know-place for know-bodies."

When Miguel made his pun, Kyle and Akimi both groaned.

But then Kyle thought of something: "This is why Mr. Lemoncello called our time-out a bonus. He knew we'd need a ton of time to find a new source of numbers."

Just then Sierra burst into the meeting room.

"You guys! I found a whole bunch of new numbers!"

"What?" said Kyle, Akimi, and Miguel. "Where?"

"Up on the ceiling!"

41

"You need to look up at the Wonder Dome," said Sierra.

"Huh?" said Kyle.

Sierra and her whole team were standing together outside the door to Community Meeting Room B. She hadn't been this happy or excited in a long time.

"Um, Sierra?" said Akimi. "Why exactly are you suggesting we all give ourselves a crick in the neck by staring at the ceiling?"

"Okay. This is a game some of us play online called What's the Connection? I put up a list of authors and you have to figure out how they're linked by the titles of their books."

"Whoa," said Akimi, sort of sarcastically. "Sounds like fun."

"It is. But believe me, it's not easy."

"What'd you figure out?" asked Miguel.

"Well, like Curtis said, Thomas Wolfe wrote *Look Homeward, Angel* and Lewis Carroll wrote *Through the Looking-Glass*. That got me thinking. And running computer searches. Stephen Sondheim wrote a book called *Look, I Made a Hat*. Maya Angelou wrote *Even the Stars Look Lonesome*, and Pseudonymous Bosch wrote *This Isn't What It Looks Like*."

"They all have 'look' in the title," said Kyle.

"What about the other five authors?" asked Akimi. "Did they write 'look' books, too?"

"No, they're up there for a different word."

"Huh?"

"Booker T. Washington wrote *Up from Slavery* and Shel Silverstein wrote *Falling Up*."

"And Dr. Seuss?" said Kyle.

"*Great Day for Up*. George Orwell did *Coming Up for Air*, and Todd Strasser has a book called *If I Grow Up*."

"So the ten statues give us two words," said Miguel.

"Yep. 'Look' and 'up.' So I did. I looked up. At the Wonder Dome. There! Did you see it? That string of numbers that just drifted across the two hundreds screen under the Star of David?"

"220.5203," said Miguel.

Akimi knuckle-punched Kyle in the arm. "This is just like that bonus code thingie you showed me on the school bus!"

"Of course," said Kyle. "This is a Lemoncello game.

He always hides secret codes in screwy places. Way to go, Sierra!"

"Thanks," said Sierra, realizing how much more fun it was to play this kind of game with real friends instead of virtual ones on the Internet.

"But we already found that same two hundreds number playing Bibliomania," said Miguel.

"True," said Kyle. "Check out the sections for numbers the cards wouldn't give us."

Everybody craned their necks and focused on the graphics swimming across the ten panels overhead.

"Here comes another one!" said Sierra. "In the six hundreds. Right underneath the floating stethoscope."

"Got it!" said Kyle. "624.193."

"Whoo-hoo!" said Akimi.

"Sierra, you're my new hero," said Kyle. "You saved the day."

Sierra blushed. "Thanks."

"The spinner," said Akimi.

"Huh?" said Miguel.

"That was another clue. The Bibliomania game was pointing us to the ceiling, too. Because in Dewey decimal mode, the Wonder Dome looks like a giant 3-D version of the board game's spinner."

"Awesome, Sierra," said Miguel. "Absolutely awesome."

* * *

217

Sierra and her teammates stared up at the ceiling for over an hour. At 12:30, they finally lay down on the floor so they wouldn't cramp their neck muscles.

Because every fifteen minutes, the animated ceiling looped through call numbers for every Dewey decimal room in the library.

Except one.

And then the sequence repeated itself.

"How come there's no three hundreds number?" said Miguel.

"Probably because that's the one book we really, really, *really* need," said Kyle.

"That Lemoncello," said Akimi. "What a comedian."

Peering over the railing on the third-floor balcony at close to two a.m., Andrew Peckleman saw Sierra Russell sitting all alone in the Rotunda Reading Room.

Andrew had spent the night on the third floor losing video games to Charles.

And being reminded about how much he needed to break into Community Meeting Room B to "borrow" any clues Kyle Keeley's team had gathered, to pay Charles back for wasting so much of "the team's time" on the *Anne of Green Gables* clue due to his "foolish fear" of heights.

Andrew had promised Charles he'd do whatever it took.

"If anyone on Team Keeley is going to help us break into their headquarters," Charles had said, "it will be the shy girl who is constantly reading. Have you noticed what Sierra Russell uses for a bookmark?"

"No," Andrew had honestly answered.

219

"Her library card, which of course doubles as a key card for Meeting Room B. Find a way to borrow it."

"Isn't that illegal?"

"Of course not. This is a library. People borrow books, don't they?"

"Well, yeah . . ."

"Did I mention that I have three thousand Facebook friends? Two thousand Twitter followers? Each and every one of them will hear what a weenie and wimp you are if you don't do this thing to guarantee that our team wins."

So Andrew made his way down to the first floor.

Sierra, as usual, was reading a book.

As he moved closer, Andrew saw a flash of white.

Charles was right. Sierra was using her shiny white library card to mark her place in the book's pages.

He made his way to the cluster of overstuffed reading chairs.

"Good book?"

His voice startled her.

"Oh. Hello. Yes."

"Mind if I join you?" He slid into a crinkly leather seat opposite Sierra. "So, um, what're you reading?"

"*Charlie and the Great Glass Elevator* by Roald Dahl."

"Oh, yeah. I've heard about that book. Where's the rest of your team?"

"They went to bed. Want to get up bright and early. Before the doors on the second floor open again."

"Yeah. Haley and Charles conked out, too. Guess it's just us bookworms, huh?"

"Well, it is kind of late," said Sierra. "I'm going to go upstairs and . . ."

"May I take a look?"

"Hmmm?"

"At your book. I've never actually read it. I just tell people I have."

"Oh. Sure." Sierra handed it to him.

"Thank you."

Andrew flipped through the pages until he found the spot where Sierra had tucked in her library card. "Wouldn't it be cool if this library had a flying elevator like in that Willy Wonka movie? Especially if you could use it to crash through the roof like Charlie and Wonka did. That'd be a pretty cool way to escape from the library, huh?"

"Yeah. I guess."

That was when Andrew made the switch. He slipped his library card into Sierra's book and palmed hers.

Charles would be so proud of him!

"So," he said, closing the book, "did you ever read *The Elevator Family*?"

"No. I don't think so."

"It's all about this family that lives in the elevator of a San Francisco hotel. And let's just say, the book has its ups and its downs!"

Andrew laughed hysterically, because it was one of the

funniest jokes he knew. Sierra sort of chuckled. He handed back her book.

Overhead, the Wonder Dome dissolved out of its Dewey decimal mode and, with a swirl of colors, became a bright green bedroom with a pair of red-framed windows looking out on a blue night sky with a full moon and a blanket of twinkling stars. In the great green room, there was a telephone, and a red balloon, and a picture of a cow jumping over the moon.

The ceiling had become the bunny's bedroom from *Goodnight Moon*.

A quiet old lady bunny in a frumpy blue dress hopped into the Rotunda Reading Room. Two tiny cats followed her.

"Great," said Andrew. "Another stupid hologram."

"I think she's cute," said Sierra.

"Hush," said the bunny. "Goodnight clocks and good-night socks. Goodnight, Sierra."

"Goodnight, Bunny." Sierra took her book and headed upstairs.

"Goodnight, Andrew," said the bunny.

"Right."

He pocketed the purloined library card. He couldn't do anything with it right away. Not while the holographic bunny's handlers were watching on the spy cameras.

But first thing in the morning . . .

"Goodnight old bunny saying hush," he called out.

And then, under his breath, he muttered, "In the morning, our competition we're gonna crush."

Up bright and early the next morning, Kyle made his way across the Rotunda Reading Room.

It was eight-fifteen. The Dewey decimal doors would open in one hour and forty-five minutes. The game would be over in less than four hours.

Kyle was totally pumped.

Sierra Russell, on the other hand, was sitting in a comfy chair reading a book.

"Hey," said Kyle.

"Hi," said Sierra, stifling a small yawn.

"Did you stay up all night reading?"

"No. I went upstairs around two. But there was a new stack of books on the librarian's desk when I came down."

"Oh, really? What'd you find?"

"Five copies of this."

She showed Kyle her book. It was *The Eleventh Hour: A Curious Mystery*.

"It's a rhyming picture book about Horace the Elephant's eleventh birthday party and the search to find out who ran off with all the food. There are hidden messages and cryptic codes all over the pages."

"Why's it called *The Eleventh Hour*?"

"The birthday feast was supposed to take place at eleven a.m. But since somebody stole all the food . . ."

Kyle laughed. "Eleven a.m."

"What?"

"The eleventh hour! The last possible moment." Kyle nudged his head up at the Wonder Dome. "How much do you want to bet that at eleven o'clock, on the dot, the clue we need most of all will pop up in the three hundreds section?"

Sierra smiled. "So this new book is a clue about our clue?"

"That's my guess. Did you eat breakfast?"

"Not yet."

"Well, what are you waiting for?" said Miguel as he strode into the room. "Today's the big day. We're gonna need our energy for the final sprint."

"He's right," said Akimi, climbing down the spiral staircase. "The doors open in less than two hours. Then we only have two more hours to figure everything out."

"But," said Kyle to his other teammates, "Sierra just figured out when we'll get the big three hundreds clue."

He gestured toward the picture book. "At the last possible minute."

"What?" said Akimi. "Eleven-fifty-nine?"

"Close. Eleven o'clock."

"Awesome," said Miguel. "It must be a very good clue."

Kyle and his team went into the café, where they found Haley Daley seated at a table, eating half a grapefruit and staring blankly through the glass walls into the rotunda.

"Hey, Haley," said Kyle. "How's it going?"

"Not bad. You?"

"Good. Win or lose, we're having a blast."

"We're the fun bunch," said Akimi.

"You guys really get along, huh?"

"Oh, yes," said Sierra. "I haven't had this much fun since I was six."

"Seriously?"

"What's the matter, Haley?" said Akimi. "Life not so good on Team Charles?"

"It's okay, I guess. I mean, we've pulled together some good clues and all. . . ."

"Well," said Miguel, "if you ever want to switch sides, we're always looking for new members."

"Can I do that? Just switch sides? Even though I know everything about what Team Charles did all day yesterday?"

"I think so," said Kyle. "I mean, there was nothing in the rules about teams."

"Huh," said Haley. "And Andrew's teamed up with you guys, too?"

"No," said Kyle.

Haley nodded toward the wall of windows behind Kyle. "Then why'd he just swipe his library card and go into your meeting room?"

Zipping across the slick marble floor, Kyle and his team, trailed by Haley, practically slid into Community Meeting Room B.

Where Andrew Peckleman stood with a notepad jotting down everything that was written on the whiteboard walls.

"Hey!" shouted Akimi. "That's cheating!"

Andrew spun around.

His eyes were the size of tennis balls behind his goggle glasses.

"Uh, uh, uh," he sputtered. "You guys left the door open!"

"No we did not," said Kyle extremely calmly, especially considering how much he wanted to throttle Peckleman. "It locks automatically; I checked."

"And I double-checked the door before we went to bed," said Miguel.

Kyle was surprised to hear it. "You did?"

"You bet, bro. It's what teammates do."

They knocked knuckles.

"Well, you don't have anything but a stupid list of stupid books and stupid authors and a stupid Bible verse. . . ."

"A verse which," boomed Mr. Lemoncello, whose face had just appeared on the video-screen wall, "you would do well to memorize, Mr. Peckleman. 'Thou shalt not steal.'"

Mr. Lemoncello was dressed in a curled white wig and a long black robe. He looked like a judge in England. He slammed down a rubber gavel on his desk. It made a noise like a whoopee cushion.

"Will everyone kindly join me in the Rotunda Reading Room? At once."

Everybody shuffled out of the meeting room and into the rotunda. They were shocked to see that Mr. Lemoncello himself was seated behind the librarian's desk at the center of the circular room. This was no hologram. This was the real deal.

Charles, all smiles, made a grand entrance, slowly descending one of the spiral staircases.

"Good morning, everybody," he called out cheerfully. "What's all the excitement? Did I miss something?"

"Just your man Andrew trying to cheat," said Miguel.

"What? Oh, good morning, Mr. Lemoncello. I didn't expect to find you here, inside the library. Isn't today your birthday, sir?"

"Yes, Charles. And there's no place I'd rather be on my

big day than inside a library, surrounded by books. Unless, of course, I could be on a bridge to Terabithia."

"Well, sir, I must say, you're certainly looking fit and trim. Have you been working out?"

"No, Charles, today I will be working *in*."

"I beg your pardon?"

"Today I will be working here, inside the library, supervising the final hours of this competition."

"Oh, I don't think it will take *hours,* sir," said Charles. "Not to brag, but I suspect some of us will be going home very soon."

"You are correct. For instance, Mr. Peckleman. He will be leaving right now."

"What?" whined Peckleman. "Why?"

"Because you cheated. You tried to steal the other team's hard-earned information."

Peckleman's eyes darted back and forth. "It wasn't my fault. It was Charles's idea." He whipped up his arm and waggled his finger. "Charles told me to do it. He *made* me do it!"

"Mr. Peckleman, please approach the bench, which, in this instance, is actually a desk. Let me see the library card you used to gain access to Community Meeting Room B."

Somewhat reluctantly, Andrew handed it over.

"Is your name Sierra Russell?"

"No, sir," Andrew said to his shoes.

"He stole my card?" said Sierra. She opened her latest book and pulled out the library card bookmark.

"Whose card do you have, Sierra?" asked Charles.

"Andrew Peckleman's."

"Aha," said Charles. "He pulled the old switcheroo, eh?"

"Because you told me to!" said Peckleman.

"Really?" Charles said, sniggering. "How dare you make such a scandalous accusation? Do you have any proof?"

"I don't need any stupid proof. You bullied me into stealing Sierra's card!"

Mr. Lemoncello banged his gavel again. "And thus ends the story of Andrew and the terrible, horrible, no good, very bad day. Mrs. Bunny?"

A hologram of the old lady bunny from *Goodnight Moon* hopped on top of the librarian's desk.

"Goodnight, Andrew," said the bunny. "Your time with us is all through."

Clarence and Clement, the security guards, appeared and escorted Peckleman out of the building.

"Sir?" said Sierra. "Would you like Andrew's library card for the discard pile?"

"No, thank you. That card is now property of Team Kyle."

Haley Daley raised her hand.

"Yes, Haley?"

Kyle saw her shoot a withering glance at Charles.

"How may I help you, dear?" asked Mr. Lemoncello.

"Well, sir, if it's okay with you, I'd like to switch sides. I want to join Kyle Keeley's team."

45

"Zap!" said Mr. Lemoncello, waving his arms like a magician. *"Zip!* You're now on Kyle Keeley's team!"

"Haley?" said Charles. "How can you desert me?"

"The same way you just deserted Andrew."

"Um, do we get *her* library card, too?" asked Kyle.

"Indeed you do. Plus any and all information she chooses to share with you. And so, Charles, I ask you: Would *you* like to quit your team and join Kyle's?"

"Excuse me?"

"You know, all for one and one for all?"

"Sir, with all due respect, that may have worked for those three musketeers in a trumped-up work of fiction, but I'm sorry, that is not how things work in the real world. Out here, it's every man for himself. What good is a prize if everyone wins it?"

"I see. But Haley knows all the clues you've collected."

"True, sir. But I doubt she realizes what any of them mean."

Kyle could see Mr. Lemoncello's nose twitch when Charles said that. And it wasn't a happy-bunny kind of twitch, either.

"It was a joke, sir." Charles must've seen the nose twitch, too.

"Oh. I see. Like the one about the boy named Charles. Hilarious. Remind me to tell it to you sometime. Anyway, be that as it may, I insist that you be given a few extra clues to compensate for the fact that all your teammates are either being kicked out of the game or abandoning your ship." Mr. Lemoncello reached under the desk and pulled out a white envelope. "This, Charles, is for your eyes only."

Charles stepped forward and took the envelope.

"Thank you, sir. That is very generous."

"I know. You may also ask me one question. But please, don't waste your question asking me, 'Where is the alternate exit?' because I do not know."

"You don't know?" Kyle said it before Charles could.

"Haven't a clue. This entire game was designed by my head librarian, Dr. Yanina Zinchenko, as my birthday present."

"But," said Akimi, "you could just ask Dr. Zinchenko how to get out, right?"

"Akimi Hughes? Are you one of those people who read the last chapter of a book first to see how it ends?"

"No, but . . ."

"Good. It's much more fun when the ending is a surprise. Dr. Zinchenko is the only one who knows how and where to exit this building without setting off all sorts of fire alarms. Any clues I personally delivered during the course of this game were completely scripted for me by Dr. Z."

"Okay," said Charles, "here's my question. . . ."

Mr. Lemoncello raised a hand. "Before you ask it, be advised: Your opponents will also hear my answer."

"Fine. Why is the book on the bedside table in your private suite *From the Mixed-Up Files of Mrs. Basil E. Frankweiler* by E. L. Konigsburg?"

"Because when I was your age, Mrs. Tobin, my local librarian, gave it to me."

Miguel raised his hand.

"Yes, Miguel?"

"Can we have one bonus question, too?" he asked politely.

"No," said Mr. Lemoncello. "However, I will give you one bonus answer, which Charles, of course, will also hear. Your bonus answer is 'lodgepole, loblolly, and Rocky Mountain white.'"

"What are three different kinds of pine trees?" said Charles, just to show off—and to let Kyle's team know their bonus answer didn't give them any kind of advantage.

"I am told that is correct," said Mr. Lemoncello, touching his ear.

He reached under the desk again and this time pulled up a three-foot-tall hourglass, a giant version of the red plastic timers that came as standard equipment in a lot of his games.

He turned it over.

"It's the jumbo, three-hour size," he said as the sand started trickling down. "Because it is now nine o'clock and you have only three more hours to find your way out of the library. Good luck. And may the best team—or, in Charles's case, the best solo effort—win!"

"Let's see what kind of *real* bonus clues Mr. Lemoncello is serving up today," Charles said to his empty conference room.

He really didn't mind flying solo. It meant he wouldn't have to share his prize when he won it.

Winner won all.

Losers lost all.

That was just the way the world rolled.

And Charles knew he would win.

After all, he was a Chiltington. They never lost.

Even if he had wasted his question about the *Mixed-Up Files* book. Turned out that Mr. Lemoncello was just a sentimental sap like Kyle Keeley. The book was there because his beloved librarian gave it to the old fool when he was the same age as all the library lock-in contestants. Boo-hoo. Big whoop.

And what was all that nonsense about pine trees?
Preposterous.

Unclasping the sealed envelope, Charles found two silhouette cards. Each of them was numbered, in case Charles couldn't figure out which books they would've been hidden in.

#8

Babied? Charles wondered. *No. Crawled!*
He examined the second free card.

#12

Three dinners? Three couples? A restaurant?
This one was difficult.

Charles decided to put the two new pieces into the puzzle, to see if their meanings would become clearer:

Charles was missing only one clue, but he had everything else.

"You can walk out the way BLANK crawled in in passed restaurant."

No. That didn't make sense.

In fact, all he was really certain about were the first two lines: "You can walk out the way."

The way what? Past the restaurant? The Book Nook Café?

And what about the image of the football player?

It came from the Johnny Unitas book. Maybe Johnny Unitas, who had played football back when Mr. Lemoncello was Charles's age, had owned a restaurant? Perhaps a popular national chain?

If so, there might've been one in Alexandriaville. Maybe right here in the old Gold Leaf Bank building.

Could the last bit be "In Johnny Unitas's Restaurant"?

Or what if Andrew Peckleman had been right all along and it was the NINETEEN that was the clue from the football player card? That would make the final line "In nineteen . . ." WHAT? *Diners? Couples?*

No.

Anniversaries!

The three couples in the bonus clue were obviously celebrating their anniversaries!

Nineteen anniversaries? Was today the nineteenth anniversary of some major event in Alexandriaville?

Charles shook his head. He knew the phrase would make sense only *after* he had completed the third line, the only one that still had a blank in it: "BLANK, CRAWLED, INN."

What if the missing image is an eyeball? Then the third line could be "I crawled *in*."

Hang on, Charles thought. The one book in the Staff Picks display case nobody had found yet was *True Crime Ohio: The Buckeye State's Most Notorious Brigands, Burglars, and Bandits* by Clare Taylor-Winters. The last image was going to be a criminal of some sort.

That one, single missing book might tell Charles who had crawled into the bank and, more importantly, *where* they had crawled in. Was this the nineteenth anniversary of a famous bank robbery?

Charles realized he needed help.

It was time to use his Ask an Expert.

That made him laugh.

Because Charles knew the top library expert in all of America, maybe the world. Someone much more important than Dr. Yanina Zinchenko.

Kyle Keeley and the rest of that bunch didn't stand a chance.

47

Eager to find out all he could in the final minutes before the Dewey decimal doors reopened on the second floor, Kyle listened as Haley Daley detailed everything she had learned on Team Charles.

Meanwhile, Akimi added Andrew's and Haley's library cards to the list on the whiteboards in Community Meeting Room B.

"We were piecing together a picture puzzle," said Haley. "It was like a memory match game, or that old TV show *Concentration*."

"We played one of those, too," said Miguel. "A rebus."

"Right. So far, I'm pretty sure it says something like 'You walk out the way bandits crawled in.'"

"'Thou shalt not steal,'" said Kyle, tapping the Bible verse they had found in the 200s room. "That points to bandits, too."

"And the blackbird," said Sierra. "It wailed like a police siren."

"Chasing bandits!"

"Hang on," said Miguel. "What about Willy Wonka? Were there criminals in the chocolate factory?"

"No," said Sierra.

"And what about all this?" said Akimi, pointing at the list of library cards. "I added the new cards but it still doesn't make much sense."

BOOKS/AUTHORS ON THE BACKS OF LIBRARY CARDS

#1 Miguel Fernandez
Incident at Hawk's Hill by Allan W. Eckert/
No, David! by David Shannon

#2 Akimi Hughes
One Fish Two Fish Red Fish Blue Fish
by Dr. Seuss/Nine Stories by J. D. Salinger

#3 Andrew Peckleman
Six Days of the Condor by James Grady/
Eight Cousins by Louisa May Alcott

#4 Bridgette Wadge
Tales of a Fourth Grade Nothing
by Judy Blume/

Harry Potter and the
Sorcerer's Stone by J. K. Rowling

#5 Sierra Russell
The Egypt Game by Zilpha Keatley Snyder/
The Westing Game by Ellen Raskin

#6 Yasmeen Smith-Snyder
Around the World in Eighty Days
by Jules Verne/The Yak Who Yelled Yuck
by Carol Pugliano-Martin

#7 Sean Keegan
Olivia by Ian Falconer/Unreal! by Paul Jennings

#8 Haley Daley
Turtle in Paradise by Jennifer L. Holm/
A Wrinkle in Time by Madeleine L'Engle

#9 Rose Vermette
All-of-a-Kind Family by Sydney Taylor/
Scat by Carl Hiaasen

#10 Kayla Corson
Anna to the Infinite Power
by Mildred Ames/Where the Sidewalk
Ends by Shel Silverstein

#12 Kyle Keeley
I Love You, Stinky Face by Lisa McCourt/
The Napping House by Audrey Wood

"Wow," said Haley. "What a mess."

"Tell me about it," said Akimi.

"I don't think it's another author-title game," said Sierra, "like up on the Wonder Dome."

"Huh?" said Haley.

"Long story," said Miguel. "We'll save it for later."

"What we need," said Kyle, "is some kind of clue to show us how to unscramble this list. Remember what Dr. Zinchenko said when the game started: 'Your library cards are the keys to everything you will need.' This clue is the big one, guys. We need to crack it."

That's when Mr. Lemoncello popped his head in the door.

"Hello, hope I'm not interrupting. We have twenty minutes till the doors open upstairs. Anybody up for an Extreme Challenge?"

48

"In case you forgot," said Mr. Lemoncello, "Extreme Challenges are extremely challenging and sometimes extremely dangerous."

"Is Charles doing one?" asked Akimi.

"He might. I'm going to ask him if he'd like to next."

Mr. Lemoncello had changed out of his judge's costume into some kind of cat burglar outfit—black pants, ribbed black turtleneck, and sporty black beret.

"Is that costume a clue?" asked Haley. "Because it goes with the whole bandit theme."

"Don't know. But Dr. Zinchenko told me to wear it for the big finale. Is there going to be a finale?"

"Maybe with Charles," mumbled Kyle. "We're sort of stuck."

"At least till eleven," added Sierra. "That's when the most important clue will appear on the ceiling."

"Really?" said Mr. Lemoncello. "That Dr. Zinchenko. The woman knows how to build suspense."

"So let's do the Extreme Challenge," said Haley. "What do we have to lose?"

"Um, the whole game," said Akimi.

"Not for all of us," said Kyle. "I'll do the challenge. After all, I'm the team captain."

"You are?" said Haley.

"We had an election," said Akimi. "Yesterday."

"Oh. Cool."

"But, Kyle," said Miguel, "if you blow the Extreme Challenge, you lose, bro."

"Not if my team wins."

"No," said Mr. Lemoncello. "If you lose, Kyle, you *lose*. You will not be allowed to share in the big prize."

"Fine."

"I'm going with you," said Haley.

"No, you're not," said Mr. Lemoncello.

"I have to. Look, we both know I'd be a *fabulous* spokesmodel for your games and stuff, but I can't just glom on to everything Kyle and his team have already dug up. I have to earn my place on this team."

"Sorry, Haley. Extreme Challenges are, and always will be, solo efforts."

"But . . ."

Mr. Lemoncello held up his hand. "No buts. Kyle must face this challenge alone. However . . ."

"Yes?"

"The rest of you can watch his progress on the video screens and cheer him on over the intercom system. You are a cheerleader, aren't you, Haley?"

"Yep," said Kyle. "But she's never cheered for me."

"Well, I will this time. I promise."

"Excellent," said Mr. Lemoncello. "By the way, Kyle, there is no backing out once you commit to the challenge."

"Fine," said Kyle. "Let's do it."

"Go, Kyle, gooooo!" shouted Haley.

Akimi flinched. "Um, a warning next time . . . please?"

"Sorry."

Mr. Lemoncello touched his ear again. "Here is your Extreme Challenge. Dr. Zinchenko tells me:

" 'The answer you seek . . .' "

He paused to listen.

" ' . . . the key to this code . . .
is a memory box . . .
that holds the mother lode.' "

"What?"

Mr. Lemoncello shrugged. "Sorry. I don't write 'em. I only recite 'em. Wait. There's more:

" 'Forget the Industrial Revolution;
my first idea is your certain solution.' "

246

The room was silent.

Mr. Lemoncello touched his ear once more and continued, " 'And now, it's time for the addendum.' "

"Huh?"

"A last-minute addition:

" *'The box had been here*
but now it is there.
Poor Kyle. Your fate
is up in the air.' "

Mr. Lemoncello stood there grinning. For several seconds.

"Is that it?" said Kyle.

"Yes. Find what you're looking for before the second-floor doors open, and it is yours. Fail, and you, Kyle, will be eliminated from the game, and your team, due to that series of unfortunate events, will be forced to struggle on without you. Good luck. You have fifteen minutes."

And Mr. Lemoncello left the room.

"Dude," said Miguel, shaking his head. "You are so dead."

"Wait a second," said Haley. "I think I know how to find what Mr. Lemoncello was talking about!"

"You do?" said Kyle.

"I better. I'm the one who moved it from 'here' to 'there'!"

247

49

"Now then, Charles," said Mr. Lemoncello, "would you like to utilize any of your remaining lifelines? Perhaps an Extreme Challenge? An Ask an Expert?"

"Yes, sir," said Charles. "And may I just say, it's kind of you to come in here and ask me that question."

"Well, it's cloudy with a chance of meatballs and I had nothing better to do."

"Pardon?"

"Nothing. Just a brief flight of fancy, my mind sailing off past the phantom tollbooth. So, which lifeline would you like to use?"

"My Ask an Expert, sir."

"Fine. See Mrs. Tobin at the main desk. I must go to my office to monitor Kyle's Extreme Challenge."

"What's he doing?"

"Trying to beat you. Tootles!"

Mr. Lemoncello raised his beret by its stem, turned on his heel, and headed for one of the bookcases on the far side of the rotunda.

Charles watched him tilt back the head on a bust and press a red button in the middle of what would have been the man's neck. A door-sized section of the bookcase swung open. Mr. Lemoncello stepped into the darkness. The bookcase swung shut.

Charles hurried to the librarian's desk at the center of the Rotunda Reading Room.

"Mrs. Tobin?" He clapped his hands. "Mrs. Tobin? Chop-chop. I'm in a bit of a rush. The doors upstairs will be open in thirteen minutes. Mrs. Tobin?"

The holographic librarian finally appeared.

"Good morning, CHARLES. How may I help you?"

"I need to use my Ask an Expert."

"Very well. Whom do you wish to consult with?"

"Someone who knows his way around a library."

"If that is all you require, CHARLES, perhaps I can be of assistance."

"I need to talk to my uncle Jimmy."

"Your uncle Jimmy? Could you please be more specific?"

"Yes. Of course. James F. Willoughby the third."

"*The* James F. Willoughby the third?"

"Yes, ma'am."

"The *head librarian* of the *Library of Congress* in *Washington, D.C.,* is your uncle?"

"That's right. If my mother's brother, Uncle Jimmy, the top librarian in all of America, can't help me find the one book I'm looking for, nobody can!"

50

"The memory box is down in the Stacks," Haley told Kyle.

So he raced down to the basement. The very long, very wide cellar was just as he remembered it: filled with tidy rows of floor-to-ceiling shelving units.

Kyle looked up at the closest security camera.

"Where to next?"

"I hid it way over on the far side," said Haley through the ceiling speakers. "On a shelf near that horrible book-sorting machine."

Kyle hurried up the center aisle.

Suddenly, a heavy metal bookcase thundered in from the right, sliding like it was on roller skates.

"Watch it!" shouted Haley.

The bookcase skidded to a screeching halt, blocking Kyle's path forward.

"Go left," suggested Miguel.

The whole team was watching and cheering him on.

Kyle went left.

And another steel shelving unit shuffled in from the side.

"Jump back!" shouted Akimi.

The shelf slammed to a stop two inches in front of Kyle's feet.

"Kyle? You okay?"

"Yeah."

"This is like the hedge maze in the Triwizard Tournament," said Sierra.

"Huh?"

"Harry Potter. Book four. *Goblet of Fire.*"

"Right. Need to read that one, too."

Kyle, of course, realized he'd just discovered the most "extreme" part of his Extreme Challenge. Each one of the sliding floor-to-ceiling bookcases was loaded down with heavy cardboard cartons, books, or metal storage bins. They probably weighed several tons each. If Kyle was in the wrong place when a shelving unit came shooting in from the side, he'd be flattened like a pancake under a steamroller.

"Warning," announced the official-sounding lady in the ceiling. "You have twelve minutes to complete this challenge."

He had to keep going. Like Mr. Lemoncello said, there was no turning back now. Unless, of course, he wanted to go home a loser.

Ha! Never!

Kyle jogged up an alleyway between two walls of book-shelves.

"Left turn!" Haley shouted. "Now!"

The wall on Kyle's right swung open, revealing six swiveling sections, each pivoting panel maybe twenty feet long, all skittering sideways and gliding backward to create new walls and reconfigured pathways.

"You've only got like ten more yards to go," coached Haley.

Kyle weaved his way around the randomly shuffling shelves.

But as soon as he was on any kind of straightaway, the walls started to rearrange themselves again.

Finally, Kyle scooted down a corridor so tight he had to turn sideways to squeeze through. The walls stuttered to a stop.

And the voice made another announcement. "Warning. You have eight minutes to complete this challenge."

"I'm trapped!" Kyle shouted. "There's no exit."

None of his teammates said anything for a real long time.

Finally, Sierra's voice rang out from the overhead speakers.

"Put your hand on the right wall," she said.

"What? Why?"

"When I was little, I played a lot of maze games. If the walls are connected, all you have to do is keep one hand in contact with one wall at all times and eventually you'll reach the exit or return to the entrance."

"Do it," coached Akimi.

"It'll work, bro," added Miguel.

So Kyle kept his right hand firmly planted on the right wall of shelves and started inching his way forward.

"Go, Kyle!" cheered Haley. "Hug that wall! Hug that wall!"

The passageway widened. Kyle kept his hand glued to the right wall and went around corners, through switchbacks, until finally, he stepped into an opening near the book return conveyor belt.

"You made it!" shouted Haley. "Whoo-hoo!"

All the shelves streamed back into their orderly church pew positions.

"Good," said Kyle. "Getting out should be easier than getting in. Where's the box, Haley?"

"I put it on the shelf."

"Which one?"

"That one."

"Warning," announced the calm female voice in the ceiling again. "You have THREE MINUTES to complete this challenge."

Kyle stared up at a nearby camera. "Um, Haley? What exactly am I looking for?"

"A cardboard box. In a drawer."

"Okay. There are like a billion of those. . . ."

"I flagged it with a piece of pink tissue."

Kyle raced to a shelf.

"TWO MINUTES," announced the calm lady.

"This one?" said Kyle.

"Yes! Look in the steel drawer."

"I thought you said it was cardboard. . . ."

"It is. Open the lid. Not that lid. The other one."

"This one?"

"No! The one under it!"

"ONE MINUTE."

"Hurry, Kyle!"

"I'm hurrying."

"Flip it open."

Kyle did as he was told. He flipped up the lid on a steel drawer and found a battered boot box.

Every member of Kyle's team shouted the same thing: "Grab it!"

"And run!" added Akimi.

Kyle did.

He tucked the boot box under his arm and ran like he had never run before.

He sprinted across the basement floor. He raced up the steps, two at a time.

When he hit the rotunda, his heart was pounding against his ribs.

"THIRTY SECONDS."

He speed-skated across the marble floor. It was so slippery he lost his balance.

He fell forward.

Dropped the box.

It flew out of his hands, hit the slick floor, and slid like a hockey puck across the threshold into Community Meeting Room B.

A buzzer sounded.

"Time is up," announced the calm voice.

"Yo," shouted Miguel, "you made it, bro!"

And Kyle started breathing again.

51

Having made his request, all Charles could do was wait.

"Apparently," said Mr. Lemoncello when he came back into the rotunda, "your uncle Jimmy is a very, *very* busy man. Reminds me of a spider I once knew. But it is a Sunday morning. We will attempt to track him down at home."

"Thank you, sir. I told Uncle Jimmy to stand by. That I might need him this weekend."

"And now—*WHOOSH!* He's as elusive as the wind in the willows. You'll have to discuss this with him the next time your family gets together for Thanksgiving dinner. Now, if you will excuse me, it is currently nine-fifty-eight a.m. Almost time to reopen the Dewey decimal chambers."

Mr. Lemoncello opened a filing cabinet and pulled out a megaphone.

"Is there some room you should be ready to run to? Isn't there some clue or book you need to go find?"

"Just one," said Charles. "And I need my uncle Jimmy to tell me which one it is. Will you keep looking for him? Please."

"Of course." Mr. Lemoncello pointed to a smudge on Charles's shirt. "If you like, I will also have Al Capone do your shirts."

All Charles could do was nod, smile, and wonder when Al Capone had opened a laundry.

52

"Everyone, please pay very close attention," cried Mr. Lemoncello through a squealing, screeching megaphone. "The Dewey decimal doors are now open and, unlike Tuck, this game will not be everlasting. Therefore, it is time to race upstairs like the rats of NIMH!"

Kyle and his teammates heard Mr. Lemoncello's announcement but stayed inside Community Meeting Room B so they could examine the dusty old boot box.

"It's from when Mr. Lemoncello was our age," said Haley. "Here. I'm pretty sure this is what we need." She handed Kyle a large manila envelope sealed up with tons of tape. "First and Worst Idea Ever" had been scribbled on the front.

"Awesome," said Kyle as he started undoing the tape. "The clue said his first idea might be our best solution."

Inside the envelope were a stack of cards, a bunch of rubber stamps, an ink pad, and a sheet of three-ring-binder paper filled with a fifth grader's sloppy handwriting.

Kyle read out loud what the young Luigi Lemoncello had written: " 'Presenting First Letters: the Amazingly Incredible Secret Code Game.' "

Haley held up some of the cards. Each one showed a cartoony drawing and a single letter: Apple = A, Bee = B, Carrot = C, and so on.

Kyle continued reading: " 'Want to send your friend a secret message to meet you after school? Just use your super-secret rubber stamps.' "

Miguel examined a couple of the wood-handled stamps. "The stamps match the cards."

"So how exactly do you use this junk to tell your friends to meet you after school?" asked Akimi.

"This is so bad," said Kyle. " 'Moon, Elephant, Elephant, Tiger. Moon, Elephant. Apple, Flamingo . . .' "

Akimi held up her hand. "Okay. Stop. I get it."

"Maybe it was for little kids," said Sierra.

"Definitely," said Kyle. "Because anybody over the age of six could crack this code in like ten seconds."

And then he froze.

"This is it!"

He went to the wall with the list of library cards. "What would happen if we played First Letters with these book titles?"

BOOKS/AUTHORS ON THE BACKS OF LIBRARY CARDS

#1 Miguel Fernandez
Incident at Hawk's Hill by Allan W. Eckert/
No, David! by David Shannon

#2 Akimi Hughes
One Fish Two Fish Red Fish Blue Fish
by Dr. Seuss/Nine Stories by J. D. Salinger

#3 Andrew Peckleman
Six Days of the Condor by James Grady/
Eight Cousins by Louisa May Alcott

#4 Bridgette Wadge
Tales of a Fourth Grade Nothing
by Judy Blume/Harry Potter and the
Sorcerer's Stone by J. K. Rowling

#5 Sierra Russell
The Egypt Game by Zilpha Keatley Snyder/
The Westing Game by Ellen Raskin

#6 Yasmeen Smith-Snyder
Around the World in Eighty Days
by Jules Verne/The Yak Who Yelled Yuck
by Carol Pugliano-Martin

<u>#7 Sean Keegan</u>
Olivia by Ian Falconer/Unreal! by Paul Jennings

<u>#8 Haley Daley</u>
Turtle in Paradise by Jennifer L. Holm/
A Wrinkle in Time by Madeleine L'Engle

<u>#9 Rose Vermette</u>
All-of-a-Kind Family by Sydney Taylor/
Scat by Carl Hiaasen

<u>#10 Kayla Corson</u>
Anna to the Infinite Power
by Mildred Ames/Where the Sidewalk
Ends by Shel Silverstein

<u>#11 UNKNOWN/CHARLES CHILTINGTON</u>

<u>#12 Kyle Keeley</u>
I Love You, Stinky Face by Lisa McCourt/
The Napping House by Audrey Wood

"Okay," said Miguel, moving to a clean space on the wall. "Here are the first letters of all the titles."

INONSETHTTATOUTAASAW??IT

"It still makes no sense," said Akimi.

"Wait a second," said Sierra. "If the title starts with an article, drop that word, and use the letter from the second word."

"Got it," said Miguel.

I N O N S E T H E W A Y O U T W A S A W ? ? I N

"Okay," said Akimi. "It's making some sense."

She went to the board and broke Miguel's string of letters into words.

I /N O N /S E T /H E /W A Y/ O U T/ W A S /A /W ? ?/ I N

"Hang on," said Kyle. "It could be . . ."

I N/ O N /S E/ T H E /W A Y/ O U T/ W A S /A /W ? ?/ I N

"What's 'In on se'?" said Akimi.

"Wait! Look!" said Miguel. "The books on the second and third library cards actually start with *numbers*!"

Kyle grabbed a marker:

I N/ 1 9 6 8/ T H E /W A Y/ O U T/ W A S /A /W ? ?/ I N

"Hang on," said Haley. "You know all those questions in the trivia contest Friday? I did so badly, I Googled a bunch of them later that night. They were all from 1968."

"You guys?" said Sierra. "I did some research, too.

Mr. Lemoncello was born in 1956. That means he turned twelve in 1968."

"Oh-kay," said Akimi. "Is this something besides a fun fact to know and tell?"

"You bet it is," said Kyle. "Nineteen sixty-eight is key. And we don't need Charles's library card to finish this phrase." He went to the whiteboard.

IN 1968, THE WAY OUT WAS A WAY IN.

"So what happened in 1968?" said Haley.

"Was that when *Charlie and the Chocolate Factory* came out?" asked Miguel.

"No," said Sierra. "Nineteen sixty-four."

"So what's up with the candy clue from the Art and Artifacts Room?"

"We messed up," said Akimi. "We need to go back and find a new rhyme for 'Andy'!"

"Really?" said Haley. "I thought he got kicked out for cheating."

"Another long story," said Miguel.

"For later," said Kyle. "Right now, we need to be on the third floor!"

Back in the Art & Artifacts Room, Kyle felt confident they were pretty close to figuring out, well, whatever it was they were supposed to figure out.

How it would help them escape from the library was still anybody's guess.

"It's ten-forty-four," said Akimi. "The last clue should pop up on the Wonder Dome in sixteen minutes."

"Okay, you guys," said Kyle. "Spread out. We need a new rhyme for 'Andy.'"

"This model of the bank building came in *handy*," added Miguel.

"The Dandy Bandits!" shouted Akimi, once again studying the display of hats.

"Yes!" said Haley, pulling off her shoe so she could show everybody her clue card.

 **+ ITS**

"Bandits! I found this in the three hundreds room."

"That's the room clue we're waiting for," said Kyle.

"Because the Dewey decimal number for True Crime books always starts with the number three," said Miguel. "When we find that book, it'll tell us how and where the 'bandits crawled in in 1968.'"

"Listen to this, you guys," said Akimi. She read a placard in the display case: "'This plaid fedora from *1968* was worn by bank robber Leopold Loblolly, one of the notorious *Dandy* Bandits.'"

"Loblolly!" Miguel shouted.

"The smell-a-vision clue," said Kyle. "That's why everything kept smelling like pine trees."

"Loblolly was one of the pine trees in the answer Mr. Lemoncello gave you guys!" said Haley.

"Whoop-whoop-whoop," said Mr. Lemoncello as, banana shoes squeaking, he stepped into the room. "Well done, Miss Daley . . . and Miss Hughes."

"See?" said Akimi. "I was right the first time we came in here. I said 'dandy' and everybody else said, 'Noooo, *candy.* Willy Wonka . . .'"

"Yes, it's all coming back to me," said Mr. Lemoncello.

"Nineteen sixty-eight. I was pondering an idea for a game at the old public library."

"And," said Kyle, "you were so totally focused, you didn't hear the police sirens screaming past the library as they raced to the Gold Leaf Bank. . . ."

"The blackbird was from Alexandriaville," said Sierra. "The police siren wail was from that day."

Miguel finished that thought: "When the Dandy Bandits tried to crawl into the bank!"

"My goodness," said Mr. Lemoncello. "How could you kids know all that?"

"From the game clues," said Kyle, "and from the story Dr. Zinchenko told us on Friday night when somebody asked her why a library building needed a bank vault door."

"She was already feeding us clues!" said Akimi.

"The time is now ELEVEN a.m.," announced the ceiling lady. "This game will end in ONE hour."

"Come on," said Kyle, heading for the door. "It's the eleventh hour. We need to go check out the Wonder Dome again."

They raced to the balcony.

"There it is!" said Sierra.

"364 point 1092!" shouted Miguel.

"Whoo-hoo!" cried Akimi. "We're gonna win!"

54

On the first floor, Charles was at long last video chatting with his uncle, James Willoughby III, the librarian of Congress, who had finally shown up for the Ask an Expert call.

"Sorry for the delay, Charles."

"That's okay, Uncle Jimmy," Charles said, straining to smile and not scream.

"The time is now ELEVEN a.m.," announced the annoyingly placid lady in the ceiling. "This game will end in ONE hour."

Charles had to hustle.

"Sir, I know you're a very important, very busy man, so I just have one quick question: If I were a book on true crimes in the state of Ohio, where would you shelve me?"

"Library of Congress classification?"

"No, sir. Dewey decimal."

"Ah. Easy. 364 point 1. What comes after the one will depend, of course, on how many books a library . . ."

Charles didn't stick around to hear the rest of his uncle's answer.

He took off running for the closest spiral staircase up to the second floor. As he ascended the steps, two at a time, he saw Kyle Keeley and his entire entourage running down a staircase from the third floor.

Charles reached the second-floor balcony first.

He darted around the bend, past the door to the 500s room, the 400s.

Keeley and his crew were coming from the opposite direction, but Charles reached the door to the 300s room before them.

He swiped his library card, yanked on the handle, and dashed into the room.

He scanned the shelves and headed to his right.

He heard Keeley enter the room.

Glancing over his shoulder, Charles saw Keeley go left.

Charles dashed up an aisle between bookcases. He read the number at the end of each row of shelves.

310.

320.

330.

One of those robots with the book baskets came rumbling across his path, but Charles was able to dodge it.

340.

350.

Keeley's footsteps pounded up the passageway on the other side of the shelving units to his left.

In the middle of the 300s room, they entered an open space with a judge's bench and witness box.

Charles was getting closer to the True Crime section.

But so was Kyle.

Charles saw Keeley read something off his palm.

He had the whole call number!

It was time to change tactics.

Charles hung back and let Keeley take the lead.

Kyle rushed toward a bookcase.

Charles sprinted after him.

"Got it!" Kyle shouted as he reached for a book on the shelf.

But before he could completely pull it out, Charles grabbed hold of the book, too.

They both yanked it off the shelf.

Kyle had the spine; Charles had hold of the top.

They tugged it back and forth.

While they wrestled with the book, Keeley's teammates caught up to them.

"Careful, Kyle," cried Sierra Russell. "Don't hurt the book."

Charles grinned. Keeley, the sentimental sap, was listening to the silly, bookish girl and easing up on his grip.

Giving Charles his chance.

He body-checked Keeley. Slammed into him with his

270

shoulder. Sent him flying, the book tumbling. Charles snatched it off the floor.

He had the book. He quickly flipped through the table of contents. Saw chapter 11 was about a robbery at the Gold Leaf Bank in Alexandriaville.

He knew he'd won the game.

Charles used his free hand to slap an "L" on his forehead.

"Loser," he sneered at Keeley.

A tiger roared, a whistle blew, and Mr. Lemoncello entered the room, accompanied by Clarence, Clement, and what looked like a rare Bengal tiger.

"Mr. Chiltington?"

Charles smiled. He knew Mr. Lemoncello was about to congratulate him for defying the odds and winning the game. He had single-handedly defeated Kyle Keeley's entire team! "Yes, sir, Mr. Lemoncello?"

"Do you remember Dr. Zinchenko's number one rule?"

"You bet, sir. No food or drink except in the Book Nook Café."

"No," said Mr. Lemoncello, touching the tip of his nose and making a buzzer noise. "Dr. Z? Tell him what he should've said."

Dr. Zinchenko's voice purred out of the ceiling speakers. "Be gentle. With each other and, most especially, the library's books and exhibits."

"I know," said Charles. "That's why I had to stop Kyle

Keeley. He was ready to rip the cover off this poor book. Heck, sir, everybody at school knows that Kyle Keeley is a maniac. He'll do anything to win a game."

Mr. Lemoncello turned to Keeley.

"Is that true, Kyle? Would you actually destroy property if it stood between you and your prize?"

"W-well, sir . . ."

Keeley was stammering. The fool didn't know how to lie.

Charles quickly opened the book to chapter 11 and slipped in his library card to bookmark the location.

"You should ask Keeley about the window he broke, sir."

Mr. Lemoncello turned to face Charles again.

"The window?"

"Yes, sir. The whole school heard about it. See, Kyle Keeley and his two brothers were playing some sort of wild scavenger hunt game and . . ."

Mr. Lemoncello pointed at the book. "That's clever. You use your library card as a bookmark?"

"Yes, sir, I sure do," said Charles, turning on the charm. "Of course, I can't take full credit for such a clever idea. On Friday night, I saw Sierra Russell doing it and . . ."

"You told Andrew Peckleman to 'borrow' her card."

Charles blinked. Several times. "I beg your pardon?"

"You broke Dr. Zinchenko's number one rule. You

were not gentle with your teammate Andrew. In fact, you bullied him into stealing Miss Russell's library card, which you knew she always used as a bookmark."

"No, sir. I did not."

"Yes, Charles. You did." Mr. Lemoncello touched his right ear. "In fact, Dr. Zinchenko has spent the past few hours combing through security tapes, and guess what she just found?"

Charles heard his own voice ringing out of the ceiling speakers:

"Have you noticed what Sierra Russell uses for a bookmark?"

"No."

"That was Andrew," said Mr. Lemoncello. "This is you again."

"Her library card, which, of course, doubles as a key card for Meeting Room B. Find a way to borrow it."

"You told Andrew to steal Sierra's library card."

"How could you record that?" said Charles. "I was whispering!"

"And *I* have very good microphones. You're done, Charles. Dr. Zinchenko? Tell our departing guest what he has just won."

"Absolutely nothing," said the voice of the Russian librarian. "But please, Mr. L, tell Charles the correct answer to the final pictogram."

"Ah, yes!" Mr. Lemoncello reached into his back

pocket, pulled out a four-by-four card, and showed it to Charles.

Charles stood there fuming.

"Anyone care to help Charles out?"

"Hmmm," said Kyle. "Is it 'six eat'?"

"You are very close," said Mr. Lemoncello.

There was a pause and then Haley laughed. "Did it come after the football player?"

"Yeah," said Charles. "So?"

"Andrew was right all along," said Haley. "The football player clue wasn't 'past,' it was 'nineteen.'"

Mr. Lemoncello shifted into his game show voice. "So, Haley Daley, would you care to solve the puzzle?"

"Sure: 'You can walk out the way bandits crawled in in nineteen six ate.'"

"I don't get it," said Charles.

"Nineteen, six-ate," said Akimi. "You know: 1968."

"Ah, yes," said Mr. Lemoncello. "The year *From the Mixed-Up Files of Mrs. Basil E. Frankweiler* won the New-bery Medal for excellence in children's literature. Another clue you completely missed, Charles."

"Wow," said Miguel. "And I thought Chiltingtons never lose."

"There's a first time for everything," said Mr. Lemon-cello. "Clarence? Clement? Kindly escort young Mr. Chiltington from the building."

"Buh-bye," said Akimi. "There goes this game's biggest loser."

55

"Open it!" Akimi said to Kyle. "We only have like forty minutes to figure out how Loblolly and the Dandy Bandits crawled into the bank back in 1968!"

Kyle flipped through *True Crime Ohio* to the place where Charles had slipped in his bookmark.

"Well?" said Miguel.

" 'Chapter Eleven. The Dandy Bandits Burrow into a Bank Vault.' "

"Even though thou should not steal," said Akimi.

"And I'll bet they crawled in, right?" said Haley.

" 'The clever thieves,' " Kyle read from the book, " 'took up residence in an abandoned dress factory next door to the Gold Leaf Bank and spent weeks tunneling from its basement into the bank vault.' "

"Which," said Miguel, "according to those old

blueprints I found, was down where the book-sorting machine is now."

"That explains the first clue," said Kyle. "The book title was *Get to Know Your Local Library*. Dr. Zinchenko meant we needed to get to know *this* library. This also explains why she wanted us to read those Sherlock Holmes stories."

" 'The Adventure of the Red-Headed League,' " said Sierra. "The story about robbers tunneling into a bank from the building next door."

Kyle nodded. "Dr. Zinchenko told me *she* had just reread it. I'll bet that's where she got the idea for this whole game."

"Hey, Charles should've stuck with crawling through sewers like he did in that video game," joked Miguel. "He might've found the Dandy Bandits' tunnel before we did."

"Come on, you guys," said Haley. "We need to be back in the basement."

"I'm coming with you," said Mr. Lemoncello. "I just have to see how this story ends!"

Clutching the *True Crime* book against his chest, Kyle led the way down to the Stacks.

"Why are you bringing that book?" asked Akimi.

"We'll put it on that conveyor belt thing," Kyle explained. "Whatever basket the scanner sends it to, I'm guessing that's where we'll find our 'black square.' "

"Our shortcut out of the library!"

"Exactly."

As the team trooped down the steps to the basement, Mr. Lemoncello turned to Kyle and said, "So, Mr. Keeley, did you have fun this weekend?"

"Yeah."

"Good. Congratulations, Miss Hughes, it seems *you* have already won."

Akimi sort of blushed.

"What do you mean?" asked Kyle.

"In her essay, your extremely good friend wrote, and I quote: 'I want to see the new library so I can tell my friend Kyle Keeley how cool it is.'"

"You wrote your essay about me?"

"Maybe," mumbled Akimi.

"Wow," said Kyle. "No one's ever done that before."

"Well, no one's ever going to do it again if you blow our chance at winning this thing. So can we please stop yakking and find our way out of here?"

"Works for me."

"Warning," said the calm voice in the ceiling speakers. "This game will terminate in THIRTY minutes."

Everybody moved a little faster.

Fortunately, when the group reached the basement, the floor-to-ceiling bookshelves didn't start sliding into another maze formation.

"The automatic book sorter is straight up this path, near the far wall," said Kyle.

They made it to the conveyor belt.

"From what I remember from the old blueprints," said Miguel, "the vault was right here, in the same spot as this machine."

"Okay, you guys," said Kyle. "Whatever robo-basket this book ends up in is probably sitting right on top of the entrance to the tunnel."

"Here goes everything." Kyle placed *True Crime Ohio* into the array of crisscrossing beams.

Nothing happened.

"What's going on?" cried Miguel. "Why isn't it working?"

"Maybe this book isn't heavy enough." Kyle pushed down on the cover of the book a bit.

Still nothing.

They stared, dumbfounded, at the book sitting on the immobile belt.

"It wouldn't *stop* moving yesterday," muttered Haley.

"That's it!" cried Akimi. She hurried to the wall and flipped the emergency shutoff switch back to the "on" position.

Several red laser scanners sprang to life under the book drop slot.

The belt started moving. Slowly.

The single book worked its way down the line like a

candy bar on a wrapping machine. When it reached the third robo-basket from the end, a set of rollers popped up and shunted the book off to the side into the waiting wire basket.

The conveyor belt stopped rolling. The robo-cart rolled away.

Nothing else happened.

"That's it?"

"Warning," said the calm voice. "This game will terminate in TWENTY minutes."

"It didn't work," said Haley.

"We're toast," added Akimi.

"Wait," said Kyle, pointing to a square tile on the floor where the robo-basket had been. It was glowing, like one of the touch-screen computers in the desks upstairs. "It says 'Howdy. Dü you like fun games? Get Reddy.' "

"Excellent!" Akimi giggled. Then she and Kyle cracked up, remembering the box tops from their first puzzle in the Board Room on Saturday morning.

"Now it says we're going to get an anagram," said Kyle.

"My favorite kind of cookies," said Mr. Lemoncello.

"Okay, everybody," said Kyle. "Gather round. Get ready."

Kyle, Akimi, Sierra, Miguel, and Haley knelt on the floor in a circle around the square. Mr. Lemoncello hovered behind them.

"Here we go," said Kyle as game instructions scrolled across the screen.

A sixty-second clock popped up at the bottom of the screen. And then a four-by-four Boggle jumble of letters:

"Luigi L. Lemoncello," mumbled Kyle.

The sixty-second clock started ticking down.

Sierra shouted out, "Lemon!" and a *ding* sounded from the speaker above. The five teammates started shouting out words:

"Cello!"

"Eon!"

"Elm!"

"Lion!"

"Mole!"

"Leg!"

"Oil!"

"Thirty seconds left," said Mr. Lemoncello.

"One!"

"Cell!"

"Cone!"

"Lone!"

"Glen!"

"Lime!"

"Eh, mole."

"We already said that."

"Melon."

"That's fifteen," said the voice in the ceiling.

"Um . . ."

"Ten seconds left."

"Anybody?"

"Five."

"Four."

"Colonel!" shouted Haley.

The computer screen flashed "Congratulations!" and "Winners!"

Somewhere, a game show audience cheered, fireworks rockets whistled through the air, and several geese honked out a "Hooray!"

"Please stand back," said the soothing voice in the ceiling.

Kyle and his teammates did as they were told.

"Warning," the voice continued. "This game will terminate in FIFTEEN minutes."

"We still need to get out, you guys!" said Akimi. "Hurry, floor. Do something!"

The eight tiles surrounding the glowing tablet also started to glow. First yellow, then orange, then purple.

"Our secret square," said Akimi.

There was a series of clicks, and the tiles began folding up on themselves and retracting into the floor, opening up like an origami trapdoor.

"Look," said Haley, "there's steps."

Mr. Lemoncello peered down into the hole at the well-lit staircase and tunnel. "My, my. Dr. Zinchenko has certainly cleaned things up since Mr. Loblolly was here."

"Of course she did," said Haley. "So we 'can walk out the way bandits crawled in in nineteen six-ate.' "

"Hurry, everybody!" said Mr. Lemoncello. "I don't want to be late to my own birthday party."

56

Kyle led the way up the tunnel and brought his team (plus Mr. Lemoncello) into an empty basement filled with mannequins and cardboard boxes.

"This must be the cellar of one of the clothing shops in Old Town," said Kyle.

"The Fitting Factory," said Haley, reading a tag on a shipping crate. "It's one of my faves."

"And," said Sierra, "back in 1968, it was the real dress factory that Leopold Loblolly and the Dandy Bandits used."

"There's some steps over here," said Miguel, climbing a wooden staircase. "And a door." He jiggled the knob. "Oh, man—it's locked."

Kyle looked up at the dingy casement windows, about ten feet above the cellar floor.

He couldn't help grinning.

It reminded him of another game he'd won once. This time, he'd just have to reverse things a little.

"Help me drag over a couple cartons," Kyle said to Miguel. "We can stack them on top of each other underneath this window."

After they built a step unit out of boxes, Kyle climbed up and examined the window latch.

"Great," he said.

"Don't tell me," said Akimi. "Another game?"

"Yep. There's a combination lock—the kind with four wheels of random letters."

"Warning," said the voice.

"What?" said Akimi. "Dr. Zinchenko put loudspeakers in this basement, too?"

"This game will terminate in FOUR minutes."

"Yo, open the lock, Kyle!" said Miguel.

"Hang on. It's some kind of word game."

"Is there a clue?" asked Haley.

"Of course." Kyle read the tiny slip of paper taped to the glass. " 'Once you learn how to do this, you will be forever free.' "

Everyone started laughing.

This last puzzle was ridiculously easy.

"Ready, children?" said Mr. Lemoncello. "All together now!"

And they all shouted it at the same time: "READ!"

Kyle thumbed the wheels to spell R-E-A-D. The lock clicked. The window opened.

And this time, he didn't need to shatter any glass to win the game.

Kyle and Mr. Lemoncello stood on top of the highest box and helped the others up and out of the basement.

When Haley crawled through the window frame, someone in the crowd that had gathered around the library for the game's big finale saw her and started screaming.

"Look! It's Haley Daley! She's the first one out. She won! With just two minutes to go!"

"Nuh-uh!" Kyle heard Haley shout in her perky cheerleader voice. "I'm just one member of a super-amazing team. We're all winners. Whoo-hoo!"

When Akimi climbed through the window, the crowd chanted her name.

"How do you people know my name?" Kyle heard her say. "Dad? Did you tell them?"

Sierra Russell was set to crawl out next.

"Mr. Lemoncello?"

"Yes, Sierra?"

"What time does the library open tomorrow?"

"For you, Sierra, nine a.m.!"

Smiling, she stepped into their hands and climbed out the window.

Kyle felt bad when Sierra stood up on the sidewalk. Who was out there to cheer for her?

But then he heard Haley shout, "Hey, you guys. You gotta meet our amazing new friend, Sierra Russell! She's so smart, she could tell you who wrote the phone book!"

The crowd went crazy. "Sierra! Sierra! Sierra!"

"Okay," said Kyle, "you're next, Miguel."

"And, Miguel," said Mr. Lemoncello, "if your summer schedule permits it, I'd love for you to head up my team of Lemoncello Library Aides."

"Thank you, sir. It'd be an honor."

"And please invite Mr. Peckleman to join you."

"But Andrew thinks this library is stupid."

"All the more reason for him to spend time getting to know us a little better. Now, off you go!"

They gave Miguel a boost up and out the window.

The chanting outside grew even louder.

"Miguel! Miguel! Miguel!"

"You guys?" Miguel shouted. "This library is like a good book. You just gotta check it out!"

The crowd laughed. Kyle groaned.

"You're next, Mr. Keeley," said Mr. Lemoncello.

"Okay. Can I ask one last question?"

"Certainly. And I hope it won't be the last."

"Are you really going to put all of us in your television commercials?"

"Oh, yes. You'll be quite famous."

"Cool."

"Indeed. Who knew spending time in your local library could be such a rewarding experience?"

Kyle smiled. "You did, Mr. Lemoncello."

"And now you do, too."

Kyle put his foot in Mr. Lemoncello's hands and grabbed hold of the window frame.

"See you at the birthday party, sir!"

"Oh, yes. And you know what, Kyle?"

"What?"

"There might be balloons!"

AUTHOR'S NOTE

Is the game really over?

Maybe not.

There is one more puzzle in the book that wasn't in the story. (Although a clue about how to find it was!)

If you figure out the solution, let me know. Send an email to author@ChrisGrabenstein.com.

THANK YOU . . .

To R. Schuyler Hooke, my longtime editor at Random House, for his incredible patience, faith, and input on this project.

To cover artist James Lancett and designers Katrina Damkoehler, Larsson McSwain, Michelle Cunningham, and Jinna Shin, who made the book look so darn good.

To my wife, J. J. Myers, who is a terrific first editor.

To Ms. Macrina, librarian, and all the folks at P.S. 10 in Brooklyn, whose library gave me the initial inspiration for this story.

To Darrell Robertson, Gail Tobin, Amy Alessio, Erin Downey, Yanna Zinchenko, Scot Smith, and all the other librarians and media specialists I have met in my travels as an author, at public libraries and in schools. When I see how you inspire the love of reading on a daily basis, I realize you are much more amazing and incredible than Mr. Lemoncello.

RANDOM CHATTER with
CHRIS GRABENSTEIN

What were you like as a kid?

Kind of chubby. Not very good at sports. But I liked to make my friends (and teachers) laugh. Sometimes I'd do this with comic books that I wrote and drew and passed around in class. I guess those were my first "published" books!

I also spent a lot of time making up imaginary stories. I could play basketball in our driveway all by myself and turn it into the most exciting championship game ever played—complete with sound effects—and do it all in my head. By the way, in those imaginary games, I was *excellent* at sports!

Did you want to be an author when you grew up?

You know, I vaguely remember reading a book in the backseat of the station wagon during my family's long and hot (it was August) car ride from Buffalo, New York, to the beaches of St. Petersburg, Florida (where my grandparents lived), and thinking, *I should write a book. About a boy. In the backseat of a station wagon. Dying of heat exhaustion and lack of cupcakes.*

Other than that, I don't really think I ever thought I could be an author when I grew up. I knew I could probably be a writer. But an *author*? I didn't own any tweed sport coats with patches on the elbows.

When I was a kid, I think I wanted to be a famous movie star. Or Johnny Carson. One of those.

Writing wasn't your first career, was it?
Well, I was always writing, but when I moved to New York City right after college (with nothing but seven suitcases and a typewriter I had received as a high school graduation gift), I spent five years doing improvisational comedy down in a basement theater in Greenwich Village and on the college tour circuit. A guy named Bruce Willis was in one of my comedy troupes. Robin Williams would drop by and hop onstage with us whenever he was in town doing a movie.

When you do improv, you make up scenes and songs right on the spot, based on audience suggestions. For instance, we'd ask the audience for a "personal problem" and then we'd make up an entire instant opera about "BO" or "acne" or whatever they shouted out.

While I was doing improv (and supporting myself with office work), I also had the great good fortune to write for Jim Henson and the Muppets. What an inspirational man. I think he named his company Henson Associates just so he could have "ha!" as a corporate logo.

I also cowrote a made-for-TV movie called *The Christmas Gift*, starring John Denver, which first aired on CBS way back in 1986. It's still on TV every year during the holiday season. Usually on the Hallmark Channel. At three a.m. I know this because my mother calls me up and tells me.

Then, in 1984, I landed a job on Madison Avenue, writing copy for the J. Walter Thompson advertising agency. I actually got the job by answering a writing aptitude test headlined "Write If You Want Work" that ran in the *New York Times*. It was full of fun questions like "How would you sell a telephone to a Trappist monk who had taken a strict vow of silence?" (I'd convince him he'd need the phone to connect to Monkmail, a new kind of email for silent monks only.)

The creative director of J. Walter Thompson, New York, wrote the test and questions. His name was James Patterson. Yes, *that* James Patterson. Before he became the world-record holder for the Most Number One *New York Times* Bestsellers Ever, he wrote commercials and ran the entire creative department at one of New York's biggest advertising agencies. I learned a lot about writing while working for Mr. Patterson, and I'm thrilled to be working with him again, coauthoring books like *I Funny* and *Treasure Hunters.*

What was your inspiration for *Escape from Mr. Lemoncello's Library?*

During an author visit to P.S. 10, a school in Brooklyn, New York, I marveled at their incredibly beautiful library. The librarian, Ms. Macrina, told me that it had been "donated by a very generous benefactor."

That got my mental wheels spinning. *What if . . . a generous benefactor, an eccentric bazillionaire, gave the town where he grew up the most amazingly awesome library ever built?*

By the way, most of my books start with a big *What if . . . ?*

And since, when I was a kid, I loved playing games like Monopoly, Sorry, and Risk, I decided to make my eccentric benefactor a wackier version of one of the Parker Brothers, the name behind many of my favorite games.

I think I named him Lemoncello and made him the son of Italian immigrants in honor of my Greek immigrant grandparents, whose last name was Lemonopoulos.

Recently, my mother told me that when she was a little girl growing up in Canton, Ohio, speaking and reading more English than her mom and dad, who were still speaking Greek, she was determined to read every book in the library. The library was where she could learn even more about her family's new home. That's one of the reasons I chose to celebrate the connection between libraries and immigrants in this book.

People have compared Mr. Lemoncello to Willy Wonka. Were you thinking of him when you wrote the book?

I was—but only to avoid making Mr. Lemoncello too much like Willy Wonka, particularly Gene Wilder's depiction of him in the old movie, which is one of my favorite films. But any time you have an eccentric bazillionaire in a fantastical setting and surround him with kids, it's hard not to be reminded of Willy Wonka. However, Mr. Lemoncello has no Oompa-Loompas to help him restock the shelves.

Kyle is very competitive with his brothers, Mike and Curtis. Do you have any brothers?

Yes! Four of them: Tom, Jeff, Steve, and Bill. Three of them are now doctors; the other is a lawyer. When we were kids, Tom, the oldest, wasn't a jock like Mike, but he was definitely the Big Brother, the guy we all looked up to, the one who did all the stuff we wished we could do. Jeff, my other older brother, was (and is) a genius like Curtis. I would get straight As at school, but it wasn't really all that impressive. Jeff, who had been in the same class the year before me, got straight A++s.

What's your favorite Dewey decimal number?

641.3373. I'm having some right now. Delicious.

Have you ever been to a library as amazing as Mr. Lemoncello's?

Actually, a lot of the libraries I visit are even more amazing. I see librarians making great suggestions about books they know kids will love. I see kids working together on school projects, and librarians helping them find the information they need, either online or in the stacks. In one of my favorite libraries, outside Chicago, they have even built Collaboration Stations in their new wing for young adults.

I like Mr. Lemoncello's motto: "Knowledge not shared remains unknown." A library is, and always has been, a place where we can come together and share what we know—as the whole human race and as individuals.

If you had as much money as Mr. Lemoncello, what would you build with it?

The world's largest and nicest animal rescue shelter with gourmet kibble and tuna for all! Fred, our rescue dog, and Parker, Tiger Lilly, and Phoebe Squeak, our rescue cats, had nothing to do with that answer.

BONUS CLUE

Have you solved the extra puzzle mentioned in
the author's note? The one that was in the book
but wasn't in the story? Here's a hint.

(Of course you have to solve this puzzle to get it!)

B = W
D = T

- C
R = D

R = H
- E

E = ST

- D
G = F

- T
- ER

I = PTE

W +

- S

W = YS

The Books, Stories, and Periodicals in
Mr. Lemoncello's Library
(How many have you read?)

- [ ] *All-of-a-Kind Family* by Sydney Taylor
- [ ] *The American Heritage Dictionary of Idioms*
- [ ] *Anna to the Infinite Power* by Mildred Ames
- [ ] *Anne of Avonlea* by Lucy Maud Montgomery
- [ ] *Anne of Green Gables* by Lucy Maud Montgomery
- [ ] *Around the World in Eighty Days* by Jules Verne
- [ ] *Baby's Mother Goose: Pat-A-Cake*
- [ ] *The Brothers Karamazov* by Fyodor Dostoyevsky
- [ ] "The Cask of Amontillado" by Edgar Allan Poe
- [ ] *The Cat in the Hat* by Dr. Seuss
- [ ] *Charlie and the Chocolate Factory* by Roald Dahl
- [ ] *Charlie and the Great Glass Elevator* by Roald Dahl
- [ ] *Coming Up for Air* by George Orwell
- [ ] *The Complete Sherlock Holmes* by Sir Arthur Conan Doyle
- [ ] *Crime and Punishment* by Fyodor Dostoyevsky
- [ ] *Cupcakes, Cookies & Pie, Oh, My!* by Karen Tack and Alan Richardson
- [ ] *Death on the Nile* by Agatha Christie
- [ ] *The Egypt Game* by Zilpha Keatley Snyder
- [ ] *Eight Cousins* by Louisa May Alcott
- [ ] *The Elevator Family* by Douglas Evans
- [ ] *The Eleventh Hour: A Curious Mystery* by Graeme Base
- [ ] *Even the Stars Look Lonesome* by Maya Angelou
- [ ] *Falling Up* by Shel Silverstein
- [ ] *From the Mixed-Up Files of Mrs. Basil E. Frankweiler* by E. L. Konigsburg
- [ ] *The Giver* by Lois Lowry
- [ ] *Goodnight Moon* by Margaret Wise Brown
- [ ] *Great Day for Up* by Dr. Seuss
- [ ] *Harry Potter and the Goblet of Fire* by J. K. Rowling
- [ ] *Harry Potter and the Sorcerer's Stone* by J. K. Rowling
- [ ] *Huckleberry Finn* by Mark Twain
- [ ] *The Hunger Games* by Suzanne Collins
- [ ] *If I Grow Up* by Todd Strasser
- [ ] *I Love You, Stinky Face* by Lisa McCourt
- [ ] *Incident at Hawk's Hill* by Allan W. Eckert

- [ ] *In the Pocket: Johnny Unitas and Me* by Mike Leonetti
- [ ] *The Jungle Book* by Rudyard Kipling
- [ ] The King James Bible
- [ ] *Little House on the Prairie* by Laura Ingalls Wilder
- [ ] *Look Homeward, Angel* by Thomas Wolfe
- [ ] *Look, I Made a Hat* by Stephen Sondheim
- [ ] *Lord of the Rings* by J. R. R. Tolkien
- [ ] "The Masque of the Red Death" by Edgar Allan Poe
- [ ] *The Mousetrap* by Agatha Christie
- [ ] *Murder on the Orient Express* by Agatha Christie
- [ ] "The Murders in the Rue Morgue" by Edgar Allan Poe
- [ ] Nancy Drew: *The Mystery at Lilac Inn* by Carolyn Keene
- [ ] *The Napping House* by Audrey Wood
- [ ] *Nine Stories* by J. D. Salinger
- [ ] *No, David!* by David Shannon
- [ ] *Olivia* by Ian Falconer
- [ ] *One Fish Two Fish Red Fish Blue Fish* by Dr. Seuss
- [ ] *Popular Science Monthly* magazine
- [ ] "The Purloined Letter" by Edgar Allan Poe
- [ ] *The Red Pyramid* by Rick Riordan
- [ ] *Scat* by Carl Hiaasen
- [ ] *Six Days of the Condor* by James Grady
- [ ] *Tales of a Fourth Grade Nothing* by Judy Blume
- [ ] *Ten Little Indians* by Agatha Christie
- [ ] *This Isn't What It Looks Like* by Pseudonymous Bosch
- [ ] *Through the Looking-Glass* by Lewis Carroll
- [ ] *Time* magazine
- [ ] *Treasure Island* by Robert Louis Stevenson
- [ ] *Turtle in Paradise* by Jennifer L. Holm
- [ ] *The Umpire Strikes Back* by Ron Luciano and David Fisher
- [ ] *Unreal!* by Paul Jennings
- [ ] *Up from Slavery* by Booker T. Washington
- [ ] *Walter the Farting Dog* by William Kotzwinkle and Glenn Murray
- [ ] *The Westing Game* by Ellen Raskin
- [ ] *When You Reach Me* by Rebecca Stead
- [ ] *Where the Sidewalk Ends* by Shel Silverstein
- [ ] *A Wrinkle in Time* by Madeleine L'Engle
- [ ] *The Yak Who Yelled Yuck* by Carol Pugliano-Martin

Books Sprinkled into Mr. Lemoncello's Dialogue

- *Al Capone Does My Shirts* by Gennifer Choldenko
- *Alexander and the Terrible, Horrible, No Good, Very Bad Day* by Judith Viorst
- *Because of Winn-Dixie* by Kate DiCamillo
- *Bridge to Terabithia* by Katherine Paterson
- *Cloudy with a Chance of Meatballs* by Judi Barrett
- *Dead End in Norvelt* by Jack Gantos
- *Ella Enchanted* by Gail Carson Levine
- *The Essential Groucho*, edited by Stefan Kanfer
- *For Your Eyes Only* (James Bond) by Ian Fleming
- *Go, Dog. Go!* by P. D. Eastman
- *Great Expectations* by Charles Dickens
- *The Great Gilly Hopkins* by Katherine Paterson
- *Heart of a Samurai* by Margi Preus
- *I Can Read with My Eyes Shut!* by Dr. Seuss
- *Joey Pigza Loses Control* by Jack Gantos
- *Maniac Magee* by Jerry Spinelli
- *Mrs. Frisby and the Rats of NIMH* by Robert C. O'Brien
- *My Side of the Mountain* by Jean Craighead George
- *Oh, the Thinks You Can Think!* by Dr. Seuss
- *The Phantom Tollbooth* by Norton Juster
- A Series of Unfortunate Events by Lemony Snicket
- *Something Wicked This Way Comes* by Ray Bradbury
- *Tuck Everlasting* by Natalie Babbitt
- *The Very Busy Spider* by Eric Carle
- *The Wind in the Willows* by Kenneth Grahame

MR. LEMONCELLO'S

LIBRARY

OLYMPICS

CHRIS
GRABENSTEIN

*For Sunshine Cavalluzzi, Sid Reischer, Stacey Rattner,
and all the awesome parents, teachers, and librarians
who do so much to make reading fun*

*And in memory of Rosanne Macrina,
the longtime librarian at P.S. 10 in Brooklyn,
who inspired so many children and one author
who was very lucky to have met her*

Just about every kid in America wished they could be Kyle Keeley.

Especially when he zoomed across their TV screens as a flaming squirrel in a holiday commercial for Squirrel Squad Six, the hysterically crazy new Lemoncello video game.

Kyle's friends Akimi Hughes and Sierra Russell were also in that commercial. They thumbed controllers and tried to blast Kyle out of the sky. He dodged every rubber band, coconut custard pie, mud clod, and wadded-up sock ball they flung his way.

It was awesome.

In the commercial for Mr. Lemoncello's See Ya, Wouldn't Want to Be Ya board game, Kyle starred as the yellow pawn. His head became the bubble tip at the top of the playing piece. Kyle's buddy Miguel Fernandez was

the green pawn. Kyle and Miguel slid around the life-size game like hockey pucks. When Miguel landed on the same square as Kyle, that meant Kyle's pawn had to be bumped back to the starting line.

"See ya!" shouted Miguel. "Wouldn't want to be ya!"

Kyle was yanked up off the ground by a hidden cable and hurled backward, soaring above the board.

It was also awesome.

But Kyle's absolute favorite starring role was in the commercial for Mr. Lemoncello's You Seriously Can't Say That game, where the object was to get your teammates to guess the word on your card without using any of the forbidden words listed on the same card.

Akimi, Sierra, Miguel, and the perpetually perky Haley Daley sat on a circular couch and played the guessers. Kyle stood in front of them as the clue giver.

"Salsa," said Kyle.

"Nachos!" said Akimi.

A buzzer sounded. Akimi's guess was wrong.

Kyle tried again. "Horseradish sauce!"

"Something nobody ever eats," said Haley.

Another buzzer.

Kyle goofed up and said one of the forbidden words: "Ketchup!"

SPLAT! Fifty gallons of syrupy, goopy tomato sauce slimed him from above. It oozed down his face and dribbled off his ears.

Everybody laughed. So Kyle, who loved being the class

clown almost as much as he loved playing (and winning) Mr. Lemoncello's wacky games, went ahead and read the whole list of banned words as quickly as he could.

"Mustard-mayonnaise-pickle-relish."

SQUOOSH! He was drenched by buckets of yellow glop, white sludge, and chunky green gunk. The slop slid along his sleeves, trickled into his pants, and puddled on the floor.

His four friends busted a gut laughing at Kyle, who was soaked in more "condiments" (the word on his card) than a mile-long hot dog.

"Was it fun?" boomed an off-camera announcer.

"Fun?" answered Haley. "Hello? It's a Lemoncello!"

That's how all the commercials ended, with Haley saying the slogan "Hello? It's a Lemoncello!" She became a TV superstar. People all across America wished they could be Haley Daley, too. Except, of course, for the kids who were extremely jealous of her and wondered why she, Kyle Keeley, Akimi Hughes, Sierra Russell, and Miguel Fernandez had been chosen to star in Mr. Lemoncello's holiday commercials.

When they found out that becoming famous TV stars was the prize the five kids had won in a game played at Mr. Lemoncello's incredible new library in Alexandriaville, Ohio—a game they hadn't been invited to play—they started demanding a rematch.

Charles Chiltington sat in his family's home theater watching his classmate Kyle Keeley rocket across a seventy-inch plasma-screen TV.

It was the worst Christmas vacation of his life.

For over a month, whenever he clicked on the television, Charles was forced to look at the five cheaters who, six months earlier, had robbed him of his rightful prize.

In that night's Lemoncello commercial, Keeley—the ringleader of the group that had "defeated" Charles in the Escape from Mr. Lemoncello's Library game—looked ridiculous dressed up in goofy goggles like a flying squirrel. But Keeley was obviously having a grand time starring in the commercial.

A commercial *Charles* should've starred in.

Keeley had needed four teammates to best Charles in

4

the past June's escape game, which was played inside the silly game maker's even sillier new library on its opening weekend.

Keeley had also needed Mr. Lemoncello's help to win.

At the very last second, just as Charles was nearing victory, the batty billionaire disqualified him on a trumped-up technicality. Keeley and his cronies went on to win the game and the grand prize.

Charles, on the other hand, went home to hear what a disappointment he was to his father.

Because Chiltingtons never lose.

Especially not to ordinary nobodies like Kyle Keeley.

For six months, Charles had been plotting his revenge on Keeley and his teammates: smart-aleck Akimi Hughes, library geek Miguel Fernandez, bookworm Sierra Russell, and most especially turncoat traitor Haley Daley, who had been on Charles's team with Andrew Peckleman until she deserted them to join Team Kyle.

"Mr. Lemoncello robbed me," Charles muttered miserably. "They should shut down his ludicrous library."

He'd been miserably muttering the same thing ever since the Lemoncello holiday commercials started airing. But for some reason, watching this annoying squirrel commercial made a new thought bubble up inside his brain.

He pushed the pause button on the DVR remote.

They should shut down Mr. Lemoncello.

That was a better idea.

The good citizens of Alexandriaville, Ohio, should not allow the demented Mr. Lemoncello to continue to control what went on inside their new *public* library.

Yes! His mind started whirring. That was the perfect angle. A public campaign to wrench control of the library away from the dangerous lunatic Luigi Lemoncello.

And Charles knew just who should lead the charge.

His mother.

She had a long history of championing public causes.

When he was in kindergarten, she had led the Anti-Cupcake Crusade, because Charles liked brownies better. When he was in third grade, his mother had made certain that the teacher who dared give Charles a B on his papier-mâché volcano was fired. And in fourth grade, she had yanked him out of Chumley Prep (and cut off their endowment) when the private school had the nerve to hire a history teacher who celebrated International Talk Like a Pirate Day.

Plus, Charles's mother did not particularly care for what Mr. Lemoncello was doing inside his zany library.

"Too much sizzle, not enough steak," she'd complained to friends in her bridge club. "They also lend out too many of the wrong sort of books."

Wheels were spinning inside Charles's head as he plotted his next moves.

With just the slightest nudge, taking the "Lemoncello" out of the Lemoncello Library would become his mother's next great cause. He was certain of it.

"Mummy?" he called out in his best your-little-boy-has-a-boo-boo voice.

When no one answered, he did it again. Louder.

"Mummy! Make it go away! I'm being traumatized! Mummy!"

His mother bustled into the TV room. "Charles, darling? What's the matter?"

Charles pointed a trembling finger at the TV screen. "Mr. Lemoncello. Make him go away. His library is a petrifying place full of cheaters!"

"I know, dear, but there's nothing . . ."

Charles started blubbering. "He cheated me, Mummy. He robbed me!"

"Yes, honey . . ."

It was time to pull out the heavy artillery.

"He lowered my self-esteem! I feel like such a failure!" He sniffled. "Because of Mr. Lemoncello, I may never go to college!"

His mother's face turned ghostly white. *Score!*

"Hush now. Mummy's here. Everything will be all right."

She hugged him tightly.

Charles grinned.

Mr. Lemoncello was toast.

Burnt toast with toe-jam jelly on top.

3

With school out for the winter holidays, Kyle and his friends were spending a lot of time hanging out downtown at the Lemoncello Library, where, because of their celebrity status, every day was a cake day.

Cake days were a Keeley family tradition. Whenever one of them did something spectacular—like his brother Mike winning a football game (again) or his other brother, Curtis, getting straight A's (again)—Kyle's mom baked a cake.

Ever since Kyle and his teammates had won the escape game, every day had felt that way. Cakey.

"You're the dude from the commercial!" at least a dozen kids said to Kyle as he strolled through the Rotunda Reading Room.

He gave them each a jaunty two-finger salute. He'd seen movie stars do the same kind of salute on TV.

"Can I have your autograph?" said a little girl.

"Sure. Here you go."

Kyle still signed each and every autograph individually.

His best friend, Akimi, on the other hand, passed out preprinted signature cards. "It's faster that way," she said.

"Hi, Kyle!" Sierra was curled up in one of the cozy chairs near the three-story-tall wall of fiction. She was reading a book, of course. Her gaze was far-off and dreamy, because when Sierra Russell was into a book, she was totally *into* it. She practically crawled between the covers to live with the characters.

"Hey," said Kyle. "What're you reading?"

"Actually, I'm rereading *Bud, Not Buddy* by Christopher Paul Curtis. It's my favorite."

"Sweet."

"Have you ever read it?"

"Not yet. But it's on my list."

Sierra laughed. Probably because Kyle Keeley had the longest to-be-read list of any kid in the country.

"There's another copy on the shelf," said Sierra.

"That's okay. I'm meeting Akimi and Miguel upstairs in the Electronic Learning Center. Mr. Lemoncello just installed a new educational video game: Charlemagne's Chivalry. I think it's about the Knights of the Round Table."

"Um, Kyle? Charlemagne was the Holy Roman Emperor. *King Arthur* had the round table—in *England*."

"See? You *can* learn something new every day. Catch

9

you later, Sierra. Don't want to keep Charlemagne or King Arthur waiting."

Kyle bounded up the spiral staircase to the third floor, signing autographs and posing for selfies with fans along the way.

He passed through the two very thick sliding glass doors that stopped the wild sounds of the Electronic Learning Center from leaking out into the rest of the building.

Once he was inside the arcade, Kyle's ears were bombarded by the blare, buzz, and bells of three dozen educational video games. His nose was blasted, too. A lot of the games in the ELC were equipped with Mr. Lemoncello's newest sensation, smell-a-vision, including one where you were a royal rat with body-odor issues, swimming through English history via the sewers of London.

"I'm sorry, I can't sign another autograph or my hand will fall off," said Haley Daley, who was holding court near the Cleopatra: Queen of the Nile game console.

Kyle didn't play that one too much, because Haley Daley always outscored him. She knew the trick for summoning crocodiles up from the Nile.

"Kyle?" Haley waved at him. "You got a second?"

"I'm supposed to meet—"

"This is super important."

Kyle made his way to Haley.

"I'm moving!" she said.

"Seriously?"

"Hello? Do you know how many offers I've had since I starred in those commercials for Mr. Lemoncello?"

"Actually, we all kind of starred in—"

"Hundreds. Maybe thousands. So my whole family's going to Hollywood. My dad found a new job in L.A. Plus, my agent is already booking guest spots for me on the Disney Channel."

"Awesome," said Kyle.

Haley Daley and her family had needed the money that came with winning the library escape game more than any other player had. It sounded like Mr. Lemoncello's generosity had really turned things around for them.

"I just wanted to say goodbye. And thanks, Kyle."

"Hey, it was a team effort. We won it together."

"Whatever. I gotta go. Need to pick out a new pair of sunglasses."

Haley dramatically waved goodbye to Kyle and all her adoring fans as she traipsed out of the Electronic Learning Center. She did that dramatically, too.

"Yo, Kyle? We need a little help over here, bro! Like now."

Miguel and Akimi were on the far side of the Electronic Learning Center playing Charlemagne's Chivalry. Miguel had the stubby controller rod gripped in front of his chest, wielding it like a lightsaber.

Kyle hustled across the noisy room.

"What's up?"

"Charlemagne needs a champion," explained Akimi. "Someone who will defend the weak and defenseless, fight for what's right, yadda yadda. The game is based on the ancient code of chivalry."

"I'm kind of stuck," said Miguel, fending off a fiery dragon with his virtual sword swishes.

"And I'm kind of bored," said Akimi. "See you two later."

Kyle turned to Miguel. "What are your options?"

"Slay the dragon or go feed the hungry peasants."

"No contest. Slay the dragon."

"You sure?"

"Definitely. If you don't, the dragon will kill the peasants. You slay the dragon, the peasants will rejoice. Peasants always love dragon slayers."

"Okay. If you say so."

Miguel thrust his imaginary sword forward. His on-screen knight pierced the dragon's hide with his steel blade.

The animated dragon fizzled out a geyser of gas and shriveled into a heap of crinkled plastic.

"Aw, man. It wasn't a real dragon. It was a big balloon. Like in the Macy's parade . . ."

A swarm of peasants armed with pitchforks stormed across the screen. They attacked Miguel's knight.

"Why didst thou not bringeth us food?" screamed the leader of the peasant army. "Death to the selfish, unchivalrous knave!"

Kyle heard the unmistakable *BLOOP-BLOOP-BLOOP*

sound of video-game death. Miguel's knight took a pitch-fork in the butt and wilted into a heap of pixels.

"Okay," said Kyle. "Now that we know what *not* to do, we'll play again and win."

"Why bother? We don't need Charlemagne to tell us we're champions. Am I right?"

Kyle grinned. "Totally."

Then the two of them knocked knuckles and chanted the lyrics to their favorite classic-rock tune: *"We are the champions, my friend. . . ."*

On the Monday after New Year's, Kyle stood shivering at his bus stop.

Ohio gets very cold and slushy in January.

Finally, the bus pulled up and swung open its door.

"Well, hel-lo," said Mrs. Logan, the driver. "It's another Lemon-cel-lo!"

Kyle shook his head. Bus drivers watched TV commercials, too.

"Good morning, Mrs. Logan," said Kyle, climbing up the steps.

"Got a riddle for you." Ever since his team had won the Lemoncello Library game, *everybody* was constantly trying to trip them up with riddles and puzzles.

"Go for it," said Kyle.

"What two things can you never eat for breakfast?"

"Easy," said Kyle. "Lunch and dinner."

14

Mrs. Logan waved her arm at him. "Ah, go sit down."

Kyle high-fived his way up the bus aisle to his usual seat, next to Akimi. Sierra sat behind Akimi, her nose buried in another book.

"What are you reading?" Kyle asked. "That *Butter Not Nutty Buddy* book?"

"Actually," said Sierra, "I'm rereading *Charlie and the Chocolate Factory,* because everybody keeps saying Mr. Lemoncello reminds them of Willy Wonka. But Mr. Lemoncello is much kinder."

"And he doesn't have Oompa-Loompas," quipped Akimi.

"Or Augustus Gloop," added Kyle.

"Actually," said Akimi, "I think Charles Chiltington was our Augustus."

"Really?" said Sierra. "He reminds me more of Veruca Salt."

Wow. Sierra Russell cracked a joke. She had definitely loosened up since joining Team Kyle.

"So," said Akimi after Kyle peeled off his parka, "did your grandmother give you that sweater for Christmas?"

"How'd you guess?"

"It looks like something you'd buy at a pet store. For a dog named Fluffy."

"I think I might lose it in my locker today."

"Good idea."

"Um, excuse me?" said Alexa Mehlman, a sixth grader seated across the aisle from Kyle.

15

"Hey, Alexa," said Kyle. "What's up?"

"I don't mean to bother you. . . ."

"It's no bother. What can I do for you?"

"Well, my uncle gave me Mr. Lemoncello's Phenomenal Picture Word Puzzler for Chanukah and I can't figure out this one rebus."

"Let me see it."

"The category is 'famous slogans,'" said Alexa, passing a cardboard square to Kyle. It was filled with a jumble of letters and pictograms.

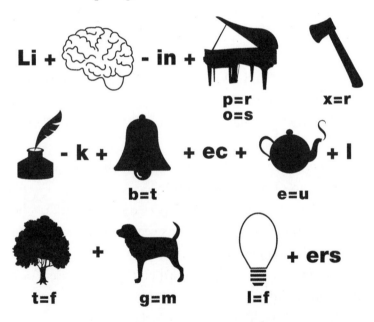

"The first word is 'librarians,'" said Akimi. "L-I plus B-R-A-I-N minus I-N gives you L-I-B-R-A. Then you add P-I-A-N-O, but make the 'P' an 'R' and the 'O' an 'S,'

16

so you end up with L-I-B-R-A, R-I-A-N-S, or, you know, 'librarians.'"

"Wow," said Alexa. "You guys are amazing."

"Not me," said Sierra. "I'm not very good at games." She dove back into her book.

The bus bounced over a speed bump and pulled into the school parking lot.

"You have ten seconds to finish the puzzle, Mr. Keeley," said Akimi. "Go!"

Kyle studied the card again and handed it back to Alexa. "'Librarians are intellectual freedom fighters.'"

"Awesome!" said Alexa. "I kept getting stuck on the bottle. I thought it was perfume, not ink. You're my hero, Kyle Keeley!"

Kyle smiled. It was good to be someone's hero.

Especially when all he had to do was play a game.

5

"You guys?"

Miguel was waiting for Kyle, Akimi, and Sierra when they walked through the school's front doors.

"You have got to see what I found!" He led them down the hall to the library. Miguel Fernandez was super enthusiastic about everything, especially libraries. That's why he'd been president of the Library Aide Society for three years straight.

"What is it?" asked Kyle as they entered the media center. "A new Dewey decimal number or something?"

"No. A whole bunch of book lovers all across America who don't like us."

"What?" said Akimi. "What's not to like? We're very likable people."

"They're wondering how come *they* didn't get to play Mr. Lemoncello's library game."

"Um, because they don't live here in Alexandriaville?" said Akimi.

"Only seventh graders at this school were eligible to enter the essay contest to win a spot at the library lock-in," added Sierra.

For the first twelve years of the Alexandriaville seventh graders' lives, school media centers were the only libraries they had ever known. The old public library, the one Mr. Lemoncello had loved when he was a boy growing up in the small Ohio town, had been bulldozed to make way for a multilevel concrete parking structure.

"They just wish they could be us," said Kyle. "You can't really blame 'em."

"It's worse," said Miguel. "They think they could've *beaten* us."

Miguel waved for his friends to follow him to the rows of computer terminals.

"I was Googling us again this morning, and all these blogs and posts started popping up. None of them are very nice."

"Greetings, heroes!" called Mrs. Yunghans, the middle school librarian, who absolutely *loved* having the most famous library card holders in America checking out books in her library. "Don't believe all those nasty things people are writing about you kids on the Web. They're just jealous."

Kyle and his teammates huddled around a monitor while Miguel clacked the keyboard.

"Check it out."

They scrolled through the top search results for "Escape from Mr. Lemoncello's Library."

"It took them a whole day to find their way out of the library?" wrote one blogger.

"I could've done it in half a day," commented another.

"I demand a rematch," said more.

"This isn't fair, Mr. Lemoncello."

"We demand a chance!"

"Put *us* in that library. We could beat Team Kyle with one 612.97 tied behind our back."

"That's the closest Dewey decimal number for hand," explained Miguel. "Actually, it refers to regional physiology of the upper extremities."

"Wow," said Kyle. "What a bunch of library nerds."

Miguel cleared his throat, prompting Kyle to quickly add, "Not that there's anything wrong with that."

"Ouch," said Akimi. "Listen to this one."

She clicked open a post with even the subject line screaming in all caps.

" 'KEELEY'S TEAM ONLY WON BECAUSE THEY CHEATED!' " she read aloud. " 'MR. LEMONCELLO IS BLATANTLY LYING TO THE WORLD ABOUT WHAT REALLY HAPPENED ON THAT DREADFUL, GHASTLY, AND ABOMINABLE DAY LAST SUMMER. HE SHOULD BE TARRED AND FEATHERED AND RUN OUT OF TOWN ON A RAIL.' "

"That's horrible," said Sierra.

"Of course it is," said Akimi. "Look who wrote it."

She pointed to the semi-anonymous signature: "C.C."

Charles Chiltington.

6

Dr. Yanina Zinchenko, the world-famous librarian, dragged a lumpy mail sack to the far end of the Rotunda Reading Room, where her boss, Luigi Lemoncello, was flying up and down in front of the three-story-tall fiction bookcases.

"I'm looking for a good book," said Mr. Lemoncello as his hover ladder jerked vertically, then skittered sideways. "But I'm not exactly sure what I'm looking for."

The hover ladders were floating platforms with handrails, book baskets, and ski-boot safety locks that allowed you to float up to retrieve any book you wanted simply by entering the book's call number into a computerized keypad. The system worked with the same magnetic levitation technology used in Germany and Japan to propel bullet trains with magnets instead of wheels.

"Perhaps I can be of assistance," said Dr. Zinchenko in her thick Russian accent. "Do you have the call number?"

"No need," Mr. Lemoncello said, laughing. "I wanted to test-drive our new 'browse' function."

After several patrons had complained that the hover ladders' demand for a specific book code eliminated the ability for patrons to leisurely peruse the shelves, the imagineers at Mr. Lemoncello's game company had come up with the new and improved hover ladders, which featured a browse button.

Once you pushed it, the hover ladder randomly flitted in front of the shelves, using advanced biofeedback technology, heart-rate monitors, and complex algorithms to figure out what sort of story you might be interested in.

"But we have a very important matter to discuss." Dr. Zinchenko pointed to the mail sack. It was the size of an overstuffed duffel bag.

"Oh, dear. A V.I.M.? I don't know if I have the vigor for a V.I.M."

"We also have visitors. . . ."

"Visitors and a V.I.M.? I'll deal with both as soon as I finish browsing."

"Mr. Lemoncello?" bellowed a voice below.

He glanced down and saw a very properly dressed lady flanked by six other very properly dressed ladies and one properly dressed man in a bow tie.

"I'll be right with you!" shouted Mr. Lemoncello as his

hover ladder caromed across the wall of books like an out-of-control Ping-Pong ball. "I'm busy browsing."

"My name is Susana Chiltington," the lady said operatically. "Mrs. Susana *Willoughby* Chiltington."

"Hello, Susana. Don't you cry for me. The doctors say they can easily remove the banjo on my knee."

Mrs. Chiltington wasn't amused.

"Perhaps you've heard of my brother?" she said. "The head librarian for the Library of Congress? James F. Willoughby the third?"

"What happened to the first two?"

"I beg your pardon?"

"Never mind. I am finished browsing. Pull me down, Captain Underpants."

The hover ladder gently lowered the happy billionaire to the floor.

"Now then, how may I help you, Duchess Susana Willoughby Chiltington the third, Esquire, PhD?"

"I'm not a . . . Oh, never mind. My colleagues and I represent the recently formed League of Concerned Library Lovers. Winthrop?"

The gentleman in the bow tie opened a leather briefcase. "As a public library, Mr. Lemoncello, this institution needs a board of trustees to oversee its finances and champion its mission."

Mrs. Chiltington snorted a little. "It is quite customary."

"So is pumpkin pie on Thanksgiving, but I prefer pineapple rhubarb," said Mr. Lemoncello.

"As concerned library lovers," said the gentleman, brandishing a thick document, "we are here today to volunteer our services."

Mr. Lemoncello ignored the man and focused on Mrs. Chiltington.

"You're Charles's mother, aren't you?"

"Indeed." She snuffled and adjusted her clothes to make certain all the seams were lined up precisely the way they were supposed to be.

"Might I humbly suggest, Mrs. Chiltington, that your considerable concern might be better spent on your son instead of my library? Now then, Dr. Zinchenko, I believe we have a very important matter to discuss?"

"Yes, sir."

Mr. Lemoncello walked over to the wall of bookshelves and tilted back the head on a marble bust of Andrew Carnegie, revealing a red button hidden in his neck.

"Mr. Lemoncello?" trilled Mrs. Chiltington. "A public library requires public oversight—guardians who will safeguard the institution's well-being and stability."

"I know! I've been thinking about that very fact for months. I've also been thinking about lunch for at least fifteen minutes. I thank you for your time and concern."

He bopped the red button.

A door-sized segment of bookshelves swished sideways. Mr. Lemoncello and Dr. Zinchenko disappeared with the mailbag down a dimly lit corridor. The bookcase slammed shut behind them.

"Mr. Lemoncello?" Mrs. Chiltington called after them. "Dr. Zinchenko?"

She banged on a row of books as if she were knocking on a door.

"Mr. Lemoncello!"

A burly security guard—maybe six four, 250 pounds, his hair in long, ropy dreadlocks—came up behind her.

"Ma'am? I'm going to have to ask you to leave the library if you keep punching the books."

Mrs. Chiltington swung around.

"I'm not . . . Oh, never mind."

She glanced at the guard's name tag.

"Clarence?"

"Yes, ma'am."

"Well, Clarence, don't worry. We're leaving. But kindly inform Mr. Lemoncello that we shall return."

"Wonderful," said Clarence. "Mr. Lemoncello loves it when people come back to visit his library."

Mrs. Chiltington gave Clarence a frosty smile.

"I'm sure he does. And next time, there will be more of us!"

7

Early in the second week of January, each member of Team Kyle received a thick envelope in the mail.

When they opened it, they found an engraved invitation:

SPLENDIFEROUS GREETINGS AND SALUTATIONS!

YOU AND YOUR FAMILY ARE HEREBY
CHERRY CORDIALLY INVITED TO THE
ANNOUNCEMENT OF MY STUPENDOUS NEW NEWS.

FRIDAY NIGHT
SHALL WE SAY 7-ISH?

THE ROTUNDA READING ROOM OF
THE LEMONCELLO LIBRARY

REFRESHMENTS SHALL BE SERVED,
INCLUDING CHERRY CORDIALS.

AND THERE *WILL* BE BALLOONS.

——————————

REGARDS,
LUIGI L. LEMONCELLO

* * *

Friday evening, Kyle and his family piled into their mini-
van and drove downtown to the library.

"Isn't this exciting?" said Kyle's mother. "I should've
baked a cake."

"Any idea what the big announcement is?" asked his
dad.

"Not a clue," said Kyle. "But we're hoping Mr. Lemoncello is going to ask us to star in more TV commercials."

"Please, no," moaned Kyle's brother Mike. "Your
head's big enough already."

Snowflakes swirled in the misty beams of light flood-
ing the front of the domed building that used to be a bank
until Mr. Lemoncello turned it into a library. Kyle noticed
several TV news satellite trucks taking up the parking
spaces along the curb.

"You better get in there, Kyle," said his dad. "We'll go
find a place to park."

"Have fun!" added his mom.

Kyle dashed up the marble steps and into the library's lobby.

Miguel and Sierra were waiting for him near the life-size statue of Mr. Lemoncello perched atop a lily pad in a reflecting pool. The statue's head was tilted back so the bronze Mr. Lemoncello could squirt an arc of water out of his mouth like he was a human drinking fountain. His motto was chiseled into the statue's pedestal:

KNOWLEDGE NOT SHARED REMAINS UNKNOWN.
—LUIGI L. LEMONCELLO

"Hey, Kyle!" exclaimed Miguel. "The place is packed. Everybody was invited! All twelve of the original players."

"Including Charles Chiltington?" asked Kyle.

"He's a no-show."

"I hope Andrew Peckleman doesn't show up, either," said Sierra with a slight shiver. Peckleman had been Chiltington's ally in the escape game and had tricked Sierra out of her library card so he could spy on Team Kyle.

"He was definitely invited," said Miguel. "But he won't be coming. Ever since he got kicked out of the game, Andrew doesn't really like libraries. He even quit being a library aide at school."

"That's sad," said Sierra.

"You guys," said Akimi, coming in from the Rotunda Reading Room, "there's all sorts of TV news crews inside. Including that reporter from CNN."

"Which one?"

"The guy with the hair."

"And there's food in the Book Nook Café," said Miguel. "Tons of it."

"So why are we hanging out here?" said Kyle. "Let's go."

The four friends hurried under the arch that led into the vast Rotunda Reading Room. The rotunda was packed. Clusters of brightly colored balloons were tethered to the green-shaded lamps on the reading desks. Hidden surround-sound speakers blasted a brassy, heroic fanfare.

Overhead, the Wonder Dome was a fluttering display of fifty state flags flapping against a cloudless blue sky, where, for whatever reason, a very muscular couple in ancient robes rode a chariot back and forth across the curved ceiling like it was a horse-drawn comet. They reminded Kyle of a Greek god and goddess straight out of the Percy Jackson books.

"Wow," said Miguel. "Do you think Rick Riordan's going to be here? That would be so awesome!"

All the animated action was displayed on ten wedge-shaped high-definition video screens—as luminous as any sports arena's scoreboard. They lined the underbelly of the building's colossal cathedral ceiling like glowing slices of pie. Each screen could showcase individual images or join with the other nine to create one spectacular presentation.

"Whoa," said Akimi. "Check out the statues. They're hardly wearing any clothes."

"And," Sierra said, "they look like they're made out of marble."

"Right," said Akimi. "*See-through* marble."

Tucked beneath the ten Wonder Dome screens in arched niches were ten 3-D statues glowing a ghostly green. Holograms.

"They all remind me of Hercules," said Kyle, taking in the dizzying array of muscular wrestlers, javelin throwers, discus flingers, and runners. "Except for the lady with the horse."

"I think that's a Spartan princess named Cynisca," said Sierra, who read a ton of history books, too. "She won the four-horse chariot race in 396 BC and again in 392 BC in what we call the ancient Olympic Games."

Akimi arched an eyebrow. "You sure she isn't that girl from *The Girl Who Loved Wild Horses*?"

Sierra laughed. "Positive!"

"Splendiferous greetings and salutations to one and all!" boomed Mr. Lemoncello's voice from the loudspeakers as the trumpets blared their final fanfare. "Thank you for joining us this evening. It is now time for my big, colossal, and jumbo-sized announcement!"

Kyle held his breath and crossed his fingers.

He really hoped he and his friends were going to star in more commercials.

Being famous was fun.

And kind of easy, too.

Blazing circles of bright light swung across the second-floor balcony to shine on Mr. Lemoncello.

Spotlights following him, he scampered to the nearest spiral staircase, slid down the banister, and dismounted with an impressive backflip. When his boot heels hit the ground, they squawked like a chicken, then mooed like a cow.

"Dr. Zinchenko? Kindly remind me never to borrow boots from Old MacDonald again."

Mr. Lemoncello wore a bright red and blue Revolutionary War outfit with a ruffled collar and a cape. A plumed tricorne hat completed the costume. He pulled out a brass handbell and rang it. Loudly.

"Welcome, boys and girls, families and friends, esteemed members of the press."

Mr. Lemoncello smiled for all the television cameras aimed at him.

"Clarence? Clement?" He clanged his bell a few more times. "Please bring in today's mail."

Clarence and Clement, the beefy twins who headed up security for the Lemoncello Library, marched into the Rotunda Reading Room flanked by six robotic carts loaded down with United States Postal Service mail bins.

"Dr. Zinchenko? How many emails have we received on this same subject?"

Dr. Zinchenko consulted the very advanced smartphone clipped to the waistband of her bright red pantsuit. "Close to one million, sir."

"One million?" Mr. Lemoncello shuddered. "And that's just the bad beginning. But, not to worry, I have come up with the happy ending! You see, fellow library lovers, kids all across this wondermous country are eager to prove that *they* are bibliophilic champions, too. Therefore, oyez, oyez, and hear ye, hear ye."

Kyle covered his ears. Mr. Lemoncello was clanging his bell like crazy.

"Let the word go forth from Alexandriaville to all fifty states. I, Mr. Luigi L. Lemoncello, master game maker extraordinaire, am proud to announce a series of games that will rekindle the spirit and glory of the ancient Olympic Games held, once upon a time, in Olympia—the one in Greece, not the capital of Washington State. Therefore,

I hereby proclaim the commencement of the first-ever Library Olympics! A competition that will discover, once and for all, who are this sweet land of liberty's true library champions. Dr. Zinchenko?"

"Yes, Mr. Lemoncello?"

"Kindly invite your network of crackerjack librarians all across this country to organize regional competitions."

"Immediately, sir."

"Oh, it can wait until tomorrow. I, of course, will pay for everything, including the Cracker Jacks."

"Of course, sir."

"Bring me your best and brightest bookworms, research hounds, and gamers. Our first Library Olympiad shall commence on March twentieth. The ancient Greeks had their summer games, so we'll take the first day of spring."

"How many members should be on each team?" asked Dr. Zinchenko, who was furiously tapping notes into her tablet computer.

"Five," said Mr. Lemoncello, "the same number as on Team Kyle. Our hometown heroes are hereby officially invited to these Library Olympics, where they will defend their crown—which, to keep things Greek and chic, will be made out of olive branches."

Kyle gulped.

Another competition?

Against the top library nerds in the country?

He didn't like the sound of that. He liked being a champion and staying a champion.

"Um, sir?" said Miguel, raising his hand.

"Yes, Miguel?"

"Haley Daley moved to Hollywood. We're down to four."

"What about Andrew Peckleman?" asked Mr. Lemoncello. "He only cheated in the first game because someone who shall remain nameless bullied him into doing it."

Mr. Lemoncello pretended to cough, but his cough sounded a lot like *"Ch-arles Ch-iltington."*

"Andrew won't play," said Miguel. "He says he hates libraries."

"Oh, my. Well, we must certainly work on changing that. For now, we will stick with *four* members on every team. Just like the four horses pulling that Spartan lady Cynisca's chariot."

Yep, thought Kyle. *Sierra was right. Again.*

"Once we find our other Library Olympians," said Mr. Lemoncello, "we'll fly them here to Alexandriaville and commence our duodecimalthon."

"Your what?" asked Akimi.

"Duodecimalthon. It's like a decathlon, only with *twelve* games instead of ten."

"Why twelve?" asked Kyle, who was already trying to figure out how many games his team would need to win to keep its title.

"Because 'duodecimalthon' sounds a lot like 'Dewey decimal system' if you say it real fast with a mouthful of malted milk balls, don't you agree?"

"Yes, sir."

"Good," said Mr. Lemoncello, raising his bell and striking a heroic pose. "The four members of the winning team shall each receive a full scholarship to the college of their choice."

The audience applauded. Some parents even whistled.

"That's right. It's very whistle-worthy. The winners will receive four years of paid tuition plus free room, board, and books. Lots and lots of books. Now go find me my champions!"

9

Dr. Zinchenko went to work with her book- and game-loving librarian colleagues in all fifty states.

The country was divided up into seven regions: Midwest, Northeast, Mid-Atlantic, Southeast, Southwest, Mountain, and Pacific. Since the Library Olympics would be held to see if any team could dethrone the stars of Mr. Lemoncello's holiday commercials, only children in middle school, like the four members of Team Kyle, were allowed to participate.

Throughout January and February, thousands of eager contestants flocked to their local libraries to play the same kind of Dewey decimal scavenger-hunt game that had been at the heart of the Escape from Mr. Lemoncello's Library game.

In Decatur, Georgia, a girl named Diane Capriola advanced to the Southeast semifinals when she worked her

way out of an Atlanta–Fulton County public library before anybody else by solving a riddle: "What occurs once in every minute, twice in every moment, yet never in a thousand years?"

"The answer, of course, is the letter 'M,'" Diane told local TV reporters. "So, I went to the reference section, opened up the 'M' encyclopedia, and—ta-da—there was a key to the back door tucked inside! When I stepped out to the sidewalk, the librarians were waiting with balloons and cake. It was easy-peasy."

In California, a boy named Pranav Pillai became a finalist for the Pacific team after he correctly deciphered that 683.3, the Dewey decimal code for *Louie the Locksmith's Big Book of Padlocks, Dead Bolts, and Tumblers,* was also the combination for the lock securing the exit of the Los Altos Public Library: 6-R, 8-L, 3-R, 3-L.

But the player librarians all over the country were raving about most was Marjory Muldauer from Bloomfield Hills, Michigan. A gangly seventh grader, a foot taller than any of her competitors, Marjory Muldauer had memorized the ten categories of the Dewey decimal system before she entered preschool.

The books in her bedroom were all organized by numbered codes. So were the spices in her mother's kitchen cabinets. And the baby food jars filled with nuts and bolts in her father's garage.

Marjory liked organizing things.

She knew her way around a library better than the robotic carts in Mr. Lemoncello's library. She read six books a day and could do two crossword puzzles at once—with a ballpoint pen.

"I'm glad that Mr. Lemoncello read my several letters and launched these Library Olympics," Marjory told a reporter from her hometown newspaper. "I could really use that college scholarship he's giving away. I'm also glad that the libraries where I've competed thus far have based their scavenger hunts on good old-fashioned research techniques. It's too bad that so many of the kids who signed up for the competition see these games as some kind of party."

"What do you mean?" asked the reporter.

"Mr. Lemoncello insists that everybody be given balloons and cake. Cake has no place in a library. Frosting is sticky. Sticky fingers damage books."

"But Mr. Lemoncello is also a great lover of libraries."

"Is he?" said Marjory skeptically. "I don't think Mr. Lemoncello loves libraries *qua* libraries."

"Huh?" said the reporter. "What does 'qua' mean?"

" 'As.' It's Latin. Mr. Lemoncello does not love libraries *as* libraries. He thinks they need to be tricked out with gadgets and gizmos and holographic displays. That library in Ohio reminds me of Disneyland with a few books. I think Mr. Lemoncello is seriously immature. He probably still believes in three-nine-eight-point-two."

"Huh?" The reporter was confused again.

"Three-nine-eight-point-two!" said Marjory. "It's the Dewey decimal number for fairy tales."

The reporter just nodded and closed her notepad.

Marjory Muldauer had that effect on people.

"Wait," Marjory told the reporter. "I'm not finished. Be sure you write this down: Kyle Keeley? You don't stand a chance in France!"

10

"Andrew used to be your friend," Kyle said to Miguel. "Maybe you could talk him into taking my place."

Kyle and Miguel were hanging out in the cafeteria, waiting for Sierra and Akimi to join them for their daily team meeting, something they'd been holding ever since Mr. Lemoncello announced his Library Olympics idea back in January.

"No way, bro," said Miguel. "We need you."

"No, you don't."

"You're our leader. *El capitán*."

"But I shouldn't be. Sure, I know how to play games. But I'm still not great at all the library stuff."

"And I'm not very good at games," said Miguel. "And I haven't read half as many books as Sierra. And I'm nowhere near as clever as Akimi. The team needs all four of us, bro."

"But have you seen some of these kids in the regional competitions? They're amazing."

"Yeah. That girl Marjory up in Michigan sure knows her way around the stacks."

"That's why you guys need Andrew Peckleman. He used to be your second-in-command on the library squad."

"I already told you: Ever since he was booted out of the escape game, Andrew Peckleman does not like libraries. Besides, he can't practice with us after school, because he has a new job."

"What kind of job?" asked Kyle.

"He's working afternoons and weekends at the motel that opened up last month across from Liberty Park. Some distant relative that Andrew and his parents didn't even know they had owns the place. A great-uncle-twice-removed or something. He hired Andrew."

"Even though he's only twelve?"

Miguel shrugged. "I guess when it's family, it's different."

"What's Andrew do?"

"Sweeps. Makes sure the ice machine isn't clogged. Fills the bird feeders."

"Bird feeders?"

"What can I say? Andrew's uncle must love birds. He even named his motel the Blue Jay Extended Stay Lodge. Come on. Forget Andrew. We're counting on *you*."

That was the problem. Kyle didn't want to let his friends down. And he'd read Marjory Muldauer's interview with her hometown newspaper online.

She was gunning for Kyle.

Kyle *so* wished he could switch places with Andrew, even if it meant sweeping up birdseed.

He hadn't told any of his teammates, but in the six weeks since Mr. Lemoncello had announced his Library Olympic Games, Kyle felt a nervous fluttering in his stomach every time he played a board game against his brothers or fielded a riddle tossed at him by a school bus driver.

The pressure was intense.

Especially since Kyle had been on something of a losing streak—something else he hadn't told Miguel or Akimi or Sierra. He hadn't beaten his brothers on family game night *once* since January. Kyle had even lost the home version of the Escape from Mr. Lemoncello's Library board game—to his mom. And Miguel had been playing with Kyle that time. True, Miguel had given Kyle some bad advice. (*Flubber* is the name of a Walt Disney movie starring Robin Williams, not a book by Judy Blume, which would be *Blubber*.) But Kyle was the one who had given the wrong answer.

The first game in Mr. Lemoncello's library had been more like a scavenger hunt, something Kyle was good at. But these new Olympic Games were going to be about serious library topics, and Kyle would be playing against some serious library whiz kids.

Akimi and Sierra came into the otherwise empty cafeteria.

"Hey, guys," said Akimi. "Sorry we're late."

"Akimi was teaching me how to play that new Lemon-cello video game where you squish all the different-colored jelly beans with a sledgehammer," said Sierra. "I made it to level three."

Kyle nodded. "Jujitsu Jelly Jam."

He didn't mention that he'd already made it to level fifty-three. Friends didn't gloat to friends.

"So what're we doing today?" asked Akimi. "More rebus puzzles? Dewey decimal drills?"

"First things first," said Miguel, jerking his thumb at Kyle. "Our fearless leader here is getting cold feet."

"Wha-hut?" said Akimi.

"Kyle wants to quit."

"I didn't say I want to quit, Miguel."

"Right. You just said you didn't want to be on the team anymore. That you wanted Andrew Peckleman to take your place."

"Which," said Akimi, "basically means you want to quit."

"I'm not a quitter," said Kyle.

"Uh, yes, if you quit, you are," said Akimi. "Sierra, correct me if I'm wrong."

"Sorry, Kyle," said Sierra. "That's the dictionary definition of 'quitter,' all right. 'A person who quits or gives up easily, especially in the face of some difficulty or danger.'"

"Snap," said Miguel. "Sierra just gave you the four-two-three on quitters."

Kyle was confused. "The what?"

44

"The four-two-three," said Akimi. "That's where you can always find a dictionary of standard English in a library."

"Oh," said Kyle. "Did not know that."

"It was on last week's study sheet," said Miguel.

"Right. Sorry. Guess I should've studied it."

"Well, duh," said Akimi. "That's why we call them *study* sheets."

Kyle pretended to laugh, but deep down, he knew the truth: No matter how hard he tried, he would never be able to win every single game he played for the rest of his life. Sometimes the cards and the dice and the questions just didn't go your way. Every chance for victory was another chance for defeat.

He didn't belong in anybody's Library Olympics.

Playing off the NCAA basketball tournament's "March Madness" theme, Mr. Lemoncello declared the first Saturday in March "Library Lunacy Day."

It was time for each of the seven regions to make its toughest cuts and choose the four members for its Library Olympics team.

At two p.m. Eastern Standard Time (eleven a.m. on the West Coast), Mr. Lemoncello himself addressed all the contestants via a video conference call. He wore a bright yellow shirt with a custom-cut tie shaped like a cello.

"Hearty and splendiferous congratulations on having made it this far in the competition. I wish I could invite each and every one of you *plus* everybody else in America to my first-ever Library Olympic Games, but, unfortunately, Ohio fire codes do not permit occupancy by more than three hundred and twenty-five million people, even

46

if they are all little women. Good luck! Have fun! And remember, books are the true breakfast of champions! You may devour them. But please don't eat them. Thank you."

In California, where all sixteen finalists were library whizzes, Sarah Trager Logan, the librarian in charge, knew teamwork would be crucial for victory inside the Lemoncello Library. That's why she made all sixteen finalists participate in a synchronized book-cart drill. It was judged by the same Hollywood celebrities who judge TV dancing shows.

In Colorado, the four members of the Mountain team would be the first four students who could solve one final puzzle. All the top contestants were given a sheet of paper with the following paragraph printed on it:

Thoze four beople who will represant awl of the bibrareans id the creat and heroik Mountain states knaw one thing aboot anything primted in a card cadalog sydtem. Without it, library users would simply be lost.

There were so many mistakes most of the contestants didn't know what it meant, what they were supposed to do, or why the judges hadn't proofread their paragraph before passing it around.

But the final four knew the mistakes *were* the secret code.

By writing down the letters that should have gone

where the wrong letters were, they came up with a simple lesson about library card catalogs:

SPELLING   COUNTS.

In San Antonio, Texas, the final contest was a fresh and very complicated rebus puzzle.

"The category is 'famous quotes,'" said Cynthia Alaniz, the librarian who would be coaching the Southwest team. "Good luck!"

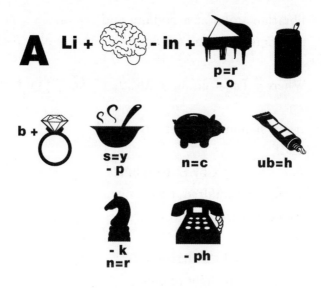

—Neil Gaiman

The eight finalists wrote their answers as quickly as they could. When they were finished, they put down their pencils and bopped bright yellow hotel bells.

The four fastest puzzle solvers nailed it: " 'Google can bring you back one hundred thousand answers. A librarian can bring you back the right one.' —Neil Gaiman"

Marjory Muldauer, who had aced every test and game thrown her way during the first eight rounds of the regional competition, was in Madison, Wisconsin, for the Midwest finals.

And she was feeling invincible.

In the Midwest's "elite eight," she played a rapid-fire "first lines" game.

49

A librarian stood at a podium and read from a note card. The contestants had to buzz in like they did on *Jeopardy!*

" 'Where's Papa going with that axe?' " said the librarian.

Marjory slammed her fist down first.

BUZZ!

"*Charlotte's Web,* by E. B. White!"

"Correct. 'All children, except one, grow up.' "

Marjory banged her button.

BUZZ!

"*Peter Pan,* by J. M. Barrie!"

"Correct. 'In the light of the—' "

BUZZ!

Marjory didn't wait for the librarian to finish.

"*The Very Hungry Caterpillar,* by Eric Carle."

"Correct. 'Mrs. Rachel—' "

BUZZ!

"*Anne of Green Gables,* by L. M. Montgomery."

The other contestants never had a chance.

To lock down her spot on the four-person team, Marjory competed against five other finalists in one last Dewey decimal challenge.

"Give me the Dewey decimal number for 'freedom of speech,' " said Tabatha Otto, a librarian from Lincolnshire, Illinois.

Two contestants began weeping.

Three wrote down the same answer: 323.44.

"Very good," said the librarian.

"But not good enough," said Marjory. "Three-two-three-point-four-four is the call number for 'freedom of action,' also known as liberty. But three-two-three-point-four-four-*three* would be 'freedom of speech.'"

And that's what she had written on her card.

Marjory Muldauer was good.

Scary good.

12

On March 18, two days before the Library Olympic Games were scheduled to start, Mrs. Yunghans, the middle school librarian, showed Team Kyle a viral video of Marjory Muldauer's brilliant performance at the Midwest finals.

"Wow," said Akimi.

"Yikes," added Miguel. "She's amazing."

"She's also incredibly tall," said Akimi. "Like a praying mantis."

"She looks sort of sad," said Sierra.

Kyle didn't say a word.

This was the last straw.

Seeing Marjory Muldauer in action, watching her guess first sentences of books with just one or two words for a clue, Kyle knew he didn't stand a chance. Not against that kind of competition. The girl knew Dewey decimal codes

down to the one-thousandths place. Kyle still wasn't sure what "the four-two-three" meant.

Plus, the Lemoncello Library had been closed to the public for a week. Mysterious imagineers from Mr. Lemoncello's headquarters in New York City had come to Alexandriaville to make what the local newspaper called "a few minor alterations." They'd been working inside the locked building under the supervision of Dr. Zinchenko, adding new surprises for the Olympic Games.

Surprises Kyle knew would totally baffle him.

He would go into the Lemoncello Library a champion and come out a chump. There would be no more cake days.

It wasn't so much that Kyle was afraid of losing (even though he was). He didn't want to be the reason everybody else lost, too.

"What kind of new gadgets and gizmos do you guys think Mr. Lemoncello has added to his library?" asked Mrs. Yunghans.

"It's top-secret," said Miguel.

"Nobody knows," added Akimi.

"Probably not even Mr. Lemoncello," said Sierra.

Once again, Kyle remained silent.

"I guess all we can do now to prep is read more books," said Miguel.

But the books would have to come from the middle school media center. The week the library was closed for its "alterations," nobody could check out books, which made the League of Concerned Library Lovers very upset.

"A public library should serve *the public*," said Charles Chiltington's mother on the radio and TV. "Not the whims of an eccentric billionaire."

Fortunately, nobody in Alexandriaville paid much attention to Mrs. Chiltington or her group. They were too excited about the upcoming Library Olympics. All the local hotels and motels lit their "No Vacancies" neons. Restaurants hired more staff. Mr. Lemoncello's wacky idea was an economic boon for the whole town.

The opening ceremonies were scheduled for the first day of spring, March 20. The twelve games of the duodecimalthon would start on the twenty-first and run for six days (two games a day). Closing ceremonies would take place the following night.

The public was invited to attend and watch. For free. The games would also be broadcast on many PBS stations, the Book Network cable channel, and NPR.

That meant everybody in America would be able to watch and/or listen to Marjory Muldauer destroy Kyle Keeley, big-time.

The Alexandriaville four, as well as the seven visiting teams, their coaches, and tutors (so they could keep up with their schoolwork for the week) would be staying at what Mr. Lemoncello had dubbed Olympia Village. It was actually the Blue Jay Extended Stay Lodge, where Andrew Peckleman had a part-time job.

And that's where Kyle was headed—as soon as Mrs. Yunghans wrapped up this final team meeting.

"You guys have done a great job," said the school librarian. "And, Kyle? We're all very glad you're still on the team."

"Thanks."

"Yo, Kyle," said Miguel, "don't let this Marjory Muldauer get under your dome. We can take her."

"You're not thinking about quitting again, are you?" asked Akimi.

That was the problem with best friends. They knew what you were thinking even when you were pretending not to be thinking it.

"I'm fine," said Kyle. "Just, you know, nervous."

"I think we all are," said Mrs. Yunghans, who'd be staying with the team at Olympia Village as one of their chaperones. "Look, guys—tomorrow's Saturday. I think we should all take a break. No more studying. No games. Just head over to Liberty Park, take in some fresh air, and don't read anything."

Sierra raised her hand. "Is that an order, Mrs. Yunghans?"

"No, Sierra. You can read if you want to. But read something for yourself—not the competition."

Kyle said goodbye to his friends, and when he was absolutely certain nobody was following him, he biked to the Blue Jay Extended Stay Lodge.

He needed to talk to Andrew Peckleman now—*before* Marjory Muldauer came to town.

The motel's sign looked like a big blue birdhouse.

The reader board out front, where the letters used to say "Ask About Our Early-Bird Specials," now read "Welcome to Olympia Village."

Kyle checked out the property. It looked like an apartment complex, with maybe a dozen or so two-story structures and parking lots spreading out in either direction from a central building that had a lobby, a dining room, and an office.

There was also a ton of bird feeders. Everywhere. Birdbaths and birdhouses, too.

Andrew Peckleman was working near the motel sign, pouring a sack of birdseed into one of the feeders. Kyle biked over to talk to him.

"Hey, Andrew."

"Kyle."

"So. Sunday's the big day."

"For what?"

"The Library Olympics."

"Oh, right."

"I was wondering . . ."

Before Kyle could say another word, a black SUV crawled to a stop behind him. One of the rear doors swung open, and out stepped Charles Chiltington.

"I'll only be a second, Mummy," Chiltington said to someone in the backseat. Kyle squinted at the tinted front windshield. The Chiltingtons had a chauffeur. The guy was even wearing one of those floppy black hats with the shiny brim.

"Hello, Keeley," said Charles, who never called Kyle by his first name (probably because "Keeley" made him sound more like a servant).

"Hey, Charles," said Kyle.

"What are you doing here?" asked Andrew.

"Following Keeley."

Andrew looked confused. "Why?"

"Because I knew that, sooner or later, he would come here and beg you to take his place in the Library Olympics."

Kyle faked a chuckle. "What?"

"My mother and I have been enjoying the regional competitions," said Charles. "You don't stand a chance against that Marjory Muldauer girl, Keeley. I know it. You know it. The whole country knows it. And since Mr. Lemoncello is so eager to let Andrew back in the game . . ."

"He is?" said Andrew. "Where'd you hear that?"

"I have my spies," said Charles.

"Spies?" Kyle said with a laugh. "Mr. Lemoncello was talking about you back in January, Andrew. When he first announced his idea for these Olympics. He knows you were bullied into stealing Sierra's card during the escape game. He'd really like to have you come back to his library."

"Well, I won't do it," whined Peckleman, pushing his goggle-sized glasses up the bridge of his nose. "Mr. Lemoncello is stupid. His whole library is stupid. And Library Olympics? That's the stupidest idea I've ever heard. You're wasting your time, Kyle. I won't take your place."

"Who said that's why I'm here?" asked Kyle.

Andrew pointed at Charles. "He did."

"Look, Keeley, *I'll* take your place," said Charles. "Mummy and her group are keen to have me on the inside, keeping an eye on Mr. Lemoncello. Besides, who knows? I might be able to whip your atrocious teammates into shape. With me at the helm, we could actually bring home the gold." He stood proudly, looking down his nose at Kyle. "Do I need to fill out a form or something?"

"For what?"

Charles rolled his eyes. "*To take your place.* We all know that's why you came here, Keeley. You're afraid. Abashed. Apprehensive. Frankly, I don't blame you. You're a loser who got lucky. Once. I, on the other hand, am a Chiltington. Chiltingtons never lose."

58

"Except when you lost," said Andrew, nervously fidgeting with his glasses. "You know. Last time."

"I did not 'lose,' Andrew. I was *eliminated* by Mr. Lemoncello."

Kyle shook his head. "I hate to disappoint you and your 'mummy,' Charles, but I didn't come here to ask Andrew to take my place."

"Oh, really?"

"Nope. And I sure don't want you anywhere near Akimi, Miguel, and Sierra. I just wanted to make sure Andrew saved Miguel and me a good room. We're checking in Sunday afternoon."

"What?" said Charles. "You're not quitting."

"Nope. Just wanted to check out our accommodations. Haven't you heard, Charles? Winners never quit, and quitters never win."

The next day, when Kyle and his teammates were dropped off at Olympia Village by their parents, the motel was swarming with kids and chaperones.

"Uh-oh," said Akimi. "They all have slick warm-up outfits."

The seven other teams were decked out in brightly colored hoodies and sweatpants. Kyle and his friends were wearing jeans, sneakers, and mismatched jackets. So were their chaperones.

"That's okay," said Sierra. "We're saving our uniforms for the parade of champions."

"Check it out, you guys," said Miguel. "There's Andrew Peckleman."

Their classmate marched briskly out of the hotel lobby wearing a bright blue sweatshirt and a Toronto Blue Jays baseball cap.

"May I have your attention, please?" Andrew shouted through a bullhorn. "May I have your attention?"

No one gave him any attention.

All the kids from out of state and their chaperones kept gabbing and giggling.

"So when do we get to check out this Lemoncello Library?" said a boy with the kind of tough edge New Yorkers always have in movies.

"I sure do want to ride one of those hover ladders," said a girl who sounded like she might be from Alabama or Louisiana.

"Dude," said a kid from California, "I'm heading straight to the Electronic Learning Center so I can half-pipe the craters on the moon."

Andrew tried again. His bullhorn squealed with feedback. "WILL YOU STUPID PEOPLE PLEASE SHUT UP?"

Every single Library Olympian glared at him.

"Thank you. Um, now, here with a few words about the motel is my boss and, uh, great-uncle-twice-removed, Mr. Woodrow 'Woody' Peckleman."

A skinny bald man—who sort of resembled a plucked chicken in a bright blue suit—strutted out the lobby door. He had a very pointy nose that looked like a beak. He twitched and fidgeted and squinted in the sunshine. Kyle half expected him to start scratching the toe of his shoe at the dirt, searching for chicken feed.

"Welcome," said Mr. Peckleman, with a voice even

more nasal than Andrew's. "The Blue Jay Extended Stay Lodge—also known, this week, as Olympia Village—is, as you may have noticed, my personal bird sanctuary. Please enjoy our feathered friends' colorful, song-filled company and merry antics." He gestured toward a nearby bird feeder. "But, please, do *not* feed the squirrels. Squirrels are nothing but thieving rodents. Rats with fluffy tails."

Oh-kay, Kyle thought. *Andrew's great-uncle is a little nutty.*

"Also," Mr. Peckleman continued, "you are free to enjoy the brand-new Lemoncello video arcade machines recently installed in the motel's game room, right off the lobby. There is no charge for any of these games."

"Woo-hoo," cried Kyle.

Now everybody in the crowd turned to gawk at him.

Right. Kyle figured his competition was more into books and libraries than video games. He felt as out of place as he'd known he would.

"That's okay," whispered Akimi. "I'll play Dragon Bop Bubble Pop with you."

"Me too," added Sierra.

"Ditto," tossed in Miguel.

"Thanks, you guys."

Suddenly, an old-fashioned horn went *AH-OOGA.*

Kyle looked at the motel entrance.

A car resembling a pouncing cat, with glowing green eyeballs for headlights, had just eased off the highway and pulled into the parking lot.

"The cat is one of the tokens from that board game," said Sierra, who had been studying Lemoncello games the way Kyle had been studying libraries and books. "Family Frenzy!"

"Correctamundo," said Akimi.

The cat car was followed by eight Winnebago-sized vehicles, their sides covered with vinyl graphics designed to make them look like bookshelves on wheels.

"And check those out," said Miguel as the vehicles gracefully glided into a reserved row of angled parking spaces.

The catmobile's paw door swung up, and out stepped Dr. Yanina Zinchenko, wearing a blazing-red flight suit. She strode through the crowd and politely took the bull-horn from Mr. Peckleman.

"Welcome, everybody, to Ohio and Olympia Village," she said. "Kindly report to the bookmobile with your region's name affixed to its side. Our library staff will give each of you a welcome packet containing the card key for your room, meal tickets, and information about this week's exciting events. The bookmobiles will be at your disposal throughout the games. They will take you wherever you need to go. They are also filled with books to make your commute more enjoyable. The opening ceremonies for the games of the first Library Olympiad will be held this evening, here at Olympia Village. Start time is eight p.m. There will be fireworks. And cake. Also balloons. So please, settle in, freshen up, and get ready for an exciting week."

Everyone applauded. Dr. Zinchenko clicked her heels and bowed.

Two smiling Lemoncello Library staffers in yellow jumpsuits with ID badges lanyarded around their necks emerged from each of the eight bookmobiles with stacks of manila envelopes.

"Let's go get our room assignments," said Mrs. Yunghans, the middle school librarian. Mr. Colby Sharp, one of the middle school's ELA teachers, would be Team Kyle's other chaperone.

Kyle, Akimi, Miguel, and Sierra followed the two adults to the bookmobile with "Home Team/Defending Champions" proudly displayed on its side.

The gangly Marjory Muldauer was standing with the two yellow-suited library staffers in front of it.

"Excuse me, Miss Muldauer," said Mrs. Yunghans, who of course recognized the girl immediately. "Are you looking for the Midwest team's bookmobile?"

"No," said Marjory. "I was just curious if any of the reigning 'champions' knew when the first perambulating library appeared in the rural villages of Cumbria County, England."

Kyle looked to Miguel and Sierra. They looked blankly at him.

"The first what?" said Akimi.

"Perambulating library." Marjory gestured over her shoulder. "A bookmobile. A mobile library?"

"Is this going to be on the final?" quipped Kyle. He was

64

trying his best to sound confident in front of his fiercest rival.

Marjory Muldauer kept her eyes locked on Kyle. "You never know, do you, Mr. Keeley?"

"Miss Muldauer," said Mrs. Yunghans, "perhaps you should rejoin the rest of your team?"

Marjory ignored her.

"It was 1857," she said. "It was a horse-drawn cart. Donated by a Victorian merchant named George Moore to 'diffuse good literature among the rural population.'"

"Well," said Kyle, "these are way cooler. And the drivers don't have to shovel horse poop all day."

Marjory Muldauer didn't laugh. She narrowed her eyes.

"I hope you enjoyed your fifteen minutes of fame, Mr. Keeley. Because when these games are over and done, *you* will be over and done, too."

She turned on her heel and walked away. Kyle actually shivered.

The girl wasn't just scary good. She was also scary.

Andrew Peckleman was in the motel game room.

"For the last time, the stupid thing is broken," he told the blond boy from Utah, who was on the Mountain team.

"How can it be broken? The motel manager said all these games are brand-new."

"Well, maybe Mr. Lemoncello made a lemon." Andrew jiggled the control knobs on the console. He jabbed his thumb at the on/off button. Finally, he gave the pressboard box a swift kick. "See? It doesn't work. Play something else."

"But I wanted to play Squirrel Squad Six."

"And I wanted to be the first librarian on Mars. Ask me how that's working out. Now go play something else."

The boy from Utah shuffled off to try Mr. Lemoncello's Disgracefully Destructive Elephant Stampede. The goal was to mash as much mall merchandise as you could with Melvin, the mischievous mastodon.

"Andrew?" called his uncle from the motel's front office.

"Yes, sir, Uncle Woody?"

"Come here, please."

Andrew stepped into the office. His uncle was at the back wall, fiddling with the combination lock on a large steel door.

"I'll just be a minute." He slid a rolling wall panel in front of the steel door. When the panel clicked into place, the massive storage locker was completely hidden behind a seamless wall featuring a framed print of two bluebirds.

Andrew's uncle pointed to a thirty-pound sack of birdseed sitting on the floor.

"I need you to refill feeders six and seven."

"Yes, sir."

"And check the batteries in the spinners."

"Yes, sir."

Each of Uncle Woody's bird feeders had a weight-activated spinner that turned it into a whirling merry-go-round the instant a squirrel set foot on it.

"I need to go chat with a few of our guests."

"About what?" asked Andrew.

"Never you mind. Go take care of the bird feeders."

"Yes, sir."

Lugging the seed bag over his shoulder, Andrew went out the side door to the swimming pool and patio area.

Since it was only the first day of spring, the pool was still covered with a tarp, but the stainless steel gas grills

on the concrete slab surrounding it had been shined and buffed. Cooks from a catering company would use them for the opening ceremonies celebration. Hamburgers, hot dogs, and s'mores were on the menu.

The outdoor fire pit—an elevated ring of rocks surrounded by lawn chairs—was stone cold. It would not be lit at any time during the Library Olympic Games because Mr. Lemoncello hated bonfires. "Throughout history," he explained in the Library Olympics welcome packet, "too many books have been burned by people who didn't like what was written inside them."

There would also be no flaming Olympic torch, just a giant, ten-foot-tall flashlight to celebrate the joy of reading under the covers. It was mounted on the back of a flatbed truck and would swing through the sky after Mr. Lemoncello switched it on, just like one of those swiveling spotlights at the grand opening of a used-car dealership.

Andrew unscrewed a cap on bird feeder number six and hoisted the bag of seed.

"Why does this hotel have so many bird feeders?" asked someone behind him.

Andrew whirled around.

It was the tall girl from Michigan. Marjory Muldauer.

Andrew adjusted his glasses. "Excuse me?"

"What's up with all the bird feeders?"

Andrew shrugged. "Uncle Woody likes birds."

"Probably because he looks like a bird."

Andrew snorted a laugh. "I know. He does!"

"I'm trying to find some coffee," said Marjory, her hands propped on her hips. Her face was scrunched up like she'd just smelled sour milk. "I need to read two more books tonight."

"Well," said Andrew, "if you really want some 641.3373, follow me."

Marjory gave him a look. "That's the Dewey decimal number for coffee."

"Yes. The beverage. Coffee the agricultural product would be 633.73."

"And," said Marjory, "coffee*houses* would be 647.95. Eating and drinking establishments."

"Yep."

"You know a lot about the Dewey decimal system for a motel employee."

"Oh, this is just a part-time job. My name is Andrew. Andrew Peckleman."

"You were one of the losers, weren't you? In the escape game."

Andrew hung his head in shame. "Yes. But ask me if I care."

"Okay," said Marjory. "Do you care?"

"No. Not anymore."

"Well, that monstrosity that Mr. Lemoncello constructed isn't really a library, Andrew. It's an indoor amusement park."

"Have you seen it?" Andrew asked.

"Not yet. But I've seen pictures. They should close

it down and turn it into a Chuck E. Cheese's—after, of course, I win my college scholarship from loony old Lemoncello."

Andrew smiled.

Because Marjory Muldauer was a kindred spirit.

He dropped the birdseed sack onto the concrete patio.

"Come on," he said. "Let's go grab that cup of 641.3373."

"And maybe," said Marjory, "we can find a few 641.8653 to go with it."

"Ooh," said Andrew. "I love doughnuts."

16

Just after dark, Kyle and his teammates put on their opening ceremonies costumes and headed out to the motel's central courtyard.

A bandstand had been erected at one end of the grassy rectangle situated in the middle of the motel's chalet-style units. Mr. Lemoncello, Dr. Zinchenko, and the mayor of Alexandriaville stood on the platform, ready to review the thirty-two Olympians.

Mr. Lemoncello was dressed in a shimmering silver toga and silver laurel-leaf crown. He looked a little like the male tribute from District Three in a *Hunger Games* parade. Dr. Zinchenko was all in red, again. Shiny red sequins. The mayor wore a black trench coat. He wasn't much on dressing up.

The eight teams marched, one at a time, into the motel's version of an arena and walked around it, just like the

athletes at the ancient Greek Olympic Games did (except those guys didn't have a sidewalk or running shoes).

A crowd of several hundred spectators ringed the courtyard, which was illuminated by colorful strings of party lights. More people were watching the festivities on giant-screen TVs set up across the highway in Liberty Park.

Kyle was carrying the "Hometown Heroes" banner. He and his teammates were wearing gray-and-scarlet tracksuits (Ohio State University's colors), brown "buckeye" nut hats, and squeaking banana shoes, exactly like the ones Mr. Lemoncello sometimes wore. The musical sneakers— bright yellow and slightly curved—were one of Mr. Lemoncello's biggest hits over the holidays. The "game" was to make the banana shoes burp-squeak out a tune by hopping, skipping, and tap-dancing the notes. For the opening ceremonies' "Parade of Champions," Kyle, Akimi, Miguel, and Sierra had choreographed the footwork to play a burp-squeak version of "Hang On Sloopy," Ohio's official rock song.

Most of the other teams wore wacky costumes, too.

The team from the Pacific states was decked out in board shorts, flip-flops, and way cool Hawaiian shirts. They blew "Surfin' Safari" on kazoos. Pranav Pillai was the kazoo drum major.

The kids representing the Mid-Atlantic region wore crab costumes, complete with deely-bopper antennae and pinchers.

The Northeasterners went with very scholarly, Harry

Potter–style robes and mumbled a chant in Latin while they marched (*"Semper ubi sub ubi"*); the Southeast team, including Diane Capriola, wore sleek NASCAR race car driver jumpsuits with all sorts of book patches sewn onto every available inch; the Southwest team sported cowboy hats, big belt buckles, and boots and did rope tricks with their twirling lassoes; all the Mountain players wore flannel shirts, lumberjack pants, fake mountain-man beards (even the girls), and furry, flap-eared hats.

The Midwest team, led by Marjory Muldauer, wore khaki pants, button-down white shirts, striped ties, and blue blazers.

Kyle thought the Midwesterners looked like marching real-estate brokers. Or Charles Chiltington's cousins.

"My dad made it!" said Sierra, waving at a man smiling proudly in the crowd. "And there's my mom," she added when the team had hop-skipped and burp-squeaked another twenty feet.

After all eight teams had marched around the courtyard three times, they lined up in front of Mr. Lemoncello's reviewing stand, ready for him to officially declare the games open and light the Library Olympics torch, which, Sierra explained, is what people in England call a flashlight.

"Welcome, one and all," boomed Mr. Lemoncello. "I am so glad to see you here this evening, because this afternoon my optometrist gave me eye drops and I couldn't see a thing! Before I officially illuminate our Olympic torch . . ."

He gestured toward the ten-foot-tall skyward-pointing flashlight.

". . . I'd like to say a few short words. 'Terse,' 'diminutive,' 'stubby,' and 'I,' which is one of the shortest words I know, until it becomes 'we,' as in 'We the people of the United States,' the same 'we' that secured the blessings of liberty for ourselves and our posterity, which, by the way, would be you, children, and not my fanny, which would, of course, be my 'posterior-ity.' "

He took a deep breath.

"Tonight, we light the symbolic flashlight of under-the-covers reading to celebrate those page-turners we can never put down, even on a school night. I am assured that our Olympic torch will never reach a temperature of Fahrenheit four fifty-one, something the Lorax, the lion, the witch, and the wardrobe were all quite happy to hear."

Mr. Lemoncello pranced across the stage to a giant cartoon version of a wall switch.

"Gamesters, if you're game, let the gaming begin!" He heaved up the humongous switch. The ginormous flashlight's beacon sliced through the night sky. "I now pronounce the games of the first Library Olympiad officially open. I also pronounce my name like a cross between a tart fruit and a mellow musical instrument. Have fun! Play fair! And remember—these games are a quest to find who amongst you is a true champion!"

A thousand balloons with glow sticks in their bellies were released into the night air. Fireworks rocketed into

the sky. The Ohio State marching band tramped into the courtyard to create an open-book formation while blaring a brassy version of "Paperback Writer" by the Beatles. Laser beams sliced through the smoky darkness in time to the music.

"And now," announced Mr. Lemoncello after the fireworks had exploded into their grand finale of floating hearts, smiley faces, and interlocking books, "the most stupendously spectacular moment of the entire night, your keys to anything and everything you ever want or need to know, boys and girls, buoys and gulls, dolphins and porpoises—may I proudly present . . . your library cards!"

17

The eight teams stood bunched in front of the reviewing stand.

Dr. Zinchenko called out names one by one.

Kyle and his friends would be last to receive their new, Olympic-edition library cards. It was like baseball. The home team always batted last.

Miguel nudged Kyle. "You think there's going to be another secret, coded clue on the back of the cards?"

When Kyle and his teammates had played the escape game, one of their biggest clues came from writing down the first letters of all the books printed on the backs of their library cards. The letters spelled out a sentence that pointed them toward the library's secret exit.

"I hope so," said Akimi. "Because none of the other teams will know how to play Mr. Lemoncello's First Letters game."

"Maybe we should tell them," suggested Sierra.

"Why?" asked Akimi. "I thought we wanted to win."

"We do," said Sierra. "But we don't want to cheat."

"Yo," said Miguel. "It's not cheating just because we know something the other teams don't."

Sierra sighed. "But it's an unfair advantage."

"True," said Akimi. "But, sometimes, those are my favorite kind."

"But remember Mr. Lemoncello's motto?" said Sierra. " 'Knowledge not shared remains unknown.' "

"Which," said Akimi, "is exactly how I want this particular piece of knowledge to remain: unknown to everybody except us!"

"You guys?" said Kyle as the line worked its way forward. "Let's wait and see. I'd be surprised if Mr. Lemoncello gave us the same kind of clue twice. He never does it in his board games."

Finally, Team Kyle's names were called.

Dr. Zinchenko handed them four cards.

"Your library cards will grant you access to all the rooms and areas where we will be playing our twelve games," she explained. "The winner of each game will receive a very special medal. The team with the most medals at the end of the week will be declared the winner, if not the champion."

"Huh?" said Miguel. "Isn't the winner automatically the champion?"

"Perhaps," Dr. Zinchenko said mysteriously. "Perhaps not. It all depends, don't you agree?"

Miguel shrugged. "I guess."

Kyle wasn't paying attention to Dr. Zinchenko. He was too focused on the fact that the library cards were, once again, numbered.

"Now, if you children will excuse me . . . ," said Dr. Zinchenko, touching her Bluetooth earpiece. "It seems Mr. Lemoncello needs me inside. He has glued his mouth shut on a caramel apple."

Dr. Zinchenko hurried into the motel.

The players on the seven other teams had already headed into the dining area off the lobby, where waiters were serving hamburgers, hot dogs, potato chips, s'mores, ice cream, cake, candy bars, cookies, caramel apples, and coconut cream pie. "There is also fruit," Mr. Lemoncello had announced, "for those who do not wish to be bouncing off the walls all night, as I will be."

Team Kyle's chaperones, Mrs. Yunghans and Mr. Sharp, came over to join them.

"Good job on the parade, you guys," said Mrs. Yunghans. "We're going inside to grab one of those burgers."

"We're right behind you," said Kyle.

"Totally," added Miguel.

The four teammates waited.

As soon as the adults were gone, they flipped over their library cards.

There were images of book covers printed on the back.

"Awesome," said Akimi. "Just like last time. You guys know the drill. We need to write down the first letters of every title."

"I've got a pen and some paper," said Sierra, digging into the hip pocket of her tracksuit.

The team laid down their cards in order. Two cards had three illustrated book covers on their backs; two cards had four:

CARD #1

The Candymakers by Wendy Mass

Holes by Louis Sachar

Inside Out and Back Again by Thanhha Lai

CARD #2

Splendors and Glooms by Laura Amy Schlitz

Incident at Hawk's Hill by Allan W. Eckert

Shabanu: Daughter of the Wind by Suzanne Fisher Staples

Nothing but the Truth: A Documentary Novel by Avi

CARD #3

One Came Home by Amy Timberlake

The Year of Billy Miller by Kevin Henkes

A Long Way from Chicago by Richard Peck

Criss Cross by Lynne Rae Perkins

Lizzie Bright and the Buckminster Boy by Gary D. Schmidt

Uncle Tom's Cabin by Harriet Beecher Stowe

Elijah of Buxton by Christopher Paul Curtis

"Okay," said Kyle. "That's T-H-I, S-I-S-N, O-T-A-C, L-U-E."

Miguel gave it a quick shot. "Thigh, sis, 'n' taco, Lou!"

"Whuh?" said Akimi.

"It's like you're at KFC and you're ordering some Original Recipe dark meat plus a taco for your sister, Louise. Or maybe you know the guy behind the counter and his name is Lou."

Akimi rolled her eyes. "Seriously, Miguel? They don't serve tacos at KFC."

"Yes, they do if it's a KFC–Taco Bell combo store, which sometimes they are."

"I don't think the First Letters game is going to work for us this time," said Sierra.

She showed them what she had written down on her slip of paper:

"This is not a clue."

"Oh," said Miguel. "Did not see that coming."

Kyle, on the other hand, sort of had.

He knew *nothing* about winning these Olympic Games would be easy.

Bright and early the next morning, Kyle, his teammates, and their chaperones climbed into their bookmobile for the drive downtown to the Lemoncello Library.

The adults sat up front with the driver.

The kids were in the back with the books and a mini-fridge stocked with chocolate milk, pop, and six different kinds of juice.

"So," said Miguel, "did Andrew's weird uncle talk to any of you guys last night?"

"He talked to me this morning," said Sierra. "When I was on my way to the breakfast room."

"What did he want?" asked Kyle.

"He told me he could give me a 'Go to College Free' card," said Sierra.

Miguel nodded. "Me too."

"And why wasn't I offered this card?" asked Akimi.

Miguel shrugged. "Maybe because I turned him down."

"So did I," said Sierra.

"What did he want in exchange for the card?" asked Kyle.

"Worms for his baby birds?" suggested Akimi.

"He didn't really say," replied Miguel. "I turned him down before he had a chance."

"Me too," said Sierra. "I also reminded him that winning a college scholarship isn't the only reason we're playing these games."

"Really?" said Akimi, arching an eyebrow. "What other reason is there?"

"To prove that we truly deserve to be crowned champions."

"Oh. Right. *That*."

"This could be part of the game," said Kyle.

"Seriously?" said Akimi.

"Yep. Mr. Peckleman is kind of working for Mr. Lemoncello this week—running Olympia Village. And in Mr. Lemoncello's Marvelously Mysterious Mine Shaft game, there are devious dwarves who offer you cheat cards that let you do stuff like use elf shovels even if you're not an elf. But elf shovels, you find out after it's too late, can't dig up diamonds, only gold, and you need a ton of gold plus two diamonds to win."

Sierra nodded very slowly. "You've played a lot of Mr. Lemoncello's games, haven't you, Kyle?"

"Enough to know that most of his cheat cards eventually come back to bite you in the butt."

When Kyle and his teammates entered the library's grand rotunda, the room was more crowded than they had ever seen it.

Spectators, staring up at the Wonder Dome, were seated at the four rings of tables. The players from the seven other teams milled around, *ooh*ing and *aah*ing at things Kyle and his friends now took for granted, like the holographic statues perched on their pedestals, peering down at the crowd below. The statues were waving at people who were waving up at them.

Kyle recognized only one of the projected images—a greenish bald guy wearing bifocals and pants cut off at the knees and tugging on a kite string. That had to be Benjamin Franklin.

"Who are those other people?" he whispered.

"Famous librarians," said Miguel. "Melvil Dewey, Eratosthenes, Saint Lawrence, Lewis Carroll—the usual suspects."

Kyle nodded. He was *so glad* Miguel was on his team.

"In honor of the ancient Olympic Games," reported Akimi, "they have all sorts of Grecian urns up in the Art and Artifacts Room. And you can check out Mr. Lemoncello's old gym shoes in the Lemoncello-abilia Room on the third floor. Bring a gas mask."

"I heard Muhammad Ali is boxing Rocky Balboa in

the IMAX theater," added Miguel. "Winner wrestles Hercules."

Up on the Wonder Dome screens, Kyle saw the enormous image of eight empty library carts and two rolling bins bulging with books. They seemed to be parked in front of the doors to the 000s Dewey decimal room on the second floor.

"Welcome, children!" cried a trembling voice. "I'm so glad you are all finally here! What took you so long?"

Kyle looked toward the circulation desk in the center of the round room. Usually, that was where Dr. Zinchenko and her staff worked, helping people find whatever information or books they were looking for. During the escape game, a holographic version of Mr. Lemoncello's favorite childhood librarian, Mrs. Gail Tobin, had popped in to help administer clues.

Today's guest-librarian hologram, the lady with the trembling voice, was somebody new.

She looked frazzled. Worn out. The way teachers sometimes look at the end of a really long day right before spring break.

"My name is Lonni Gause," said the shaky see-through librarian. She was nervously nibbling a pencil as though it were a cob of corn. "I was the very last librarian at the old Alexandriaville Public Library—the one they bulldozed down so they could build a parking garage." She started sobbing. "Oh, the horror! The horror!"

"Thank you, Mrs. Gause," said Dr. Zinchenko, strid-

ing into the room from a section of the fiction bookshelves that swung open like a hidden passageway in a castle. "Welcome to day one of our competition, Library Olympians. Today we begin our quest for champions!"

"Yes!" cried the holographic librarian. "We need champions. We also need defenders! We needed them all those years ago when, first, books started disappearing off the shelves and, then, the wrecking balls rumbled up Main Street. Oh, the horror. The horror!"

Dr. Zinchenko pointed and clicked a miniature remote at the wailing librarian. The librarian disappeared.

"Perhaps we'll hear more from Mrs. Gause. Later. Now, however, it is time for our first game. Will all thirty-two contestants please report to the second-floor balcony? Spectators? You may witness the event, live and in high-definition color, up on the Wonder Dome."

"This way, you guys," Kyle said to the kids from out of town as he headed toward the nearest spiral staircase. All the Library Olympians followed and clomped up the metal steps.

"Kindly report to your assigned library cart," said a soothing female voice oozing out of the second floor's ceiling speakers. "And remember, free people read freely."

Marjory Muldauer, walking with her Midwest teammates, chuffed a sarcastic laugh. "Thanks for the sappy bumper sticker, ceiling lady."

The second floor was a carpeted, circular balcony, with the same circumference as the Rotunda Reading Room

85

below. The twelve-foot-wide balcony was lined with evenly spaced massive wooden doors that opened up into the ten Dewey decimal rooms.

Eight library carts—three tiers of slanted shelves on wheels—were lined up in front of the door to the 000s room. Across from them stood two canvas bins, both loaded with books.

Each library cart was labeled with two laminated cards: one with the name of a team, the other designating a range of Dewey decimal numbers. The Hometown Heroes' empty cart was labeled "900–999."

"That's for history and geography," Miguel reminded Kyle.

"Welcome to our first event: the Library Cart Relay Race," said Dr. Zinchenko, coming through another secret panel. This one was cut into the back of the curved fiction bookcases, which climbed past the second floor on their way up to the dome. "To win this game, your team must be the first to complete four laps of the second-floor balcony without spilling any of the three dozen books stacked on your rolling shelves, no matter the obstacles."

Marjory Muldauer's arm shot up.

"Yes?" said Dr. Zinchenko.

"There aren't any books on the library carts."

"No? Oh, that's right. The library has been closed for a week, so all of the recently returned books—exactly two hundred and eighty-eight different titles, thirty-six from each of eight different Dewey categories—are presently

stored in one of those two rolling bins. You must find the books that belong in your group, carefully load your cart, and, then, each team member must complete one full lap of the balcony and cleanly pass the cart off to the next relay racer. The team that finishes first will take home today's first medal and move closer to their college scholarships. I suggest choosing your swiftest cart pusher for the final leg."

"That's you, Akimi," said Kyle. "You're the fastest."

"I'm the slowest," said Miguel.

"I'm pretty slow, too," added Sierra. "I'm more of a reader than a racer."

"That's okay," said Kyle. "You two will be in charge of finding our books for us."

"The numbers should be on the spine," said Miguel. "Look for anything that starts with a nine."

"By the way," said Dr. Zinchenko, "to make this game more challenging, we have temporarily covered up all the call numbers on the spines of the books in the bins."

"Oh-kay," said Akimi. "So much for that idea."

"Find books about historical events and places you've always wanted to visit," suggested Sierra.

"How about the bathroom?" said Kyle, feeling queasy. "I wouldn't mind visiting it right now."

"Relax, bro," said Miguel. "Sierra and I will load the cart. You and Akimi need to run real fast once it's good to go."

"You take the first leg," said Akimi. "Try to buy us an early lead."

Kyle nodded. He was pretty swift. Not as fast as Akimi, but thanks to his big brother Mike the Jock, he was used to running wind sprints. "I'll give it my best shot."

"Please stand by," said the soothing ceiling voice. "Once your cart is fully loaded, do not block, trip, or shove the other teams. Do not interfere with their cart handoffs."

"In other words," said a new voice in the ceiling—Mr. Lemoncello's—"play nice, cart runners—not to be confused with kite runners, a book you should all definitely read when you're a little older. Dr. Zinchenko? Let the book-sorting shindig begin!"

Dr. Zinchenko raised her arm. She was holding a fancy tasseled bookmark between her fingers as if it were a small flag.

"On your mark," she said. "Get set. Go!"

She lowered the bookmark.

The race was on!

19

Kyle and Akimi hung back while Sierra and Miguel dug through the book bins with a couple dozen other eager Dewey decimal decoders.

A short, scrappy kid from the Southeast team leapt into one of the rolling canvas containers and tossed out language books (the 400s) to his teammates.

Marjory Muldauer simply stood next to the book heaps and pointed. "That one. That one. That one, too."

"That's our first twelve!" said Miguel when he and Sierra filled the lowest shelf of the library cart with their first two armloads of books. "Only two dozen more to go!"

If somebody put a wrong book on a cart, the lady in the ceiling said, "Sorry, Northeast team," or "Sorry, Pacific team." Then she urged them to "please try again."

Sierra and Miguel didn't make a single mistake. Neither did Marjory Muldauer.

The guys from the Pacific and Northeast teams goofed up the most. They kept mixing up their 100s (philosophy and psychology) with their 200s (religion).

"Go!" said Miguel, loading the thirty-sixth book about history and geography onto Team Kyle's cart.

Kyle took off at the exact same second as the first relay racer for Marjory Muldauer's Midwest team.

The front left wheel on Kyle's rumbling three-tiered wagon was wobbly. Like a grocery cart with a squished grape stuck to one of its tires.

The whole library cart was shimmying.

But he didn't slow down.

After he passed through the tunnel behind the fiction shelves and hit the doors to the 300s room, he was in the lead.

He aimed for the inside railing, figuring the tighter the circle he ran, the faster he'd complete his lap.

Pranav Pillai from the Pacific team came tearing up on his left. They must've sorted out their confusion about the 100s and 200s faster than Kyle had thought they would.

Then Pillai did something absolutely amazing. He twirled around in place—while running. He moved his hands over each other and behind his back as he executed a total 360-degree rotation.

Kyle had to slow down a little to nod and give the guy some props.

"Later, dude!" Pillai hollered as he flew past Kyle. He swerved inside to hug the balcony railing that Kyle had wanted to hug.

That's when Kyle remembered that to make the Pacific team, you had to pass the West Coast librarian's final test: a synchronized library-cart drill. The California, Oregon, and Washington State kids weren't pros, but they were definitely the best library-cart handlers in the building.

By the time Kyle completed his circuit around the balcony and reached the 000s door to hand off the cart to Miguel, the Pacific team's second runner, Kathy Narramore from Oregon, was already four doors ahead of him. When she saw a crimp in the carpet, she did a front flip over the rolling buggy so she could pull it behind her for a while before she did a somersaulting backflip so she could push it again.

Meanwhile, Miguel hit the bump and sent a stack of books tumbling off the cart's slanted shelves.

By the time Miguel finally reloaded the cart, pushed it around the balcony, and handed it off to Sierra, the Pacific team's fourth and final runner was ready to lap her.

Sierra made it as far as the 500s door when the Pacific team's closer sprinted across the finish line.

Akimi never even got into the race.

The Hometown Heroes had lost.

The Pacific team took the first medal of the duodecimalthon.

"Congratulations on your Gold medal," said Dr. Zinchenko as she draped a ribboned medallion over each of the winning team members' heads.

"No worries," said Kyle, trying to buck up his teammates, even though he was starting to have those "champions become chumps" feelings again. "We'll take the next one."

"Definitely," said Miguel.

"Unless," said Akimi, "it involves running with a rolling suitcase."

During the lunch break, the Pacific team kids did interviews with NPR, PBS, and the Book Network.

"That used to be us," groused Akimi.

"Come on," said Kyle. "You didn't think we'd win every single game, did you?"

"No. I didn't think it. But I was kind of counting on it anyway."

"My bad," said Miguel. "I lost all that time when I hit that bump."

Kyle glanced at Sierra. She had a smile on her face. Because she was reading again, and apparently, *The Fourteenth Goldfish* by Jennifer L. Holm was a very amusing book.

At two p.m., all eight teams were once again summoned to the second floor.

The library carts, each one still loaded down with three dozen books, were parked, once again, in front of the 000s door.

"Great," muttered Akimi. "A rematch."

"Teams," said Dr. Zinchenko, "it is now time for our second contest. In game number two, you must put all of your books back on the shelves in the exact spot where they belong. Therefore, you will need to first properly determine the full Dewey decimal number for all thirty-six of your assigned books and then place them in their proper shelf slots in your Dewey decimal room."

Kyle looked at Miguel.

"We can do this," said Miguel. "It's why we ran all those drills after school."

"Teams?" said Dr. Zinchenko. "Please return to your carts."

The eight teams clustered around their carts to size up their thirty-six titles.

Miguel, Sierra, and Akimi tilted their heads and squinted. Kyle could tell they were already noodling out numbers.

Great. They could do that part. Kyle would be in charge of running real fast and slamming the books into the shelves.

They had a chance.

A good chance.

It took Team Kyle only one hour and twenty-two minutes to correctly code and reshelf all thirty-six books.

Unfortunately, the Midwest team, led by Marjory Muldauer, did it in under an hour.

Marjory and her teammates would be awarded four Olympian medals.

"Looks like that's one for us"—Marjory smirked at Kyle—"and none for you."

The medal ceremony took place under the Wonder Dome, which, to honor the idea behind the second game, was operating in its spectacular Dewey decimal mode. The ten pizza-slice video screens scrolled constantly changing images associated with each category in the library cataloging system.

"Hey, Kyle," Miguel whispered as Dr. Zinchenko draped an Olympian medal around Marjory Muldauer's neck. "How come they have different names for the medals? Why aren't they all just, you know, 'gold'?"

Kyle shrugged. "Maybe to make it easier for us to remember that we lost *two* different games today."

But tomorrow would be another day.

With two new games to play.

Kyle just hoped his team didn't lose both of those games, too.

Charles Chiltington brought a tray of cucumber finger sandwiches (with the crusts trimmed off) into the living room, where his mother was hosting a meeting of the League of Concerned Library Lovers.

The seven ladies and one gentleman in a bow tie were huddled around a laptop, their horrified eyes glued to the screen.

"This is an abomination!" said one of the committee members, watching a recap of the Lemoncello Library Olympics' first day of competition on the Book Network's website.

Charles knew what "abomination" meant (anything greatly disliked). He used big words whenever possible. It impressed teachers, especially when you used words they didn't understand. Charles kept a list: "panacea," "panoply," "pedantic." And those were just the ones that started

with "p." He was very sesquipedalian (given to the use of long words) where others were perspicuous (clear in expression and easily understood).

He was also elated (very happy, jubilant, in high spirits) to hear all the adults complaining about Mr. Lemoncello and his egregious (shockingly bad) library.

"It's preposterous," said the gentleman in the bow tie. "Racing around in circles with library carts? Restocking shelves? Are these children applying for part-time jobs? Because they're all far too young to be legally employed."

"Ugh," said Mrs. Tinker. "That Mr. Lemoncello fellow is so incredibly irksome. So is that Russian gal, Dr. Zinfadelski."

"I'm so very confused," said Mrs. Brewster. "Why on earth would a library need a director of holographic imagery?"

"Because it's Disneyland in there!" shouted Mrs. Tinker. "Disneyland, I say!"

"Then we're agreed," said Charles's mother. "Something must be done."

"And may I," said Charles, "as a youth of Alexandriaville, quickly elucidate how fortunate I feel to have you wise and sagacious elders looking out for my best interests as well as the interests of all the young children yet to come?"

Charles knew being smarmy was the best way to get adults to do exactly what you wanted them to do.

"Thank you, Charles," said his mother. "Rose, please

make a note in the official meeting minutes. Resolved: We, the League of Concerned Library Lovers, must, by any means necessary, seize control of Alexandriaville's new public library and wrest it away from that borderline lunatic Luigi Lemoncello."

There was a light rap on the living room door.

"Excuse me," said Chesterton, the butler. "This gentleman insists that he is here for your meeting."

"Are you folks the Concerned Library Lovers?" asked a scrawny old man with a pointy beak who stood timidly in the doorway beside the butler. The man was dressed in a bright blue Windbreaker and was fidgeting with the sweat-stained Toronto Blue Jays baseball cap he held in his hands.

"Do we know you?" asked Charles's mother.

"I don't think so. My name is Peckleman. Woodrow J. Peckleman."

"Of the Geauga County Pecklemans?" twittered Mrs. Tilley.

"No, ma'am. From right here in Alexandriaville. Well, I grew up here, but then I flew the coop."

Charles sniggered. He couldn't help it. Mr. Peckleman looked like a chicken.

"I own the Blue Jay Extended Stay Lodge," said Mr. Peckleman.

"That's Olympia Village," said Charles. "You're Andrew's long-lost great-uncle-twice-removed, correct?"

"That I am."

"Pardon me for asking," said Charles's mother, "but what brings you here, Mr. Pecklestein?"

"It's Peckleman, ma'am. And I won't beat around the bush. I don't like what they're doing inside that Lemoncello Library downtown."

"Neither do we."

"I know. I've seen you folks on TV. Now, like I said, I used to live here in Alexandriaville. Years ago. Grew up with Luigi. Knew him when he was just a little boy, not some kind of fancy billionaire. And let me tell you folks something: Luigi L. Lemoncello was just as irresponsible back then as he is now. Why, in fifth grade, he made up multiplication and division games to make learning math 'more fun.' Pah. Math isn't supposed to be fun. It's math!"

"That's all well and good, Mr. Peckleman, but . . ."

"You people want him out of that library, am I right?"

Charles's mom coyly twiddled her fingertips against her cheek. "Perhaps."

"Well, I know how to do it."

"Really? And what do you require from us in return?"

"Not much. I just need you to talk to that brainy gal from Michigan for me. The tall one on the Midwest team."

"Marjory Muldauer?"

"Yes, ma'am. I've been scoping out all the library lovers bunking at my motel. Looking for just one of 'em to help me do what needs to be done. So far, over a dozen have turned me down. But I have a hunch that Miss Muldauer won't."

"What makes you say that?"

"She's not very fond of all the silly sideshow antics down at Luigi's library. I suspect she wouldn't mind seeing the place run by more responsible adults."

"But, Mr. Peckleman, why do you want *me* to speak with this girl on your behalf?"

"Because, Mrs. Chiltington, she'll listen to someone refined and educated like you. And when *you* offer her a 'Go to College Free' card, I have a feeling Miss Muldauer will become the answer to both our prayers."

21

Team Kyle's bookmobile ride from Olympia Village to the Lemoncello Library was extremely quiet on the second morning of the competition.

Finally, Akimi spoke up. "Wonder what kind of wacky games we can lose today."

"Both of them," said Miguel. "And it'll probably be my fault again, too."

Kyle was also feeling pretty low. But since he was still the team's captain, he decided he needed to give a pep talk. Maybe he could even convince himself that they still had a shot.

"Take it easy, you guys," he said. "Look—if you were playing Mr. Lemoncello's Family Frenzy and the first and second time you rolled the dice, you landed on Sewer Repairs and Dog Pound, would you quit?"

"Yes," said Akimi. "I'd consider it an omen."

"I wouldn't," said Sierra. "Especially since you still have so many more turns to go before anyone wins."

"Exactly," said Kyle. "Well, we've got ten more turns. Right now, the score is Pacific one, Midwest one. All we have to do is win one game and we're tied for first place."

Miguel stroked his chin. "Hmm. When you put it like that . . ."

"We're still currently tied for last place," said Akimi.

"So is everybody else," said Kyle as the bookmobile pulled up to the front of the library. "So let's go in there and change that!"

"Fine," said Akimi, who was pretty immune to pep talks. "Whatever."

The setup in the Rotunda Reading Room was slightly different for the second day of the competition.

The two circles of desks closest to the center of the room had been roped off to the crowd of spectators, many of whom were now upstairs on the second and third floors with the news cameras, peering down at the action from the upper decks.

Kyle noticed that Mr. Peckleman, the motel owner, was in the crowd clustered at the remaining tables on the first floor. He was staring up at the Wonder Dome in awe.

"Ah, the sandhill crane migration!" Kyle heard him exclaim to nobody in particular. "Isn't it marvelous?"

The entire underbelly of the Wonder Dome had been

transformed into a fluttering flock of birds, soaring across an unbelievably blue sky, swooping through a clay-colored desert landscape.

"Welcome, bookworms!"

Kyle looked up.

Mr. Lemoncello had just climbed on top of the balcony railing outside his private suite—on the third floor! He was wearing a leather aviator helmet with goggles and had a pair of feathered wings strapped to his back.

"Today," announced Mr. Lemoncello, "in our third and fourth games, you will use the library to help your imagination take flight, much as I am about to do."

"No!" screamed Mrs. Lonni Gause, the frazzled holographic librarian, who popped into view behind the circulation desk. "Don't jump! You'll end up a heap of crumpled bones, just like the old library ended up a heap of crushed rubble! And they'll be back! The book haters with their bulldozers! They always come back! I hear them rumbling up Main Street now!"

"Fear not, Mrs. Gause," cried Mr. Lemoncello. "If anyone should ever again threaten this library, I will fly to its aid, much as I should've flown to it all those years ago. But alas, I was too busy doing business in Beijing to come home and save my beloved library, leaving you to ask, 'Where's Waldo?' even though my first name was, and still is, Luigi. Moving on. I'd like to quote the lyrics of Rodgers and Hammerstein—something that's extremely easy to do when you're in a library near 782.14 and all

those magnificent Broadway show tunes—'I flit, I float, I fleetly flee, I fly!' "

Mr. Lemoncello leapt off the railing.

Two thousand spectators gasped. Several hid their eyes. Too bad. They missed the whole thing.

Mr. Lemoncello floated in a graceful arc, then soared up to join the migrating Canadian geese now flocking in a V formation on the Wonder Dome video screens.

After leading the geese toward Montreal, Mr. Lemoncello drifted down to buzz and salute the statues perched atop the pillars at the base of the dome. The holographic heroes were different again. Kyle turned around so he could read all their names: Amelia Earhart, Charles Lindbergh, Neil Armstrong, Bessie Coleman, Jimmy Doolittle, Howard Hughes, Sally Ride, Billy Mitchell, the Tuskegee Airmen, and some kind of monk whose pedestal was labeled "Eilmer of Malmesbury."

"They're all famous aviators," said Miguel as Mr. Lemoncello executed a tucked-knee roll and soared around the rotunda like Peter Pan.

Actually, he flew *exactly* like the star of a touring production of *Peter Pan* that Kyle had seen at the civic center.

Because now, in the shafts of sunlight streaming through the arched windows at the base of the dome, Kyle could see cables hooked to a harness under Mr. Lemoncello's wings.

As he spread out his arms and fluttered toward the floor, the audience applauded wildly.

"Thank you, thank you," said Mr. Lemoncello when his feet finally touched down.

He slipped out of his flying harness, and his wings shot back up toward the ceiling.

"Yowza! That's almost as much fun as the hover ladders. Almost. Teams, your first challenge today is to make your ideas take flight, something that's very easy to do inside a library."

"So long as nobody bulldozes it down!" cried Mrs. Gause, whose flickering image was still being projected behind the circulation desk.

"Yes. Thank you for that, Lonni." Mr. Lemoncello pushed up his goggles. "Dr. Zinchenko? Will you kindly take over? I must go assemble our esteemed panel of judges."

"Of course." Dr. Z popped up behind the center desk like a hand puppet. Mrs. Gause disappeared.

"Amaze me!" cried Mr. Lemoncello as he dashed toward the towering fiction bookshelves and disappeared through another secret door that whooshed sideways in the shelves.

"Teams," said Dr. Zinchenko, "on each of your worktables, you will find a sheet of eight-and-a-half-by-eleven paper, one standard paper clip, three inches of tape, one plastic bag containing a dollop of glue, and a stapler loaded with three staples."

Kyle and his teammates checked out their reading desk. Everything on Dr. Z's supply list was arranged in a tidy row.

"To win today's first competition, you must design the paper airplane that stays aloft the longest. In the case of a tie, our esteemed panel of judges will also award points for style and what aviators call derring-do."

At the Midwest team's desk, Marjory Muldauer shot her hand into the air and waved it around annoyingly.

"Yes? Is there a question?"

"Just one," said Marjory, folding her arms across her chest. "What does building a paper airplane have to do with the study of library science?"

"Simple," said Dr. Zinchenko. "The flight test will take place in three hours, at precisely one o'clock. You may use the intervening time and the library's vast resources to do research before building your planes. Or not. The choice, as always, is yours."

22

The 700s room on the second floor (named for the Dewey decimal designation for the arts) was crowded with Library Olympians.

Every team had raced up the steps, hoping to be the first to grab *The Paper Airplane Book* by Seymour Simon. Its call number was 745.592.

Fortunately, the Lemoncello Library had eight copies of the book on its shelves.

"You guys?" whispered Miguel after the team had grabbed their copy of the book and huddled together under a Nerf basketball hoop in a secluded nook so they could talk without all the other teams overhearing what they were saying. "Everybody's reading this same book."

"Because there are all sorts of neat paper airplane designs in here," said Sierra.

"But," said Kyle, "if we follow one of these sketches, our plane will end up being just like everybody else's."

"We need my dad," said Akimi.

"Huh?" said Miguel.

"Well, not my dad, exactly. But someone with his architect-slash-engineer brain."

Miguel slapped his forehead with his palm. He had an idea.

"Aerospace engineering," he whispered.

"Six hundred and twenty-nine point one," added Sierra.

It was Akimi's turn to say, "Huh?"

"Sorry. That's the Dewey decimal number for aviation engineering."

"Oh. Right. I knew that."

"It's next door," said Kyle, checking out the other teams. All seven of them had settled in at collaboration stations to pore through the paper airplane book. "Follow my lead, guys."

He loudly closed their copy of the paper airplane book. "Okay, team. I think that'll work. Come on. Let's go fold some paper and use our paper clip."

"And the glue," said Akimi. "Don't forget, we have a whole dollop of glue."

The four teammates sauntered out of the 700s room. Miguel whistled casually. Sierra hummed along.

The other teams were too busy debating the design of their paper airplanes to pay them much attention.

When Kyle, Akimi, Miguel, and Sierra slipped next door to the 600s room, the place was empty. Since the 600s were all about technology and applied sciences, the team passed several animated exhibits and dioramas depicting inventions and one about industrial gases, which used Mr. Lemoncello's patented smell-a-vision technology and reeked of rotten eggs.

"Great," muttered Akimi. "We had to come in here on sulfur day."

When they turned the corner at the end of a bookshelf labeled "629–632," they saw a holographic image of a bald man with a paintbrush mustache projected behind a desk. He wore a three-piece wool suit and fiddled with a small rocket.

"That looks like Robert Goddard," said Akimi. "My dad told me about him. Goddard invented the first liquid-fueled rocket."

"He's also on an old airmail stamp," said Miguel.

The others gave him quizzical looks.

"Stamp collecting is a very interesting hobby."

"Robert Goddard really was a rocket scientist," said Akimi. "Maybe he can help us design a better paper airplane."

The teammates moved closer to the hologram's very real metal desk.

"Hello," the hologram said, "my name is Robert. You can call me Bob. I designed and built airplanes and space-ships. When I was your age, I was considered a nerd. Now I'm on an airmail stamp."

"See?" said Miguel. "Told you."

"Professor Goddard," said Akimi, "what's the best design for our paper airplane?"

"That depends on your objective. Are you going for distance or aeronautical acrobatics?"

"Distance, sir," said Akimi. "Whoever can keep their paper plane aloft the longest wins."

"Then you should be folding what we rocket scientists call a glider."

"Because it glides?" asked Kyle.

"Precisely. I suggest going with a Seagull. Remember to line up the wing flaps for good balance. Set the dihedral angle flat or slightly up, the vertical stabilizers to approximately forty-five degrees to the plane of the wings . . ."

"The plane has a plane?" Kyle was totally lost.

"Keep going," said Akimi, who apparently understood engineer mumbo jumbo.

"Do not use the elevators or your craft will stall."

"No worries," said Miguel. "We always use the spiral staircases."

Akimi and Goddard stared at him.

"Never mind these guys," said Akimi. "I understand what you mean. My dad designed the library's front doors."

"Incorporating the old bank's vault door?"

"Yep."

"I am impressed," said Bob. "Will you be the one launching the craft?"

"Yes," said Kyle, Miguel, and Sierra.

"Excellent. Use a soft or medium throw by gripping the underside of the nose. This aircraft flies best when launched level or at a slight up angle from a high place. A detailed schematic with complete instructions is available in the top drawer of my desk. Good luck. And happy paper-folding!"

Robert Goddard vanished.

Kyle pulled open the desk drawer.

There were eight copies of the Seagull paper airplane design.

"I guess there's one for every team," he said.

"If they think to come in here," said Miguel.

But none of them did.

They were too busy, back at their worktables down in the Rotunda Reading Room, folding the paper airplanes they had chosen from that one book in the 700s room.

At one p.m., the eight teams brought their finished aircraft up to the third floor.

The eight designated fliers stepped up to the balcony railing, where they were joined by Dr. Zinchenko and the panel of holographic judges: Orville and Wilbur Wright, Amelia Earhart, Neil Armstrong, and Leonardo da Vinci.

The spectators were ringed around the rotunda, eagerly anticipating the paper aircraft taking flight.

Leonardo, decked out in his flowing robes and floppy Renaissance cap, gave the prelaunch countdown: "*Cinque, quattro, tre, due, uno*—blast off!"

Eight paper airplanes took off. The crowd cheered, rooting for their favorite fliers.

"That's one small toss for a sheet of paper," said Neil Armstrong, "one giant heave for paperkind."

Most of the paper airplanes drifted in looping circles, spiraling down the three stories under the dome in one or two minutes.

Akimi's carefully constructed Seagull, however, stayed aloft for four whole minutes. The audience gasped in astonishment as it glided along, scarcely losing altitude. Finally, after what seemed like forever, it gently drifted to the floor, where it made a soft landing.

"Woo-hoo!" shouted Kyle.

He looked down and saw Akimi's father in the audience on the first floor. Akimi's dad marched over to the winning glider, proudly plucked it off the floor, and gave his daughter a thumbs-up!

"Thanks, Dad!" Akimi shouted.

Orville and Wilbur Wright announced that the hometown team's glider had just set a new "hand-folded paper plane" indoor flight-time record.

"And it didn't get lost," added Amelia Earhart.

Akimi accepted the team's Top Gun medal from Dr. Zinchenko.

And just like that, the Hometown Heroes were tied for first place.

23

"And now," announced Dr. Zinchenko, "it is time for today's second game. This way, please."

The teams followed her from the third-floor railing to the nearby Electronic Learning Center. All the video games and flight simulators were dark. The arcade was eerily quiet. Kyle noticed something new in what had always been his favorite room in the library: One whole wall was covered, floor to ceiling, with a panoramic (but blank) video screen. As Kyle squinted at the wide swath of shiny white, he noticed a series of evenly spaced glowing green LEDs at eye level on the wall.

Kyle couldn't move closer to examine the screen, because the area fifteen feet in front of it had been fenced off with a series of brass poles and velvet ropes.

Suddenly, the floor on the other side of the ropes opened. Up came the smiling head and extremely long

neck of a life-size *Apatosaurus*—what everybody used to call a *Brontosaurus*, thanks to *The Flintstones.*

The giant dinosaur had leaves stuck between its teeth. Its breath reeked of rancid salad, smelling worse than the middle school cafeteria that time all the refrigerators stopped working on Taco Tuesday.

"Woo-weee!" cried Mr. Lemoncello, who, in a complete cowboy costume, was riding in a saddle strapped around the giant audio-animatronic *Apatosaurus*'s neck. "I knew the dinosaurs were extinct, but I didn't know they were extra stinky, too." He took in a deep breath. "Ah, isn't smell-a-vision wondermous?"

He unbuckled some sort of seat belt and hopped out of his saddle.

"Thank you, Brontie," he said to the big *Apatosaurus*. "By the way, I love your sister Charlotte. Now, please—go floss."

The enormous creature roared pleasantly, rattling all the blank video screens in the game room, then disappeared back into the floor, which closed up around it like a collapsing ring of tiles.

"Since today is all about flights of fancy and fancy flights, our next contest is to see which of you would make the paleontologically perfect prehistoric pterodactyl."

Mr. Lemoncello flung open his arms toward the wide screen filling the back wall.

"This room was recently equipped with my Imagination Factory's brand-new, revolutionary Gesticulatron

Gameware. Motion sensors in that hugerific video wall can read a gamer's body language and use human gestures to control the actions of your avatar inside the video game. Yes, with the Lemoncello Gesticulatron Motion Detector, you can fly through the sky like Harriet the Spy, if Harriet the Spy could fly."

Marjory Muldauer sighed very audibly and, once again, shot her arm into the air.

"I see from my own internal gesticulation sensors that we have a question," said Mr. Lemoncello. "Either that or Ms. Muldauer is attempting to hail a taxi indoors."

All the other kids (including Marjory's teammates) chuckled.

Marjory ignored them.

"Yes, Ms. Muldauer?" said Mr. Lemoncello.

"What does flying like a dinosaur have to do with libraries?"

"Actually," said Mr. Lemoncello, "pterodactyls were not dinosaurs but rather flying reptiles that existed from the Late Triassic through the Jurassic and most of the Cretaceous eras. They missed, however, the disco era, for which they were extremely grateful. All of this information I first learned, years ago, at my local library. Now we can learn even more by bringing these extinct creatures back to virtual yet historically accurate life. This is how the library of the future can present the facts of the past. Dr. Zinchenko? Kindly explain how this next game will be played." He tugged at his fringed leggings. "I'll

be monitoring this fourth contest from my private suite down the hall. I need to change out of my chaps before I chafe."

Spurs jingling, Mr. Lemoncello moseyed out of the Electronic Learning Center.

"For our next competition," announced Dr. Zinchenko, "each team will choose one player who will report back here in two hours. Your chosen flier will, with arm gestures and body movements, control the flight of a single pterodactyl. The player to reach the finish line of our airborne obstacle course first will be today's second medalist. Launch time is four p.m. Until then, all of the library's vast resources are available to you. Including, of course, all the games here in the Electronic Learning Center."

The blackened video screens on all the game consoles filling the room sprang to life. Dings, pings, bells, whoops, and techno music filled the air.

"Awesome," said a kid from the Southeast team when the Mars rover simulator whirred awake. "Who wants to race around the rings of Saturn with me?"

Kyle was tempted.

In fact, he was practically drooling.

Then Akimi tapped him on the shoulder.

"You're flying our pterodactyl, correct?"

"Sure. If you guys think I should."

"Yo," said Miguel. "It's a video game. You're our gamer."

"The only flying I've ever done," said Sierra, "was with

115

Max, Fang, Iggy, and Nudge in James Patterson's Maximum Ride books."

Kyle stared at all the kids blasting through outer space, flinging catapults of fire at castle walls, or scuba diving with dolphins on the glowing game screens surrounding him.

"So," he said, sighing, "where do I learn about dinosaurs?"

"The five hundreds room," his three teammates said in unison (because they'd all paid attention during those after-school Dewey decimal drills).

"It's downstairs," said Akimi. "Right below us. You can't miss it. There's a big *Apatosaurus* named Brontie inside."

24

With his teammates' help, Kyle found several books about flying creatures from the prehistoric era.

Pterodactyls had wings formed by a thin skin and muscle membrane stretching from one of their elongated fingers to their hind limbs. They looked like four-legged, pointy-nosed kites.

"They ate meat and fish," said Miguel. "Guess they wouldn't go for that birdseed Andrew's always pouring into Mr. Peckleman's bird feeders back at the motel."

"Why does that crazy old guy like birds so much?" said Akimi, flipping through a dinosaur picture book. "There are gobs of white bird poop splatted all over the cars in the motel parking lot."

"He's a birdbrain," said Miguel. "Get it? Bird-brain?"

"Yeah," said Akimi. "I got it."

"Have you ever played one of these motion-sensor games?" Sierra asked Kyle.

"Once. My cousin has a Kinect on his Xbox 360. We played a game where you karate kick and shoot lightning bolts at each other."

"Cool," said Miguel.

"Totally. But I'm guessing Mr. Lemoncello's Gesticula-tron technology is way more sophisticated."

Kyle's team wasn't the only group in the 500s room doing dinosaur research. Several other teams had had the same idea. Just about every book about pterosaurs (from the Greek words for "wing" and "lizard") was flying off the shelves.

When it was nearly four o'clock, a slender boy in blue jeans from the Southwest team sauntered over to Kyle, Akimi, Sierra, and Miguel, who were slumped in beanbag chairs resembling dinosaur eggs.

"Excellent display of aviation engineering," he said. "Your glider design was flawless."

"Thanks. I'm Akimi Hughes." She shot out her hand. "I was chief engineer on the paper airplane project."

"I'm Angus Harper. From Texas."

"My dad's an engineer," said Akimi, sounding sort of self-satisfied. "Guess I'm just hardwired to design stuff."

Harper nodded. "My dad's a test pilot. He's been givin' me flyin' lessons since I was six."

"You're kidding," said Kyle, closing his dinosaur book.

"Nope. I've already been offered an appointment to the United States Air Force Academy."

"Even though you're still in middle school?" said Sierra.

"Well, I guess some of us are just 'hardwired' to be flyboys."

"So," said Miguel, clearing his throat, "who's going to fly the pterodactyl for your team?"

"I reckon I might give it a whirl. See you folks upstairs."

Angus Harper ambled away.

"So," Kyle said to Sierra, "tell me about those kids in Maximum Ride. How exactly did *they* fly?"

"Genetic mutation," said Sierra.

"Oh. Guess we don't really have time for that. . . ."

"Don't worry, bro," Miguel told Kyle. "If the Texas Tornado takes the next medal, we'll still be tied for first place."

"Yeah," said Akimi. "With three other teams."

At exactly four p.m., Kyle stood on a pair of glowing green footprints in a line with seven other contestants facing the blank video wall.

Television cameras were set up in the Electronic Learning Center so spectators, in the library and at home, could watch the great flying reptile race. The illuminated floor markers put six feet of space between each player. That way, they'd have plenty of room to flap and flail their arms.

Angus Harper was on Kyle's right.

A girl from the Northeast team, wearing a hijab, was on his left.

She was staring at Kyle.

"Um, hi," he said. "I'm Kyle."

"Yes. I am aware of this fact."

"So, uh, what's your name?"

"Abia Sulayman. And you will soon be eating my exhaust fumes."

Kyle nodded. "Good to know."

Dr. Zinchenko paced in front of the players, her hands clasped firmly behind her back.

"The motion sensors in the screen will detect your arm, head, and torso movement," she explained. "Do not step off your footprint markers at any time during today's race. If you do, you will lose control of your flying reptile and it will crash. If you wish to go left, lean that way. To go right, lean right. Raise your head to gain elevation; look down at the floor to dive or swoop. When you flap your arms, your pterodactyl will flap its wings. Any questions?"

"Yes, ma'am," said Angus. "How do we gun our bird? I feel the need—the need for speed."

"To accelerate, simply flap your arms faster. However, be advised: The faster you fly, the more energy your pterodactyl will consume. Your winged avatar will have a 'life battery' icon glowing on its back. If you burn through your fuel, you will also crash. The object of this game is to be the first to safely reach the volcano crater on the island at the far side of the sea."

As Dr. Zinchenko spoke, the wall behind her turned into a spectacular prehistoric world. Kyle could see dinosaurs munching on tall tree branches far off in the rain forest. Then a *Tyrannosaurus rex* roared and stomped through the leafy jungle, causing a leaping herd of *Velociraptors* to screech and flee. It was like being inside that movie *Jurassic Park*. All the creatures Kyle had read about and studied in the dinosaur books downstairs were now swarming across the giant video screen in front of him.

"Give me eight pterodactyls," Dr. Zinchenko called out. Instantly, eight winged creatures appeared on the screen, one stationed in front of each player.

"Flap your arms," instructed Dr. Zinchenko.

The eight players did. The flying reptiles beat their wings up and down in sync with their human counterparts.

Suddenly, a massive image of Mr. Lemoncello's face appeared on the video wall.

"Release the kraken!" he cried.

And the pterodactyl race was on.

25

Kyle flapped his arms and raised his chin.

His flying reptile soared toward the sky.

The game was responding like his cousin's Xbox, only Mr. Lemoncello's body-motion sensors were, as Kyle had suspected they might be, much more sophisticated and sensitive.

He tilted his body sideways and his dino-bird sliced through the narrow opening in a vine-tangled clump of prehistoric trees.

After clearing that obstacle, Kyle quickly ducked left to escape the gaping jaws of a lunging *Tyrannosaurus rex*. Eight of those screeching, short-armed monsters had appeared to snap at the eight flying pterodactyls.

Three of Kyle's competitors went down, including the kid from Marjory Muldauer's team.

Angus Harper and Abia Sulayman were just off Kyle's wings. He cleared the *T. rex* trap and reached a sandy beach where some smaller dinosaurs were building nests. Kyle waved his arms and soared across the choppy sea.

On the distant horizon, Kyle could see a volcano spewing molten lava. The finish line.

He flapped his arms faster.

When he did, the battery icon on the back of his pterodactyl dipped down to three-quarters. Dr. Zinchenko had been right. Flying fast drained your dino-bird's life force even faster.

Suddenly, another "flying reptile" from the dinosaur books appeared in the sky: a giant *Pteranodon* with a thirty-foot wingspan. It was four times as wide as the other fliers and shrieked at the runts in the pterodactyl pack.

Kyle kept his cool and aimed his reptile into what he hoped would be the *Pteranodon*'s blind spot. The bigger beast gobbled down one flier, which freaked out Stephanie Youngerman from the Mountain team. She shrieked, jumped off her floor mark, and crashed into the ocean.

Only Kyle, Angus, and Abia were left in the race.

"If I was flying any faster," Angus shouted, "I'd catch up with tomorrow!"

"Where you would meet me!" cried the girl.

The two kids flailed their arms furiously. Both of their avatars shot off like rocket ships, streaking the cloudless sky with white contrails.

Kyle could see Abia tuck in her arms and shoulders, making her profile sleekly aerodynamic. She inched ahead of Angus.

Kyle tried his best to mimic Abia's moves but was buffeted in the wake created by her back draft. He moved his arms up and down and up and down until he looked like a berserk bicycle pump.

He whooshed forward faster but his battery icon dipped down to one-quarter. Its green light was on its way to red.

And the volcanic island was still miles away.

No way would Kyle make it without running out of juice.

He pulled back on his speed, wishing this flying pterodactyl game came with power pellets of some kind. In most video games, there was some way to restore life force after you'd been weakened, and play on. But in this game, there was nothing except the two other pterodactyls, the ocean, and the distant volcano.

Then Kyle remembered something from his library research.

The pterodactyl was a carnivore.

It ate meat and fish.

Maybe there were some virtual fish in the virtual ocean below.

It was worth a shot.

He lowered his chin and sent his dino-bird swooping into a dive, then leveled it out when it was just a few inches above the video ocean's churning waves.

The water was swarming with fish.

Kyle opened his mouth.

The pterodactyl opened its long spiky jaws.

Kyle did a goosenecked head bob.

The pterodactyl bobbed and scooped up a mouthful of fish.

Kyle heard a *WHIRR-DING!* sound effect as his red battery icon glowed green and grew from nearly empty to completely full. Raising his head, Kyle gained altitude and zipped across the sky.

He leveled off and aimed for the volcano. Abia Sulayman, who was maybe three hundred feet ahead of him, stalled in midair. Her battery icon was solid red. Kyle shot past her. She dropped like a chunk of fossilized dinosaur bone.

Ahead, Angus Harper appeared to be flying on vapors—barely sputtering, lurching and jerking forward.

His battery icon went red just as Kyle zipped past him.

"You must've cheated!" Harper screamed right before his pterodactyl plummeted to its watery grave.

"Nope!" shouted Kyle, executing a pretty nifty barrel roll by swiveling his hips. "I just did my homework!"

When Kyle's pterodactyl reached the volcano, a hot-air balloon rose from the smoldering basin. In the balloon's wicker gondola was a video-game image of Mr. Lemoncello dressed like the Wizard of Oz.

"Hearty and splendiferous congratulations, Kyle Keeley," boomed Mr. Lemoncello. "You played hard but

you studied harder. You are the true Lord of the Fliers. Therefore, by the power vested in me by the electric company, even though they didn't know I would be wearing a vest today, I hereby award you the Olympian Researcher medal for meritorious fish mongering. Tonight, at Olympia Village, in honor of your cleverosity, you and your teammates shall feast upon fish sticks and Filet-O-Fish sandwiches."

Kyle hoped there might be some kind of cake for dinner, too, because he and his teammates definitely had something to celebrate.

All of a sudden, they were in the lead!

26

Marjory Muldauer watched as the triumphant Kyle Keeley and his happy crew of crumbums climbed into their bookmobile.

All four were merrily flapping their arms, giving each other high and low fives.

Marjory still couldn't believe what she had just witnessed. Kids waving their arms up and down to make fake video creatures fly to a phony volcano?

Shame on you, Mr. Lemoncello, she thought, seething. *If I didn't need a scholarship to even think about attending college, I'd quit these inane games!*

Marjory and her teammates climbed into their bookmobile for the ride back to Olympia Village, which, in her opinion, was really just a cheesy, mid-level extended stay motel—the kind of place typically frequented by sketchy traveling salespeople and high school athletics teams.

Marjory grabbed a book off a shelf in the back. *Bleak House* by Charles Dickens. It matched her mood.

"Shake it off, you guys," coached Margaret Miles, the librarian who was one of the Midwest team's chaperones. "So what if the Ohio kids won two medals today? There are eight more games left to play. This thing is far from over."

"That Kyle Keeley kid is good," said Nicole Wisniewski, one of Marjory's wimpy teammates. "He was smart, the way he recharged his pterodactyl's battery."

"He's a gamer," Marjory snapped at Nicole. "Of course he won the video game. But he doesn't know diddly about the Dewey decimal system. That's why I beat him in the book reshelving game."

"Actually," said Nicole, "we all beat him."

Marjory blew her teammate a wet raspberry. "Yeah. Right. Like you guys would've had a chance without me."

"Marjory?" said Ms. Miles. "Remember, there is no 'I' in 'team.'"

So? thought Marjory. *Because there is definitely an "m" and an "e" for me!*

To chill out after such a lousy day, Marjory headed into the motel lobby and started reorganizing the rack of tourist brochures.

All the other Library Olympians, including Marjory's worthless teammates, were at the pizza place next door to the motel, having dinner and probably playing more mind-numbing video games.

Andrew Peckleman, the boy with the Olympic-sized goggle glasses who worked at the motel, came into the lobby when she was about halfway done.

"Are you going with an alphabetical classification system or something a bit more complex?"

"I'm categorizing them according to attraction type," said Marjory. "Outdoor activities, historical sites, shopping opportunities—subcategorized, of course, into fashion, antiques, and souvenirs."

"Of course," said Andrew.

"And, over here, you'll find dining options."

Andrew smiled. "Isn't informational organization awesome?"

"Yes," said Marjory. "It's certainly more intellectually stimulating than video games."

"Rough day at the Library Olympics?"

"Ha! That Lemoncello Library is as ridiculous and absurd as Mr. Lemoncello himself."

"True," said Andrew through his nose. "I'm afraid Mr. Lemoncello doesn't like libraries qua libraries."

Marjory nearly gasped. "You use the word 'qua'?"

"Yes," said Andrew, finger-sliding his glasses up the bridge of his nose. "But only when its usage is appropriate."

A lady wearing a fur-fringed jacket floated into the lobby.

"Hello, Andrew."

"Oh, hello, Mrs. Chiltington. What're you doing here?"

"I came to see Miss Muldauer."

"Who are you?" asked Marjory. "And why do you have a dead animal wrapped around your neck?"

"There's a slight nip in the air, dear. Andrew, would you kindly excuse us? I need to talk to Miss Muldauer in private."

"But . . ."

"Andrew?" his uncle Woody called from outside the front doors. "We need to go grease the baffles on the bird feeders."

"Right now?"

"The sooner, the better. I noticed a squirrel having an upside-down feast on feeder number eight. We need to put an end to that. A slicker surface might do the trick."

"But . . ."

"Say goodbye to Marjory, Andrew," suggested Mrs. Chiltington.

"Okay. See you later, Marjory. I have to go to work."

Mrs. Chiltington waited for him and his uncle to walk down the driveway.

Then she pounced.

"Miss Muldauer, may I be frank with you?"

Marjory shrugged. "I don't care."

"I came here this evening as a representative of the League of Concerned Library Lovers."

"Who are they?"

"A group of local citizens who love libraries and

consider Mr. Luigi L. Lemoncello to be a threat to all that we hold dear."

"The man is a major-league wackaloon," said Marjory.

"That he is." Mrs. Chiltington glanced around to make absolutely certain they were alone in the lobby. "I was wondering if you might be able to help Mr. Peckleman and I with a small . . . *project?*"

"I'm kind of busy trying to win these games."

"This won't take much of your time. I promise. But if we work together, I feel confident, we will both be quite satisfied with the end result."

"What do you mean?"

"With your assistance, Marjory, I firmly believe we will convince Mr. Lemoncello to abandon his infantile and dangerously contagious ideas about how a library should be run. Certain things don't belong in our temples of knowledge. Things like flying dinosaur video games."

"So why do you need me?"

"Because the books in the Lemoncello Library are currently off-limits to everyone except you thirty-two Olympians."

"What?" said Marjory, arching an eyebrow. "You want me to check out a book?"

"That's right, Marjory. A book. Just one."

"We can't. Not during the games."

"You strike me as a clever young lady. Surely you can find a way to skirt the rules?"

"But what about my scholarship?"

"Do this for me, and you won't need Mr. Lemoncello's money. Mr. Peckleman and I will personally guarantee funding for your college education. Call it a 'Go to College Free' card. My family is extremely wealthy, Marjory. Has been for centuries."

Interesting. By removing one book from the stacks, Marjory could help these locals put an end to Mr. Lemoncello's misguided notions about how a library should be run and, at the same time, earn herself a full-ride college scholarship.

"So, what makes this one book so special?"

"It is, as they say, the straw that will break the camel's back. Once it leaves the Alexandriaville Public Library, we feel quite confident that Mr. Luigi Lemoncello will want to leave, too."

Kyle wasn't worried when Dr. Zinchenko made her morning announcements at Olympia Village on day three of the
games.

"Today's two competitions will both be centered on
books."

Kyle knew Sierra Russell could handle anything bookish the game makers threw at her.

"Today's your day to shine," he told her.

"I'll do my best," said Sierra.

When the bookmobiles arrived at the Lemoncello
Library, the security guards, Clarence and Clement, gave
each team member a brand-new smartphone.

"You will need it for today's first game," said Clarence.

"But you get to keep it, too," added Clement.

Sweet, thought Kyle. Even if his team lost this round,
they'd all just scored some excellent swag.

The eight teams were assigned work desks in the rotunda. Spectators crowded around the edge of the circular room.

"Please access the Web browser on your phones," said Dr. Zinchenko from her position behind the central desk, "and go to Lemoncello.it."

Kyle did. Then he helped Sierra do it, too. Miguel and Akimi were fine on their own.

"Please enter game code one-zero-zero-two-four."

All the players did.

"Excellent," said Dr. Zinchenko.

Overhead, the Wonder Dome turned into a giant game screen reading "Welcome to the Battle of the Books."

"Please enter your first and last names and, when you have done so, tap 'Join Game.' When you are all online, I, as the quizmaster, will show you a series of ten questions, each one with four possible answers. For each question, you will have ten seconds to make your selection on your phone screen. Lemoncello.it will instantaneously calculate your score based on correctness and speed of answering. It will then post a leaderboard for the top five players. In the event of a tie, the team with the most players in the top five will be awarded today's first medal, the Libris."

Up on the Wonder Dome, thirty-two brightly colored names in a balloon font popped into view as the players finished tapping them into their phones.

"Let us begin," said Dr. Zinchenko. "First question: In which book does a character bounce a pinecone off some-one's head?"

Tense, clock-ticking music throbbed out of the Rotunda Reading Room's hidden speakers.

Four answers were displayed on the dome, each identified with a geometric shape. A square for *Ungifted* by Gordon Korman, a triangle for *A Tangle of Knots* by Lisa Graff, a hexagon for *Twerp* by Mark Goldblatt, and an oval for *The Postcard* by Tony Abbott.

"The square," whispered Sierra.

Kyle, Akimi, and Miguel didn't waste any time second-guessing her answer, because the countdown clock had already slid from ten seconds to five by the time they'd finished reading all the possible answers.

A gong sounded when the timer hit zero. The red square for *Ungifted* lit up and was given a check mark as the correct answer. According to the scoreboard on the ceiling, thirty of the thirty-two players had answered correctly, including, of course, all four players from Ohio.

"Way to go, Sierra!" said Kyle.

"Question two," said Dr. Zinchenko. "The Watson family went to Birmingham, Alabama, in 1963. In what city did the Watson family actually live?"

Four choices filled all the phone screens: Detroit, Kansas City, Kalamazoo, and Flint.

"Flint," said Sierra.

All the players on the hometown team tapped the oval icon for Flint.

Sierra's answer, once again, was correct.

"Boo-yah," said Kyle.

Suddenly, Marjory Muldauer, two desks away, leapt up from her seat.

"Dr. Zinchenko?"

"Yes, Ms. Muldauer?"

She pointed at Sierra. "That girl from Ohio is telling her teammates what answer to give."

Trembling slightly, Sierra stood up, too. "Is that against the rules, Dr. Zinchenko?"

Kyle stood up beside her. "Because you didn't say we couldn't help each other."

"Yeah," said Miguel, standing up, too.

"What they said," added Akimi as she stood to join her teammates.

"You are correct," said Dr. Zinchenko. "I did not specifically state that collaboration would be prohibited."

"But it's cheating!" hollered Marjory. She whirled around and glared at Kyle. "This isn't flap-your-arms-and-do-the-chicken-dance, Kyle Keeley. This is serious. 'Battle of the Books' serious. Everybody on your team needs to know the material, inside and out."

"I agree with Miss Muldauer," boomed Mr. Lemoncello. His huge face, looking weirdly warped around the edges, was now filling all the video screens under the dome. "As much as I love teamwork, for this game, you all need to fly solo, like Han in Star Wars, although he always had Chewbacca in the copilot seat. But that is neither here nor there, because it is in a galaxy far, far away. Play on, Olympians. And henceforth, there shall be no consultation

amongst teammates. Kindly keep your eyes on your own phone."

The Battle of the Books continued.

Kyle got a couple of answers right on his own, but he took longer to respond than everybody else, so his name never appeared on the leaderboard again. After the ninth question was answered, Marjory Muldauer, Sierra Russell, and a girl from Knoxville, Tennessee, named Jennifer Greene were all tied for first place.

"Here is your final question," said Dr. Zinchenko. "Once again, you will have ten seconds to choose your answer. In which book is a toddler worshipped by cockroaches?"

Wow! Kyle actually knew that one, because the past summer he'd read the book. He quickly tapped the purple hexagon for *Gregor the Overlander* by Suzanne Collins, who had also written *The Hunger Games*.

The gong sounded.

Kyle's answer was correct.

Sierra's, however, wasn't.

"I'm sorry," she said. "I read that book when I was six. I forgot. . . ."

"It's okay," said Kyle.

Meanwhile, at the Midwest team's table, people were jumping up and doing bad potato-masher dances.

Jennifer Greene from the Southeastern team must've chosen the wrong answer, too. Because according to the leaderboard, Marjory Muldauer had just won the games' fifth medal.

28

"We're still tied for first place," Kyle reminded Sierra.

Sierra lowered her eyes. "But I let you guys down."

"Not really," said Akimi. "Did you see any of us winning that last game? I thought the cockroach book was *Harry Potter and the Prisoner of Azkaban,* because they eat Cockroach Clusters at Honeydukes."

"We'll win the next medal," said Miguel. "You'll see."

"Moving on to game six," said Dr. Zinchenko, still stationed behind the circular librarian's desk at the center of the room. "Please focus your eyes on the area between the lobby archway and the entrance to the Children's Room."

Clarence and Clement came into the rotunda to clear a path. Spectators gladly moved out of their way. The musclemen were both pretty ginormous.

"Players?" said Dr. Zinchenko. "This will be another

solo competition. Please pick one player to represent your team. A parade of costumed characters as well as stagehands carrying props will soon march from the lobby, promenade along the back wall, and exit into the Children's Room. Your chosen player will assemble the characters and props into titles of famous children's books. The player who can correctly figure out the titles and identify their authors the fastest will win our sixth medal, the 'I Did It!' "

"I played a mix-and-match game like this once in a magazine," said Miguel.

"Good," said Sierra. "You should be our player for this round."

"No way. You fall off a horse, what do you do?"

"Bruise your butt?" said Akimi.

"No," said Kyle with a laugh. "You climb right back into the saddle."

Miguel agreed. "This is your saddle, Sierra."

"I don't want to lose another game. . . ."

"You won't," said Kyle. "You're our number one bookworm. In a good way."

"Not in the icky insect-that-bores-through-paper way," added Akimi.

"Thanks," said Sierra. "I think."

"Let the title parade begin!" commanded Dr. Zinchenko.

A recorded brass band struck up a Sousa march as a bizarre assortment of costumed characters and prop

carriers strolled out of the lobby, around the edge of the circular room, and into the Children's Room.

Kyle couldn't make any sense of what he saw:

A white knight.

Two stagehands rolling a chest of drawers on wheels.

A knitter working on a very long Christmas stocking that dragged behind her on the floor.

A plate of eggs colored green.

A girl carrying a shiny purple purse.

An actress dressed up like a witch.

A boy dressed like a poor orphan in one of Charles Dickens's novels, carrying the letter "E."

Three waddling actors in penguin costumes.

A bouquet of daylilies.

An actor wearing a lion costume.

A slice of ham on a plate.

A man pushing a popcorn cart.

A paper moon.

And finally, one of the Alexandriaville reference librarians, Mrs. Maria Simon, carrying a crumpled copy of *Time* magazine.

"Oh-kay," said Kyle. "That was kind of random."

"No," said Sierra, her confidence returning. "It's pretty easy. You just have to put the pieces together. I can do this."

"Good," said Akimi. "Because I sure can't. All I got was *Green Eggs and Ham* by Dr. Seuss."

"What?" said Kyle. "How?"

"Yo," said Miguel. "One dude had a plate of green eggs, another had a slice of ham?"

"Oh. Right."

One by one, the teams sent a player into the Children's Room. When it was Sierra's turn, she went in and quickly came out with her list of book titles and authors:

1. *Goodnight Moon* by Margaret Wise Brown
2. *Green Eggs and Ham* by Dr. Seuss
3. *Lilly's Purple Plastic Purse* by Kevin Henkes
4. *The Lion, the Witch, and the Wardrobe* by C. S. Lewis
5. *Mr. Popper's Penguins* by Richard and Florence Atwater
6. *Pippi Longstocking* by Astrid Lindgren
7. *A Wrinkle in Time* by Madeleine L'Engle

"Whoa," said Akimi. "Wait a second. How'd you get 'Pippi Longstocking'? I remember the lady knitting the 'long stocking,' but how'd you get the 'Pippi' part?"

"Easy," said Sierra. "The Dickensian orphan boy was Pip from *Great Expectations,* and he was carrying the letter 'E,' making him Pip-E or, you know, Pippi."

"Brilliant," said Miguel. "I would've missed that one. I might've missed Mr. Popper, too. He was the guy pushing the popcorn wagon, right?"

Sierra nodded. "And, of course, Mrs. Simon with the crumpled copy of *Time* magazine was *A Wrinkle in Time* by Madeleine L'Engle."

"Nice," said Kyle. "Way to climb back on that horse."

The other seven players eventually put together the same list of titles that Sierra had.

But none of them did it as fast.

The home team picked up the "I Did It!" medal, and just like that, they were back in the lead.

29

On the fourth day of the competition, however, Kyle and his teammates didn't fare so well.

They lost the Bendable Bookworm medal to the Northeast team after a fierce game of Dewey Decimal Twister. The girl from Rhode Island, Cheryl Space, was extremely flexible.

The Mid-Atlantic team, led by a skinny kid from Maryland named Elliott Schilpp, who could do some serious damage to a plate of food, scored the Eating It Up medal for reading while eating.

In that game, played in the Book Nook Café, each team had to eat pizza while reading a Newbery Honor book from way back in the 1960s that none of the players had ever read before. When the pizza was gone, they had to answer a whole series of comprehension questions. The Mid-Atlantic gang devoured their pepperoni pies the

fastest and then nailed every single question about *When Shlemiel Went to Warsaw and Other Stories* by Isaac Bashevis Singer.

Kyle congratulated the kids from Maryland, Virginia, Delaware, and Pennsylvania.

"Thanks," they said, burping up pizza gas.

On the bookmobile ride back to the Olympia Village motel, Kyle realized that, at the end of the fourth day and eighth game, there were only two days and four games left.

Marjory Muldauer and the Midwest team hadn't picked up any new medals on day four, either, so Team Kyle was still in the lead.

The Hometown Heroes had three medals.

The Midwest team, starring Marjory Muldauer, had two.

The Pacific, Mid-Atlantic, and Northeast teams each had one.

"You guys?" said Kyle after doing the mental math. "We only need to win *two more medals* and we're the champions!"

Once again, Miguel started chanting that old song by Queen, "We Are the Champions."

Akimi joined in. Sierra, too.

Then the teammates belted out the chorus in four-part harmony.

"We are the champions, my friend!"

Kyle grinned.

He was definitely looking forward to his next cake day.

30

"What did you and Mrs. Chiltington talk about?" Andrew Peckleman asked Marjory Muldauer.

They were sitting together on the patio near the motel's stone-cold gas-powered fire pit.

"How much we both hate what Mr. Lemoncello's doing at his so-called library. Do you know what insane game they had us play today? Reading while eating."

Andrew shook his head in disbelief.

"And the food was pizza! Greasy, slimy, cheesy pizza!"

"Pizza spillage can cause major damage to books," said Andrew. "I've seen it. Back when I was a library aide at the middle school."

"I complained about the messiness, but Mr. Lemoncello popped in on a video screen to remind us that all the books being used in the read-and-eat contest were paperbacks."

"As if that makes a difference."

"Exactly. Loopy old Lemoncello said paperback books were meant to be taken to the beach, where they'd have suntan lotion, melting ice cream cones, and sand dribbled all over their pages."

"How ridiculous."

"I know. But Lemoncello said books did no one any good sealed up tight. He said books need to 'have their spines cracked, their covers opened, and their pages ruffled for them to come alive.'"

"The man's a menace," said Andrew.

"He's a lunatic."

"He needs to be stopped."

"Don't worry. We're working on it."

"Really? How?"

Marjory studied the nerdy boy in his goggle glasses. Yes, he seemed to be a true library lover, but Marjory couldn't trust him. She couldn't trust anybody—not when the future of library science was at stake.

"I can't say," she told Andrew. "But don't be surprised if Mr. Lemoncello leaves town. I understand he's turned his back on Alexandriaville before."

"Well, he left when he was like eighteen," said Andrew. "He moved to New York City to start his game company."

"And," said Marjory, "from what I've heard, he never once came back here until he cooked up his crazy scheme to build a new library in the old bank building as a big publicity stunt."

"Where'd you hear that?"

"Mrs. Chiltington."

"Huh. Mr. Lemoncello told us he built the library to honor the memory of Mrs. Gail Tobin. The librarian who helped him so much when he was our age."

"Ha! You believe that? That's just the clever spin Mr. Lemoncello's marketing department put on this scam." Marjory stood up. "But don't worry, Andrew. Your public library will soon be a true public library. Mr. Lemoncello will turn it over to a local board of trustees and flee."

"And he won't be coming back?"

"Highly doubtful."

"Wow. Thanks. I guess."

"You're welcome. Excuse me. I need a 641.2."

"Sure. Enjoy your beverage."

Marjory marched into the motel lobby, hoping to find a cold bottle of water. But, of course, the only free beverages the Lemoncello Library Olympics people had put on ice in the open coolers were chocolate milk, strawberry milk, and ten different kinds of soda pop, including something called Mr. Lemoncello's Lemonberry Fizz. All of it junk.

"And a lemon is not a berry, Mr. Lemoncello," Marjory muttered. "Look it up. Six-three-four-point-three-three-four. Lemons as an orchard crop. That means it's a fruit!"

Suddenly, a voice boomed through a megaphone. "Who would like to play another game?"

Mr. Lemoncello. It sounded like he was right outside.

"Will all Library Olympians kindly join me at the swimming pool? It's time to *dive* into another game!"

"Come on, Marjory," called Margaret Miles, the Midwest team's coach, hurrying across the lobby. "We're only down by one."

"I thought we were only supposed to play two games per day."

Margaret Miles laughed. "You know Mr. Lemoncello. He's all about keeping things a little unpredictable."

Which is precisely why he shouldn't be allowed anywhere near a library, thought Marjory.

Libraries were all about order, control, precision, and predictability!

And that's exactly how Mrs. Chiltington and her League of Concerned Library Lovers would run things when they became the board of trustees in charge of what used to be the Lemoncello Library.

To help them succeed (and to earn her scholarship from the Willoughby-Chiltington Family Trust), all Marjory had to do was remove one book from the library's shelves.

She had no qualms about it. No doubts or misgivings.

After all, that was what a library was supposed to do: lend out books, not dribble pizza sauce all over their pages.

She planned on borrowing the book Mrs. Chiltington had requested the very next day.

Marjory would earn her "Go to College Free" card.

And if things went the way Mrs. Chiltington said they would, the Alexandriaville Public Library would finally be free of Luigi Lemoncello.

31

"Surprise!" cried Mr. Lemoncello.

Marjory was standing on one side of the motel's swimming pool with the other contestants and their coaches. The blithering buffoon, Mr. Lemoncello, and his head librarian, Dr. Zinchenko, were standing on the other.

"As a library reaches out to the community surrounding it," said the bizarro billionaire, "so do the games of the first Library Olympiad!"

"So we're, like, gonna be playing game number nine right here?" said the blond boy from California, whom Marjory had already decided was an idiot. "Tonight?"

"Absolutamundo," said Mr. Lemoncello. "And although it's not easy being bad, this next game is. Easy, not bad. Then again, I already know all the answers, which makes any quiz easier, wouldn't you agree?"

Dr. Zinchenko tapped a switch box with the toe of her

red high-heeled shoe. An electric air pump *varoom*ed to life to inflate an enormous movie screen that rose beside her like a giant gorilla balloon outside a used-car lot.

"Our ninth game," said Dr. Zinchenko, "is inspired by the Dewey decimal classification 510."

"Mathematics!" shouted Marjory a half second before anybody else.

"Correct," said the librarian. "Solve two of these mathematically inspired picture puzzles before any of the other teams and you will earn our ninth medal, the Rebus!"

"Remember," said Mr. Lemoncello, "you only need two to win, which means we need at least nine puzzles. I think. I'll have to ask Morris, the moose. He's good with math. Anyway, here it is, your first puzzle! Dr. Zinchenko?"

She read from a stack of yellow note cards. "Name this fortress of intellectual freedom fighters."

Mr. Lemoncello snapped his fingers and the fully inflated video screen displayed an equation made up of pictures:

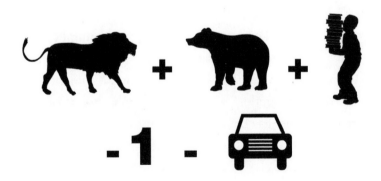

Marjory thought the game was absurd, but her mind went to work anyway. It was like a math equation. LION plus BEAR plus GUY WITH STACK OF BOOKS minus ONE minus CAR equaled what?

No. Wait. The third symbol had to be just one word, like all the others. The guy was carrying the books. CARRY?

Marjory added and subtracted the letters as quickly as she could. She mashed the letters all together: LION-BEARCARRY minus ONECAR.

L I O̶ N̶ B E A R C̶A̶R̶ R Y

That left L, I, B, A, R, R, Y.

An extremely easy word jumble.

"A library!" she shouted an instant before Kyle Keeley shouted it, too.

"I heard Miss Muldauer first," said Mr. Lemoncello. "That's one for the Midwest, America's heartland, home of all this great nation's Valentine's Day decorations. Well done!"

Marjory smirked.

If she could figure out one more puzzle, she'd win this game and, once again, be tied for first place.

She no longer needed to win Mr. Lemoncello's Library Olympics for the scholarship money.

But since she was already in the game, she wouldn't mind crushing Kyle Keeley.

Kyle was starting to panic.

If Marjory Muldauer solved the next "mathematical" picture puzzle, her team would have *three* medals, just like Team Kyle.

They'd be all tied up.

Again.

And once they were tied, it'd be much easier for the Midwest team to slip into the lead. Kyle's cake day might never come.

"Time for our second mathematically inspired picture puzzle," announced Mr. Lemoncello. "This one is the answer to a trivia question. Dr. Zinchenko, if you please?"

Dr. Zinchenko read a question off another yellow card. "In the year AD 35, the Roman emperor Caligula tried to ban a book because it expressed Greek ideals of freedom, which Caligula did not like, because Rome was occupying

Greece at the time. Which book did the Roman emperor try to ban?"

A new image filled the inflated screen:

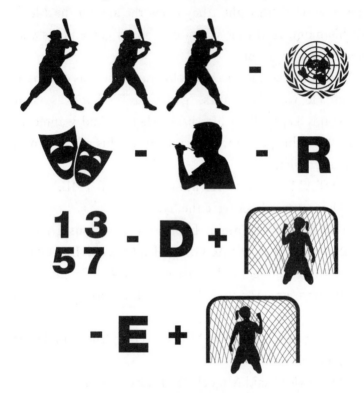

Kyle stared at the second puzzle.

He needed to decipher it, fast. No way was he letting Marjory Muldauer snag this one, too.

Three home runs minus the symbol for the United Nations.

That had to be HOME RUNS minus UN, or HOMERS!

"I think I know this," whispered Sierra.

Kyle's world shifted into super slow motion. In his head, he heard Miguel saying, "I think the answer is *Flubber*." The last time a game was on the line and Kyle listened to someone who "thought" they knew the answer, he'd lost. To his mom. And that was just a board game. This was way more important.

Kyle ignored Sierra. Made his mind race as fast as it could. He was the team's "game guy." That was what everybody kept telling him back when he had wanted to quit. Well, this puzzle was a game. It was his job to win it, no matter what.

THEATER minus EAT minus R equaled THE.

The last two lines were the hardest

ODD (numbers) minus D plus GOAL minus E plus a backward GOAL, or LAOG, equaled ODGOALLAOG.

Sierra tried to get Kyle's attention again. "Caligula was the Roman emperor in AD 35 and the book he banned was—"

"Hang on," said Kyle. "I just need to unscramble the last jumble."

"Yo, Kyle?" said Miguel. "Sierra has the answer."

"So do I," said Kyle. He turned to face Dr. Zinchenko and hollered, "Homer's *The Good Ol Gala*!"

"Wha-hut?" said Akimi the second Kyle blurted it out.

"Sorry," said Dr. Zinchenko, "that answer is incorrect."

"Homer's *The Odyssey*," said Marjory very coolly.

"Ha! That's wrong!" cried Kyle. "She didn't even use the 'G,' 'O,' 'A,' or 'L' from 'goal'!"

"Of course I didn't," said Marjory. "Because I believe that symbol is supposed to represent the word 'yes,' which backward would be 's-e-y.' But I didn't need the puzzle pictures. I knew the answer because, unlike some people, I've actually read a few history books."

"That's how I knew it, too," sighed Sierra.

"Ms. Muldauer's answer is correct," said Mr. Lemoncello. "The Midwest team has won two out of two, and therefore, they have also won the Rebus medal. And, if my own mental math is correct, the Midwest team now has three medals, which equals the same number currently held by the hometown team. It's a three-for-all! A tie! Wow, isn't math marvelous?"

"Way to go, *mon capitaine*," said Akimi, knuckle-punching Kyle in the arm. "Next time, try to remember you're on a *team*."

Kyle and his teammates, along with all the other Library Olympians, were allowed to sleep in the next morning, because thanks to the surprise poolside contest, there would be only one game played that day.

Of course, Kyle didn't want to sleep in. He wanted to get back in the arena ASAP and retake the lead.

He didn't like being tied with Marjory Muldauer.

He didn't like knowing his team had lost the poolside pop quiz because he'd blurted out the wrong answer and hadn't let Sierra say the right one.

He also didn't like being *this close* to losing.

Kyle and Miguel were sitting in the Olympia Village dining room, pushing the bobbing yellow marshmallows around in their Lucky Lemoncello Lumps cereal bowls.

"Sorry about blowing it last night," he said to Miguel.

"Don't apologize to me. Tell Sierra."

"I will. But now we still have to win *two* of the last three games."

"Not necessarily, bro. If one of the teams with no medals or just one medal beats us, we're still in a tie with—"

"Miguel?" Kyle snapped. "We *need* to win two more games."

"Yo. Ease up, Kyle."

"Ease up? If we lose this thing, do you know what people are going to say about us? That we just got lucky the first time. That Charles Chiltington probably would've won the escape game if Mr. Lemoncello hadn't kicked him out on a technicality."

"Yeah. They might say that. Or they might say, 'You win some, you lose some.' But what counts is how you play the game."

"Well, I am not playing to lose, Miguel."

"Hey, neither am I. And I'm not playing alone."

"I know. And we need you to step it up a little."

"What?"

"You're the only member of our team who hasn't won a single medal."

"Gee, Kyle, thanks for reminding me."

"Have you guys seen Marjory Muldauer?" asked Akimi as she and Sierra joined the boys at the breakfast table. "I like to keep my eye on our competition at all times."

"What about all these other kids?" said Sierra, gesturing to the tables filled with the country's top young bibliophiles. "They're our competition, too."

Akimi blew that off with a wave of her hand.

"Come on, Sierra. Little Miss Library from Michigan has won every single one of the Midwest team's medals for them. She's our only real threat. Especially if Kyle keeps hogging the ball and missing his shots."

Kyle sighed. "I'm really sorry about shouting out the wrong answer last night, Sierra."

"Apology accepted," said Sierra. "Next time, maybe you could, I don't know, trust me?"

Kyle nodded. "Definitely."

Akimi craned her neck and checked out all the other tables. "So where is Marjory?"

"She went to the library early," said Andrew Peckleman, who was rolling a rubber barrel between tables to collect people's breakfast trash. "She wanted to do some studying, so my uncle drove her over there."

"What's she studying?" asked Kyle.

"How to beat you," whined Andrew.

"And how's she going to do that, Andrew? What'd she find to study at the library when none of us even know what the tenth game is going to be?"

"I don't know. Do I look like a mind reader?"

"No, Andrew, I'd say you look like a garbage man."

"Kyle?" said Sierra, shaking her head. "That wasn't nice."

"In fact," said Akimi, "it was downright nasty."

"Yeah," said Miguel, with his arms crossed over his chest. "What is with you today?"

"Sorry, Andrew," said Kyle. "I'm just a little on edge."

"Well, you should be," said Andrew, adjusting his goggle glasses. "Because Marjory Muldauer is going to kick your butt, and I can't wait to watch her kicking it. Now, if you will excuse me, I have more garbage to collect."

Andrew pushed his barrel away.

Akimi glared at Kyle. Sierra stirred her cereal. Miguel shook his head.

"Andrew's a decent guy, Kyle," said Miguel, sounding disappointed. "He didn't deserve that."

"I know. I'm sorry. We just really, *really* need to win today's game—whatever it is."

34

The library was extra packed with spectators for the fifth day of the Olympic games.

Television cameras were everywhere.

Word must've spread that unless one of the other medaled teams miraculously swept the final three competitions, the championship was down to two true contenders.

"Welcome back, everybody!" said Mr. Lemoncello, addressing the contestants and the crowd from the second-floor balcony, where he was seated in a canvas director's chair. He was wearing a floppy beret and an ascot like movie directors sometimes do—in cartoons. "I hope you're all having fun!"

"Fun?" shouted Mrs. Chiltington, who was back, once again, with her pack of protestors. "Libraries should be about books, Mr. Lemoncello. Not fun!"

Even from a distance, Kyle could see some kind of dark cloud shadow his hero's eyes.

"Good to see you again, too, Archduchess Von Chiltington. And may I say, for the record, as well as the CD, I agree with thee."

"Ha! Prove it."

"My pleasure." He turned to address the assembled Library Olympians. "Today, for game number ten of the duodecimalthon, we'll do a little role-playing. You Olympians will play librarians, and I will play the patron who has come here seeking a very particular, very special *book*."

He shot Mrs. Chiltington a toothy smile, then pivoted back to the players.

"But I can't remember the title or the author or whether this *book* . . . "

Another smile for Mrs. Chiltington, who wasn't smiling back.

". . . is fiction or nonfiction. Your mission, should you choose to accept it, is to find this one needle in our haystack of five million different titles."

Mr. Lemoncello whipped off the beret and tugged on an Ohio State Buckeyes baseball cap.

"I will now play the patron. Before I do, however, I'd like to express my sincere gratitude to my brilliant acting coach, the renowned thespian Sir Donald Thorne, for his assistance in helping me craft my portrayal of this role."

Mr. Lemoncello cleared this throat and started speaking with a flat and friendly Ohio accent.

"Excuse me, Ms. and/or Mr. Librarian, can you help me find a book? All I remember is that it's kind of white and brownish on the front. It might be about the opposite of wildlife mixed up with a James Joyce novel, but Joyce didn't write it, although I think a woman did. I also remember something about a fruit no one has ever heard of before the year 2014. It's about yea thick. The book. Not the fruit. Can you please find it for me? Right away?"

Mr. Lemoncello whipped off the baseball cap and put the director's beret back on.

"The first team to locate the book and bring it to me wins our tenth medal, the Thank You medal. You will also, of course, win your patron's eternal gratitude. Okay, maybe not eternal, but he'll probably say 'thanks' when you hand him the book. Maybe. They do that, sometimes."

The thirty-two players stood frozen, staring up at Mr. Lemoncello.

Mr. Lemoncello didn't say anything else.

"Is that it?" asked Stephanie Youngerman from Boise, Idaho.

"Yes," said Dr. Zinchenko, stepping up to the railing on the second floor beside Mr. Lemoncello.

Then she was silent, too.

"Okay, you guys," Kyle whispered to his teammates. "Let's get busy."

"What should we do first?" asked Sierra.

"Weep," said Akimi. "That's the lamest clue I've ever heard."

"Nuh-uh," said Miguel. "I have a few ideas."

Kyle and his teammates headed to a desk in the outer ring so they could converse privately.

Marjory Muldauer led her team to a desk on the opposite side of the circle. Pretty soon, all the teams were grabbing desks and firing up the tablet computers built into the furniture so they could explore the library's online card catalog.

"So what fruit was first discovered in 2014?" asked Akimi, zeroing in on that part of the clue. "Craisins?"

"Hold up," said Miguel. "You're being too literal."

"Miguel's right," said Kyle. "Mr. Lemoncello is way too wacky to mean exactly what he said."

"So what *are* we looking for?" asked Sierra. "A new apple? A new banana? A new strawberry?"

"Bingo!" said Miguel. "That's it!" He started tapping the built-in tablet computer's screen.

Sierra was stunned. "Really? What'd I say?"

" 'New strawberry,' " said Akimi. "Which, I'm sorry, but I don't really think is a 'bingo' kind of answer."

"Because," said Miguel, as quietly as he could, "we don't need a new strawberry. We need a different kind of 'new berry.' "

"Which one?" said Kyle. "Blueberry? Raspberry?"

Akimi snapped her fingers. "Huckleberry! Because this is a library and *Huckleberry Finn* is in here."

"No, you guys." Miguel found a stubby pencil and a slip of scrap paper. "The 2014 Newbery Medal winner. *Flora and Ulysses* by Kate DiCamillo."

Akimi's eyes lit up. " 'Flora,' meaning 'vegetation,' is the opposite of 'fauna,' meaning 'wildlife.' "

"And," added Sierra, "James Joyce, the great Irish novelist, wrote a book called *Ulysses*."

"And Kate DiCamillo sounds like a lady's name that isn't Joyce," said Kyle.

"Triple bingo," said Miguel, scrolling through the card catalog entry for the book. "Dang."

"What?"

"All the copies in the Children's Room are checked out."

"Did they also put a copy on the fiction shelves?" asked Sierra.

"Yes! Just one. I guess so adults can check it out, too. That means the only copy in the whole building is right over there."

Miguel head-bobbed toward the bookcases that wrapped around the back third of the Rotunda Reading Room and climbed all the way up to the base of the Wonder Dome.

"We're gonna need a hover ladder," said Kyle.

"And this code." Miguel showed his teammates a slip of paper with "F.D545f 2013" written on it.

"Punch it into the hover ladder pad!" Akimi said to Miguel. "Go get our book."

"No way," said Miguel. "I'm scared of heights. *You* do it, Akimi."

"No way. Go on, Kyle."

Kyle shook his head. "You guys were right this morning. I don't want to be a 'ball hog' again."

"This ball you can hog. Go!"

"Hurry," said Sierra. "I think some of the other teams just figured it out, too."

Kyle dashed across the marble floor.

So did Stephanie Youngerman, the girl from Boise.

And Elliott Schilpp, the skinny genius from Maryland who had won the pizza-eating contest.

Uh-oh, thought Kyle. *The Mid-Atlantic team already has one medal. If they win this game, they actually have a shot at being crowned champions.*

Kyle ran faster. Fortunately, there were eight hover ladders, one for each team, lined up under the three-story-tall bookcases.

"Only one ladder per team," announced Dr. Zinchenko.

The instant she did, each of the other teams sent someone scurrying over to float up the fiction wall. Even if they didn't know what book they were looking for, they knew it wasn't in any of the Dewey decimal rooms now that the hover ladders had more or less been declared game pieces.

Kyle reached for a hover ladder.

But Marjory Muldauer grabbed its handles first.

"Sorry, Keeley. This ride is taken."

So were the next three down in either direction. Thanks to Marjory Muldauer, Kyle would have to dash to the very end of the line.

He ran past Stephanie Youngerman, who was furiously tapping in the winning code on her hover ladder's control pad.

Elliott Schilpp was jabbing in a number, too.

Stephanie Youngerman lifted off first.

By the time Kyle reached his hover ladder and typed in the book code and waited for the safety boots to clamp shut around his shins, three other teams were already floating up the wall: Mountain, Mid-Atlantic, and, of course, Marjory Muldauer for Midwest.

Kyle's platform finally drifted up from the floor and set off on a diagonal tangent for the 2014 Newbery Medal winner—and a very possible midair collision with the three other players, who were all aiming for the same target.

To his left, Kyle heard keys clacking.

Marjory Muldauer was typing a different code into her pad.

Her hover ladder stuttered to a stop, then shot sideways at a forty-five-degree angle. Kyle stayed on his direct trajectory to *Flora and Ulysses,* but within seconds, his hover ladder's infrared collision sensors picked up the approach of Marjory's platform.

"Yield to traffic," cooed a computerized voice from the tiny speaker in Kyle's control panel.

Marjory thumbed her red emergency stop button.

Her hover ladder froze, right where it would block Kyle's ascent.

"Yield to traffic." His hover ladder's safety features had put him in a lockdown mode.

Marjory pretended to be studying the books in front of her.

"That's not where the book we're looking for is and you know it!" Kyle shouted at her.

Marjory didn't say a word. In fact, she looked a little airsick.

Kyle twisted his body so he could see around Marjory's stalled ladder and watch the final seconds of the race to F.D545f 2013.

Stephanie Youngerman's hover ladder screeched to a halt and she shot out her arm to grab the book.

Then she started sliding books around on the shelf. Shoving them sideways. Looking behind them.

"I'm here!" she shouted. "But the book isn't."

The crowd of spectators gasped.

Mr. Lemoncello surprised all the floaters by swinging open a window-sized door cut into the bookcases. He poked his head out maybe three feet away from where *Flora and Ulysses* was supposed to be shelved. "I beg your pardon?"

"Flora and Ulysses," said Stephanie Youngerman.

"The 2014 Newbery winner. It's not here. Kate DiCamillo's other books are. *Because of Winn-Dixie. The Tale of Despereaux.* But there's only an empty gap where *Flora and Ulysses* is supposed to be."

"But this is impossible," said Mr. Lemoncello. "Dr. Zinchenko? Don't we have two dozen copies of that book?"

"Three, sir," said Dr. Zinchenko after popping open another window in the bookcase. "They are all checked out. That was our last copy."

"This is preposterous!" declared Mrs. Chiltington, striding forward to the front of the viewer gallery on the first floor. Her son Charles and a group of well-dressed ladies and one gentleman in a bow tie pushed their way forward with her.

"Missing books? Silly dinosaur video games? Money wasted on talking statues and holograms and secret panels in bookcases that could've been more wisely spent on extra copies of popular children's books?"

Mrs. Chiltington propped her hands on her hips and scowled up at Mr. Lemoncello.

"This library is a disgrace, sir. An absolute disgrace!"

"Perhaps you are right, Contessa Chiltington," said Mr. Lemoncello, sounding extremely sad—something Kyle had never heard him sound before. "A library without books? That is, indeed, a disgrace. An absolute disgrace."

Kyle watched Mr. Lemoncello halfheartedly award the Thank You medal to the Mountain team.

But his mind drifted back to the hover ladder race.

Marjory Muldauer had blocked him on purpose. She wasn't even trying to go for the book.

Why'd she do that? he wondered. *Why'd she want the Mountain team to win this round?*

"Hip, hip, hooray," said Mr. Lemoncello as he limply shook the winner's hand. "You won the tenth medal. Yippee, huzzah, and various other exclamations of glee. You were the first to reach the empty slot where the winning book should've been, which makes me want to sing, '*Brown bear, brown bear, what do you see? An empty hole where a book ought to be.*'"

Mr. Lemoncello turned to face the crowd.

"Thank you, Library Olympians and library lovers, for

joining us here today. Come back tomorrow for the final two games of the first Library Olympics. Now go away! All of you! Go!"

The crowd was stunned into silence.

The control room crew quickly pumped show tunes through all the speakers under the dome to cover the awkward silence. The ten holographic statues ringing the rotunda turned into the Trapp Family Singers and Uncle Max from *The Sound of Music*. They waved cheerfully and sang, *"So long, farewell, auf Wiedersehen, goodbye!"*

"That concludes today's competition," said the soothing lady's voice in the ceiling. "The score, after ten of the twelve games of the first Library Olympiad's duodecimalthon: Pacific, Northeast, Mid-Atlantic, and Mountain teams—one medal. The Midwest team and the Hometown Heroes—three medals."

"So," said John Sazaklis, the anchor for the Book Network's live coverage of the games, "it seems we're looking at a battle of the bookworms between the two top teams. They're all tied up, three to three. And there are only two games left."

"That's right," said his sidekick, renowned librarian Helen Burnham. "Of course, one of the four teams with a single medal could dazzle us all and sweep the final two competitions. It's still possible that this thing could end in a three-way tie."

"Exciting."

"You betcha, John. There's only one thing we know

for certain. The South will not rise again. Both the Southeast and the Southwest teams have remained medal-less in these games. I'm afraid those kids have no chance at being declared Mr. Lemoncello's library champions."

"Too bad. I really like their cowboy hats and NASCAR tracksuits."

37

A half hour later, the library was empty except for Team Kyle, Mr. Lemoncello, Dr. Zinchenko, and the engineers locked behind the red door in the library's control room.

Kyle and his friends wanted to be there for Mr. Lemoncello in what looked like his hour of despair.

"I'm sure whoever checked out *Flora and Ulysses* is enjoying it immensely," said Sierra Russell. "I know I did."

"Thank you, Sierra," said Mr. Lemoncello, who was breaking his own library rules, spooning a half gallon of ice cream straight out of its carton while he sat slumped in one of the comfortable reading chairs at the base of the fiction wall. He wore a bib to stop the ice cream from dribbling on his clothes.

"You're really only supposed to eat food in the Book Nook Café, sir," said Miguel.

Mr. Lemoncello ignored Miguel and shoveled up another gob of birthday-cake ice cream.

Meanwhile, Dr. Zinchenko had commandeered a hover ladder and sailed up to the spot where the missing book should've been shelved.

"The book was here last week," said Dr. Zinchenko, examining the gap between Kate DiCamillo titles. "I know it was. I made certain of it, right before we locked down the library to the public. Since then, the only ones allowed near the books have been our thirty-two young Olympians. . . ."

"Fascinating," said Mr. Lemoncello, not sounding fascinated at all. He shoveled more confetti-sprinkled ice cream into his mouth.

Dr. Zinchenko started her slow descent. "I must talk to security about this."

"Don't bother, Dr. Zinchenko," said Mr. Lemoncello. "This is a library. Books check in but they don't check out. No, wait. That's a Roach Motel. I forget what happens at a library. Maybe Mrs. Chiltington is correct. Maybe we should find some more mature adults to run this place. We really had three dozen copies of that same title and now they're all gone?"

"Yes, sir."

Mr. Lemoncello heaved a heavy sigh.

"This is horrible," shrieked the holographic librarian Mrs. Gause, as once again she flickered to frazzled life behind the circulation desk. "This is what happened last

time! First, books started disappearing. History books. One title in particular. All ten copies. Nobody cared. The whole town turned its back on its library. Very important people convinced the mayor to cut our funding. Before long, you couldn't even find a bookmark or an empty jar of library paste. Then *BOOM!* Here come the bulldozers and the wrecking ball! So long, library; hello, parking lot. Oh, the horror. The horror."

"Thank you, Mrs. Gause," said Mr. Lemoncello, gobbling down his ice cream even faster. "Good to hear from you again. Control room?"

Mr. Lemoncello flicked his wrist.

The hologram vanished.

Kyle approached his hero.

"Do you need anything, Mr. Lemoncello? Anything at all."

Mr. Lemoncello looked up from his tub of ice cream. The twinkle was gone from his coal-black eyes.

"Just what I've been looking for all along, Kyle. My true champions."

"Don't worry, sir. We won't let you down. We'll win both of the last two medals. I promise."

Mr. Lemoncello looked at Kyle, shook his head, and sighed again.

The Hometown Heroes' bookmobile ride from Olympia Village to the Lemoncello Library the following morning was as dreary as the weather.

Kyle and his teammates stared out the rain-streaked windows and watched familiar streets roll by.

"How weird will it be," said Akimi, "if the next time we head downtown to the library, we're not famous anymore? What if we're just a bunch of losers?"

"Thanks for that inspirational thought, Akimi," said Miguel. "You should really consider a career as a motivational speaker."

"What if something worse happens?" said Sierra. "What if all that stuff Mrs. Gause mentioned happens again? What if Mr. Lemoncello decides to close his library?"

"Why would he do that?" asked Kyle.

"Because he's tired of people taking out books and not bringing them back. He looked so sad yesterday."

"Yo," said Miguel. "He's a bazillionaire. He can always buy more books."

"You guys?" said Kyle. "Dr. Zinchenko said the *Flora and Ulysses* book was in its spot on the fiction shelf a week ago. And no one has been able to check books out since then except—"

"The thirty-two Library Olympians!" said Akimi, finishing Kyle's sentence, the way friends sometimes do.

"Yo!" said Miguel. "That means somebody on one of the other teams took the book out of the library. One of the kids Mr. Lemoncello spent so much time and energy searching for."

"No wonder he was so upset about a single missing book," said Sierra.

"Yep," said Kyle. "One of his specially selected library nerds stole that book." He turned to Miguel. "No offense."

"None taken."

When the team trooped up the slick marble steps into the library's lobby, they saw Charles Chiltington, his mother, a bunch of stuffy-looking ladies, and that one guy in a bow tie. This time, they were ringed around the Mr. Lemoncello fountain, which wasn't gurgling water like it was supposed to.

Each member of Mrs. Chiltington's crew was carrying a one-word protest sign. Together, they read "Is THIS ANY

LIBRARY? WAY TO RUN A." Bow-tie man, who was holding the "LIBRARY?" placard, was standing in the wrong spot.

Kyle and his teammates lingered in the archway just long enough to hear what Mrs. Chiltington and Charles were saying to the Book Network reporter interviewing them.

"If this library is to be a true public institution," said Charles's mother, "then it requires public oversight. It should be governed by a board of community trustees, not by a one-man band."

"Especially," said Charles, "when the batty bandleader is a disingenuous and mendacious charlatan."

"Are you suggesting that Mr. Lemoncello is both a liar and a fraud?" asked the reporter.

"Heavens no," said Charles. "Don't be preposterous."

"But that's what those words you just used mean."

"Charles is simply upset," said Mrs. Chiltington, draping a protective arm around her son. "That's why we're here today. Our children deserve a proper library, not an indoor amusement park. Mr. Lemoncello is exposing their impressionable minds to things such as a smell-a-vision version of some book called *Walter the Farting Dog* that children and their impressionable noses simply should not be exposed to."

Then she smiled and blinked. Repeatedly.

Kyle and his teammates shook their heads and continued into the Rotunda Reading Room.

"Hey, Kyle!"

It was his brother Mike.

"Don't disappoint us!"

And his other brother, Curtis.

"Win, baby, win!" screamed Mike, pumping his arm. "Woo-hoo! O-H, I-O! O-H, I-O!"

They were with Kyle's mom and dad in the capacity crowd that was bunched behind velvet ropes for the final two events of the duodecimalthon. So was everybody else's family. And friends. It seemed like the whole town of Alexandriaville had turned out for the big finale.

"No pressure or anything," said Akimi.

"Yo," said Miguel, pointing up at the Wonder Dome. "Check it out. I bet they did that to cheer up Mr. Lemoncello."

"I was hoping there might be balloons," said Kyle as he admired the ceiling.

"It's beautiful," said Sierra.

It looked like Dr. Zinchenko had instructed her video artists to run a Balloon Fiesta simulation for the final day of the Library Olympics. The Wonder Dome had been magically transformed into a brilliant blue sky filled with brightly colored hot-air balloons. The video loop made the Rotunda Reading Room feel as if it were a gondola gently swaying beneath a motley-colored airship drifting along on a warm breeze.

It was awesome.

"Turn! It! Off!" decreed a voice from the third-floor balcony.

Kyle looked up. Mr. Lemoncello stood at the railing. He was dressed in a black suit, black shirt, and black tie. He looked like he was on his way to a funeral.

The Wonder Dome went dark. It was just a curved white ceiling.

"I was so looking forward to this day," sighed Mr. Lemoncello from his lofty perch. "Today is the day I thought I would finally discover my true champions."

He looked down at the thirty-two Library Olympians.

Kyle thought he knew why his hero seemed so sad. One, or maybe more, of the thirty-two kids Mr. Lemoncello had entrusted with all the wonders of his library had betrayed him. They had taken away a book they weren't supposed to even touch.

"But instead of being giddy," Mr. Lemoncello continued, "I feel like a Watership. Down. Dr. Zinchenko? Will you kindly run game eleven? My internal Olympic torch is dimming and is in desperate need of fresh batteries. Therefore, I will be in my private suite working on the clues for game twelve, the final and most important game of the Lemoncello Library Olympics."

Mr. Lemoncello waved a feeble wave and disappeared into his private suite on the third floor.

Dr. Zinchenko, also dressed in black—a shiny, short leather dress—strode into the Rotunda Reading Room. Even her glasses had black frames instead of their usual red ones.

"Will the following teams please choose a represen-

tative for the eleventh game of our duodecimalthon: the Midwest, the Northeast, the Mid-Atlantic, the Mountain team, the Pacific team, and the local team from Alexandriaville, Ohio."

Marjory Muldauer shot her arm into the air.

"Yes, Miss Muldauer?"

"What's this game going to be about? Drinking milk shakes while floating books in a hot tub?"

"No, Miss Muldauer, although your sarcasm is duly noted. Game eleven will celebrate your freedom to express yourself with snarky scorn as well as everyone else's freedom to read. Today's first game will be all about *banned* books."

39

Sierra turned to her teammates. "Who should play for us?"

"Either you or Miguel," said Kyle.

"Definitely," agreed Akimi.

"I vote for Sierra," said Miguel. "You've read more books than the rest of us combined."

"Are you guys sure? Because I didn't do so well in that Battle of the Books game."

"And I did terribly in the poolside puzzle fiasco," said Kyle. "Remember?"

Sierra smiled. "I may never forget it."

"Yeah. Me neither. Come on. You'll be great. I don't know anything about band books. Did John Philip Sousa write one?"

"*Banned* books," said Sierra.

"See? You're doing better than me already."

"Teams?" said Dr. Zinchenko. "Please send your designated player to the circle of desks closest to mine."

Sierra looked at her teammates one last time. They were all smiling and nodding. She started walking to the inner ring of reading desks.

"Go, Sierra!"

That was her dad. Cheering for her.

"Good luck, honey!"

Her mom, too.

Each of the six remaining teams was assigned its own desk. Sierra sat down at hers. Marjory Muldauer was at the desk to her right. Elliott Schilpp, the nice guy from Maryland who really liked pizza, was on her left.

Each desk had its own built-in touch-screen computer.

"This contest will include an immediate elimination factor," announced Dr. Zinchenko from her swivel stool behind the central librarian's desk. "If you answer a question incorrectly, you will be asked to leave your desk. Quietly. As those of you playing for the Northeast, the Mid-Atlantic, the Mountain, and the Pacific teams undoubtedly recall, you only have one medal each. If you are eliminated from this game, it will be mathematically impossible for your team to go on and win the duodecimalthon. Therefore, if you lose, your team loses its chance at being crowned champions."

The four players nodded. They all understood the very high stakes of this eleventh game.

"However," said Dr. Zinchenko, "should you win this game as well as our twelfth game, we will have a three-way tie for first place and enter into a sudden-death over-time situation. That thirteenth game, if necessary, will take place tomorrow."

"Don't worry," sneered Marjory. "We won't be playing any games tomorrow."

"Let us begin," said Dr. Zinchenko, completely ignoring Marjory Muldauer. "I will read a multiple-choice question. Use the touch-screen computers in your reading desks to select your answer."

Sierra took in a deep breath.

"Question number one: In 1985, Shel Silverstein's *A Light in the Attic* was banned from a school in Wisconsin because:

a) the attic was cluttered and dangerous.
b) the children in the book were filthy and never combed their hair.
c) the book encouraged children to break dishes so they wouldn't have to dry them.
d) the book used foul language.

Please enter your answer now."

Sierra had read about this book-banning incident. She tapped "C." Her computer screen glowed green. She was correct.

The Northeast and Mountain teams, however, chose

the wrong answer. The screens on their computers turned bright red.

"Thank you for playing," said Dr. Zinchenko. "Kindly rejoin your teammates. And thank you for participating in the first-ever Library Olympiad. You and your teammates will receive lovely parting gifts."

"Whoop-de-doo," said Marjory. "Next question, please."

"Of course. Question number two: Why was Dr. Seuss's book *The Lorax* banned?

    a) There is no such creature as a Lorax.
    b) The drawings were too frightening for
       young readers.
    c) The rhymes and silly names were too weird.
    d) It offended forestry workers.

Choose your answer now. You have thirty seconds."

Sierra wasn't certain about this one. The first three answers could be reasons to ban *any* Dr. Seuss book. But *The Lorax* was all about "Truffula" trees and saving the environment. Forestry workers might not like that.

She went with "D."

Her touch screen glowed green.

So did Marjory Muldauer's.

The Pacific team answered incorrectly.

"Sorry," Sierra said to Pranav Pillai as he left his table.

"Thanks. Good luck!"

"Three players remain," said Dr. Zinchenko. "Here is your third question: Why was Junie B. Jones, a series of children's books by Barbara Park, banned from libraries? Was it because:

- a) Junie B. Jones is a mouthy brat?
- b) characters use words such as 'stupid' and 'dumb'?
- c) the author takes liberties with traditional spelling?
- d) the main character makes bad choices?
- e) all of the above?"

Since Sierra had loved the Junie B. books when she was younger, she knew the correct answer was "E) all of the above."

So did Marjory Muldauer.

Elliott Schilpp, however, did not. His red screen meant the Mid-Atlantic team was out of the competition.

It also meant the whole Library Olympics came down to the Hometown Heroes versus the Midwest.

Sierra Russell versus Marjory Muldauer.

40

"And then there were two!" shouted Mr. Lemoncello from his third-floor balcony. "This finale is far too exciting to miss!"

"Are you feeling better, sir?" asked Dr. Zinchenko.

"Much!" He looked down at Sierra and Marjory. "I've been watching you two on TV! There's nothing like a pair of brilliant young minds set free in a library to perk me up! Plus, I've decided to hire detective Sammy Keyes, who found the hotel thief, to help me find the book thief, which, of course, is now available on DVD in our movie department on the first floor."

He scampered down the spiral staircases.

Kyle heard a funny *burp-squeak-burp* sound and smiled. Mr. Lemoncello was still dressed all in black, but he'd put on his banana shoes.

As he made his way around and around and down the

two flights of curling, corkscrewing steps, his shoes were honking out a song: "The Wheels on the Bus Go Round and Round."

Good, thought Kyle. His hero was back!

Mr. Lemoncello sprinted to the center of the Rotunda Reading Room, leapt up, and somersaulted over the librarian's desk. When he landed on the other side, his banana shoes let out a gassy *PPPFFFFFFIIP.*

The audience laughed, applauded, and cheered.

Well, everybody except Mrs. Chiltington and her friends. Kyle could see them shaking their heads disgustedly.

"I'll take over from here, Dr. Zinchenko!" said Mr. Lemoncello.

"Very well, sir." She handed him her stack of question cards.

"Hello, Sierra."

"Hello, sir."

"Marjory."

She waggled her fingers at him like she was bored.

"Okeydokey, pokey," said Mr. Lemoncello. "You two look lonely. Teammates? Come on down."

Kyle, Akimi, and Miguel dashed down the aisle between desks to join Sierra.

"I'm good," said Marjory, stopping her teammates in their tracks. "I don't need any help."

"Very well," said Mr. Lemoncello. "Let me recap."

He reached under the librarian's desk and pulled out

a purple flower-petal swim cap, which he tugged down snugly over his curly white hair.

"Your two teams are currently tied, with three medals each. We have two games remaining: this one and then the one that comes after it, which would be the next one. This is extremely exciting, wouldn't you agree?"

"Yes, sir," said Kyle and his teammates.

Marjory Muldauer shrugged. "Can we move on to the next question?"

"Moving on," said Mr. Lemoncello. "This next question is not—I repeat, *not*—a multiple guess. You must tap in your answer using the keypad on your tabletop's tablet computer. We're still in the category of banned books, only this time they're more than banned, because these poor books were burned. Here is your question: On what date did the Dominican priest Savonarola collect and publicly burn thousands of lewd books in Florence, Italy?"

Kyle looked at Sierra.

She nodded.

"Go for it," said Kyle.

Sierra typed in her answer: SHROVE TUESDAY, 1497.

Kyle could hear the computer's *click-clack* sound effects accompanying Marjory's glass-tapping as she entered her answer, too.

"Is that your final answer, Sierra?" asked Mr. Lemoncello.

"Yes, sir."

"Miss Muldauer?"

"Well, duh. I typed it in, didn't I?"

"Indeed you did. Dr. Zinchenko?"

"The answer we were looking for is Shrove Tuesday, 1497!"

"Woo-hoo!" shouted Kyle.

"That's the answer Sierra Russell gave me," said Mr. Lemoncello, checking his own computer screen. "Miss Muldauer, I'm afraid your answer is incorrect."

"No, it's not."

"I'm sorry, Miss Muldauer," said Dr. Zinchenko. "You did not type in 'Shrove Tuesday, 1497.'"

"I know. Because that answer isn't specific enough."

"I beg your pardon?" said Mr. Lemoncello, taking off his bathing cap. "My ears were covered by rubberized flower petals. Are you saying my head librarian, Dr. Yanina Zinchenko, has incorrectly identified the answer as 'Shrove Tuesday, 1497?'"

"It's an okay answer," said Marjory. "If you're lazy. My answer, however, is more correct. February 7, 1497. Yes, it was also Shrove Tuesday, now commonly referred to as Mardi Gras, but your question specifically asked for a *date*, not a day."

The whole crowd gasped.

Kyle could feel his heart racing in his chest.

Was Sierra's answer technically incorrect?

If so, did that mean his team lost another medal?

"This is quite the quizzical, perplexable, and curious conundrum," said Mr. Lemoncello. "Fortunately, we are

in a library, where librarians may not know everything but they certainly know how to find it. Dr. Zinchenko?"

"I will go upstairs to the triple zero room, locate the appropriate encyclopedia volume, and check both 'Savonarola' and 'Shrove Tuesday.'"

"Aha. Might I suggest you start with the 'S' volume?"

"Such was my plan, sir."

"Excellent pre-research planning, Dr. Zinchenko. We wait with bated breath, so kindly hurry before things get too fishy down here."

Heels clicking on the marble floor, Dr. Zinchenko made her way to the nearest spiral staircase, then clanked up the steps to the second floor.

Mr. Lemoncello turned to the closest television camera. "Don't go away. We'll be right back with the correct answer to our last question right after this word from our sponsors."

"This is public TV," whispered the camera operator. "We don't do commercials."

"Oh. Well, can't you do a pledge drive or something? Or should I just make funny faces?"

"Funny faces would be fine, sir."

While Mr. Lemoncello mugged for the camera, Miguel turned to his teammates. "Dr. Z is headed upstairs for the zero-three-zeros. That's the Dewey decimal classification for encyclopedias and books of facts."

"Actually," said Marjory, leaning back smugly, "she will be looking for zero-three-*two*, encyclopedias in American

English. You people need to start being much more specific; otherwise—"

Suddenly, there was a shriek from the second floor.

Dr. Zinchenko raced to the balcony railing. "They're gone!"

"What?" cried Mr. Lemoncello.

"All the 'S' encyclopedias, sir. They're missing. Every single one!"

"What? How is that possible?"

"I don't know, sir. We never check out encyclopedias. Somebody must have stolen them!"

Kyle was sort of relieved.

If the encyclopedias Dr. Zinchenko needed were missing, maybe they'd just move on to another question. Hopefully, another one Sierra knew the answer to.

"Guess we need to move on to the next question card," Kyle said to Mr. Lemoncello.

"Not so fast, Keeley," said Marjory. "Since Mr. Lemoncello was so sweet to give us smartphones when we played that Battle of the Books game, I used mine to Google 'Bonfire of the Vanities, 1497,'" because that's what the Italians used to call the burning of objects they considered immoral. If I may quote: 'The most infamous bonfire took place on *February seventh, 1497,* when the Dominican priest Savonarola collected and publicly burned thousands of objects like art and books in Florence, Italy, on the day of the Mardi Gras festival.' It doesn't even mention Shrove

Tuesday. It does, however, confirm that my answer, February seventh, 1497, is correct."

Perched on a stool behind the librarian's desk, Mr. Lemoncello looked completely dumbfounded.

Miguel pointed at Marjory. "You used your phone to find the answer! You cheated."

"No, I did not. I only used it to *confirm* my answer."

"I am so sorry, sir," said Dr. Zinchenko, still bracing herself against the banister on the second-floor balcony.

"As am I," said Mr. Lemoncello, his shoulders sagging. "As am I."

"You should be more than sorry!" shouted Mrs. Chiltington from the gallery. "You should be ashamed, Mr. Lemoncello. This is no way to run a library! Missing children's books *and* encyclopedias?"

"This is egregious!" shouted Charles.

"The people of Alexandriaville deserve better!" added his mother.

"This is also heinous!" said Charles. "And atrocious, too."

Mr. Lemoncello held up a shiny green medal. "I suppose I could cut this thing in two and award one half to each of you. But I might need a laser beam or a hacksaw. . . ."

"Why would you give Sierra anything?" demanded Marjory. "You asked for a date; I gave you a date. She gave you nothing except the name of a holiday."

"And a year," said Akimi. "Sierra got the year right, too."

Marjory snorted. "Too bad she couldn't come up with the month and day like I did. Then she'd actually have *a date*!"

"I suppose you are correct, Miss Muldauer," said Mr. Lemoncello. "Sound the jubilee; the Midwest team wins another medal."

"This isn't fair!" grumbled Miguel.

"There's still the twelfth game," said Kyle. "If we win it, we'll be all tied up again."

"And we can do that sudden-death overtime thing," said Akimi.

"Miss Muldauer?" said Mr. Lemoncello. "Please step forward and receive your prize."

Marjory strutted to the center of the room.

"For answering our most important questions most correctly, it is my honor to award you the most important medal of all the very important medals awarded thus far: the Yertle the Turtle."

"Huh?" said Marjory. "Why'd you give it a dumb name like that?"

"Because, Miss Muldauer, Dr. Seuss's book was considered extremely controversial when it first came out in 1958, for including the word 'burp.'" Mr. Lemoncello belched. "Sorry. Guzzled too much Lemonberry Fizz while I was recharging my batteries. *Yertle the Turtle* has also been banned because of its political messages."

"Whatever," said Marjory.

She snatched the medal out of Mr. Lemoncello's hand,

twirled around, and dangled her new prize in front of Team Kyle.

Kyle tried to ignore her. "What's the next game?" he asked Mr. Lemoncello.

Just then, a voice rang out behind Kyle.

"Stand aside, please. Coming through."

It was Clarence, the security guard, wading through the crowd of spectators.

"Mr. Lemoncello?" he said, waving a stack of papers. "You need to see this."

"What is it?"

"A list of all the titles currently missing from the library shelves. Dr. Zinchenko asked us to put one together after that last *Flora and Ulysses* book disappeared from the fiction wall."

"That looks like a mighty thick stack of paper, Clarence."

"Yes, sir. Ten pages."

"Any encyclopedias on your list?"

"Every single 'S' volume in the building."

Mr. Lemoncello shook his head and drooped in his seat.

"Enough. I'm done. I can't fight this fight alone anymore."

He slowly rose off his stool and gave his town-crier bell a weak jingle.

"Hear ye, hear ye. Oyez, oyez. The games of the first Library Olympiad are hereby suspended. If you have trou-

ble understanding the word 'suspended,' kindly look it up in a dictionary, but forget checking an encyclopedia, because all the 'S' volumes have gone missing."

"Does this mean I win?" shouted Marjory.

"No, Miss Muldauer. It means I am tired of playing games here in Alexandriaville. Nobody wins. Everybody loses."

"What about those college scholarships you promised?" said one of the other members of the Midwest team.

Mr. Lemoncello turned to his head librarian.

"Dr. Zinchenko? Kindly give a 'Go to College Free' card to each and every Library Olympian."

She started passing out small orange cards.

"Tomorrow," said Mr. Lemoncello, "you shall all receive a full scholarship *if* you remember to bring that card with you to the closing ceremonies. If you should somehow lose it between now and then, I might pretend I don't know who you are, what you want, or what it was I promised to give you."

Dr. Zinchenko handed Kyle his "Go to College Free" card.

It was the size of a "Luck" or "Fortune" card from Mr. Lemoncello's Family Frenzy board game.

But this rectangle of flat cardboard was worth thousands and thousands of dollars.

Still, Kyle wished Mr. Lemoncello didn't look so sad. He wished he had drawn a "Find the Missing Books" card instead. He wished they could all go back to playing games.

When the thirty-two "Go to College Free" cards were handed out, Mr. Lemoncello narrowed his eyes and peered at the players.

"Hearty and splendiferous congratulations to you all," he said without any of his usual zip. "However, I have a sinking feeling that at least one of you doesn't really need a scholarship from me anymore."

Kyle watched the audience shuffle out of the building.

Most of the Library Olympians were thrilled to hear that they'd be picking up an all-expenses-paid college scholarship even without winning the most medals.

The Chiltingtons and their well-dressed friends were overjoyed for other reasons.

"Marvelous work, Miss Muldauer!" said Mrs. Chiltington when Marjory and her team passed by on their way to the front door. "Simply marvelous! You completely demoralized the man."

"Fantastic finish," added Charles. "Getting Lemoncello to cancel these so-called Olympic Games? Couldn't have done it in an abler manner myself."

"Mr. Lemoncello looked so sad," giggled Mrs. Chiltington. "I wouldn't be surprised if he packed up all his toys and went home to New York City!"

"If he does, it might be for the best," Marjory told her small cluster of fans. "For far too long, Mr. Lemoncello has pretended to be a library lover when, in truth, this was all a clever publicity stunt so he could sell even more of his preposterous games!"

The League of Concerned Library Lovers clapped daintily.

"Maybe now you concerned citizens, those of you who love libraries qua libraries, can run this institution the way we all know it should be run. If you turn this book-filled building into a true temple of learning, people all over Ohio will say, 'Is that library down in Alexandriaville any good?' To which you can reply, 'Hello? It's *not* a Lemoncello. It's a library!' "

Her admirers' hands pitter-pattered together again.

Marjory nodded graciously, then headed through the lobby with the rest of her team. Actually, the other kids from the Midwest team weren't really walking *with* Marjory, just in the same general direction.

"Where'd Mr. Lemoncello go?" asked Akimi.

"I saw him and Clarence head upstairs," said Sierra. "Probably to console Dr. Zinchenko."

"Definitely," said Miguel. "Librarians always flip out when books and encyclopedias mysteriously disappear off their shelves."

Mrs. Yunghans and Mr. Sharp, the hometown team's two chaperones, came to join the players at the reading desk.

"You guys ready to bookmobile it back to Olympia Village?" asked Mr. Sharp.

"Not just yet," said Kyle. "We want to make sure Mr. Lemoncello is okay."

"All right," said Mr. Sharp. "But it's barbecue night at the motel."

"We're not really in the mood for barbecue," said Akimi.

"They have ice cream, too," said Mrs. Yunghans.

Akimi crinkled her nose. "I think I'm suddenly lactose intolerant."

"We won't be long," said Kyle, tucking his orange scholarship card into his shirt pocket. "Come on, you guys."

As his team trooped up the spiral staircase to the second floor, Kyle looked down at the Rotunda Reading Room and realized how hollow the library seemed without anybody in it.

No one was riding the hover ladders or grabbing a snack in the Book Nook Café or hanging out in the community meeting rooms or rushing upstairs to do research at a collaboration station or heading to the third floor to check out the newest educational video games in the Electronic Learning Center.

The holographic statue nooks were empty and dark.

The Wonder Dome was just a blank canvas. A TV set after the power goes out.

Without people or laughter or learning, the domed building was just a fancy tomb filled with dry and dusty books.

43

"Mr. Lemoncello?" Kyle shouted, his voice echoing under the dome. "Dr. Zinchenko?"

"We are back here," replied Dr. Zinchenko. "Outside the zero-zero-zero door."

Kyle and his teammates made their way around the circular balcony.

Mr. Lemoncello, Dr. Zinchenko, and Clarence were standing in the same spot that had served as the starting line for the Library Cart Relay Race. They flipped through Clarence's thick stack of papers with serious expressions on their faces.

"Hey, Mr. Lemoncello," said Kyle.

Mr. Lemoncello raised his left hand to silence Kyle and continued frowning at the list of missing books.

"Are you telling us one individual removed all thirty-six copies of *Flora and Ulysses*?" asked Dr. Zinchenko.

"Thirty-five of them," said Clarence. "Somebody else grabbed the last copy off the fiction wall. But our main suspect checked out multiple copies of other titles, too. Tracking his records, we see he's been working on his personal book removal project for close to a month."

"Are the books overdue?"

"Not yet, Dr. Z," said Clarence. "He auto-renewed them all online. We can't be certain, but we think he's also the one who removed all those 'S' encyclopedias."

"This is actually old news," said Mr. Lemoncello. "You see, Clarence, Dr. Zinchenko—I've known all along who was behind this nonsense. And why. Stopping him and bringing back all the missing books was to be our final challenge in the Library Olympics. I've already been handing out clues left and right. But I don't think I can continue with that plan. If he and his associates can recruit a child—a Library Olympian, no less—or a group of children for their cause, what hope is there?"

"We'll help you, sir," said Kyle.

"Will you, Mr. Keeley? I've already given away the grand prize. Thirty-two of them, in fact. I can't give your team a *grander* prize or even a grand piano."

"That's okay. We just want to keep playing and prove we're really champions. Besides, I thought finding the missing books was supposed to be the twelfth game."

"It was. Another treasure hunt of sorts."

"So if we find the books, we'd win the twelfth medal."

"And then we could do a sudden-death overtime against Marjory Muldauer," added Akimi.

Mr. Lemoncello shook his head. "What if I told you that you might need Miss Muldauer to safely retrieve all the books?"

Akimi made her famous "gag me now" gesture.

"I know, I know," said Mr. Lemoncello. "It's impossible. Asking you and the other Library Olympians to work together for a higher, common purpose? Forget I even mentioned it. Dr. Zinchenko?"

"Sir?"

"I've made up my mind even though I have not yet made up my bed. I, Luigi Libretto Lemoncello, hereby officially declare the games of this first Library Olympiad to be over. Done. Kaput. There will be no winners. This library has failed to find its true champions. Tomorrow night, at the closing ceremonies, kindly hand out one college scholarship to each and every player who presents you with an orange card. I'm afraid I won't be able to attend the festivities. I'll be out of town. Either on a bridge to Terabithia or flying home to New York City. In fact, I may never return to Alexandriaville or Ohio again."

This was just about the worst news Kyle had ever heard.

"Mr. Lemoncello?" he said. "If you know who checked out all the books, why don't you tell the police and have the guy arrested?"

"The books are not yet overdue," said Dr. Zinchenko.

"And, if I might cite the American Library Association's code of ethics . . ."

"Please, Dr. Z, cite away," said Mr. Lemoncello.

"Here at the Lemoncello Library, we protect each library user's right to privacy and confidentiality with respect to information sought or received and resources consulted, borrowed, acquired, or transmitted."

"Seriously?" said Akimi.

"Oh, yeah," said Miguel. "It's the library law."

Kyle tried one more time. "But, Mr. Lemoncello . . ."

His hero raised that hand again.

"It was fun, Mr. Keeley, but now we're done. Dr. Zinchenko? Monday morning, kindly instruct my lawyers to draw up the necessary papers appointing Mrs. Chiltington and her League of Concerned Library Lovers as the Alexandriaville Public Library's first board of trustees. Then take down my statue and pack up anything with my name on it, including my last case of Mr. Lemoncello's Lemonberry Fizz."

"But what if we find the missing books?" Kyle pleaded.

"I told you—I'm through handing out medals. There are no more prizes, Kyle. No more ice cream, cake, or balloons."

"I don't care." Kyle turned to his teammates. "How about you guys?"

They all shook their heads.

"Nope," said Miguel.

"The medals clash with my earrings," added Akimi.

"Fine," said Mr. Lemoncello. "Suit yourself. Play my final game, find the missing books before tomorrow's closing ceremonies, and I might—I repeat, *might*—reconsider turning my library over to Mrs. Chiltington. I might also consider staying in Ohio on a permanent basis."

"Thank you, sir," said Kyle. "Because we don't really need to win any more medals or scholarships. But we definitely need you. And our library."

Around midnight, after celebrating the defeat of Mr. Lemoncello with Charles and Marjory over a few bottles of root beer, Andrew Peckleman still needed to sweep up around the motel.

Even though it was very late, he heard voices coming from his uncle's office, so he worked his broom and dustpan closer to the door.

He heard his uncle Woody, Marjory Muldauer . . .

. . . and Mrs. Chiltington?

Andrew pressed his back against the wall and listened.

His uncle was chuckling. "Luigi is really leaving town?"

"So it would seem," said Mrs. Chiltington. "I just received a call from that Russian woman, Dr. Zinfluenzo. She suggested that I come by the library first thing Monday morning. Apparently, Mr. Lemoncello's lawyers are drawing

up papers to transfer the stewardship of 'his' library to its new board of trustees."

"That's you and your friends, right?" said Marjory.

"Yes. The League of Concerned Library Lovers will make certain that the new Alexandriaville Public Library undertakes a major course correction and no longer subjects children to corrupting influences and mindless frivolity."

"And to think," said his uncle, "Luigi's unraveling really started with one book. The one you plucked off the shelf for me, Marjory. It was the straw that broke the camel's back."

"How did you know losing *Flora and Ulysses* would have that effect on him, Mr. Peckleman?" asked Marjory.

The old man cackled. "Because Luigi's smart. He figured out that one of you library-loving kids was helping me hoard every single copy of that terrible book. It broke his heart. Crushed his spirit."

"Well . . ."

Andrew could hear a slight quaver in Marjory's voice. She took a deep breath.

"I'm very glad I could help you two save a library from turning into a cheap, Floo-powdered World of Wizardry tourist trap," she continued, her voice shaky. "However, now that Mr. Lemoncello is relinquishing control, we should take back that book I borrowed. Maybe I can drop it off in the sidewalk book-return slot when no one is watching."

"No need for us to do that, dear," said Andrew's uncle.

"I disagree," said Marjory. "I can't just walk back into the library with the book."

"Of course not. What I meant to say is there is absolutely no need for us to *ever* take back a single copy of that particular book. The library has plenty of other books. No one will miss one more."

"It's true," said Mrs. Chiltington. "There are so many wonderful children's books. I have suggestions for others we should stock, as well."

"But *Flora and Ulysses* won the Newbery Medal," said Marjory. "There should always be at least one copy on the shelves in any library."

"Perhaps," said Mrs. Chiltington. "Perhaps not. It seems rather childish to me."

"It's a children's book. It's meant to be childish."

"Miss Muldauer," said Mrs. Chiltington, "I'm sure our new librarians will give your concerns about this *Flora and Ulysses* the attention they deserve. However, since you live in Michigan and not here in Ohio, you may not be fully aware of our local tastes and opinions about which books do and do not belong on our library shelves."

"Besides," said Andrew's uncle, "I don't like that book. It's one of the worst of its kind."

"There are other books that *I* don't like," added Mrs. Chiltington. "For instance, that *Yertle the Turtle*. It is rather subversive. Not at all what our children need to be reading if we expect them to grow up properly. There are

also some local history books that are quite biased in their interpretation of the past. One entitled *Ohio River Pirates and Scallywags,* for instance, is full of lies, innuendo, and misinformation. It should, once again, be pulled from the shelves."

"B-b-but . . . ," stammered Marjory.

"Thank you, Miss Muldauer, for all your help. Thanks to you, our lovely new library shall soon become a true library. With none of Mr. Lemoncello's lunacy."

Andrew quickly swept away from the door.

He couldn't believe his ears.

His great-uncle-twice-removed and Mrs. Chiltington were trying to ban certain books from the Alexandriaville Public Library.

Books they didn't like.

The two of them were nearly as bad as all those book burners and banners Andrew used to hate back when he loved libraries.

Which, actually, he still kind of did.

First thing in the morning, the bookmobile dropped off Kyle and his teammates in front of the library.

"I'll wait here," said the driver.

"Thanks," said Kyle.

He and his teammates bustled up the front steps and entered the library.

The statue of Mr. Lemoncello was gone.

Someone had slathered wet cement over the "Knowledge Not Shared Remains Unknown" motto chiseled into the fountain's base.

"Mr. Lemoncello has left the building," said Clarence, coming out of the control room off the lobby.

"We can see that," said Kyle. "Somebody took out the statue."

"Mr. Lemoncello," said Clarence. "He wanted to ship it back to his factory in New Jersey. They have a garden."

211

"Who erased his slogan?" asked Sierra.

"The new board of trustees. They don't officially take over till sometime Monday, but they've already started making changes. They have a new slogan: 'Shush!' Now they're inside, trying to figure out how to dismantle the hover ladders."

"Oh, no they're not," said Kyle. "The hover ladders are awesome!"

Kyle stormed into the Rotunda Reading Room with Miguel, Akimi, and Sierra right behind him.

Charles Chiltington was jabbing at one of the hover ladder bases with a pointy-tipped screwdriver.

"Knock it off, Charles," said Kyle.

"Oh, hello, Keeley. What are you doing here in mother's library?"

"It's not her library," said Akimi.

"Well, it will be soon enough," said Charles. "When I'm finished grounding these ridiculous contraptions, I'll be heading upstairs with my wire cutters. Mummy wants me to snip the power cables to all those senseless video games."

"That is so *not* going to happen," said Miguel.

"Really? Who's going to stop me?"

"I will!" said the holographic librarian, Lonni Gause. She didn't seem to be flickering as much as she usually did.

"What?" laughed Charles. "I don't mean to be rude, lady, but you're not real."

"That's right. I'm a virtual librarian. That means I live up in the cloud inside a computer—a computer connected to the four hundred and ninety-eight different security cameras currently operational inside this library. I'm also linked to the Web and know exactly how to send streaming video footage of you vandalizing that expensive equipment to the local and state police. It's amazing what you can do when you share knowledge with others."

"You wouldn't dare. My mother is—"

"Just another library card holder until Monday."

"The make-believe librarian is correct, Charles," said Mrs. Chiltington as she came out of the Book Nook Café, sipping a cup of tea with her pinky finger extended.

"I should've known," gasped Mrs. Gause. "It's you again!"

Mrs. Chiltington smiled and sipped her tea.

"Yo," said Miguel. "No food or beverages are allowed in the library. You have to drink that in the Book Nook Café or dump it down the sink."

Clarence and Clement strode into the Rotunda Reading Room.

"Somebody sipping tea where they shouldn't be sipping it?" asked Clarence.

"Yes," said the holographic librarian. "Kindly escort Mrs. Chiltington and her disruptive son out of the building. And whatever you do, don't let that woman anywhere near the nine hundreds room!"

"There's no need for an escort," huffed Mrs. Chiltington. "We know the way out. Come along, Charles dear. But, Mrs. Gause?"

"Yes?"

"First thing Monday morning, I'm personally pulling your plug."

As soon as the Chiltingtons were gone, Kyle turned to Mrs. Gause.

"We want to play the final game."

"The book quest?"

"Yes, ma'am. We figured that if it was supposed to be the twelfth game, like Mr. Lemoncello said it was, there might be some clues to start us off."

"I'm not aware of any new clues. Just the ones he's already handed out."

"What about those security cameras that caught Charles?" asked Kyle. "Did they record who took the last *Flora and Ulysses* off the shelf? Mr. Lemoncello said it had to be one of the Olympians. Maybe one of the losing teams did it so nobody else could win."

"Um, Kyle?" said Akimi. "How would they know what book to take?"

"I don't know. Maybe they hacked into Dr. Zinchenko's computer."

Akimi arched an eyebrow. "You're making this up as you go, right?"

"Yeah."

"Unfortunately," said Mrs. Gause, "all the fiction wall

cameras were not functioning from the start of the Library Olympics until ten minutes ago."

"Look, Mrs. Gause," said Kyle, "we need to find those missing books. Before tonight."

"And we want you to find them," said Mrs. Gause.

"Indeed we do," said one of the holographic statues, which had just appeared under the Wonder Dome. Benjamin Franklin.

Now all the other nook statues came to illuminated life and started shouting. "Save this library!" "You can do it, lads and lasses!" "Your library is your paradise!"

"It's all the famous librarians again," said Miguel.

"The task you four are attempting is very difficult," said Mrs. Gause. "It's also extremely complex. It might take you *and* all of the other teams to unravel this particular puzzle."

"Everybody's still at the motel," said Akimi, "because Dr. Z is handing out those scholarships tonight at the closing ceremonies."

"Well," said Mrs. Gause, "you don't really need *all* of them. Just the winners. The ones who received medals?" Then she winked. Several times.

"The medals!" said Kyle. "Of course. All those goofy names. They're clues. Mr. Lemoncello said he'd been handing clues out right and left. He's been setting us up for this final game since the first day of the Library Olympics."

Suddenly, the Wonder Dome was filled with an "instant

215

replay" video collage of Mr. Lemoncello handing out eleven different medals.

"So," said Miguel, "anybody remember what all those different medals were called?"

"Sorry," said Sierra. "I guess we should've taken notes."

"Come on, you guys," said Kyle. "We're going back to Olympia Village. We have some medals to inspect."

46

"What are we going to learn from all the medals?" asked Sierra as the bookmobile raced back to Olympia Village.

"I don't know," said Kyle.

"Maybe there's something etched on the back," suggested Miguel. "Maybe parts of a map, like in that movie *National Treasure*. And if you arrange all the medals correctly, it'll make a treasure map that will lead us to the secret hiding place for the missing books!"

"Seriously?" said Akimi.

"Hey," said Kyle. "It's a possibility. We have to consider every angle."

"Even the screwy ones?"

"Yo," said Miguel, "we're talking about Luigi Lemoncello. Screwy is usually his first choice."

"Do you think Marjory Muldauer is going to let us even look at the four medals she won?" asked Sierra.

"No way," said Akimi. "If she finds out we're try-ing to win the twelfth game, even though there isn't any prize . . ."

"Except saving Mr. Lemoncello's library," said Kyle.

"A library that, by the way, Marjory Muldauer despises," added Miguel.

"My point exactly," said Akimi. "She isn't going to play along with us, Kyle."

"Well, we have to try. Mr. Lemoncello said we might need Marjory to 'win' this round. Not that we're actually going to *win* anything."

When they reached Olympia Village, most of the other teams were hanging out in the dining area, scarfing down bacon and playing with the waffle machines.

"Um, you guys," said Kyle, standing near the fireplace at one end of the room, "don't mean to interrupt your breakfasts, but we sort of need your help."

"What for?" asked Elliott Schilpp, the kid from Mary-land, who seemed to enjoy bacon as much as he enjoyed pizza.

"Someone has been taking books out of the Lemon-cello Library," said Akimi, "and not bringing them back."

"Finding the missing books was supposed to be the twelfth game in the Library Olympics," explained Kyle.

"So do we win an extra prize if we help you folks figure this thing out?" asked Angus Harper from Texas.

"Not really," said Akimi. "Neither will we. Mr.

Lemoncello's basically canceled the whole Library Olympics dealio."

"But we need to find them anyway," said Kyle. "Otherwise, Mr. Lemoncello is going to leave town and his awesomely incredible library will get turned into Mrs. Borington's Snoozeville Book Depository."

"They'll bring in old-fashioned librarians to shush people," added Miguel.

"Well, if we don't win anything extra by helping you guys," groused the guy from New York City, "why should we help? We've already scored our college scholarships."

"Actually," said Kyle, "you *will* win something else if you help us do this thing."

"Yeah? What?"

"You'll all get to come back to Alexandriaville as often as you like and have fun doing research or learning junk about flying prehistoric reptiles or talking to famous holograms, like this amazing rocket scientist we met, or just reading a good book you found while you were floating along and browsing the fiction wall in Mr. Lemoncello's amazingly incredible library."

The whole room was quiet. There wasn't even a fork clink or a milk slurp.

Finally, Angus stood up. "Sounds good to me."

Stephanie Youngerman from the Mountain team was on her feet next. "What do you guys need?"

"Ah, what the hey," said the kid from New York. "Sign me up."

"Me too!" said Elliott Schilpp, his mouth full of bacon.

"Thanks, you guys," said Kyle. "First we need to see everybody's medals. Including the ones the Midwest team won."

"Oh, you mean the ones Marjory Muldauer said she won all by herself?" said a girl in a Wisconsin Badgers baseball cap.

"Don't worry," said Margaret Miles, a chaperone for the Midwest team. "I made Marjory turn them over to me."

"Is Marjory around?" asked Kyle.

"She went for a walk with our other chaperone," said Ms. Miles. "Father Mike from Regis Catholic Middle School in Cedar Rapids, Iowa. They should be back soon."

That's when Andrew Peckleman stepped into the dining room.

"Kyle?" he said. "We need to talk."

47

"We're kind of in the middle of something, Andrew," Kyle said politely.

Andrew put his hand alongside his mouth and whispered, "I know who grabbed that last copy of *Flora and Ulysses*."

Kyle motioned for Andrew to step out of the room with him.

"First off," said Kyle, "I'm really sorry about that garbage man crack I made the other day."

"You were under a lot of pressure. I know how that feels. When we played the escape game, Charles Chiltington put so much pressure on me I thought I might turn into a diamond."

Kyle must've looked confused.

"You know," said Andrew. "The way Superman can squeeze a lump of coal so hard that it turns into a diamond?"

"Riiight," said Kyle. "So, who swiped the book off the shelf?"

Andrew took a moment. "Marjory Muldauer. That's why she's with the priest. I think she feels bad and is giving him her full confession!"

"But why would she take the book?"

"Because my uncle Woody told her to."

Is that why Mr. Peckleman offered cheat cards to Miguel and Sierra? Kyle wondered. *Maybe he wasn't working for Mr. Lemoncello but against him!*

"Late last night," said Andrew, "I heard them both talking with Mrs. Chiltington about taking the book off the shelf. Uncle Woody had already checked out the other thirty-five copies, and he probably would've checked out the last one, too, except regular people weren't allowed in the library for a whole week while they fixed up the place for the Olympics."

Now Kyle wondered if this was why Marjory had blocked him instead of going for the book during the hover ladder race.

She had known the last copy of *Flora and Ulysses* wouldn't be on the shelf, because she'd already removed it. She probably didn't think she was a good enough actress to be the one who found the empty slot. But she didn't want Kyle finding it, either, because she assumed Mr. Lemoncello would give a medal to whoever found the spot where the book was supposed to be.

"Okay. So why did your uncle want the last copy of *Flora and Ulysses*?"

"I'm not sure," said Andrew. "But I am formulating a theory. It has to do with all those other books and encyclopedias you guys say are missing from the library. Do you have a complete list?"

Kyle shook his head. He should've thought of that.

How were they going to return all the missing books if they didn't even know what books were missing?

Then it hit him.

"Clarence does!"

"Who?"

"The head of security. Come on."

Kyle and Andrew went back into the dining area.

"You guys?" said Kyle.

"What's up?" asked Akimi.

"Andrew and I need to head back downtown. Sierra? Can you come with us?"

Sierra looked at Andrew, the boy who had stolen her library card during the escape game.

"I never really wanted to steal your library card," said Andrew. "Honestly. Charles made me do it."

"I know," said Sierra. Then she took a deep breath. "Should I tell the driver to fire up the bookmobile?"

"Definitely," said Kyle. "Go with Sierra, Andrew. I'll meet you guys out front."

"What's up?" asked Miguel.

"We have a lead on who might've checked out all those books."

"So what do you need the rest of us to do while you guys are gone?" asked Akimi.

"Round up all the medals. Make a list. See if there is some kind of pattern or hidden code."

"Or a treasure map etched on their backs!" said Miguel.

"Riiight. Or that. You guys have your phones?"

"Totally," said Akimi.

"Cool. Whoever finds out something first—"

"Calls the other ones."

Clarence met Kyle, Sierra, and Andrew in the lobby.

"We're looking for the missing books," said Kyle.

"Well, not to bust your chops, Mr. Keeley," said Clarence, "but I think you're looking in the wrong place. The books aren't here in the library. If they were, they wouldn't be missing."

"We know," said Kyle. "But we need to see your list."

"Why?"

"I have a theory," said Andrew.

Clarence gestured for the three treasure hunters to follow him through the red door into the control room.

"Here's the list. Hope it helps. I'll be out in the lobby if you need anything else."

Clarence left. Andrew and Sierra studied the pages.

"Aha!" said Andrew. "I was right."

"Good going, Andrew," said Sierra. "It's so obvious."

Kyle looked down at the list.

He had no idea what they were talking about.

48

"Have you read *Flora and Ulysses*?" Andrew asked Kyle.

Kyle looked at the floor and sort of shuffled his feet. "I wanted to. But all the copies were checked out or missing and . . ."

"It's about a squirrel, Kyle," said Sierra with a smile.

"So are all these other books," said Andrew.

Sierra read a few titles off the list. "*The Tale of Squirrel Nutkin* by Beatrix Potter. *The Bravest Squirrel Ever* by Sara Shafer. *Earl the Squirrel* by Don Freeman."

"*Earl*'s a great audiobook, too," said Andrew. "Uncle Woody also checked out every single book from the five hundreds room about squirrels—all three subcategories under 599.36 for Sciuridae."

"For *who*?" said Kyle.

" 'Sciuridae' means 'squirrel family,' " explained Sierra.

"Indeed it does," said Andrew, smiling at Sierra, who, believe it or not, was smiling back at him. "Uncle Woody took everything Mr. Lemoncello had about tree squirrels, ground squirrels, *and* flying squirrels."

"And then," said Sierra, "he went downstairs and scooped up all the Rocky and Bullwinkle DVDs."

"Because Rocky is a flying squirrel!" added Andrew eagerly. "He also removed all the 'S' encyclopedias. . . ."

"Because they'd have squirrels in them," said Kyle, finally catching on. "But why does your uncle need all these books? Is he some kind of squirrel nut?"

Andrew laughed. "Touché, Kyle. Very clever."

Sierra laughed, too. "I get it. Squirrel—nut."

"And Uncle Woody was *squirreling* away all the squirrel books he could!"

"So," said Kyle, "for whatever reason, your uncle loves squirrels so much he has to hoard every single squirrel book he can find?"

"Oh, no," said Andrew, sounding deadly serious again. He adjusted his glasses with his fingertip. "My uncle doesn't love squirrels. He *hates* them. What he loves are birds."

"Right," said Kyle. "All those bird feeders on the motel property. Calling it the Blue Jay Extended Stay Lodge. The way he looked at those birds up on the Wonder Dome that day."

"Correct. Uncle Woody thinks squirrels are 'nothing but thieving rodents' and 'rats with fluffy tails.' They make a mess of all his bird feeders."

227

"So since he hates squirrels, he doesn't want anybody else reading about them?"

Andrew shrugged. "I guess. Like we said, he's kind of nutty."

Kyle snapped his fingers. "This is why that Squirrel Squad video game never worked in the motel game room."

"Uncle Woody probably snipped the power cord."

"Do you know where he put the books?" asked Kyle.

"No," said Andrew. "I only started figuring this out early this morning, after I heard Uncle Woody talking to Marjory about *Flora and Ulysses*. However, if you guys will have me, I'd like to help you find the missing books."

"You would?"

"Certainly. No matter how much I disagree with Mr. Lemoncello and his loony ideas about libraries, I totally respect his right to stock his shelves with whatever books he chooses—and our right to read them."

Sierra was beaming when Andrew said that.

Kyle's phone started chirping. It was Akimi.

"What've you got?" he asked her.

"Meet us in Liberty Park, across the street from the motel."

"We're on our way." He ended the call. "Come on, you guys!"

"Where are we going?" asked Andrew.

"Liberty Park."

"Why?"

"I have no idea."

49

Kyle, Sierra, and Andrew piled into the bookmobile and took off.

"The park is right across the street from my uncle's motel," said Andrew. "Maybe he buried the squirrel books in the sandbox or something."

"All of them?" asked Sierra.

"Hang on, you guys," said Kyle as he thumb-dialed Akimi.

"Where are you, Kyle?" said Akimi the instant she answered.

"On our way."

"Well, hurry. We're all kind of confused."

"Who's with you?"

"Miguel and one player from each of the other teams."

"Nice. Whose idea was that?"

"Mine."

"Sweet!"

"Yeah. I can be very diplomatic when I'm about to lose my favorite library in the whole world."

"So what's up with Liberty Park? What sent you there?"

"The medals!" said Akimi. "Stephanie Youngerman from the Mountain team is an excellent code cracker. She's the one who figured it out."

"Figured what out?"

"Okay, here's the list of medals in the order they were given out: Gold, Olympian, Top Gun—"

"We won that one."

"We also won the Olympian Researcher. After that, Marjory scored the Libris. Then came the 'I Did It!,' the Bendable Bookworm, Eating It Up, Rebus, Thank You, and Yertle the Turtle medallions."

"Are they anagrams or something?"

"Nope. It's another version of Mr. Lemoncello's First Letters game. When you write down the first letter of all eleven medals, guess what it says."

Kyle had already scribbled out the answer on a scrap of paper: "Go to Liberty."

"Exactly," said Akimi. "And you said Mr. Lemoncello never repeats himself, never uses the same kind of clue twice."

"Well, he didn't. Not the exact same way."

"Whatever. But now that we're over here at the park, we don't know what we're looking for."

"Books about squirrels."

"Wha-hut?"

"That's what Andrew Peckleman figured out. His uncle Woody hates squirrels, on account of all his bird feeders. So he doesn't want anybody else in town reading about them, either."

"Why? Does he think that if all the squirrel books disappear, the squirrels will disappear, too?"

"Maybe."

"The man is definitely nutty," said Akimi.

Three minutes later, the bookmobile squealed to a stop outside Liberty Park, which was actually more of a playground with trees and picnic tables.

"You guys find anything?" Kyle asked Miguel.

"No. No signs of digging."

"Why are you looking for signs of digging?"

"Buried treasure, man. Like in *Treasure Island*."

"I don't think Mr. Peckleman would've buried his books over here," said the Texan, Angus Harper. "Somebody would've seen him doing it."

"You're right," said Kyle. "He wouldn't take that big of a risk."

"So why did Mr. Lemoncello send us here?" asked Diane Capriola, from the Southeast team.

"Liberty Park!" said Stephanie Youngerman. "It's another anagram!"

Everybody whipped out their smartphones and started using the notes app to rearrange the letters.

"Perky tribal!" shouted Miguel.

"Library kept!" said Stephanie Youngerman. "It has 'library' in it!"

While the other treasure hunters kept calling out weird word combinations, Kyle slowly rotated in place, scanning the park and the playground.

"What's that?" He pointed to a green humped structure with a bobble head attached to one side by a stubby neck made of coiled spring.

"That's for kids to climb on," said Andrew. "It's supposed to look like a turtle."

"And," said Kyle, "when Mr. Lemoncello gave Marjory Muldauer her Yertle the Turtle medal, he said it was the 'most important medal of all the very important medals awarded thus far.' Come on."

Kyle led the way to the shell-shaped turtle toy. Pranav Pillai, from the Pacific team, scooted under it.

"Score!" he shouted.

"What'd you find?" asked Kyle.

Pranav slid out from under the turtle and showed everybody what he'd found: a bright yellow envelope with "Clue" stamped on its front.

50

Kyle looked at what was written on the yellow card tucked into the yellow envelope:

41.376495

−83.651040

"Guess we better head back to the library," he said with a sigh. "More Dewey decimal numbers."

"Whoa, hang on," said Miguel.

"Those are not Dewey numbers, my friend," said Pranav Pillai.

"There aren't any negative numbers in Mr. Dewey's library classification system," explained Elliott Schilpp.

"I believe Mr. Lemoncello is inviting us to play a geocaching game," said Angus Harper. "Because those numbers sure look like GPS coordinates to me."

"What's geocaching?" asked Sierra.

"An outdoor recreational activity," said Pranav Pillai, "where one uses a GPS device and other navigational techniques to hide and seek waterproof containers that each have a logbook sealed inside, where you can sign your name to indicate that you found it."

Kyle smiled. A lot of these library experts sounded like dictionaries.

Angus Harper pulled out his smartphone. "And it just so happens that I have a GPS navigation app on my phone. Most fliers do. We tap in longitude 41.376495 and latitude negative 83.651040 and—*BOOM!*—this map shows us where to go."

A red pin dropped on the app's map, indicating a spot just across the street from Liberty Park.

"That's near the motel!" said Miguel.

"Looks like the mailbox out front!" said Andrew.

"Let's go check it out," said Kyle.

The group of twelve new teammates trooped down to the crosswalk, where they waited for the light to change.

"You can't miss the mailbox," said Andrew. "It's shaped like a bird."

The light changed.

Kyle and Akimi led the charge across the street to the boxy blue mailbox. It had wooden wings nailed to its sides and a tail feather on its rear. To open the drop-down front, you had to tug on the bluebird's beak.

"Another envelope," said Abia Sulayman when Kyle opened the mailbox.

"Is it official USPS mail?" asked Stephanie Youngerman. "If so, it is a federal offense for us to open it."

"No," said Kyle. "It's another yellow envelope with 'Clue' stamped on the front."

"Open it," urged Angus.

Kyle tore open the envelope.

"It's a bunch of riddles," he reported. "Three of them."

Diane Capriola, who had won her spot on the Southeast team by solving riddles, stepped forward.

"Let me see that," she said.

Kyle was pretty good with riddles, too, but he handed the envelope over to Diane.

"First riddle," she said. " 'What has four wheels and flies?' "

"An airplane!" blurted Miguel.

"Hold that thought," said Diane. "Second riddle: 'You'll find your next clue in the red stump.' "

The other eleven kids started looking around the motel grounds, searching for a brightly painted tree stump.

"And finally, riddle three: 'Everything I do goes to waste.' " She closed up the envelope. "All three clues are sending us to the same place."

"The woods?" said Nicole Wisniewski, who was still looking for the red stump. "I'm not big on woods. I'm from Chicago."

"No," said Diane. "The third riddle is a pun. The second riddle is a jumble. And the first riddle is for kindergartners."

"So, Kyle," said Akimi, "that means you can probably handle it."

Kyle grinned. "That's okay. I'm sure Diane knows the answer."

"Yep," she said. "The Dumpster."

"This way," said Andrew. "It's behind the kitchen."

He led the way around the main building to a small loading dock in the back.

"Oh, I get it," said Miguel. "The Dumpster has four wheels and attracts flies."

"Also," said Sierra, " 'Dumpster' and 'red stump' are spelled with the same letters."

"Yep," said Diane, "and everything a Dumpster does 'goes to waste.' "

"Good work," said Kyle. "Now who wants to lift the lid?"

Even closed, the Dumpster reeked of rotting fruit and rancid dairy products.

"You," said Akimi, pointing at Kyle with one hand while swatting at the foul air and buzzing flies with the other. "You're the team captain."

"Of our hometown team," said Kyle, "but not this one. This is more like one of those superhero teams in the comic books."

"We could be the Justice League of Libraries," said Pranav Pillai eagerly.

The guy sounded like he *really* liked comic books.

"All in favor of Kyle Keeley being our captain, no matter what our team is called, please raise your right hand," said Akimi.

Everybody, including Andrew Peckleman, shot one hand into the air. They were using their other hands to hold their noses or fan the air in front of their faces.

The vote was unanimous.

Kyle was elected captain. He would open the Dumpster.

He might also need to climb inside it.

Even though he was lifting a lid on a fly factory, Kyle was feeling pretty pumped.

This new team of super library geeks seemed invincible. They were Mr. Lemoncello's Champion Crusaders, standing up for what was right in a world gone wrong. Sharing knowledge to boldly conquer the unknown.

Or something like that.

Kyle watched a lot of movie trailers.

A warm blast of sour-milk-rotten-lettuce-dirty-diaper air made Kyle's eyes water as he raised the rubbery lid on the Dumpster.

Fortunately, a plastic-wrapped envelope labeled "Clue," with something rectangular in it, was attached to the lid's underside. There would be no need for Dumpster diving.

Kyle tugged the envelope free and heard the unmistakable sound of Velcro strips separating. He tossed the

package, which felt like a wrapped-up book, to Andrew. Kyle let go of the lid and the Dumpster's rubber cover slammed.

"Can we go somewhere a little less rank to open it?" asked Akimi, trying to breathe only through her mouth.

"Definitely," said Kyle.

The whole team scurried away from the loading dock and back to the parking lot outside the motel lobby.

"Where's your boss?" Akimi asked Andrew.

"He must be running errands. His truck is gone."

"Open it," Kyle said to Andrew.

Andrew tore at the tape and plastic bag protecting the thick yellow envelope with "Clue" inked on the front. Inside, he found a book.

He read the title out loud: " *'Louie the Locksmith's Big Book of Padlocks, Dead Bolts, and Tumblers'?*"

Pranav Pillai smiled at the book. "And so, old friend, we meet again."

"What do you mean?" asked Akimi.

"To earn my place on the Pacific team," said Pranav, "I had to use the Dewey decimal code on this very book."

He flipped the book sideways and read its spine.

"Oh, my. This is incorrect."

"I'll say," said Abia Sulayman. "It should be in the six hundreds with books about technology, not the nine hundreds with history and geography."

"What's the call number?" asked Andrew.

Pranav read it off: "Nine-four-three-point-seven."

"That is soooo wrong," said Andrew.

"True," said Pranav. "But it could be wrong on purpose. You see, when I played the escape game in Silicon Valley, the Dewey decimal number for the locksmith book was also the combination for the lock on the library door."

"So whatever lock we're looking for," said Sierra, "couldn't have the same combination as that one."

Andrew slapped his hand to his forehead, nearly smashing his goggle-sized glasses.

"The storage locker! I'm sorry, you guys. I should've thought of this sooner."

"That's okay, Andrew," said Sierra. "You thought of it now. Go on."

"Well, my uncle Woody has this humongous safe. The vault door is the size of a motel room door. It's hidden behind a sliding panel in the front office."

"Then this is most likely the combination," said Pranav.

"The office looks empty," reported Nicole Wisniewski, peering through the windows. "We should go check it out."

"All of us?" asked Elliott Schilpp.

"Yep," said Kyle. "There's strength in numbers."

"Kyle's right," said Akimi. "If Andrew's creepy uncle . . . No offense, Andrew. . . ."

Andrew held up his hand. "None taken."

Akimi continued: "If the birdman of Alexandriaville comes back, a dozen kids should be able to hold him at bay."

"We could tell him we just spotted an ivory-billed woodpecker or a blue-throated hummingbird," said Abia Sulayman.

"Huh?" said Akimi.

"Both species are very high on every birdwatcher's 'must see' list. I am something of a birder myself."

"Come on," said Kyle. "Let's go crack open that safe."

The twelve treasure hunters made their way through the lobby and into the motel office.

"That's the wall," said Andrew, pointing to the sheet of paneling sporting a framed portrait of two bluebirds.

"Which way does it slide?" asked Kyle.

"To the right," said Andrew.

He and Kyle put their hands on the wall and shoved it sideways.

The panel rolled away and revealed a tall steel door with a combination lock right above a thick metal handle.

"Okay, Pranav," said Kyle, "you're on."

Pranav Pillai stepped forward and spun the dial three times to clear it. Then he worked the combination.

"Right to nine. Left to four. Right to three. Left to seven."

He pressed down on the handle.

It didn't budge.

"Try it again," suggested Kyle. "But reverse it."

"Ah, yes," said Pranav. "An excellent suggestion."

He spun the dial to clear it, then worked the new combination.

"*Left* to nine. *Right* to four. Left to three. Right to seven."

Something clicked.

Pranav pressed down on the handle.

The door to the vault swung open.

52

The motel safe was huge, the size of a whole room, which was what it probably had been until Mr. Peckleman converted it into a steel-walled high-security vault.

It was also empty except for a couple of stacks of birdseed sacks. Kyle couldn't believe it.

"There's nothing in here," he said.

"But it looks like there used to be," said Angus Harper. "Check out those marks on the carpet." He pointed to the floor.

"Indentations that might've been made by heavy boxes," said Elliott Schilpp.

"Book boxes," added Sierra.

"No!" somebody screamed outside the motel. "You can't do it!"

"That sounds like Marjory," said Nicole Wisniewski. "She screamed at us all the time."

"Come on!" said Kyle.

The twelve treasure hunters tore out of the office, raced across the lobby, and headed out to the patio, where all the other Library Olympians and their chaperones were standing in a circle, staring at something that was making their jaws drop.

Kyle heard a crackle and a pop.

He pushed his way through the crowd.

Mr. Peckleman stood next to the blazing fire pit, laughing hysterically.

Marjory was there, too. Tears streamed down her cheeks.

"I'm begging you, sir," Marjory said. "Don't do this."

"What's going on?" demanded one of the chaperones.

"We're going to get rid of these wretched squirrel books, once and for all," cackled Mr. Peckleman.

"Oh, no you are not," said Akimi, shoving her way to the front of the crowd to join Kyle near the roaring fire pit.

Kyle could see garden carts, a little red wagon, and a wheelbarrow loaded down with books. On top of the pile closest to him was *Flora and Ulysses*.

"Marjory told me all about how you tricked her into stealing that book," said a man in a priest collar, who Kyle figured had to be Father Mike, chaperone for the Midwest team. "I'm going to call the police."

"Try it, Padre," snapped Mr. Peckleman, "and I start tossing books on the bonfire the second your finger touches your phone. I figure I can burn through most of 'em before

the police even show up. They're very busy this afternoon down at the Lemoncello Library. It seems an anonymous tipster just phoned in a report of a major book burglary."

"That was you!" whined Andrew. "How can you do this, Uncle Woody?"

"Easy. You see, I agree with that lunatic Lemoncello: 'Knowledge not shared remains unknown.' Well, if I destroy this so-called knowledge about squirrels, no one will ever know it existed." He held up a copy of *Flora and Ulysses*. "A squirrel who writes poetry? *Pah!* Squirrels are nothing but thieving rodents. Rats with fluffy tails! They're bullies who steal food from innocent birds."

"Look, Mr. Peckleman," said Kyle, "just because you don't like books about squirrels . . ."

"Nobody else should, either! Don't you see, Mr. Keeley? I'm trying to protect you children. You shouldn't be forced to read lies about a squirrel named Earl who wears a red scarf and can't find his own acorn. Your young eyes should not be exposed to videos about a flying squirrel who shares his home with a talking moose."

"That's a cartoon," said Kyle. "It's not real."

Kyle didn't know what to do.

Mr. Peckleman was nuttier than any of them had suspected.

And the fire pit was really blazing.

If the police were busy downtown at the library, investigating the theft of the missing books, it would take them maybe ten minutes to race all the way up to the motel.

245

Mr. Peckleman could burn a ton of books in ten minutes.

Kyle had to do something. Saving Mr. Lemoncello's library had to include protecting its books, even the ones some people didn't like.

"Look, Mr. Peckleman, let's make a deal. . . ."

"Oh, that's right. Andrew told me about you. You're the game boy. You think you can make some kind of trade with me like you would if we were playing Monopoly?"

"Why not? What are you afraid of?"

"Not you, Kyle Keeley. Or any of your friends. What I am doing is right!"

"Then let's play a game. If we win, you don't burn a single book."

"And if *I* win?"

Kyle looked to Akimi.

She nodded.

He turned to Mrs. Yunghans.

"Do what you have to do, Kyle. We're running out of time."

Finally, Kyle looked at Marjory Muldauer.

She nodded, too.

"Okay, Mr. Peckleman," said Kyle, "if you can beat us in a game—"

The old man jabbed a finger at Kyle. "I get to choose the game, right?"

"Fine. But remember—if we win, you have to leave the books alone."

"Yes, I heard you the first time," said Mr. Peckleman. "But what do I get if I win?"

Kyle swallowed hard. "The books."

Mr. Peckleman's eyes bugged out and he sneered. "I already have the books. I want something more! Something to make this game a little more . . . exciting."

Kyle was stumped. He didn't know what else to offer.

A breeze fanned the flames. Made them leap higher.

That's when Marjory Muldauer stepped forward.

"If you win," she said, "you can burn this, too."

She held up her "Go to College Free" card.

53

"Oh, this is interesting," said Mr. Peckleman, rubbing his hands together and leering at the card in Marjory's hand. "Very interesting, indeed."

"Wait," Kyle said to Marjory. "That card's worth thousands of dollars."

"Actually," said Marjory, "it's worth 234,428 dollars. I plan on attending Harvard. For four years."

"Well, that makes your card even more important. You can't just throw it away."

"Yes, I can. Some things are even more important than a free college education. Including 323.443: 'freedom of speech.'"

She handed her card to Mr. Peckleman.

Everyone gasped.

Kyle glanced at the books. He couldn't believe what

he was about to do. He couldn't believe he was even *thinking* about doing it. His brothers would tease him about it for the rest of his life, because it was definitely crazy.

But that didn't stop him.

"Fine," he said, pulling his college scholarship card out of his shirt pocket. "If you win, you can burn mine, too."

Akimi stepped forward. "And mine," she said.

"And mine," said Angus Harper.

"And mine," said twenty-eight other voices as every single one of the Library Olympians stepped forward to hand Mr. Peckleman their orange prize coupons.

"Excellent," giggled Mr. Peckleman, crumbling the thirty-two cards in his hand, wadding them up into one extremely flammable paper ball. "You're on, Mr. Keeley. Mr. Lemoncello won't give you your scholarships. Not without these. Cards must be present to win."

"What's the game?" demanded Kyle.

"Let's see. How about a riddle?"

"Fine. We've got several players who are excellent at solving riddles."

"Who cares? You're the one who made the challenge."

"I know, but . . ."

"What? Afraid you might lose and ruin all of your friends' dreams of a college education at the same time?"

"Riddles aren't my best sport."

"Too bad. I insist on trial by single combat. A duel

between two champions that will decide the fate of everyone and everything else. No one may interfere or offer advice. You, Kyle Keeley, are on your own."

Kyle felt that nervous flutter in his stomach again. Trying to be a hero wasn't always easy or fun.

He looked at his best friend, Akimi.

"Do it."

"You can take him, Kyle," said Andrew.

"Go on, Keeley," said Marjory Muldauer. "Even I'm rooting for you."

Kyle turned to face Mr. Peckleman.

"Okay. I accept your challenge. If I answer your riddle correctly, you don't burn a single book. We take them all back to Mr. Lemoncello's library."

"But if you can't answer my riddle," sneered Peckleman, "if you fail, you and your library-loving friends have to stand here and watch me destroy all of these horrible books and all of these lovely orange cards."

"Deal."

"Oh, this is going to be fun," said Mr. Peckleman. "Let me think. . . . I need a really good riddle . . . one that's almost impossible to solve. . . ."

Kyle waited, giving a little voice deep inside his head time to remind him that *every chance to win is also a chance to lose.*

So Kyle told that little voice to shut up.

Because he needed every brain cell he could spare focused on Mr. Peckleman's riddle.

"All right, Mr. Keeley. Here is your riddle: You are a prisoner in a room with two doors. One leads farther down into the dungeon and certain death; one leads to freedom. There are two guards in the room with you, one at each door. One guard always tells the truth. One always lies. You don't know which is which. What single question can you ask one of the guards that will help you find the door that leads to freedom?"

Oh, man.

Kyle wished somebody else had made the challenge.

But they hadn't. He had.

Concentrate, Kyle told himself. *You can do this thing. Okay.*

If Kyle wanted to find out which guard told the truth and which one told lies, he could ask, "If I asked the other guard whether you always told the truth, what would he say?" If the guard he asked said, "No," that would mean he was definitely talking to the truth teller. If the guy said, "Yes," that would mean he was the liar, because he never told the truth, about himself *or* the other guard.

Kyle's head was starting to hurt.

"I'm waiting, Mr. Keeley," said Mr. Peckleman, pinching the thin picture book *Earl the Squirrel* between his thumb and forefinger so he could dangle it over the fire pit.

"Gimme a second."

But Kyle had only *one* question to find the right door.

He couldn't do a two-step dance and first find out who

was the truthful guard and then ask him which door to use.

So . . .

He had to ask . . .

"My single question," he said, "to either one of the guards . . ."

Everyone was hanging on his every word.

". . . would be . . . 'If I were to ask the other guard, which door would *he* say leads to freedom?' I would then choose the door opposite of the one the guard told me."

"Are you certain, Mr. Keeley?"

"Yes! Because if the guard I ask is the one who always tells the truth, he would tell me the other guard, the lying guy, would point to the door of death. If I asked the guard who always lies, he would also point me to the door of death, because he's a liar. So in either case, I'd choose the door the guard *wasn't* pointing to."

"He's right," declared Marjory. "Right?"

Mr. Peckleman lowered his book.

But not into the fire.

He gently placed it on top of the heap in the little red wagon.

"Well done, Library Olympians. Bravo!"

All of a sudden, Mr. Peckleman had a British accent.

"By being willing to sacrifice everything you thought you came here to win, you have all proven yourselves to be true champions."

Kyle half expected the guy to say "pip pip, cheerio" or something.

Instead, he heard sirens approaching.

The police.

They were flanking a car shaped like a big boot and another one that looked like a pouncing cat.

54

The boot was another playing piece from Mr. Lemoncello's Family Frenzy board game.

So Kyle had a pretty good idea who was driving the bootmobile.

His hero. Luigi L. Lemoncello.

The boot car turned into the motel driveway with Dr. Zinchenko's green-eyed catmobile following close behind.

Kyle couldn't figure out what was going on. Mr. Lemoncello had said he was leaving town. Going to New York or Terabithia, which sounded like it might be in Indiana.

The police cars escorting the two game pieces on wheels had flapping Library Olympics flags attached to their bumpers. They weren't coming to the motel to arrest

Mr. Peckleman. They were just part of Mr. Lemoncello's motorcade.

The boot car skidded to a stop near the patio. Dr. Zinchenko's cat car crawled to a halt behind it. Mr. Lemoncello popped open the boot ankle and stepped out.

"Donald?" cried Mr. Lemoncello, his voice booming across the parking lot. "Extinguish thy flame!"

"I fly with haste to do thy bidding," said Mr. Peckleman, sounding all of a sudden like he was in a play by Shakespeare. He bent down and flipped a switch on the fire pit. The flames disappeared in a poof!

"Gas logs," said Mr. Lemoncello. "Just another part of our glorious charade."

"Huh?" said Kyle.

Mr. Lemoncello was dressed in a bright yellow tracksuit and a half-lemon crash helmet, which he unbuckled and tucked under his arm as he strode onto the patio.

"Please cover those books with their protective tarps," coached Dr. Zinchenko, who was dressed in her standard red leather minidress, scarlet stockings, red high heels, and red-framed librarian glasses.

"Thy wish is my command, milady!" Mr. Peckleman ruffled open a bright blue tarp with a theatrical flourish and draped it over all the squirrel books.

Mr. Lemoncello approached Andrew Peckleman.

"Andrew?"

"Yes, sir?"

"My grandmother isn't Strega Nona, and you don't have a long-lost great-uncle-twice-removed named Woody."

"I don't?"

"No. Meet Sir Donald Thorne, one of the finest actors in all of England!"

Sir Donald, who everybody had thought was Uncle Woodrow "Woody" Peckleman, took off his Blue Jays baseball cap and twirled it in front of his face as he took a bow.

" 'All the world's a stage,' " he said. " 'And all the men and women merely players.' "

"Sir Donald also coached Dr. Zinchenko and me so we might play our own parts with passion and panache." Mr. Lemoncello started imitating himself, acting much more melodramatically than he had in his original performance. "Oh, boo hoo. I, Luigi Libretto Lemoncello, hereby officially declare the games of this first Library Olympiad to be over. Done. Kaput!"

"Wait a second," said Akimi. "That was all an act?"

"Indeed."

"You were very convincing, sir," said Sierra.

"Sir Donald is an excellent coach."

"And thou, sir, art an excellent pupil." Sir Donald took another bow.

"Thank you," said Mr. Lemoncello, taking his own little bow.

256

"But why were you pretending to give up on the library?" asked Kyle.

"To make absolutely, positutely certain that all of you would not do the same. Now, before I made my dramatic exit, I promised I would appoint a new board of trustees for my library on Monday. All public institutions similar to ours have such boards. . . ."

"Indeed they do," added Dr. Zinchenko. "Mostly to raise funds and to make certain the institution fulfills its mission."

"Well," said Mr. Lemoncello, "my library never has to worry about raising funds. Did I mention I'm a bazillionaire?"

"Yes," said Abia Sulayman. "We have heard."

"However, I do need a board of trustees to champion my cause here in Alexandriaville. That's the real reason I hosted these Library Olympics. I told you it was a quest for champions. And it was. I was looking for library lovers willing to stand up and fight for what's right, no matter the cost or personal sacrifice." He paused and looked directly at Marjory. "Even if they did not agree with my way of doing things."

"I'm sorry I took that book," said Marjory.

"We figured somebody would once Mr. Peckleman started passing out his 'Go to College Free' cards. It was a test. To see if you, or anyone else, were here for the wrong reasons. I'm overjoyed that, in the end, you fought so hard

to save these books, because believe it or not, Marjory, I, too, love libraries qua libraries. I just don't like saying 'qua.' It makes me sound like a duck."

Everyone, including Marjory, laughed.

"Now then," said Mr. Lemoncello, putting down his crash helmet so he could clasp his hands behind his back and address his Library Olympians, "seeing the results of this final game, I feel confident that I have finally found my first board of trustees. In the end, you all worked together to save the library even though there was no prize except the knowledge, joy, and wonder contained inside the pages of its books."

"But, um, we're not adults," said Akimi.

"Thank goodness. Adults can be so serious and dull. And as you all know, reading and learning are anything but dull!"

"You really want me on your board?" asked Marjory.

"Oh, yes. Couldn't do it without you. Or Andrew."

"I wasn't in the Olympics," said Andrew.

"Minor technicality. You're a trustee now, Mr. Peckleman. Congratulations!"

"But I live in Michigan," said Marjory.

"And my library has state-of-the-art technology, including very high-speed Wi-Fi, so we can all chat via your brand-new smartphones. I need your help—Marjory, Andrew, all of you—to make certain my library is the best that it can be. All I ask is that you always champion freedom of speech, freedom of expression, and freedom of fun!"

"Well, I guess a little fun is okay," said Marjory. "As long as there's always a quiet place for people to read."

"It's why the Electronic Learning Center has sound-proof walls." Mr. Lemoncello opened his arms to the group. "So, will you thirty-three new trustees share this quest for truth and knowledge with me?"

"We will!" everyone answered, including Marjory Muldauer, who actually seemed to be enjoying herself.

55

Kyle thought the closing ceremonies were a blast.

Mr. Lemoncello handed out thirty-three full college scholarships before switching off the giant swirling flashlight. A DJ spun dance tunes. There was a huge sheet cake shaped like an open book. On it, written in yellow on a sea of fudgy frosting, were these words: "Open a Book and Open Your Mind."

"Congratulations, Mr. Keeley," said Dr. Zinchenko, who was slicing the cake and passing out pieces. "Oh, I nearly forgot. Mrs. Gause wanted me to give you this. I checked it out of the nine hundreds room."

She handed Kyle a book.

"Mrs. Gause?" said Kyle. "The holographic librarian from when the old library was torn down?"

"That's right. She thought you might like to know why."

Kyle studied the book's cover: *Ohio River Pirates and Scallywags*.

"It's a history book, obviously," said Dr. Zinchenko. "It was written by a teacher at Chumley Prep. I think you'll find chapter eleven to be very enlightening. It's all about a bandit named Ugly Chuck Willoughby, who led the Hole-in-the-Rocks gang, a group of pirates who plundered flatboats along the Ohio River in the late 1700s."

"Wait a second," said Kyle. "Isn't Charles Chiltington's super-rich uncle, Mrs. Chiltington's brother, named Willoughby?"

"Yes. James Willoughby the third. This book will tell you exactly *how* the Willoughby family fortune got its start and why Mrs. Chiltington was so disappointed to find the book on the shelves of the new Lemoncello Library."

"Did she want it banned from the old library, too?"

"Of course. And when Mrs. Gause refused to do her bidding . . ."

"Mrs. Chiltington sent in the bulldozers."

"Actually," said Dr. Zinchenko, "*Mr.* Chiltington is the one in the construction business. Together, they were hoping to rewrite the history that didn't fit their family myth."

"So this book is the real reason why Mrs. Chiltington wanted to take over the Lemoncello Library, isn't it?"

Dr. Zinchenko smiled. "Knowledge can be a very powerful and, for some, frightening thing, Kyle. Especially when it's shared with the whole world, including your neighbors."

"Thank you for this," said Kyle.

He tucked the Ohio history book under his arm and, balancing his cake plate, went over to where Mr. Lemoncello was chatting with Sir Donald Thorne, the actor who didn't look so much like a chicken now that he was out of costume and had taken off his fake rubber nose.

"Oh, you should have seen me when I held that book over the flames, Luigi! I was amazing."

"Yes, Donald," said Mr. Lemoncello politely. "I'm sure you were."

"And when I tricked Mrs. Chiltington into thinking we were co-conspirators? That was some of my best work ever."

"Yes, Donald . . ."

"And my eyes. This is how I bugged them out when I was pretending to be a few sandwiches short of a picnic."

"Very convincing, Donald . . ."

Mr. Lemoncello sounded bored, so Kyle butted in.

"Mr. Lemoncello?"

His eyes brightened. "Excuse me, Donald. Urgent business. I must speak with a member of my new board."

Mr. Lemoncello touched Kyle's shoulder and urged him to step away from Sir Donald Thorne.

Quickly.

"What is it, Kyle?"

"Can I ask you a question?"

"Certainly. In fact, as a trustee of the Lemoncello Library, you are duty bound to come to me with any and all questions you might have."

"Well, sir, was part of this whole Olympic Games thing an attempt to get Andrew Peckleman to like libraries again? Is that why you had Sir Donald pretend to be *his* great-uncle instead of, say, mine or Miguel's?"

Mr. Lemoncello smiled slyly. "Why, Kyle Keeley, do you really think I am that cunning and clever?"

"Yes, sir. That's why your games are so good."

Mr. Lemoncello laughed and nodded toward the far side of the patio, where Andrew Peckleman and Sierra Russell were sharing a piece of cake and laughing.

"My guess is they're talking about their favorite books," said Kyle.

"And my guess," said Mr. Lemoncello, "is that Andrew will be coming to the Lemoncello Library every single Monday, Wednesday, and Friday after school."

"You think so?"

"Certainly. That's when Sierra's there."

Epilogue

On the first day of spring break, two weeks after all the visiting Olympians had gone home, Kyle Keeley biked downtown to the Lemoncello Library.

Charles Chiltington was outside, as usual, walking back and forth on the sidewalk, carrying a protest sign that said "Mr. Lemoncello's Library Is Execrable."

Kyle parked his bike and waved. "Hey, Charles."

"Keeley."

"You want to come inside and check out our reference section? Maybe borrow a thesaurus?"

"What?"

"I totally respect your freedom of expression, Charles. I just think you might be able to express yourself more clearly if you didn't use big words on all your signs. See ya!"

Kyle bounded up the marble steps and entered the

lobby, where the statue of Mr. Lemoncello—with his head tilted back and water spewing out of his puckered fish lips—was gurgling away again. They'd fixed up his slogan about knowledge not shared on the base and added a new one on the side:

A LIBRARY IS AN ARSENAL OF LIBERTY.

In the Rotunda Reading Room, patrons were happily hover-browsing the fiction shelves. Clarence and Clement were checking their email on the built-in desktop tablet computers. Some college kids were huddled around another table, doing some sort of serious research project. And Mrs. Lonni Gause, the holographic librarian, was helping out behind the circulation desk without fear of being bulldozed. Because this library had true champions, intellectual freedom fighters who would do whatever it took to protect it: Mr. Lemoncello, of course, and all the library lovers from the first-ever Library Olympiad, plus Andrew Peckleman.

"Yo, Kyle?" said Miguel as he and Akimi came down one of the spiral staircases. "There's a brand-new game up in the Electronic Learning Center."

"You stand on a platform, slide your feet, and go skating down a frozen canal with Hans Brinker," added Akimi.

"You start out on wooden skates," said Miguel, "but you can win silver ones. Just like in the book."

"It's a brand-new Lemoncello concept," said Akimi.

"Audio-animatronic books. You get to act out a whole novel along with its main characters."

"You also get to skate," added Miguel.

"You guys have fun," said Kyle. "I promised Dr. Z I'd help out in the Children's Room for a couple hours today."

"Cool," said Miguel. "I'm doing that tomorrow. With Sierra and Andrew." He waggled his eyebrows knowingly. "Catch you later, bro."

"Later."

Kyle went into the Children's Room, where kids were reading books with their moms and dads or watching a puppet show or listening to a storyteller or singing along with Mother Goose and her goslings.

"Excuse me," said a small voice behind Kyle.

Kyle turned around. "Can I help you?"

"Is this book any good?"

A tiny boy was holding a copy of *Flora and Ulysses.*

"Oh, it's excellent," said Kyle. "I read it last week. It's all about a squirrel who gets sucked up inside a vacuum cleaner and turns into a poetry-writing superhero."

"Awesome!"

The kid ran to the checkout desk with his prize.

Kyle watched him go and felt great.

Actually, he felt fantastic.

It was definitely another cake day.

THE THIRTEENTH GAME

Are the games really over? Of course not. Here's one final puzzle:

> *Twenty things you just read,*
> *Twenty things Mr. Lemoncello said,*
> *Were once not allowed to be read*
> *Because of what other people said.*

Can you find them all? If so, send an email with your list to author@ChrisGrabenstein.com.

AUTHOR'S NOTE

Writing this book about banned books (which, yikes, might be banned in some places because of its subject matter) made me remember when I was in the fifth grade and bought (with my allowance money) my first subscription to *MAD* magazine. I think it cost less than five dollars for the whole year.

Every month, *MAD* was filled with hysterical satire of TV shows and movies, sarcastic spoofs, and funny fake ads. The thing was pure irreverence in ink and paper.

MAD (along with the *Rocky and Bullwinkle* cartoons) did more to spark

my love of words and humor than anything else during my middle school years.

I remember my monthly installment of *MAD* magazine arrived by mail in a plain brown wrapper because some adults thought its satire and lack of respect for authority made it questionable, maybe even subversive. Many of those adults also thought the magazine should be banned, that impressionable children (like me) should not be allowed to read it.

But read it I did. (Maybe even more hungrily because I knew reading it was considered a form of rebellion.)

My own parents had no problem with my reading *MAD*. I think my father, having seen combat in World War II, had that Greatest Generation's skepticism about blind obedience to rules and those in authority.

When I did improvisational comedy in a Greenwich Village theater—what the *New York Times* described as "basically impudent madness" in a review of our show— we were called the First Amendment Improvisation and Comedy Company. Nightly, we exercised our First Amendment right of freedom of speech to poke fun at politicians and current events and goofy trends and just about anything that needed fun poked at it. We were a living, breathing *MAD* magazine.

And now that I am an author, I always feel a small surge of pride when I read that tiny type printed inside all of my Random House books: "Random House Children's

Books supports the First Amendment and celebrates the right to read."

Doing research for this story, I was amazed at how many children's books have been banned over the years. Not just in the past but as recently as yesterday.

I found myself agreeing with former American Library Association (ALA) president Carol Brey-Casiano, who said, "Not every book is right for every person, but providing a wide range of reading choices is vital for learning, exploration, and imagination. The abilities to read, speak, think, and express ourselves freely are core American values."

I like this bumper sticker of a slogan, too: "Free your mind. Read a banned book."

The ALA sponsors an annual Banned Books Week in September. It's a great time for teachers, students, and librarians to discuss what the First Amendment truly means.

Mr. Lemoncello will definitely be celebrating it this year at his library.

There will be balloons. Cake, too.

And lots and lots of books. Even ones Mr. Lemoncello doesn't really like.

Read more:

ala.org/advocacy/bbooks/banned
teachhub.com/banned-book-week-activites

MR. LEMONCELLO'S LIBRARY OLYMPICS
BOOK LIST

Here's a complete list of the books mentioned in *Mr. Lemoncello's Library Olympics* that you can find in *your* library. (How many have *you* read?)

☐ *The Adventures of Captain Underpants* by Dav Pilkey
☐ *Anne of Green Gables* by L. M. Montgomery
☐ *The Bad Beginning* by Lemony Snicket
☐ *Because of Winn-Dixie* by Kate DiCamillo
☐ *Birdman of Alcatraz* by Thomas E. Gladdis
☐ *Bleak House* by Charles Dickens
☐ *Blubber* by Judy Blume
☐ *The Book Thief* by Markus Zusak
☐ *The Bravest Squirrel Ever* by Sara Shafer
☐ *Bridge to Terabithia* by Katherine Paterson
☐ *Brown Bear, Brown Bear, What Do You See?*
   by Bill Martin Jr. and Eric Carle

- [ ] *Bud, Not Buddy* by Christopher Paul Curtis
- [ ] *The Candymakers* by Wendy Mass
- [ ] *Charlie and the Chocolate Factory* by Roald Dahl
- [ ] *Charlotte's Web* by E. B. White
- [ ] *Criss Cross* by Lynne Rae Perkins
- [ ] *Earl the Squirrel* by Don Freeman
- [ ] *Elijah of Buxton* by Christopher Paul Curtis
- [ ] *Fahrenheit 451* by Ray Bradbury
- [ ] *Flora and Ulysses: The Illuminated Adventures* by Kate DiCamillo
- [ ] *The Fourteenth Goldfish* by Jennifer L. Holm
- [ ] *The Girl Who Loved Wild Horses* by Paul Goble
- [ ] *Goodnight Moon* by Margaret Wise Brown
- [ ] *Great Expectations* by Charles Dickens
- [ ] *Green Eggs and Ham* by Dr. Seuss
- [ ] *Gregor the Overlander* by Suzanne Collins
- [ ] *Hans Brinker, or The Silver Skates* by Mary Mapes Dodge
- [ ] *Harriet the Spy* by Louise Fitzhugh
- [ ] *Harry Potter and the Prisoner of Azkaban* by J. K. Rowling
- [ ] *Holes* by Louis Sachar
- [ ] *The Hunger Games* by Suzanne Collins
- [ ] *Incident at Hawk's Hill* by Allan W. Eckert
- [ ] *Inside Out and Back Again* by Thanhha Lai
- [ ] *It's Not Easy Being Bad* by Cynthia Voigt
- [ ] Junie B. Jones series by Barbara Park
- [ ] *The Kite Runner* by Khaled Hosseini

☐ *A Light in the Attic* by Shel Silverstein
☐ *Lilly's Purple Plastic Purse* by Kevin Henkes
☐ *The Lion, the Witch, and the Wardrobe*
  by C. S. Lewis
☐ *Little Women* by Louisa May Alcott
☐ *Lizzie Bright and the Buckminster Boy*
  by Gary D. Schmidt
☐ *A Long Way from Chicago* by Richard Peck
☐ *The Lorax* by Dr. Seuss
☐ *Lord of the Flies* by William Golding
☐ Maximum Ride series by James Patterson
☐ *Morris the Moose* by B. Wiseman
☐ *Mr. Popper's Penguins*
  by Richard and Florence Atwater
☐ *Nothing but the Truth: A Documentary Novel* by Avi
☐ *The Odyssey* by Homer
☐ *One Came Home* by Amy Timberlake
☐ *The Paper Airplane Book* by Seymour Simon
☐ Percy Jackson series by Rick Riordan
☐ *Peter Pan* by J. M. Barrie
☐ *Pippi Longstocking* by Astrid Lindgren
☐ *The Postcard* by Tony Abbott
☐ *Sammy Keyes and the Hotel Thief*
  by Wendelin Van Draanen
☐ *Shabanu: Daughter of the Wind*
  by Suzanne Fisher Staples
☐ *Sound the Jubilee* by Sandra Forrester
☐ *Splendors and Glooms* by Laura Amy Schlitz

☐ *Strega Nona* by Tomie dePaola
☐ *The Tale of Despereaux* by Kate DiCamillo
☐ *The Tale of Squirrel Nutkin* by Beatrix Potter
☐ *A Tangle of Knots* by Lisa Graff
☐ *Treasure Island* by Robert Louis Stevenson
☐ *Twerp* by Mark Goldblatt
☐ *Ulysses* by James Joyce
☐ *Uncle Tom's Cabin* by Harriet Beecher Stowe
☐ *Ungifted* by Gordon Korman
☐ *The Very Hungry Caterpillar* by Eric Carle
☐ *Walter the Farting Dog*
    by William Kotzwinkle and Glenn Murray
☐ *Watership Down* by Richard Adams
☐ *When Shlemiel Went to Warsaw and Other Stories*
    by Isaac Bashevis Singer
☐ *Where's Waldo?* by Martin Handford
☐ *The Wonderful Wizard of Oz* by L. Frank Baum
☐ *A Wrinkle in Time* by Madeleine L'Engle
☐ *The Year of Billy Miller* by Kevin Henkes
☐ *Yertle the Turtle and Other Stories* by Dr. Seuss

THANK YOU . . .

To the many, many people who helped make this return to Mr. Lemoncello's Library possible.

My wondermous wife, J.J., who reads everything I write before anybody else. If you like my books, it's because she did such a great job editing the first draft. If you don't like them, it's all my fault.

My terrifically creative and supportive Random House editor, Shana Corey. Brainstorming with her is always extremely funderful.

My astounding associate publishing director Michelle Nagler. I love associating with her.

My fantastical designers Katrina Damkoehler, Michelle Cunningham, Larsson McSwain, and Jinna Shin, and James Lancett, the equally fantastical illustrator for another incredible cover.

My amazing literary agent, the dapper Eric Myers, who has helped me publish nearly forty books over the past ten years.

My team of crackerjack librarians: Amy Alessio, Gail Tobin, Erin Downy Howerton, and Margaret Miles. Without their invaluable assistance, Marjory Muldauer would be all over me for my inexact Dewey decimal numbers. I'd also like to thank librarian Darrell Robertson, whose scavenger hunt game for the first Lemoncello book has been downloaded by nearly a thousand libraries across the country.

My awesometastic "beta readers" in California—the entire Cavalluzzi family: Sunshine, Tony, J.D., Lucy, and Micah. What an amazing family. They even do book-themed dinners and picnics!

My many friends and supporters at Random House Children's Books who have shown Mr. Lemoncello their love: Laura Antonacci, Jennifer Black, Dominique Cimina, Rachel Feld, Lydia Finn, Sonia Nash Gupta, Judith Haut, Alison Kolani, Kim Lauber, Mallory Loehr, Barbara Marcus, Orli Moscowitz, Lisa Nadel, Paula Sadler, Danielle Toth, Adrienne Waintraub, and Ashley Woodfolk. Yes, it takes a village to keep this library open.

The American Museum of Natural History and the New York Public Library for the inspiration of their exhibits "Pterosaurs: Flight in the Age of Dinosaurs" and "The ABC of It: Why Children's Books Matter."

Finally, thank you to all the teachers, parents, bookstores, and librarians who made *Escape from Mr. Lemoncello's Library* leap to life for young readers through games, extra rebus puzzles, rollicking read-alouds, gala celebrations, bunches of balloons, and incredible scavenger hunts. Thanks for making reading so much fun!

Bonus Clue

Hail, Caesar!

Here's a coded hint for winning the thirteenth game.

Your lucky number is XX.

**(And don't forget Caesar was a Roman,
so he liked to use roman numerals.)**

Gl. Fygihwyffi bum u qcfx cguachuncih.

By xlijm migy zugiom ncnfym chni bcm
wihpylmuncih.

By xcx cn nqyhns ncgym qbcfy mjyuecha ch
nbcm viie.

Mi qbs xih'n sio ai vuwe uhx nuey uhinbyl fiie?

Zchx qbun nbys bupy ch wiggih, cz sio quhn
ni qch.

Uhx qbyh sio nbche sio'py ain cn, domn myhx
siol uhmqyl ch!

Need a DECODER WHEEL?

Trace or make a copy of the two wheels. Cut out both wheels and place the smaller one on top of the larger one. Attach the two at their centers with a paper fastener. To start, line up the *A* on the outer wheel with the *A* on the inside wheel. Then use your lucky roman numeral to turn-turn-turn and begin decoding!

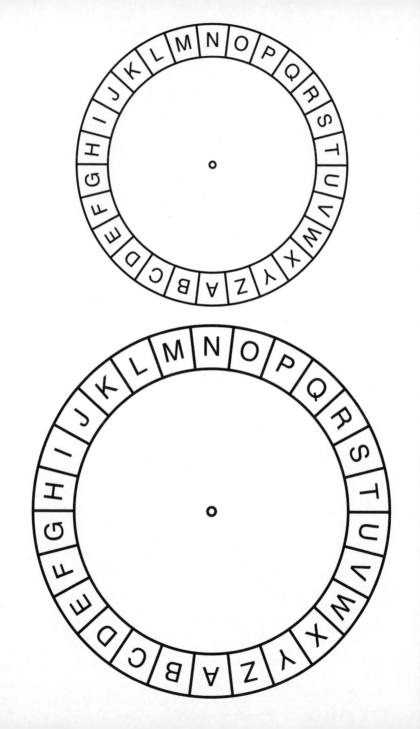